PART OF THE FAMILY

Now a freelance journalist, Charlotte Philby worked for the *Independent* for eight years as a columnist, editor and reporter, and was shortlisted for the Cudlipp Prize for her investigative journalism at the 2013 Press Awards. A former contributing editor and feature writer at *Marie Claire*, she is founder of the online platform Motherland.net, and has contributed to all the majors newspapers, as well as the BBC, Channel 4 and numerous magazines and books. Charlotte is the granddaughter of Kim Philby, Britain's most famous communist double-agent, the elusive 'third man' in the notorious Cambridge spy ring. She has three children and lives in London.

Praise for *Part of the Family*:

'Everyone has an agenda in this intriguing exploration of deceit and duplicity, as Philby ratchets up the paranoia to Highsmithian level'
GUARDIAN

'An enigmatic and slippery beast, a cool new generation of spy novel. Just as the characters play cat and mouse with one another, so does the author with her readers – it's a guessing game right to the end and I turned the last page with my heart pounding. Recommended'
LOUISE CANDLISH

'A compelling and emotionally resonant mixture of spy thriller and domestic suspense' ***DAILY TELEGRAPH***

'I devoured this beautifully written, intricately wrought and unique blend of spy thriller and domestic suspense. The twists keep coming, right down to that chilling last line' **ERIN KELLY**

‘Like *The Night Manager* rewritten by Patricia Highsmith, this is a distinctively female take on spying’ ***MAIL ON SUNDAY***

‘Dark and addictive and magnificent’ **JOANNA CANNON**

‘A genre-busting spy novel that amps up the tension and will leave you trusting no one’ ***RED***

‘Spying has been her inheritance and this brilliant, beautifully crafted debut novel uses it to the full – and so much more besides’
JON SNOW, Channel 4 News

‘A writer of promise’ ***FINANCIAL TIMES***

‘Compelling and complex – a compulsive read’
HARRIET TYCE, author of *Blood Orange*

‘An espionage/domestic noir crossover in which betrayal is as inevitable as it is compulsive’ ***i PAPER***

‘Compulsive and chilling’ ***GOOD HOUSEKEEPING***

‘A page-turning thriller’ **BBC RADIO 4 *OPEN BOOK***

‘Philby clearly understands something about deceit and betrayal, making this a page-turner with several cliffhanger moments, including the ending’ ***DAILY EXPRESS***

‘Intricate, enigmatic, and compelling … Philby is perfectly placed to blend spy thriller with domestic tension’ ***PRESS ASSOCIATION***

‘[A] page-turner full of intrigue and deception … a compulsive read’
PRIMA

‘Fantastic … [a] slick spy thriller’ ***WOMAN’S WEEKLY***

‘A carefully constructed study of duplicity in which the uneasy mood of moral compromise and betrayal never abates’ ***THE HERALD***

‘Absolutely riveting … It will keep your heart pounding to the very last page’ ***MEATH CHRONICLE***

PART OF THE FAMILY

CHARLOTTE PHILBY

First published in hardback as
The Most Difficult Thing

THE BOROUGH PRESS

The Borough Press
An imprint of HarperCollins*Publishers* Ltd
1 London Bridge Street
London SE1 9GF

www.harpercollins.co.uk

This paperback edition 2021
1

First published by HarperCollins*Publishers* 2019

A catalogue record for this book is available from the British Library

ISBN: 978-0-00-842441-1

Set in Adobe Garamond by Palimpsest Book Production Limited, Falkirk, Stirlingshire

Printed and bound in the UK by CPI Group (UK) Ltd, Croydon CR0 4YY

For Rosa

'To know yourself is the most difficult thing'

Thales of Miletus

Prologue

I felt my abdominal muscles twinge as I lowered myself to sit. The bench by the lamp post at the foot of the bridge, just as planned.

It had been almost two months since the surgery but still the scar was so raw that I felt tearing across my abdomen if I so much as lifted one of the twins at the wrong angle. Letting my eyelids drop for a moment, I pushed the thought of the girls out of my mind.

Open the box, close the box. Just as the doctor had taught me.

They were not so much benches that lined the stretch of pavement along this part of the Thames. More slabs, like a procession of concrete coffins quietly guarding the water.

It was dusk. Winter. The terminal gloom had long set in, and with it the sort of damp cold that gnawed its way into your bones. A thin gust of wind snuck through the opening in my cardigan as I pulled the grey cashmere closer across my breasts, still swollen.

'For God's sake, Harry,' I cursed him silently, my eyes rolling up towards the stone-coloured sky.

For as long as I can remember, I have always been early. It is a pathological politeness that brings with it control; no one wants to be the last person to step into a room. It was one of the things we shared, at the beginning, he and I. How many times had I arrived early to meet him, before all this had started, only to find him already lurking under an amber glow at the end of the bar?

Yet it was nearly five, and the pavement around me was virtually empty but for a steady stream of deflated tourists and office workers scuttling towards the Tube.

What was he playing at? David would be home from work by six, as had been his wont since the babies had arrived and, almost overnight, he too had been reborn, his naturally attentive, easy parental love a reminder of everything I could never be.

I had told Maria I was just going shopping for babygros. What was Harry doing? Careful not to make any sudden movements, which I had come to accept would be followed by a sharp stab of pain, I pulled my phone from my navy leather handbag, my hand trembling.

No new messages.

My fingers were a bluish-red. I had hardly left the confines of the house since the birth, two months ago, aside from those ritualistic processions along the darker recesses of Hampstead Heath, under the instruction of the nanny. *The Nanny*. The truth was, she was always so much more than that. Ever-competent Maria silently heaving the double buggy down the front steps, seeing me off from the shadows of the doorway.

I loved the way the air chilled my lungs. Even the buildings on Millbank, which loomed over us from the other side of Lambeth Bridge, seemed to shiver. I had forgotten how cold it got out here. How easy it is to forget.

Hoping I'd maybe missed something in the string of messages that had passed between Harry and me, I flicked my fingers across the screen. Nothing. How many times had I reread his messages? How many times had I crept across the hallway while the girls slept, my toes curling into the carpet, sliding the lock closed behind me, carefully retrieving the phone from where I kept it, stuck behind the drawer of the cupboard where the bathroom cleaning products were kept – somewhere I could guarantee David would never look?

Telling myself I would wait five more minutes before considering my next step, I flicked through a stream of encrypted messages. Once again, my attention was caught by a single image: a photograph, blurred, but clear enough – my father-in-law, the grandfather of my children, shaking hands with a man in a dark suit – his thick black beard a smear of tar across a smudge of flesh.

Out of the corner of my eye I noticed the streetlights flick on along the river. Looking up, I saw him. Those fierce blue eyes drilling a hole in my chest. Breathing sharply, as if struck, I said his name: 'Harry.'

PART ONE

CHAPTER 1

Anna

Three Years Later

The house is still, as it always is at this hour. Once again, I have hardly slept, taking a moment to savour the peace, the calm before the storm: this moment in which I am neither who I was nor who I will become. My eyes skitter across the silver clock by my bed, the one that had belonged to David's mother: 5.40 a.m. The date is already firmly etched in my mind, as it will be for as long as I live.

Dawn has always been my favourite time of day. As a child I would wander the narrow hall of my parents' house under a hazy bruise of light, gazing through the window overlooking a cul-de-sac of privets and exhaust pipes, imagining myself somewhere else.

David is still asleep. I sit, slowly, careful not to rouse him, his body a mound of flesh under a blanket of Marimekko florals.

I have spent most of the night going over the plan in my head, sealing every second of it into the recesses of memory, ensuring it could never be prised out again should I be caught. Caught. It's not a word I allow myself to linger on too long.

Creeping from the bed, with its expensive linen sheets and tasteful throws, I sit at the stool in front of the small oak dressing table with its neat displays of family life. Trophies, trinkets of a world I have made my own. Among them, a bronze frame with a photo of David and me in front of the vista of his father's house in Greece. One of many of his family's boltholes that we have jetted between over the years, the planes leaving tracks like scars through the sky, visible only to those who glance up at just the right moment.

So young we were then, clinging to one another in front of the pool, the Greek sun bleaching out our features. David's body turned towards mine, claiming me. Our first holiday together had been a victory, almost. This was where it all had really begun. I was his prize, he had said it a hundred times, but he never knew that he was also mine. Not yet, but he will.

The thought jars in my mind, and I lift my head, catching my reflection in the oval mirror. For a moment I am transfixed. The same light blonde hair, pale green eyes, high cheekbones. Hardened, now. The years of insomnia have caught up with me, in the hollows of my eyes. The corners of my mouth, cracked from years of fixed smiles.

My phone is plugged into the charger on the wall. Silently, I lift it, glancing at David's sleeping body in the mirror – the soft line of which I could draw from memory – before tapping my password into a second phone, stashed in the pocket of my silk dressing gown. My fingers leave a streak of sweat across the screen. The phone is the same model, same sleek black cover as my other one. Same pin number – the date Harry and I first met. Fundamental differences you would have to peer inside to see.

Once again, I flick through a stream of messages from Harry, distracted for a moment by a chip in my blood-red nail polish. Hearing David stir in the bed, I expertly lock the phone while concentrating my face in the direction of the neat row of perfumes and creams in front of me, replacing it in the pocket of my gown as I stand.

'What time is it?'

David's voice drifts across the room, still thick with sleep.

'Nearly six. My flight isn't until twelve but I have work to catch up on; Milly's off on maternity leave today.'

I picture my assistant, whose belly I have watched swell and groan under its own weight over the past months. I picture the young woman's blotchy red cheeks, which she attempts, feebly, to mellow with slightly too-orange foundation; her increasingly uncomfortable gait.

Over the past weeks, I could almost feel her pelvic bones grating as she delivered proofs of the next issue of the magazine to my office.

Of course Milly believed she would be back within a few months of having the baby, four to six months' maternity leave, she had told HR. I don't believe it for a second. Not that it matters. Either way, I won't be seeing her again.

'I'm going to have a shower.' David's voice interrupts my thoughts.

Smiling convincingly back at him, I lay my hand on a pile of magazine pages, 'Of course, I won't be long with this.'

An hour later, I am standing by the door, ready to leave.

'You look nice.' David sweeps down the stairs, his polished brogues crushing against chenille carpet, nudging one of the girls' scooters back in line against the wall in the hallway as he passes; the scooters he had insisted on buying them for their third birthday, a few months earlier, ignoring my concerns that they were too young.

I am dressed for the office. An Issey Miyake cream trouser suit fresh from the dry-cleaners. Shoulder-length hair tucked behind my ears. A slick of Chanel lipstick. The same perfume I spritz and step into every morning, the smell chasing me through the house, a reminder of who I am now.

It was what the papers always commented on, when a picture of me found its way into the society pages of some supplement or other. Perhaps they did not know what else to say: 'Anna Witherall, editor wife of TradeSmart heir David Witherall, perfectly turned out in . . .' Ethereal beauty. Enigmatic charm. These were the words they used. Lazy attempts to place a finger on my ability to stand out and disappear at the same time.

As David makes his way towards the open-plan kitchen – a wall of sliding glass at the back, lined with California poppies – I stand in the hall, making a show of the final check of my handbag. Inside my bag, my fingers are shaking.

Passport, keys, purse. Just another day.

'I really think you should stay at Dad's while you're there, it will be much nicer than a hotel,' David calls across the kitchen as I slip my feet into a pair of black leather mules, which stand side by side next to the girls' shoes, Stella's scuffed at the toe.

I feel the colour rise in my cheeks, and look down again so that he won't notice. 'Do you think?'

It is exactly what I have been relying on, of course. Knowing my husband as I do, I can predict that he will push for me to stay at his dad's place; desperate for this connection to me, this ownership of my life, even when I am abroad.

'There is actually a ferry, isn't there, which runs directly from Thessaloniki to the island . . .' I add casually, as if the thought has just occurred to me.

It takes four hours and fifty-five minutes, port to port. Not that I will be taking it, of course.

'Honestly,' I pace my words carefully, 'your father won't mind?'

David doesn't look up from his newspaper. 'I told you, he won't be there, he won't be in Greece for at least another month. I'll send a message to Athena, tell her to make up the bed.'

Before I can answer I feel the phone purr in my pocket. I look down, keeping my breath light. WhatsApp message from Unknown Number.

Thinking of you.

Inhaling, I close my eyes before placing the handset in my bag along with my usual phone and house keys, and head into the kitchen, all tasteful teal cupboards and oak countertop. A chrome Smeg fridge plastered in naive children's drawings, daffodils turning on the table, scattered with the detritus of breakfast.

Neatly dressed in matching pinafores, my daughters are slumped in their chairs, their eyes glued to the iPad their grandfather insisted on buying them. Their grandfather. The thought brushes against my knees and my legs bow. Feeling a rush of blood to my head, I place my hand on the countertop to steady myself, breathing deeply.

Looking up, I prepare to blame a stone in my shoe, a spasm of the spine, but no one has noticed.

This is it. I let my eyes shift between David, the competent father, and the girls. My girls. Still but not quite babies.

Something looms above them, a hint of the women they will become, the women I will never know. Rose's left eye twitches as it always has when she is tired or worrying about something. Even now she is like a person with the weight of the world on her shoulders. A typical first-born, even if only by a minute. Stella, beside her, oblivious always. How long will she remain so? I feel the unwanted thoughts rise in my mind, and expertly push them down again, back into the pool of simmering acid in my gut.

'Anna?'

I blink for a moment at the sound of my husband's voice. How long have I been standing here?

'I'll get the door for you. Are you sure you don't need a lift to the station?' Is there a hint in his tone? Does he sense what is about to happen? For a second I wonder if I see something in his expression, but then I look again and it has gone.

Grateful for the distraction, I keep my voice light, though my lips are so dry I feel a sharp crack as they tighten. Keeping my hand steady, I shake my head and take a fresh slice of toast from David's hand.

'I'm sure.'

I thought it would really take something to kiss my children goodbye one morning and walk out the front door, knowing I wouldn't be back. But in the end, it was simple. The door had already been opened; all I had to do was walk.

CHAPTER 2

Anna

There is no going back now. The taxi glides away from the house, down the street towards South End Green, retreating effortlessly from my family home, away from the expensive brickwork and tended gardens I will never see again.

The sound of the indicator clicks out a steady rhythm. My body quietly shaking, I turn my head so that my driver will not look at me and see what I have done, I watch my life streak past through the window, the bumping motion of the car, the low hum of conversation from the radio.

The girls hadn't lifted an eye as the horn beeped from the road. Why should they? To them, today is just another day. How long will it be until they learn the truth? How long until the illusion of our lives together comes crashing down, destroying everything I have created, everything that I hold dear?

'Why couldn't he get out and ring the bloody doorbell?' These were David's parting words.

I have called a different cab service from my usual. My face is automatically drawn to the locks on the car door as the motor flicks silently to life, the wheels rolling between the parade of five-storey terrace houses, into the unknown.

Moving through South End Green, I am bemused by the familiar bustle of London life – the sound of discarded cans rattling against the gutter, the boys in bloomers and long socks stuffed into the back of shiny 4x4s, an old woman with an empty buggy pushing uphill against the wind – the world still rolling on as if nothing has changed.

The traffic is heavy. When the car turns off, unexpectedly, at Finchley Road, my hand grips the door handle.

'Short cut.'

The voice in the front seat senses my fear but it does little to allay my nerves.

As the car turns, my eyes are distracted by the sudden movements of the trees, the light sweeping over the rear-view mirror. When it levels out again, I see the driver's eyes trained on mine for a fraction of a second, in the reflection, the rest of his face obscured.

It is an effort to keep my legs steady as I step out of the car at the airport, every stride pressing against the desire to break into a run.

The terminal is a wash of blurred faces and television screens. Slumped bodies, caps tilted over eyes, neon signs, metal archways. My body endlessly moves against the tide, my eyes flicking left and right beneath my sunglasses. There is a sudden pressure on my shoulder and I spin around but it is just a rucksack, protruding from a stranger's back.

There is something satisfying about flying, I find: the routine of it, the rhythm; answering questions, nodding in the right place, yes, shaking your head, no. I am grateful for it now – for the process, a welcome distraction from what will come.

Nevertheless, my mind won't settle. All I can do is run through the plan once more. There will be hours of waiting at the airport before my flight to Skiathos. My time there will be brief, a night at the most, and from there I will travel on using the ticket I will buy in person at the airport, a day later, in my new name – the one emblazoned in the pages of the passport Harry had couriered to the office days earlier.

By the time I reach security, the urge to get to the other side is almost as strong as the desire to stay.

The queues this morning are sprawling. Breathing in through the nose, out through the mouth, as the doctors taught me, I remain composed, even when confronted by an abnormally cheerful security officer.

'Going somewhere nice?'

For a moment, my mind flips back to this morning. From this vantage point, I watch what happens as if I am a witness – soldered to the sidelines, my tongue cut out. Unable to intervene, I watch myself leaning forward to kiss my daughters on their foreheads, lingering a second longer than usual. Neither had moved, barely raising their eyes from the iPad, which David had propped up against a box of cereal, a cartoon dog tap-dancing on the screen.

I watch the corners of their mouths twitch in unison, their spoons suspended in front of their faces, engrossed in their own private world. Behind them, the glass doors leading out to the garden that I would never see again.

'I love you.' Had I said it aloud? I had tried to catch my daughters' eyes for a final time, my fingers curled tightly around the edge of the breakfast table. But they were lost in their own arguments by then, oblivious to what was happening before them.

Startled, I blink, lifting my eyes once again so that I am now focusing on her face.

'Sorry, I . . .' Breathing in, I remind myself to stay calm. There is no reason for her to question any of this.

'Thessaloniki. It's for work, I'm a writer. There's an art fair, I'm interviewing one of the curators.' It is an unnecessary detail and for a moment I curse myself, but the security officer has moved on, no longer interested.

It is a balance; truth versus lie. The tiny details are the ones that guide me through. Things can be processed in small parts, after all. But too much truth and the whole thing comes unstuck.

It is true that the magazine is intending to cover the Thessaloniki event, and I am lined up to write the piece. That way, if on the unlikely off-chance David had ever bumped into one of my colleagues and mentioned it, I would be covered. What David does not know is that the show is not due to start for another three days, and by then, I will be long gone.

Once I am on the other side, I quickly check for my original passport, which I will dispose of once I reach Greece. I head to WHSmith to buy a paper. I can't concentrate but I need something that will help me blend in, distract my eyes.

Scanning the neatly compartmentalised shelves, my attention is drawn to the luxury interiors title of which I am editor. Was.

I remember how the office building seemed to swell up from the pavement, the first time I saw it. Entering the revolving doors off Goswell Road, turning left as instructed, the palm of my hand nervously pressing at the sides of my coat. Acutely aware of how young and unsophisticated I must have seemed, I had forced my spine to straighten, my consonants to harden.

The office, a wash of soft grey carpet and low-hanging pendant lights, a wall of magazine covers, was a picture of good taste, framed on either side by views of the city.

At first I had felt like an intruder, following the immaculately presented editorial assistant through the warren of desks scattered with leather notepads and colour-coded books. But then there was a wave of pride, too, that I might finally feel part of something.

It had been a struggle not to fall apart when Meg told me, with a blush of shame, that she had been offered the chance to stay on at the paper, while I was thanked for my time and moved along. We had been having drinks with David at the pub near her flat when she announced it, before brushing it off as if it were no big deal.

I managed to hold it together just long enough to hug her before slipping away to the bathroom and weeping hot, angry tears into my sleeve. It would have been impossible for the two of them not to notice the red stains around my eyes when I emerged five minutes later, claiming to have had an allergic reaction to my make-up.

By the time I reached the Tube platform, later that evening, I was numb, unable to feel the tears dropping from my eyes. Would Meg have asked me to move in if she had not been feeling guilty about the job? I would question it later, just as I would question everything else. Back then, though, I was in no doubt – she was as committed to me as I was to her.

When David rang the day after Meg's announcement about her new job on the news desk, I ignored his call before turning my phone to silent. It was a Saturday and the only noise from the street outside my parents' house came from the neighbours herding their children, laughing, into the back of a black hearse-like car. Aside from the occasional movement on the stairs, inside the house stung with silence.

When he rang again, an hour or so later, his name flashing on the screen like a hand reaching in from another world, I pressed decline, too bereft to speak, and just like that he was gone. I was halfway to the bakery, to ask for my old job back, when I heard a ping alerting me to a new message.

Pulling out the phone, annoyed that he wouldn't leave me alone with my misery, I read his words and stopped in my tracks.

'She's an old family friend.' His voice rose above the swish of traffic when I called back a few minutes later, moving slowly along the grey paving slabs of Guildford town centre. 'I hadn't seen her in years but she is married to one of the bosses at my firm and we bumped into one another. I told her you had done a degree in English and about your internship at the paper, and . . . She wants to meet you.'

David's voice was soft, listening intently at the end of the phone for my reply.

The interview had been arranged for the following week. Clarissa, I discovered, was exactly the kind of woman one would imagine to run a high-end magazine, exuding money and confidence and an overpowering smell of petunia. But she was kind, too, and generous. 'Any friend of David's . . .' she had beamed, radiating warmth.

The memory of her words sends a pang of sadness through me. Picking up a magazine at random, I use the self-service checkout before making my way to the boarding gate.

I find my seat in Business Class, store my neat black suitcase overhead, and wait for the comforting purr of the engine. As the rest of the passengers fiddle with their seats, I draw out the phone from my bag and compose a message to Harry.

On my way.

'Cabin crew, prepare for take-off.'

I raise my drink to my lips, the clatter of the ice vibrating against my glass. Gratefully, I absorb the captain's words, their familiarity grounding me in my seat, creating a rhythm against which my breath rises and falls, in desperate chunks.

They are the same words I have heard on countless flights with David and the girls over the years. Maldives. Bali. The South of France. Of all the places we have been together, it is Provence that I think of now. Maria steadily marching the girls up and down the plane, her monotonous hush-hush enveloping me in a blanket of calm.

I close my eyes but the memory follows me. The girls' faces trailing the cloudless sky through the car window during the drive from the airport to yet another of David's father's houses. This one is cushioned by lavender fields, the smell clinging to the air. The gravel crunched underfoot as we made our way from the cool air of the Mercedes towards the chateau, through a web of heat. My father-in-law was waiting under the arch of the doorway.

I watched him, my skin prickling as he swaggered out to meet us, the underarms of his crisp white shirt drenched in sweat. 'My dear Anna!'

'Clive.' Had his name stumbled on my lips?

The panama tipped forward on his head, jarring against my cheek as he leaned in to kiss me.

'Two times, darling, we like to play native around here . . .' His voice was booming. 'And where are my girls? Oh, let me have a good look at them.'

Clive blew an ostentatious kiss to Maria, and I worked hard to repress my jealousy at the thread that ran between them, the years their families had been connected in a way that would somehow always trump what David and I had. Maria, carrying one of my girls in the car seat, moving so comfortably alongside my husband, our other daughter asleep in his arms.

Clive took his son by the wrist, and as if reading my need for inclusion, said, 'Well, I'm glad to see they still have their mother's looks . . .'

Steadily, I let myself picture my daughters. Stella, all cheekbones and arch features, strident from the inside out. Her fall to earth padded by the arrival of her sister, a minute earlier.

Stella would be fine. Stella was always fine, always the one to take the best from a situation, and make it hers. But Rose. My eyes prickled.

There was something about Rose that demanded you take care of her, from that first day at the hospital. Even when it was Stella who had needed me. Even though it was Stella who had been the one to give everyone the fright, it was Rose whose cries, when they came, small and unsure, unnerved me. Everything about her was milder, from the delicate features to the way she hung back, always letting her sister wade in ahead, gung-ho. The truth is, I see more than just my own face in Rose, and that is what scares me most.

'Can I interest you in any duty free?' The flight attendant flashes a fuchsia smile, beside the trolley.

I am grateful for the interruption.

'Thank you, I'll take a packet of Marlboro.'

My fingers are shaking as I hand my card to the outstretched hand before me. Taking the cigarettes, I feel the weight of them in my hands.

SMOKING SERIOUSLY HARMS YOU AND THOSE AROUND YOU.

The warning on the cigarette carton goads me. Toxic. *Just like you.* I hesitate. Not me, I remind myself. This is not my doing.

I imagine Clive, the outline of his face filling my mind as a jet of stale air seeps through the vents above my head, the thought of him powering me on. A few moments later, I lean my head back, allowing my thoughts, once more, to drift to the girls. It is like that story Maria used to read to them when they couldn't sleep.

We can't go over it. We can't go under it . . . We've got to go through it.

I think of the three of them, she and the girls, perched on their bed along the hallway from mine. Sometimes, in those early days when I could still hardly bear to look at my daughters, I would lower myself into the nook of the doorway, listening to her sing or read to them. Closing my eyes, I would imagine their little faces staring up at me instead of her, their tiny fingers resting on mine.

'Anything else?' The flight attendant's eyes are fixed on me. Briefly, I imagine myself lurching forward to grab her by the starched collar of her shirt, my voice curdling in my throat as I scream so close to the woman's face that she can smell the fear on my breath. I can almost hear the words I might say: *Turn back, I've left my children and I don't know whether they're safe.*

But my voice, when it comes, is clipped and courteous, the strains of Queen's English I've assimilated over years of working under Clarissa providing the perfect camouflage for the cracks in my confidence.

'That's all, thank you.'

As she turns, I feel tears prick behind the folds of my eyelids, and this time I let them come.

Closing my eyes, I picture the girls seated next to me on this very flight as they have been so many times before. Their ears immediately clamped shut with padded headphones. The sound of cartoons seeping out from the side. David, as ever, oblivious to the sound.

I feel my throat close. Letting the tears roll, I turn my face to the window of the plane, giving myself a minute before I wipe my cheeks with the sleeves of my shirt, pushing my back straight upright and forcing the tears to stop.

Open the box, place the thought into the box. Close the box. Just in time.

I open my eyes again just as the roar of the engines kicks in.

'Madam, would you mind putting your seat forward for landing?'

I manage a congenial smile, and swallow.

'Of course.'

CHAPTER 3

Anna

Then

The newspaper office at South Quay stood at the end of an otherwise barren street, set back from the road, not so much insalubrious as unloved.

'You look smart.' Meg winked at me after a moment as we made our way up the front steps, a piece of gum rolling lazily against her tongue.

She was being kind but still I felt my cheeks flush, cursing the cheap suit-jacket and shirt I had hastily bought the moment she told me about the internship she had secured us, picking it out in the shopping centre in Guildford, only to discover on the first day that no one at the paper wore suits to the office apart from the news editors and the receptionists.

It had been both baffling and also completely believable when Meg announced, within six months of leaving university, that she had secured us both a placement at a national newspaper. That was the kind of power she had in those days, the kind that meant she could do anything and it should never surprise you.

She had met one of the editors at the members' club she had been working at since moving to London; she shrugged when I pressed her on how she had got me a placement too.

'But he hasn't even met me . . .' I countered reluctantly, trying to balance my gratitude with the sense that something was not right.

'I sent him your CV.'

'You don't have my CV.'

'And?' She grinned, lifting her chin as she pulled on her cigarette, and I left the matter there, knowing how easy it was to write a fraudulent résumé. Knowing how willing people were to believe.

The wind snapped at our heels as we crossed the bridge, Meg leaning into me, the warmth of her body soothing my nerves. How I envied the ease with which she moved; how comfortable she was in her own skin, her nylon mini-skirt hitched around skinny thighs, thick black tights, DMs.

Noting my expression, she snatched my arm and squeezed it against her own. 'I'm serious! You look hot. You're like Maggie Gyllenhaal in that film David made us all watch in Freshers' Week, but less slutty, obviously.'

We had still been practically strangers then, the three of us, wedged awkwardly together on cushions in the hallway of our shared house, watching *Secretary* on David's laptop, busying our fingers with a bowl of nachos. Unaware of the roots that were taking hold, blind then to how tightly they would bind us together.

Feeling my cheeks flush, I changed the subject as we made our way through stiff automatic doors.

'Have you been given any actual writing to do yet?'

She rolled her eyes. 'Just more transcriptions for the Arts desk, it's bullshit. I tried to talk to the Environment guy about a story idea but he just fobbed me off.'

I tried to hide my relief.

'Still it's better than a real job, I suppose. For now, at least.' She moved towards the door.

My nails pressed into my palms as the familiar panic rose in my chest, fingers searching for a ledge to break the fall.

For now? The thought of how much I had already spent on the month-long train ticket from Guildford to the Docklands – almost all of the little money I had saved while working double shifts at the bakery in town – all that I had already done, on the basis that there would be a paid job at the end of this, a career, a chance to get away, made my gut twist.

'You don't really think that?' I tried to sound calmer than I felt. Despite three years of friendship, I still could not let Meg see the true extent of my need. Had she spotted it, the day we left our shared flat in Brighton, she heading to London to chase the career she had always known was rightfully hers, while I returned to Surrey, my face burning with the loss of a life that had always felt borrowed?

I pictured it now, the flat we shared at the top of a crumbling Regency town house, wedged beneath two more of its kind on a thin strip of side-street leading from St James's Street down to the sea. I loved that flat, with its slanting floorboards and faded magnolia walls; I loved my bedroom, which overlooked the back of the house and a tiny courtyard below – more of a pit than a garden, a dry rectangle well speckled with cigarette butts and seagull feathers. I loved the way I could look out of the window from our battered Chipperfield sofa, onto Kemptown with its bars and pubs which throbbed with noise no matter what time of day or night, and not recognise a soul.

If the worst came to the worst, Meg had told me one night not long after we arrived in London, then she would simply go back to Newcastle. She would take bar work there and stay with her parents while she worked on the book she was destined to write. Though we both knew it would never come to that. Meg was one of those people who appeared to create the existence they wanted, without effort.

I imagined her mother, a shorter, squatter version of my friend – the same ready smile, fiery red hair. I thought of my own mother, thin with worry, her loss etched into the corners of her eyes. The years of silent dinners behind neatly pruned privets, hedging me in together with the memory of what I had done, or, rather, what I had not.

The smile had been pulled tighter than ever across my mother's lips the day I returned home, the day university – and its promise of escape – came to a crushing end. It clawed at the corners of her eyes as she watched me placing the box of my possessions onto my bed, the room having been stripped of any trace of me the moment I had left. Just as she had purged any trace of Thomas from the house within days of him leaving us.

My breath sharpened as I thought of my parents. *Them*, the only alternative to *this*. An invisible tightening around my neck reminded me that I could not let this opportunity slip through my grasp.

Meg's voice cut through my thoughts, steadying my heartbeat as we stepped into the foyer where a TV screen was playing the BBC News channel on the wall above the reception desk.

'Here you go.' The receptionist handed back to us the security passes we were made to collect daily and wear around our necks at all times. Looking down at the hollow outline of my face on the paper print-out, my eyes moved instinctively to the word 'Temporary'.

We stepped into the lift and Meg moved her fingers to press the button for Floor 1, the newsroom, before changing her mind and pressing Floor 2 instead.

'We're at least having a quick fag before we go in,' she said, stepping out of the lift.

The smell of stale smoke hit us before the doors had finished opening. Turning left into the smoking room, there were plastic chairs edging the walls, rectangular metal tubs strategically placed across the blue carpeted floor.

Meg leaned down to grab a copy of the morning's paper from a pile by the door, before crossing the room towards a seat by the window.

The room was airless, years of nicotine clinging to every surface.

Silver bangles jarring against one another on her wrists, Meg pulled out a ten-box of Marlboro Lights, drawing one out for herself and another for me. The cigarette was thick between my fingers as I leaned into the flame, holding back my hair, which had recently been cut from waist to shoulder length in an attempt at sophistication.

'That's a fucking scoop,' she said, pressing the fag between her teeth as she pulled her phone out of her pocket.

My eyes moved over the front page of the paper. Below the headline *'Exclusive: Leading Charity in Cahoots With Arms Dealer'*, my attention was drawn by a small black-and-white headshot of a young man with thick, dark hair grazing his neckline. Next to his face, there was the name of the reporter on the piece – Harry Dwyer.

Beside me, Meg's phone beeped again, but I was distracted by the man's face, the arch of his nose, the full curve of his lips.

'It's David. He's started his job at that bank in Canary Wharf . . . wants to know if we're up for a drink after work . . . Oi, are you listening?'

It took a moment for Meg's words to register and when they did I felt the familiar dull ache in my chest.

There was nothing more daunting than the prospect of going out and spending even more money I didn't have, before running to catch the last train home. Nothing apart from the prospect of home itself – the deafening silence a constant reminder of the person who wasn't there.

'You know David will be throwing cash around,' Meg laughed, reading my mind. 'Why don't you stay with me at my cousin's flat after? She's not going to be there. Save you going all the way back to your aunt's house?'

I smiled, flushing at the memory of my lie.

'Sweet.' The silver ring in Meg's nose rose up as she smiled, typing furiously into her phone.

Pressing 'send', she stood. 'Right, I'm going to have a piss before we start. You coming?'

'Yeah, I'm just going to finish reading this. I'll see you up there.' Something about the story, the man's face, wouldn't let me go.

Following an extensive year-long investigation, this newspaper can exclusively reveal that members of a leading social justice charity accepted a series of bribes from arguably the world's most prolific warmongers . . .

After a moment, I stood and pulled the front two pages of the paper, Harry Dwyer's piece in its totality, from the rest and folded it neatly, careful not to make an impression along the image of his face, as I placed it in my bag. Unaware of the chain of events I had, without the slightest comprehension, just set in motion; the wheels that were gaining traction, preparing to spin dangerously out of control.

David was waiting for us outside the pub, when we arrived later that evening.

'Jesus, man, what are you like? Couple of weeks in the City and this happens?' Meg ruffled his hair, where the undercut from just a few weeks earlier had been replaced by an expensive barber's take on short back and sides. 'Still haven't lost the leather bracelet though, I'm glad to see . . .'

'What? I thought you'd be into it?' David raised his eyes as he pulled her into a bear hug, the flame of the outside heater licking against night air. He paused before moving to me, his expression shifting into something softer.

'Anna.' He took my hand, gently, pulling me towards him, holding me as if I was something that might otherwise break.

'Right – drink, bar!' Meg slipped her arms through mine and David's, squeezing gently, the three of us falling into rhythm as we moved through the pub door, and I squeezed back, grateful that we were simply there, all three of us. Knowing, in my bones, even then, that it was too good to last.

'What have you done with my lighter?' Meg was scrabbling around the empty glasses and crisp packets an hour or so later, in the pub garden, when I spotted him, seated with his back to us at one of the far tables.

Despite the angle, I recognised him instantly – even from where I was sitting, which meant I could only see a sliver of his face, the same face I had studied on the front page of the paper that morning.

He would not believe me when I told him this later. How is that possible? he would shake his head and laugh, though not unkindly. Maybe he was right. Maybe what I felt then was something deeper; not so much recognition as a sense of foreboding.

Meg spotted him a moment later. I stayed where I was, rooted to the ground as she circled towards Harry Dwyer, in search of a lighter. I couldn't see his expression as he held out the flame towards Meg's face, but after a moment she pulled back, as if to get a better look, and as she spoke, a small smile curled at the edges of her mouth.

'I'm Meg.' The words blew off her lips, like kisses. My palms burned as he accepted her outstretched hand.

'Come and join us.' She was drunk, though she would have done the same thing sober.

'Don't be like that.' I did not hear his reply but after a moment he stood reluctantly, his thumb scratching his cheekbone as he followed Meg back towards our table. His eyes were red and he looked tired. I wanted to hold his hand.

'Guys, this is Harry. Harry works at the paper . . .' Meg leaned into him, laughing. 'He's quite the star reporter, don'tcha know?'

Harry muttered something I could not make out. He was drunk too, and weary. When he smiled, I could see he wanted to leave. I could hardly look at him and yet I could not look away; there was something so powerful in my response to him that I could not trust myself to speak. But then I did.

'Do you want a drink?' My voice was louder than I had expected.

He paused, looking at me for the first time, before nodding, his mouth breaking gently into a smile as the moon behind his head disappeared into a cloud.

CHAPTER 4

Anna

In those early London days, the office was a bus ride from the flat Meg and I shared, a boxy two-bed above a kebab shop on Camden High Street. It was Meg's cousin's flat really. Although she had not lived there for months, Lucy's presence was etched across the living room in cheap, colourful wall-hangings from her travels in Asia; ineffectual attempts to distract from the grubby off-white walls and the draught which rattled in from the road below.

To the outside world, it was a dive. To me, it was home. Mine and Meg's.

It was a Friday night when Meg announced that Lucy had decided to stay on in Sydney with her boyfriend, leaving the flat in Meg's care. The very same night that Harry landed back in our lives, like a bomb.

The two events, unconnected on the surface, squeezed me in from either side.

We were sharing a bottle of wine – my treat, courtesy of my new job – in the pub on Arlington Road, around the corner from Meg's flat. As was her style, the offer for me to move in was presented not so much as a proposition but as a fait accompli.

'How could you say no?' She paused halfway through pouring my glass. 'Even if the prospect of living with me isn't enough on its own, which it obviously should be, then just think how much you'll be saving on travel from your aunt's house, presuming that's where you were planning on staying . . . From the sound of it, your dad's not going to be stationed back in the UK any time soon. I know it's a tiny flat and it's a shithole but it's cheap – and you get to live with me!'

The pub doors swung open, a bluster of wind edging through the heavy velvet curtain.

'Look, Lucy isn't charging me full whack. If we split the bills, you'd be doing me a favour, and I want you to live with me . . . Fuck sake, man, say yes?'

Meg had this way of making me feel like I was the most important person in the world. I thought of my parents, the nights I had cried myself to sleep after it happened, desperate for one of them to hear my heart tearing above the sound of their own; for them to come to me and tell me it was not my fault. For a split second, my brother's face flashed in front of me, but the spectre disappeared at the sound of Meg's voice.

'Shit, are you crying?' She leaned across the table and took my arm. 'I'm not that bad!'

I pressed my sleeve briefly at the corner of my eyes, laughing, and when I looked up again, my skin bristled like a fox catching the first scent of the hounds. Harry: the man who would be the death of me.

It was the first time I had seen him since that night in the pub in the shadow of Canary Wharf, though my eyes had sought him out at the office the following day, self-consciously pulling at the sleeves of the jumper I had borrowed from Meg – deep red with a slight scratchiness to the wool. I even stayed late, making excuses to move around the office, in the hope that I might spot him; propelled by a naive notion that he might be looking for me, too.

Rather than giving up, something in me accepted his absence as a challenge. That evening after work, my legs moved more briskly than usual as I made my way back from Guildford station, energised by the thought of him. It was just past eight by the time I closed the front door and already the house was swallowed by darkness, a low light emanating from the living room.

I walked purposefully across the hall so that they would hear my steps momentarily hovering outside the room, giving my mother the chance to call out, to ask if I had had a good day. But the door remained shut, the only sound the canned laughter clattering out from the television.

Upstairs, at the end of the corridor I flicked on the lamp beside my bed, the featureless room coming into stark focus. The single bed, neatly made, a single chest of drawers uncluttered by anything other than a small make-up bag and a stick of deodorant, which my mother had pointedly removed from the bathroom and placed on my bed on my first day home, without a word. The spectacle of my return flaunted in our shared spaces was apparently too much for my father to bear.

By the bed there was the computer I had been given my first week at Sussex, as part of my grant. Pressing the door closed, I turned it on, my fingers trembling as I typed 'Harry Dwyer' into the search engine, holding my breath as a photo appeared on the screen. The first image might have been a disappointment if I had not been so desperate for any trace of him.

It was taken from a news conference: Harry in the crowd amidst a small throng of reporters. The image was poor quality, Harry's face distracted by a scene just out of shot.

After a moment, I pressed the arrow on the screen and another, less recent, photo appeared of Harry having just scooped the Young Journalist of the Year prize for a piece on internal wranglings at Number 10. He was twenty-three at the time, which made him nine years older than me. For a moment I thought of my own path: the year spent working at the chain bakery in town after leaving school with an unblemished if unremarkable academic record; fending off awkward advances from Tristan, the general manager, who snorted when he laughed, and stood too close behind me at the counter, making comments about the position of my hairnet by way of exerting his power.

The three years at university, where my greatest single achievement had been meeting Meg and David and having, for the first time in my life, found both friendship and the space to breathe, space to become the person I was beyond the frameworks by which others interpret and define us. The fact that Sussex had accepted me onto an English and media degree without asking for an interview had not so much given me confidence in my ability as it had confirmed to me that I would get by better in life if people weren't given too much information. On paper, the surface facts of my life – childhood in Surrey where my father ran a local business; my mother, otherwise a stay-at-home wife, lending a hand – were acceptable: I was acceptable. Delve any further, and . . . I inhaled hard, not allowing my mind to slip back to Thomas. Look forward, I reminded myself, focusing on Harry's face, absorbing his successes, allowing myself to live vicariously through them, even if just for a moment.

Admittedly, it was a long way from the life I was living now. If you were to line up our achievements side by side, and draw lines between them – a habit I found impossible to break – you would notice a distinct distance between where I was now – commuting four hours a day to transcribe other people's interviews and make endless cups of tea – and where Harry had been at the same age. But a lot could change in a year; I was dependent on that possibility. Though of course back then I couldn't have known quite how much.

There was a stirring on the stairs, and instinctively I sat upright, pressing open a new tab on my web browser. Though I need not have bothered; as always I heard the footsteps speed up as they passed my door, despite my father's attempts to make his feet lighter in the hope that I wouldn't notice him, urged forward by his terror of being made to look me in the eye.

Refusing to give my father another thought, I returned to the previous tab. With another click of the mouse, I was met by a brief journalistic profile of Harry and his time as a reporter at the paper, alongside the same byline photo that had first caught my eye on the front page that morning in the smoking room. And then, with another simple click, there it was, on the second page of Google, a brief mention in the media pages of a rival paper:

Harry Dwyer was unceremoniously sacked today, just hours after his most recent scoop. The paper's editor, Eddy Monkton, is believed to have seen off the Irish-born writer in characteristically pithy style, telling his former star reporter, 'Dwyer – you're fucked'. A talented self-starter, Dwyer rose through the ranks after dropping out of school and taking a job in the canteen of his local paper. Monkton refused to comment on the parting of ways.

But . . . how? My mind searched for answers to the impossible question of how this could be. How our lives could have intersected as they had and then, just like that, have been torn apart again. This had to be wrong. Determined to prove it so, I continued to trawl for clues until long after the light in the hallway had been clicked off – but there was nothing else to be found. No other mention of his being sacked, and no further explanation.

It is a visceral memory, the sadness I felt in that moment; I can still feel it, the deflation at knowing that if this brilliant, beautiful man no longer worked for the paper, there would be no chance of bumping into him again. It was real, that memory, it is impossible to believe it was not – and yet I will question it later, just as I have learnt to question everything. In the darkness to come, I will ask myself if I could have felt so instinctively connected to him at this point – or was I simply retrospectively filling in the details to suit the version of events that I needed to create in order to justify what I had done?

In any case, the sight of him in the Crown and Goose that night, his arm propped against the bar, a pint in front of him as he scanned the pages of the *Evening Standard*, seemed not so much astonishing as merely confirmation of the connection I had felt in the beginning.

Of course, what I should have asked myself was, what were the chances of him turning up like that in our local pub? And the real question: if I had known the answer, would I have run for my life?

'What are you staring at?' Meg turned, following my gaze, a smile creeping over her mouth as she spotted him too.

'No way.'

I could not be sure if she was smiling for herself or for me. Despite the special connection I felt to Harry, it was clear I was not the only one to notice his rough impression of beauty. It was hard to ignore the looks he elicited as we all sat together in the bar that first night, the flutter of eyes noticing him as Meg stood and moved towards him, seemingly unfazed.

When he looked up, an amused smile formed at the edge of his lips. It was a struggle to pull my eyes away. After a moment, I heard the scrape of a bar-stool and when I looked up again he was standing above me.

'You remember Anna?'

'Of course.'

Harry reached down and for a moment I thought he was going to kiss me, but instead he drew out a chair and sat.

'We're celebrating,' Meg announced, leaning a hand casually on his shoulder, the intimacy of her movements making me wince.

'Oh really, why's that?' It was David's voice this time. Arriving straight from work, he was dressed in a Barbour coat and navy scarf, his shirt untucked. A matter of months since leaving university, the mutation had already subtly begun, the sartorial shift from trustafarian to trust-fund manager made in incremental steps. At this stage, he was still a boy doing a poor impression of a man.

'Anna has just agreed to move in with me.' Meg raised her eyes at me, flashing a smile and leaning in to kiss David's cheek.

'Cool. Well if we're celebrating we better have champagne – and shots.'

David laid his coat on the chair beside mine before turning to acknowledge Harry. Something in his face shifted; I can't have been the only one who noticed.

'Hello again, I didn't realise . . .'

'Nice to see you.' Harry held out a hand, his self-assurance filling the room.

David paused, a moment too long, before accepting it, briefly, and then moving towards the bar.

By the time we left the pub, Camden High Street was a heaving mass of bodies and light, the smell of lead clung to the air. We were moving in a line, a marauding army stumbling towards an unknown threat. Unaware that the enemy already lay within.

'Where are we going?' David's voice followed Meg and me as we stepped into the road, the sound of horns blaring across the street.

'Fuck knows!' Meg called back and we fell sideways, in unison, our bodies crippled with laughter, the sound of us, warped and distant, blowing back at me as if from the other side of the street.

'Watch out.' Harry's hand hooked under my arm, guiding us across Parkway. Only once we had reached the phone box outside the pub did he let us go.

Meg whispered something to David, linking her arm in his before turning back briefly to the pair of us.

'We're just going to get something,' she winked.

'Are you sure you don't want to come with us, Anna?'

David's eyes held onto mine.

'She'll be fine.' Harry's voice was assured, the sound of it steadying me.

I leaned back against the phone box, my eyes straining to keep him in focus, the sound of a bottle smashing in the forecourt of the Good Mixer pub, followed by a wave of laughter.

When he looked down, I turned my face away, self-conscious despite the sambuca, wary of how I must look under the sharp streetlight. Hoping that if I didn't meet his eye, maybe he wouldn't see me so clearly.

'Why are you doing that?' He seemed amused.

'What?' I laughed awkwardly, aware of my teeth.

'That thing,' he laughed, mimicking me, ostentatiously sweeping his head to the side.

'I'm not.' I pushed my hand out to quieten him and my fingers landed on his chest, the breath clamming up in my throat as he leaned slightly into my palm.

There was a moment's silence then, the lights from the high street casting a golden haze that warmed the sky above our heads. The movement on either side of us slowed until it was just us, my face finally settling into perfect stillness under the softness of his gaze.

'Sorted!'

Meg's voice cut across us, and it was Harry who looked away first. Pulling my hand back, I turned to see David, his pupils black and bulging.

Within seconds of David and Meg reappearing, Harry had peeled away from me towards a door to the left of a bar with no signage, taking centre-stage on the short strip of terraced buildings running the length of Inverness Street. David's grip held me back as a young man, slumped over and supported by friends, his top flaked with vomit, wobbled precariously in front of us.

'Sorry, babe,' one of them called out as we stepped back to make way.

Brushing past them as quickly as I could, I watched Harry and Meg disappear ahead of us into the club, Harry's hand pressing against the small of her back as he guided her in from the street.

He is just looking out for her, I told myself. There is nothing more to it than that.

'Maybe we should go somewhere else, it looks crazy busy in there. I've got some . . .'

David hesitated as we reached the entrance where little more than a handful of smokers gathered outside, hemmed in by a single rope. But I kept walking.

'I don't want to leave Meg,' I replied without turning around.

Down a narrow flight of stairs, the club was heaving with people, a dark warren of rooms, loud and airless, house music vibrating against low ceilings and windowless walls.

The bar stood at the back of the central room, thick with bodies. The heat suddenly overwhelming, I wished I wasn't wearing a shirt on top of my vest-top. David moved towards the bar, pulling me protectively by my waist. 'What do you want to drink?'

'Water,' I called over the throb of noise, my eyes frantically weaving through the crowd, desperate to find Harry and Meg, but all I could see were strobe lights and contorted faces, spilling over one another.

When David finally handed me my drink, I sipped gratefully before screwing up my face.

'What is this?'

'Vodka and soda . . . I . . .' he called over the noise, which drowned out his voice as I pushed my head back, so thirsty I drank it all in one go.

'Steady,' he pulled the drink away from me, laughing nervously, but I pulled it back and drank the dregs.

'You should pace yourself . . . How are you feeling?' he asked a few minutes later, his mouth pressed against my ear.

'Let's dance!' I shouted back as the whole room exploded with movement, a wave of euphoria rising in one endless swell of rhythm and sound. Pulling off my top layer, I turned, my arms stretched wide, my teeth grinding out of beat, and found David, his arm around my back, his breath against my face, the smell of sambuca on his lips.

I cannot be sure how long we stayed like that, our bodies swaying in primal movements, before a sickness hit my stomach, acid rising, scraping at the inside of my throat, the walls suddenly pushing towards me.

Stumbling backwards, my leg pressed against a leather bench which I had not been expecting and I sank back onto it, grateful but also unable to sit still, my skin burning and then cold, so that I pushed myself to standing. I could feel the strap of my top slinking off my arm, but there was nothing I could think to do to pull it up again.

The room was a slush of noise by now, indistinct notes thrashing against one another as I felt my way along the wall towards the exit, my breath tightening as strangers' bodies crushed against my own.

Finally, my fingers curled around something cold and angular. It was another wall, leading away from the crowd and into a smaller corridor, which was dark and thankfully cool. It was quieter here and I was alone. For a moment I half-stood, half-crouched, my back against the wall, the breath slowing in my chest, before, from the end of the corridor, I felt movement and I knew that I wasn't alone. With an animal sense, I recognised the presence of another person, even as my eyes still struggled to adjust. Then a shuffle of feet, and another, followed by a voice.

'Anna?' It was Meg, her face moving towards mine, and then another voice behind her reaching in through the mist. Harry.

'Shit, it's Anna!' Meg's hands gripped my body as I slumped, David stepping in in time to break my fall.

CHAPTER 5

Anna

When I came to, the room was quiet.

Even with my eyes closed I could register a sense of space above my head. My body, heavy and unfamiliar, pressed down against the springs of a mattress.

'Anna? Thank God, man.'

I stretched my neck, my movements slow and unfamiliar as Meg's voice emerged, along with her pale face as she bent over me.

Sitting, I pulled the sheets around a T-shirt I didn't recognise. It was her flat we were in – my flat, now – the curtains sagging against the window.

'I took your clothes off, they were covered in sick.' She did her best to make it sound casual.

'I'm cold.' My voice was raspy and Meg nodded, seemingly pleased by the specificity of the instruction, jumping up and leaving the room without another word. Seconds later there were more footsteps, heavier this time, less certain, moving towards the bed.

'David, maybe wait a minute, yeah?'

Meg followed him back into the room, the duvet from her own bed bundled in her arms. But he was oblivious, his bloodshot eyes trained on mine.

'I'm so sorry.'

He lowered himself as I pulled the covers tighter around my chest, still dazed, distracted by the taste in my mouth.

The outside world was an uncertain grey, I couldn't tell if it was dawn or dusk.

'I don't know what you're talking about.'

'The MDMA, it was just a dab in your drink, I warned you . . .'

I felt myself back in the airless bar, David's voice mouthing words I could barely hear as my eyes scanned the room desperately for signs of Harry. I had smiled as I turned back to him, masking my disappointment as I took the drink from his hand and downed it, my eyes wincing at the bitter aftertaste.

'Leave me. I'm fine, it's fine, I just need to sleep . . .'

'I'm sorry, honestly Anna, I thought you knew . . . I thought it was what you wanted.' His face was stained with desperation.

'Just let me sleep. Please.' I turned away from them both, the sound of their footsteps moving into the hallway, fading again a moment later.

When I woke again, the flat was silent, and the memory of the night before came back to me in waves.

Placing a pillow in front of my face in a futile attempt to stem the flow of thoughts, tears of shame pricked the corners of my eyes, the humiliation churning in my gut, heavy and hot.

How much had Harry seen? Was I sick in the club or only once we had come home? *Fucking* David. I said the words aloud. I never took drugs, never risked putting myself in a position where I wasn't in control. I couldn't. And yet, how was he to know? I had let them believe that I did, him and Meg. I remember the sharp taste of a pill on my tongue, on nights out in Brighton, those few seconds before I turned and spat it into my hands, disposing of it before either of them saw, terrified they would spot that I wasn't one of them.

The flat was empty, silence ringing through the air as I moved slowly towards the kitchen.

On the table, there was a note.

Hope you're feeling OK. Pizza and juice in the fridge. Make yourself at home. Mx.

Beside it, my keys, purse and phone, which Meg must have pulled from my pockets after stripping me down.

Desperate for a distraction, I pressed the home button on my phone and watched the screen light up. Rather than a message from my parents wondering where I was, I was met only by the date and time flashing on the screen against the backdrop of a photo taken by David on Brighton Pier, two summers previous – Meg and me, the wind whipping against our cheeks, our faces contorted in a scream.

It was the same day Meg had first asked me about David.

'So what you going to do?' We settled ourselves at a table in the corner of the Hop Poles while David went to the bar.

'What do you mean?'

Meg rolled her eyes disbelievingly.

'About David . . .' She waited, and when I didn't speak, continued, 'He fucking loves you, man.'

I snorted. 'Don't be ridiculous.'

'Oh please, tell me you're joking.'

'What?'

'Jesus, you're serious. Anna, the boy is infatuated. Have you noticed that he can't be more than two feet away from you at all times?'

Along with incredulity I felt a prick of pride. My voice was less convinced as I continued, 'Yeah well, I don't know, maybe that's because he likes you and I'm always with you—'

'Anna.' Meg slapped her hands against her face. 'Honestly, do you really not realise . . . You don't. Wow. I mean you're smart but sometimes you're so fucking dumb. He's in love with you. If you can't see that then you really need to learn to read people better.'

The digits overlaying the image read 20.12. Sunday night. For the first time in my life, I had slept through an entire day.

Sipping gratefully at a glass of too-warm water from the tap, I moved from the counter towards the sofa.

Meg must have had a clean-up while I slept as the detritus that was usually scattered across the floor had been stacked into a pile in the corner of the room, the remote control neatly aligned on the coffee table in front of the sofa.

Scanning mindlessly between channels, I settled on a film I did not recognise, my thoughts gradually fading into nothingness before a harsh buzzing noise reverberated through the intercom, causing me to jump.

Pressing the volume on the television to mute, I lay back on the sofa, holding the edges of the blanket I had dragged in from the bedroom, waiting for whomever it was to give up. A moment later, though, the bell sounded again, longer this time.

Aware it might be Meg, having forgotten her keys, I reluctantly stood, brushing away the covers before moving to the window.

The light inside the flat was off. The only potential clue to my presence was the glow emanating from the screen behind me as I nudged the curtain with my fingers, pressing my cheek against the glass. Looking down, my eyes ached as they struggled to focus, my breath forming a screen on the pane in front of me.

Using my thumb, I smeared the condensation away. As if sensing my movement, his face flicked up at me.

'Fuck.' I pulled back.

The buzzer sounded again. I couldn't let him see me like this, but what choice did I have? Besides, I had already made the decision as I moved across the room towards the door. Pressing my hand against my thigh, I leaned forward into the mouthpiece, pressing the button before I could change my mind.

'Hello?'

'Anna?'

My palms were prickling. My face, in the reflection of the screen on the intercom, was hollowed out, and tacky with sweat.

'It's Harry.' There was a pause, and then, 'It's bloody cold out here – are you going to let me in?'

My finger hovered for a moment over the button, before pressing down again.

'What are you watching?' Before I had time to fully register his presence, he was moving across the room as if being here was the most natural thing in the world.

'A film.' I turned to the counter, pulling desperately at my hair, twisting it into a bun.

'You alone?'

'Yeah.'

It was too late to turn away, to shield him from the circles under my eyes, the unwashed skin.

'Would you like tea?'

He nodded, his eyes smiling. 'You feel like shit, right?'

'I don't know what happened, I'm not usually—'

'Course you're not.' His laugh was familiar. 'I'm just glad you're OK. That's what I came to check. The club, I couldn't find you anywhere and then I saw Meg and she said you weren't well and had to go home and . . .'

The moment our eyes locked there was a rush through my body and I instantly felt like a fool for imagining whatever it was I had imagined might have happened between him and Meg in the time that they were lost in the club.

He settled himself on the sofa as my grip tightened slightly around the handle of the kettle.

'How did you know where I lived?'

'You pointed it out last night, on the way back from the pub.'

'Really?' It was unlike me to forget things. Besides, everything else from the night before remained clear, before the club. Or did it? How would I know – was it possible to intuit where the holes in your memory lay? Harry's claims were hardly surprising given the number of shots we'd consumed at the bar. Something about his presence had lured me into a state of off-guardedness, my usual restraint failing to kick in. The drinks had been endless, David galvanised by the presence of another male into buying round after round, each more elaborate than the last. If nothing else, this was a lesson. Or fate, perhaps. If I hadn't passed out, would Harry have been here now? At the time, the thought struck me as reassuring.

He took the cup of tea I had made for him from my hand and our fingers touched.

'Have you eaten?'

'I still feel pretty sick.'

'You've got to eat.' He stood up straight, pulling his wallet from his pocket. 'And have a drink. Trust me, it will make you feel better.' He winked, taking a sip of his tea and passing it back to me.

'I'll be back in ten, buzz me in?'

I watched him pull the door closed behind him, and it was all I could do not to scream.

CHAPTER 6

Anna

'So how's work?'

The question came out before I realised what I was saying. We were facing each other on the sofa, the box of pizza wedged between us, a half bottle of brandy on the coffee table, alongside the mug of hot chocolate he had stirred it into at first, to soften the impact.

Harry's face straightened all of a sudden, and he shrugged. 'Ah, you know . . .'

It was silly to imagine he would want to go into the details of his being fired with a relative stranger, yet I could not help feeling disappointed at his lack of confidence.

Sighing gently, he placed a half-eaten slice of Margherita back on the box, taking a swig of his drink. 'Well, if you really want to know, I've been sacked.'

He continued chewing, his eyes locking on mine, and I held my body straight.

'Are you serious?'

'Deadly.'

'When?'

A half-smile appeared on his face.

'The day before I met you guys, believe it or not. That's why I was . . . You know, shit-faced, on my own . . . That's not my usual style, I'll have you know. I had come in for a meeting with the editor, trying to get my job back, but what can I say, the man's a prick.

Still, he ran my story the same day though, didn't he? Not too moral to miss out on a final scoop . . .'

He shrugged again, taking another bite of pizza.

'What happened?'

He paused then, as if he had changed his mind. For an alarming moment I thought he was going to stand, but he simply lifted an arm to his cheek for a moment before carrying on.

'That story, the one about the undercover charity investigation? One of the protestors I embedded myself with is claiming we were in a relationship.'

There was an authority to his delivery that dampened the shock.

'OK.'

'Well, it might have been, except it turns out she was fifteen at the time.'

His words hung in the air.

'The time of what?'

'There's a photo, she says it shows us "being intimate". I mean, Jesus, it's nothing. I've seen it, we're just talking. But she says it was more than that. Her parents, they threatened the paper, said if I wasn't disciplined, they'd take the case to court. It would be my word against theirs, but apparently that doesn't mean anything. With things the way they are in the industry, there isn't the kind of cash needed to defend a law case. And, like I said, the editor's an arse. He had been looking for an excuse to get rid of me . . .'

Harry's face lifted suddenly, turning, his eyes narrowing. 'Shit, I don't know why I told you that. I'm sorry. It's intense, I know. I just . . . Something about you, I just felt I could . . . I'm sorry, I shouldn't have put that on you, we hardly know each other.'

His face was parallel with mine, something passing between us.

'It's bullshit, you should know that. I mean, Jesus . . .'

I nodded, my hand instinctively moving towards his, 'I do.'

As he opened his mouth to speak again, a key jangled loudly against the front door. Lurching back, his legs swung forward off the sofa as Meg's face appeared.

There was a moment of doubt and then she spoke, her features recomposing themselves.

'Hi!' Her eyes briefly flicked between the two of us, and then she smiled. She did not ask aloud what Harry was doing there. At the time I didn't either.

Harry had suggested it, all of us meeting up again the following week. We had been saying an awkward goodbye that evening in the flat, he, Meg and me. By then, my hangover had been usurped by an urgent fizzing in my gut.

'I'll be working near here in the afternoon if you fancy a drink afterwards?' Harry had looked at me and then, out of politeness, at Meg.

'Bring your friend David too if he's around . . .'

If he spotted my disappointment at the mass invite, he didn't show it.

David was already there when I arrived at the pub, as planned, the following Friday. It was the first time I had seen him since the incident at the club and he was holding his hands under the table when I arrived. Standing up, he presented me with a large, purple, gold-embossed bag, the plush cardboard soft and soothing as it swept against my fingers.

'I just wanted to apologise for what happened. I—'

'David, what . . .'

His face fixed on mine as I tugged at the ribbon that had been pulled tight in a perfect bow, protecting whatever was inside, unable to keep the smile from lifting the corners of my mouth.

The material was a light grey wool, which hung just above my knees, with a soft shearling lining. From the label, it must have cost more than the rest of my wardrobe combined.

'It's – well, it's perfect, but . . .' He must have seen the flicker of uncertainty in my face as he stood, casually, wary of applying too much pressure.

'It's no big deal. If it's not right the receipt's in the bag. I just thought . . . Meg's taking forever, shall we order? I'm starving.'

It was then that I looked up and noticed Harry and Meg, already seated at the bar on the other side of the pub, Meg facing away from us. At that moment, Harry looked up and our eyes met, his gaze followed a second later by Meg. I could have sworn it was disappointment I saw in her eyes, but then her face lifted into a smile and she jumped off the stool, striding towards us, her eyebrows rising as if to say, 'Where the hell have you been?'

CHAPTER 7

Anna

The air was heavy and damp that winter, the perfect backdrop to the months of boozy nights that followed in pubs across London, the four of us drinking until the small hours before falling away to our respective beds. But then, as time passed, the initial thrill of our weekly group gatherings was worn away by erratic working hours and office parties, until one night it was just Harry and me sitting across from each other at a table in the corner of the Crown and Goose, where an irate chef passed out plates of food through a minuscule hatch.

We shared one bottle of wine, and then another, our fingers resting side by side on the round wooden table, oblivious to the comings and goings of the other drinkers as they passed back and forth on their way to the bathroom, the urgent ring of the kitchen bell clattering above our heads.

By the time we rose to leave, I was surprised to find the bar swollen with people. Stepping out into the street, the twinkling fairy lights entwined along the shop fronts, Harry stopped and pushed me gently back against the wall of the pub. Holding me there for a moment, my neck in his hand, he paused before kissing me, his lips soft but persuasive.

And that was it, our fate sealed. I had waited for that confirmation of what I had felt for months, and when it came it was as if it had never not been there.

* * *

Meg had gone back to Newcastle for a couple of weeks, so the flat was ours alone, that first night together. I woke the following morning to a feeling of utter contentment, until I turned to find an empty space in the bed next to me. Running my fingers over the grooves where his body had been, I briefly wondered if I had imagined it all.

My sense of unease grew when I called his phone later that morning, and the next day, only to reach his voicemail, the recorded message playing a jeering loop against my ear. When he re-emerged, a few days later, he was apologetic but reassuring. There was a job he was doing, which had pulled him away unexpectedly. He was sorry he couldn't be in touch.

'You know what it's like.'

It took everything I had to play down my disappointment, but I knew better than to let the extent of my feelings show. So instead I nodded along – even agreeing when he insisted that we could not tell anyone about us, swearing myself to secrecy.

The case against him was ongoing, he offered by way of explanation. If the defence found out he was dating a former intern – and that was how they would frame it, he said – then they would have a field day.

I was a consenting adult, it was ridiculous. But maybe something about the situation suited me too. It was not as if I was leading David on, exactly, but he had done so much for me already and the idea of him knowing I was with someone else . . . It would not have been fair.

What bothered me most, though, was how unjustly Harry had been vilified, how quick his colleagues had been to turn against him.

'But you didn't do anything,' I raged one night as he reminded me once more of the charges he could be up against. My counter-arguments were always weak, and he looked at me like I was a child he cared for but who knew nothing of the world.

'Oh, Anna, of course I didn't sleep with her – but do you really think that means anything?'

He shook his head despairingly.

'The girl who made this claim against me, or rather the girl whose parents made this claim . . . They don't care that she had told me she was twenty-one. They don't care that *she* was the one who duped *me*.'

To be honest, I could have contested him on that point if I had wanted to. He was the investigative reporter; it was he who had infiltrated the organisation, using whatever means he could to extract the information he wanted. Even if that meant earning the trust of a young woman who believed he was after her, rather than what she could do for him.

Yet how could I say any of that without sounding unsupportive? Harry did not need another person rallying against him. More importantly, I understood why he did it. What he did, it was about the story, the pursuit of truth and justice, regardless of the cost. That was simply the person he was.

The threads in my stomach pulled tighter as I stepped off the bus that morning in Bethnal Green, on my way to his flat for the very first time. My breath in the January air was a curling finger of smoke drawing me forward, as I followed the directions he had sent, past the coffee shop with the couples in beanies sipping hot drinks on a terrace makeshifted out of old wooden crates; young men with bloodshot eyes sucking on roll-up cigarettes, already weary of the winter that still had some way to go.

Hidden on the other side of a scruffy communal garden was a square of grand red-brick houses, stained black where they met the pavement by centuries of tar and a drift of pigeon feathers. Adjoining it, an elegant Victorian mansion block curved and disappeared towards the next street. Harry's flat was on the second floor, that much I knew, and with that tiny detail I had already drawn a picture in my head, instinctively filling in the gaps.

So many times our evenings together had been curtailed by a sudden phone call that would see him downing his pint and standing to pull on his coat, leaning in to kiss me, reluctantly, his lips hovering over my mouth, telling me he wished he could stay. In those moments,

I would picture him coming back to this flat, to the bedroom I imagined filled floor-to-ceiling with books, photos of his childhood stacked precariously on a mantel, shirts thrown over the back of an easy chair. But never did I question where he went in the intervening hours. Maybe I told myself it did not matter, or maybe I was scared what the answer would be.

On the doorstep, I took a moment to gather myself, a row of numbered buzzers in a panel on my left, drawing a deep breath before pressing the bell. There was a moment of silence then a crackle and Harry's voice.

'Hello?'

'It's me.'

He paused and then his breath lightened. 'Hello you.'

The sound of his feet drumming against the stairs echoed my heartbeat. When he opened the door, his face broke into a smile. Neither of us spoke as I stepped inside the hallway, which was even colder than the street.

He laced his fingers in mine and led me past piles of post and folded buggies and bikes, our feet quietly moving up the stairs.

It was another hour before we let each other go long enough for me to take in his flat.

The hallway, where our clothes now lay discarded, was tall and white, uncluttered by pictures or coat-hooks. At the far end of the hall, there was a kitchen, with a little round table and four chairs. Just enough cutlery and cups, a single frying pan and a sieve. Everything with its own place and purpose.

The only thing that was out of place was a single box of condoms, which he had gone to lengths to dig out; his ability to think so cautiously, even in the heat of the moment, pricked at me once it was over. At that moment, entangled in his arms, I would have risked anything never to let him go; it was the first clue, if only I had been willing to see it, as to how uneven the balance of power between us was.

'Must be a reaction against my house, growing up,' Harry said, watching my eyes react to the sparseness of it all, the precision. It was the first time he had mentioned his childhood and I stayed silent, willing him to carry on.

We were moving through to the living room now, my eyes scanning the original fireplace, unused; just a few books neatly stacked over purpose-built shelves. Hungrily, I drank in any detail I could latch my eyes upon.

Comparing the scene before me with the image of the flat I had created in my mind, I found my imagined version already slipping away.

'When you're one of six and there are other people's things everywhere, I suppose a kind of efficiency grows out of craving your own personal space,' Harry said.

I thought of the silence of my parents' house, the endless space.

'You grew up in Ireland, right?'

'Galway.' He turned to the door, the look passing over his face telling me he'd had enough of this kind of talk, and I was happy to follow him back to safer ground. Any question I asked him was liable, after all, to be turned back on me.

'And this is my bedroom.'

Harry had moved across the hall and was standing in the doorway of the final room. There was a small double bed against one wall, a desk against the other, piled high with papers.

His eyes followed mine, over the bed, which was low to the ground, the sheets white and nondescript. Beside it, on stripped wooden floorboards, there was a square alarm clock and a notebook. Nothing else to betray the details of a life.

Moving towards the desk, my eyes trailed the papers neatly covering the surface.

'So, what is it you're working on?'

He moved to intercept me, pulling me towards him as I reached the desk.

'If I told you that, I'd have to kill you.'

* * *

There was something so powerful about him, so far beyond my reach. And yet the truth was we weren't so different, he and I. For all his bravado, for all his success. People like David, their lives were defined by what they had; Harry's life, like mine, was defined by what he had lost.

'It was a Saturday morning,' Harry confided one night, our noses pressed together in the darkness of his flat, the occasional flash of a car headlight through the bedroom window the only sign that in this moment we weren't the only two people left on Earth.

'I'd been moaning on and on about a toy car I wanted. Little red thing I'd seen in the window in town a couple of days earlier. Wouldn't quit. In the end, my pa says, "If it'll shut you up, I'll get you the damn car." He walked out the house, and that was it. Ten minutes later, he lost control of the steering wheel and . . . Three people died.'

There was a pause and I felt the pain that moved across his face.

'Oh, Harry.' I moved so close to him that I could feel the muscles in his body contract with grief.

'It was my fault.' His voice was so quiet, but I felt the tears soaking into my scalp. 'You can't imagine what that's like. To know—'

'That was not your fault, Harry, don't you ever think that.' I clung him, hushing his cries with my own, as if soothing my younger self.

I squeezed him harder then, feeling my own confession pour from my lips; the relief of saying the words out loud tinged with fear. Our secrets reaching out for one another, their grip so tight I could hardly breathe.

CHAPTER 8

Anna

If it had happened a few months earlier, I would have told Meg about Harry and me, regardless of what I had promised. How different things might have turned out if I had. There was nothing she and I did not share, back then, nothing we wouldn't have told each other, until suddenly there was.

At first I put the cracks that began to show in Meg's armour down to the pressures of office life – the spikiness that had always been offset by a natural generosity and easy humour falling away into something that would have been otherwise unexplainable.

David had picked up on it too, on the occasions when we still found time to hang out together, the three of us, between the various pulls of our respective working lives. He had tried to raise it with me but I had played the ignorant, telling myself I would not discuss Meg behind her back but knowing deep down that I just did not want to think about it.

And then, one day, the blinkers were torn off.

I was sitting at the table in the kitchen of our flat, typing up a piece on monochrome accenting. Behind me, a single panel of wall was lined incongruously with illustrations of botanical branches: a single roll of statement wallpaper which I had plucked from a box of samples at the office, with Clarissa's encouragement; one of a number of disjointed acquisitions with which I had started to embellish the flat over the past months. I was squinting at the computer, trying to block out the churn of Camden High Street filtering in through the sash, when Meg walked through the front door, slamming her keys onto the counter, pulling open the door to the fridge and closing it again.

'Where have you been? Are you OK?'

It had been two or three days since I had last seen her, only an unfinished cup of coffee on the counter when I woke that morning offering any sign that she had been home at all.

She looked odd, changed somehow, in a way that I could no longer ignore: her fingers scratching at her thighs, front teeth chewing her bottom lip. There was a darkness that had taken hold, its shadow stretching beneath her; an anger, barely contained, slowly tightening its grip.

'Why?'

'You just seem a bit . . . I tried to call.'

'I'm fine, I'm tired. Work's full on . . .' Her eyes skittered around the room as if in search of an answer.

'David rang, a minute ago, wanted to know if we were going to his party.'

Even as I said it, I knew I was setting myself up for a fall. Harry was away on a job, and although house parties were not my scene, especially not without Meg there to create a distraction, something had made me say yes.

'Can't, there's something I've got to do.' Meg's voice was distant.

'What is it?'

It stung that I even had to ask.

'Just something for work.'

She walked out of the kitchen, and even though her bedroom stood directly on the other side of the wall, she could have been on the other side of the world.

When she came back out, half an hour later, her expression had softened slightly.

'Sorry, I'm not myself at the moment, it's just a lot of pressure.'

She held my gaze for a second before snapping her face away again.

Without looking me in the eye, she stepped forward and kissed my cheek. There was a flicker of electricity between us and then she turned, the door slamming shut before I had time to reply.

The bus stop stood opposite our flat on the high street, illuminated in a sickly streetlight. Fifteen minutes later I stepped off the bus at South End Green, where the road veered right towards Hampstead Heath station.

Keeping the pub on my left I followed the right fork which led up to the Heath.

In all the years David and I had known each other, I had never been to his London house. After leaving halls, he had his own apartment in Brighton, on one of the smarter Regency squares, a very different proposition to the house we had shared the year previously.

The flat had been bought for him by his father, he let slip one afternoon. We were lazing on the nobbled rectangle of grass that stood between a U of buildings, sharing a bag of chips from soggy newspaper, the sea lapping at the shore on the other side of the main road. Back then, David still told himself he was uncomfortable with the level of wealth his father had started to accrue as his business grew from small-time independent to leading international trading company TradeSmart. The irony of his faux-liberal university lifestyle, banging on about the importance of fair trade while snorting lines of cocaine from supply chains involving child exploitation and murder, paid for by Daddy's money, was not so much lost on him as ignored.

He had been the first person I met, the day I arrived at Sussex. Freshers' Week, Falmer campus. Summer had stretched on that year, grass lining the lazy knolls that formed a ripple in front of the university, swarming with bodies, snatching up the final rays. Morcheeba drifting across the hills. Endless drum'n'bass.

My halls were on the far side of campus, just before rows of housing melted away into fields.

'So, this is your room,' explained the self-assured young man who greeted me at the door. He had watched my eyes for a reaction as I scanned the room with its worn carpets and fireproof doors.

'Sorry, I'm David,' he had added, stretching out his hand. 'I'm your RA. This is my second year so I'm here to, you know, make sure you have everything you need . . .'

'I'm Anna.' I smiled self-consciously, trying out my new name for the first time.

'What are you studying?' His eyes were trying hard to catch mine.

'English Literature.'

'Cool, I'm doing Business Studies . . . Are your parents bringing the rest of your things later?'

I paused, shaking my head, and kept walking. 'It's just my dad but he's abroad. RAF.'

I could hear the hesitation in my voice, but David never questioned it, and why would he?

As David continued talking, my eyes settled on a blur of hills rising to meet an expanse of blue sky, through the window, unaware of the dark clouds looming in from the edge.

The light was fading as David's road came into view, in an enclave of North London reserved for old money and increasingly new.

The house was a four-storey Victorian semi-detached, three times the size of my parents' home, chequered tiled steps leading up to the entrance. It was beautiful, the house a child might draw, plucked straight from a ghost story.

I took the stairs to the house slowly; light and voices emanated from the hallway through the open front door, music spilling over the wall from the garden.

David was there, waiting for me, a smile stitched across his face as I tentatively pushed at the open door.

'You came!'

He kissed my cheek, his skin soft and grateful, my proximity to him reassuring.

'This is your house?'

'This is it.' Leading the way, past a sweeping staircase with double-height ceilings and down through the kitchen, David paused to pour me a drink.

'So here we are.'

We were standing in the garden, which was not much smaller than the ground floor of the house. The lawn stretched down to a red-brick wall with an arched doorway leading out onto the Heath.

On the terraced area, where we now stood, there were paper lanterns punctuating the view from one side of the house to the other. In the middle of the garden someone had attempted to create a pit and amidst the ash, a fire licked at the air. A group of people I didn't recognise were sitting around it, flicking joint roaches into the flames.

'Anna, I'm . . .' Watching my face turn back to his, David took a step forward, a look stirring in his eyes. Ever since that night at the club, something had shifted between us and aside from the gifts that passed between us like relentless peace offerings, he had been careful not to push.

'Meg couldn't come,' I changed the subject before I could stop myself, immediately feeling like a traitor to my friend for raising the subject.

'What's with her at the moment?' David's face changed. 'Every time I see her recently she's . . .'

'She's just, you know, work.'

David raised his eyebrow. 'I don't know, it seems like more than that. We're all busy . . .'

'How is work?' It seemed fitting to change track.

'Good, yeah, I mean it's banking, it's not exactly . . . But it's good, you know, doing something for myself, making my own money.'

I nodded, wondering how much David earned. Not that he needed money of his own, clearly.

As if reading my mind, he continued, 'My dad wanted me to go into the family business but . . . I don't know, I want to do my own thing. The idea of just following my father's footsteps . . .'

He blushed, shrugging.

'Good for you.' Discreetly, my eyes cast their way up the back of the house, the vast wooden shutters, creepers growing up the walls. The top-floor windows gazed out with hollow eyes over the black expanse of Hampstead Heath.

'So this is the house you grew up in?'

David took a swig of his drink.

'Yup. My grandparents bought it in the 1950s, and when they died, my dad inherited it.'

'And he doesn't mind you having a party . . .?'

'He doesn't live here any more. He's got a flat in town, but he's away most of the time, so it's just me.'

'How come?'

'Work. He's mainly working in Africa and Asia at the moment. His company has an office over here, but mostly it's . . .'

The music stopped suddenly, as if someone had lurched the needle from the record, followed by a wave of indignation from the crowd. Behind David's shoulder I could see more people spilling into the garden as the music started again, something soulful this time.

'If you ever want to come over . . .'

'Thanks.' I smiled, not sure what else to say as I watched the party from a distance, David's guests' uplit faces devoid of features, like apparitions passing under a cloud.

It was nearly 1 a.m. by the time I left the party. David had called me a cab, his hand lingering on mine as I ducked into the car, his eyes following me down the road.

Within minutes of driving, the wide open streets of Hampstead gave way to Malden Road, sprawling council blocks obscuring my view of the sky. Camden High Street, with its all-night bars and the endless roar of the night bus trundling along tarmac scarred by hidden potholes, faded to a reassuring throb as I pressed closed the door from the street.

A strip of light gently glowed above the tatty carpet at the top of the stairs, warm and inviting, but when my feet reached the upstairs landing, something already felt wrong. I pushed open the front door to find the room darker than I had imagined. Meg's body, her back to me, was unnaturally taut at the table, an open bottle of wine beside her.

In another life, I would have called out to her. I would have watched her turn to me, holding up the bottle, signalling for me to bring down a glass. Now, though, her body was still. For a moment I felt my joints freeze, imagining the worst, but then she moved, a small, almost imperceptible intake of breath, and my chest loosened, just enough.

Not knowing what else to do, I went to the counter to pull down a mug, waiting for her to make the first move. Holding the cup under the tap, I discreetly glanced at the window, catching an outline of her silhouette.

Taking a gulp of water, I turned to face her. From here, she looked pale and still.

'Meg?'

When I ran towards her, her head collapsed into my chest, her body heaving with silent tears.

'Sshh, what is it?' It was the first time I had ever seen her cry. The first time in my life that I had been alone with someone in tears, whom I was allowed to touch.

Meg shook her head.

'Anna . . . I . . .'

The words dried up after that. I briefly tried to speak, to fill the silence with the sounds she needed to hear. I wonder now how different things might have been if I had. But my throat clammed up. Instead, I led her to her bed and pulled the blankets around her neck, lying down beside her, my arms wrapped in hers, until her breath slowed into sleep.

Meg was standing by the counter when I emerged in the kitchen the following morning. She was facing the window, the glass streaked with rain.

'I have to go.' She did not look at me as I pulled a mug from a pile on the draining board.

'OK, I'll be off soon, too. I'm going into the office to catch up on a few things.'

Clarissa had assured me there was no need to work this weekend, but we had a big commercial pitch coming up and I knew she planned to go in and crack on – and I knew how much it would please her to see me there as she arrived, perched in front of my computer, notes neatly stretched across my desk. If I was going to climb the ladder the way I needed to, I had to show how keen I was, how much more I was capable of than endless admin.

'I'm leaving London.' Meg turned away from me, her voice matter-of-fact.

'What do you mean?'

'I've been offered a job in Bristol.'

Finally, she turned back to face me, her skin bare, free of the heavy eyeliner she always applied within minutes of showering.

'What? When?' My eyes scoured her face for signs of something I could hold onto.

'I can't talk now. This flat, it's—'

'Bristol?'

'You can stay on, if you can cover the rent on your own, or . . . It's paid up until the end of the month. We'll talk later. I've got to go.'

'Meg, what the fuck? Where are you going?'

I followed her to the front door, willing her to turn around as she gripped the handrail, her free arm raised defensively as she reached the bottom of the stairs.

But I didn't follow her. Instead, I went to the office, rather than waiting there in the flat for her return, making the effort she would have made to stop me from leaving, had the shoe been on the other foot. If I had, could I have saved us all?

Harry's phone was off when I tried it at lunchtime, on my way to the noisy coffee shop where I ordered a salad box for Clarissa before heading back to the office. Again, I was met by the monotony of his answerphone as I wrestled with the front door later that evening, the smell of frying meat following me in from the kebab shop, my voice struggling to remain light.

'Harry, it's me, just seeing how you are. I'm at the office but I wondered what you were doing tonight, or tomorrow. Call me . . .'

I paused before I hung up, slipping the phone back into my pocket, darkness descending as I shut the door against the street.

Even before I reached the upstairs landing, something felt different. In the dark, fumbling for the light switch, my key turning quietly in the lock, I pushed the door open with a nervous hand.

'Meg?'

Inside, the flat was still and instinctively I knew.

I called her name again, already knowing it was too late. Feeling it, the guillotine falling, severing the space between then and now.

CHAPTER 9

Anna

It was October, that first year at university in Brighton, and a late burst of summer sun meant the city was awash with life: swarms of Italian tour groups smoking cigarettes in the grounds of the Pavilion; elderly couples walking in companionable silence along the shore, hands held behind their backs.

The beach had been a heaving mass of bodies by the time I arrived late that afternoon. Walking across the pebbles, I was aware of the glances from a group of guys sprawled out by my feet as I made my way towards the pub where we had arranged to meet. It was less than a month into our first term and Meg had suggested a group of us have afternoon drinks before heading to a drum'n'bass night at the club on the sea front.

Scared of getting it wrong, of being exposed for the fraud I was, I had spent the previous week watching the other students stumble along the path in front of my window, gathering hints about what to wear. In the end I had chosen denim cut-offs, a slick of pink lip gloss, hair pulled away from my face.

David's skin was lightly tanned and his sandy-coloured hair shaven, self-consciously, into a low undercut on one side of his head.

'So, what are your plans for Christmas?' he asked that afternoon as we sat opposite each other outside the Fortune of War, the two of us the first to arrive.

I took a long sip of wine, watching his pupils dilate like two dark wells in the glare of the sun.

'Not much. Studying. My dad's still in Singapore, so I'll stay with my aunt.'

'You said your dad's in the RAF?'

I smiled, taking a sip of my drink.

'So where do you stay when you're in the UK?'

'I have an aunt, in Surrey. It's dull but convenient.'

We were silent for a moment, him drawing lines with his finger on the sweat of his glass.

'How about you?'

He looked up again, a flicker of embarrassment immediately succeeded by pride.

'Maldives, probably. My dad has lots of international clients and that's where they . . . It's work for him, but you know, could be worse . . .'

My mind flicked to my parents' dining room, the sound of my mother's best cutlery scratching against our plates at the mahogany table laid for three – the empty chair filling every inch of the room.

I had nothing to say, but needed to push the conversation on, away from my life.

'So you travel a lot?'

David shrugged. 'We spend most of the summer between the South of France and Greece. My dad has a place on the edge of this island, in the Sporades.' He looked at me, as if to ask if I had heard of them.

I took another sip of my drink, waiting for him to continue.

'It's a few islands along from Skiathos. Our one's much smaller, though, low-key.'

'Cool.' I nodded, working to suppress my jealousy as a cube of ice slipped down the back of my throat.

By the time Meg arrived, followed by a stream of faces I didn't recognise from campus, David had already bought three rounds, insisting he was closer to the bar whenever I made a half-hearted attempt to stand. The moon hovered precariously above the water as we made our way along the beach, hours later, towards Concorde 2.

'Have you seen LCD Soundsystem live before?' David asked, holding back as Meg and some of the others took off their shoes, screaming with laughter as they waded through the low waves, their voices drowned out by the thrashing beats as we approached the club.

The temperature had dropped dramatically and I felt ripples moving across my arms and legs as I pushed my hands into the pockets of my shorts. David at once started to unzip his hoodie.

'Take this.' His eyes worked hard to hold mine as I went to take the sweater. His mouth opened to speak but then Meg appeared, her wet clothes clinging to her skinny frame. Without saying anything, she laughed, tugging the hoodie from his fingers and wrapping it around her.

'Jesus, Meg,' the disapproval in my laughter was laced with awe, my envy of her total lack of inhibition so potent that I could almost taste it.

Even as I pushed open the door to Meg's room, the rumble of Camden High Street clattering through the glass, I knew she was already gone. Even before my eyes adjusted to the light, to the empty wardrobe, the bed stripped bare.

'Meg, where are you? You can't do this. You have to call me. Please.'

My mouth pressed against the phone, tears streaming down my cheeks.

Harry's number went straight to voicemail. The urge to run to his flat might have been overwhelming if I had not already known what a false move it would be. As he said himself, he was hardly ever there, his freelance investigative career taking him off in far-flung directions that he refused to discuss. Besides, from the time we had spent together, it was clear he did not respond well to being needed, always preferring to be the one to give chase.

Without Meg, the flat was too big and yet the walls seemed to press in on me, her absence everywhere I looked.

Outside, Camden Town was a drizzling sky, illuminated grey pavements, Saturday night drinkers passing by in a sea of strangled faces, their corners smudged.

I pulled out my phone. Other than work, there were four numbers in my past calls list. Harry, Meg, Mum, David.

Leaning my back against the wall to steady myself, I pressed 'call'.

He answered after two rings. 'Anna? What time is it . . .'

'Hi.' My voice broke then.

'What's wrong?' I could feel him freeze whatever he was doing, his attention, as always, focused on me.

'It's Meg . . .' The words caught in my throat.

'Where are you?'

'I don't know what to—'

'Anna, just tell me where you are and I'll be there in a minute, just tell me . . .'

'I . . .' But the words wouldn't come; the lights on the street were too bright, a blast of noise exploding from inside the Irish bar along the high street as the doors swung open.

David's voice was calm and firm at the end of the line. 'OK, look, just jump in a cab, OK? Find a taxi, I'll stay on the line. Come to the house, I'm waiting. Everything's going to be all right.'

Compared to the last time I had seen it, the wide entrance hall felt eerily devoid of life. As I stepped inside, the air lightly hummed with the smell of stale booze and stale bodies.

'Sorry about the mess.' David led me through the hallway, scooping up half-drunk glasses as he went, placing them on the kitchen table.

'Can I get you a drink?'

He moved to the fridge, his hair flattened on one side from where he must have slept. When he turned, he was holding two bottles of beer. 'There's not much else. I could pop out to the shop.'

I shook my head, gratefully accepting the drink, wondering for a moment how he could live like this while holding down a job in the City.

'What is going on?'

He leaned back against the table as I took a sip of beer.

'Meg's gone.'

He moved onto the other foot, 'What do you mean, gone?'

'She's gone. Taken all her things. She said something about a job in Bristol this morning and then when I got home after work, she had cleared out.'

'She can't have done.'

'She left a note.'

'What did it say?'

'Nothing. "Take care of yourself." I just don't fucking get it – why would she just leave?' I raised the bottle to my lips again, the glass knocking against my tooth.

'You've tried calling her? I'll try now . . .'

He walked into the living room, the phone pressed against his ear, and I followed. There was something mausoleum-like about the inside of the house, like a set of family life, frozen in time. Framed pictures of David as a baby were neatly scattered across the surfaces of a huge pine dresser. Heavy woven rugs, William Morris curtains, an oil painting hanging above the fireplace.

'It's going to voicemail.'

'Where is that?' I was transfixed by a painting hanging above the fireplace, dusty strokes of blues and rusty greens.

'That is the view from my parents' house in Greece when they first bought it. It was just a shack really.' He spoke as if to himself.

'It's beautiful.'

'My mum fell in love with it, she did loads of these after we first moved in. For a while . . .'

'Your mother painted this?'

'That's how they met. My mum grew up on the island and when she was in her early twenties she used to have a stall at the top of the village, selling her paintings. Dad was on holiday, stumbled upon her shop and . . .'

The thought of Meg popped back into my mind and I shook my head.

'She said I have to move out, unless I can cover the rent on my own, which obviously I can't . . .'

Pushing his phone back into his pocket, David looked at me.

'Move in here.' He said it straight away, as if the sounds had been poised on his lips all his life.

'I mean it, why not? Move in.'

Even if I had wanted to hold back, my face would not contain itself. Lips curling at the edges, my chest lifted my whole body with something between gratitude and excitement, and something else too – an unease, a feeling I could not place, creeping in from the side.

'Really, but . . .?'

David rose then, unwilling to hear it. 'No buts.'

A moment of doubt, that is all there was. And then I felt myself nodding, pushing away the lingering sense of discomfort, stifling it with all my will until, just like that, it was gone.

CHAPTER 10

Anna

The weeks passed slowly and then quickly in the months following Meg's disappearance.

David spoke to Meg's mother who told him she was surprised Meg had not been in contact with either of us directly and confirmed she was in Bristol, working for a paper, and was, for want of a better explanation, probably just busy.

Why had I refused to call? I told myself I was too hurt, but perhaps even then I was instinctively fearful of what I might find out.

There was a moment, one morning at the office not long after she left, when I found my hands hovering above the keyboard of my computer, her name at the tip of my fingers. But what would be the point? I moved my attention towards something else. I was not on Facebook, and neither was she; what would be gained from trawling the internet for her most recent press cuttings, other than confirmation that she had moved on – and that I should, too?

At first, I had taken Harry's response to the news I was moving in with David as a form of contempt. There was a note in his voice that I did not recognise when I told him of my new living arrangements, and it pleased me.

'I never knew you and David were so close . . .?'

'We're not. Well, not like that, obviously. He's an old friend, and he's living in this massive house on his own and . . . where else am I going to go?'

I swallowed, knowing I was crossing a line.

'Anna, you know if I could, I would ask you to stay at mine. But it's not . . .'

'It's fine.'

'Would it help if I said I was jealous?'

'Maybe.' I smiled reluctantly, leaning forward to kiss him, but he was less easily distracted than I was.

'So, this house, it belongs to David's parents but they don't live there?'

I was touched that he cared enough to want to understand my life.

'Exactly. His dad is mega-rich, he's usually away on business and when he's in town he has a flat he uses. So that just leaves David and the house . . .'

'And now you.' He thought for a moment before nodding. 'OK.'

It did not hint at anything out of the ordinary at the time, the excitement shining in his eyes as he raised his glass to his lips, his eyes holding mine as he drank.

It was a while later that he pushed the parameters of our relationship beyond the generally permissible limits, broaching the matter one night as we lay side by side, our legs entwined, between the sheets.

'I know I said I was jealous of the idea of you and David sharing a house, but I wouldn't mind if you and he . . .'

My body tensed. Sensing my reaction, he placed his hand gently in the small of my back.

'That's not because I don't want you – you know that, right? It's just . . . You and me, there's no question over what we have.'

Swallowing, I chose to ignore that questions blew between us like sheets billowing precariously on a line.

His lips pressed against mine and the thought was pushed away. He was a free spirit, that was all it was. There was no reason to feel alarmed.

'It's just, if it makes life easier, you know? I have no problem with it.'

I tried to forget Harry's words over the following weeks, but no matter how hard I tried to run from them, they chased me. The thought of his indifference, the ease with which he could accept the possibility of another man's body on mine, following me into sleep . . . But there was an excitement too. The seed of a possibility of something I could sense if not name.

And over time, I suppose, the idea lost its menace. Was it that simple? Perhaps it wasn't, but in the end it felt like little more than an inevitability.

We had been sitting on the sofa, David and I, flicking through magazines, a half-smoked spliff resting in the ashtray on the coffee table. It was not planned, not consciously at least. David leaned forward to reach his glass of water and I felt my fingers stop him, my hand on his shoulder. Then, as if it was the most natural thing in the world, I was leaning in, my fingers lifting to his face, cupping his chin.

His mouth was dry from the weed, and I moistened it with my tongue, leaning him back against the sofa and lifting his shirt in slow, gentle tugging motions. His eyes were bloodshot and his face temporarily frozen. Throughout, I felt his want driving me, spurring me on, wondering how many times he had envisaged this moment.

Once he had finished I sat up and lifted the spliff from the ashtray, lighting it and inhaling deeply while he trembled on the sofa.

It was two months to the day after my first time with David that I stumbled upon the notes on Harry's desk. We were lying on his bed watching a film on the laptop balanced on the duvet between us, the sound of a party flooding in from the flat above.

'Do you want me to ask them to turn it down?' I had asked as he fidgeted beside me, his hands refusing to settle.

'What?'

'The music . . .'

He looked confused and then batted his hand. 'It doesn't bother me.'

For a moment he was silent, and then he continued, shaking his head dismissively. His timing was perfect.

'Sorry. It's nothing, it's just work.'

'Anything I can help with?'

'It's just this story I'm working on.' Leaning forward, he took a swig from his glass. 'It's nothing. Let's just watch the film.'

The following morning I woke to find him already seated at his desk on the other side of the bedroom, his body folded over the table.

I loved watching him work, the way he argued with himself under his breath, chewing the tip of his pen, as he did now, absent-mindedly circling words on the page.

I pushed myself up to sitting. 'What are you doing?'

'You're awake.'

He turned slightly from his chair, keeping his eyes fixed to the page. 'I'm going to make coffee,' he added without moving.

I smiled to myself, leaning back, breathing deeply, drinking in his smell, letting the coolness of the sheets settle against my skin.

'It's OK, I'll make it.' I went to stand but he got up first.

'No, no, it's fine. You stay there.'

I watched him walk through the bedroom door to the kitchen in boxer shorts and a T-shirt, the cotton rubbing against the curve of his shoulder blade.

Contentedly, I let my eyes drift around the room, soaking up the old press cuttings, a couple in frames against one wall, a thick stack of books on either side of the fireplace.

It was not like me to overstep boundaries with Harry. But it was in both our interests, I told myself as my toes pressed silently onto the floor next to the bed, the wooden boards soft against the soles of my feet.

Still, I was reassured by the sound of the kettle lightly humming in the kitchen as I wrapped the bedsheet around myself, turning slightly to the empty doorway before moving towards his desk.

I stopped again, giving myself a chance to back out; but it was not as if I was snooping, I reminded myself as I lowered myself slowly into his empty seat, which was still warm. It was hardly rummaging through his secret possessions; it was just a pile of papers and a pad, his writing, unconcealed, the thick, loopy scrawl of someone who thought too quickly.

I did not touch anything, I did not have to turn my head to read it. It was just there, in the middle of a series of words connected by arrows, streaking angrily back and forth across the page, the word 'TradeSmart' circled in pen.

My whole body tensed. That could not be right. I looked again, picking up the notepad this time, turning it so that the words were in sharp focus in front of my face.

As I raised the pad, a photo fell loose, landing face up on the floorboards by my feet. I looked down, and the image stared back at me. The single image of a boy, his extremities protruding from under a white sheet – a child of six or seven.

If it wasn't for the skin, which was black, and the hair, which clung to his head in tight curls, it might have been Thomas. My own brother's face, his skin unnaturally white that day, beneath a scattering of freckles across the bridge of his nose, had shared the same slackness of the jaw, the same unmistakable absence of life. His blond hair stuck to his forehead where he had pushed away the heat of the summer's day with a tiny wrist.

'Your coffee?' Harry stopped when he saw my expression.

My eyes were unable to leave the photo. As if looking in from somewhere else, I heard myself gag, watched myself stand too quickly and then the chair falling away behind me.

'Anna?'

Harry rushed towards me and I pulled myself away, making it to the bathroom just in time.

He had not been angry about me prying and, like a fool, I had taken his softness as a sign of his love. Rather, he had merely sighed, as if there was an inevitability about what was to come.

Leading me into the living room, he held a cigarette packet in his hand as we sat opposite each other on the sofa, spinning the box slowly between his fingers as he spoke.

After some deviation, we got to the point.

'The thing is, Anna, for the past four years I've been part of a team looking at a company called TradeSmart.'

'I know who they are.'

'Of course you do.'

He dropped his eyes, looking away momentarily, releasing a small sigh.

'Well, as you may or may not know, David's dad's company, they're a massive FTSE 100 organisation. A leading logistics and commodity trading company, by their own account.'

He lit a cigarette, his forehead creasing, sliding the pack along to me.

'Clive Witherall, David's father, he's . . .' He paused. What was he thinking in that moment? Did he ever doubt me – did he ever wonder if it was safe to carry on? Or was I so clearly enraptured by then that he already knew what I would be prepared to do?

'We haven't met.' I filled in the gaps.

He carried on after a moment, holding my eyes.

'Well, as you might be aware, to the outside world, Witherall is a bit of a saint. Philanthropist, socialite . . . Runs a couple of orphanages in Central Africa, patron of several charities, friend to the great and the good, whatever else you like.'

He took a drag of his cigarette between words, exhaling a thin, steady stream of smoke.

'You've probably seen him on TV. He's a cocky fucker, always up on his soap-box, brazen as anything. What he's less keen to stand up and talk about, though, is the fact that TradeSmart, for all its talk of corporate social responsibility and ethical foundations, is responsible for dumping a shitload of toxic waste at the edge of villages in Equatorial Guinea, through a series of local contractors. The fallout of which has meant thousands of people have died.'

I shifted uncomfortably in my seat, unsure what to say.

'Shit. That's terrible.'

'It is terrible. I mean, we're talking babies, children, women . . . and hundreds more left with horrific health problems.'

I had no idea where this was going; I was just so happy, so grateful, to be party at last to his inner life. Perhaps once he learned he could trust me, then we could become a proper couple. I could move in, introduce him to my work colleagues . . .

Even then, my mind had skated to David but only for a second. The presents, the house? For Harry I would have given it all up in a second.

'That's so fucked up. I can't believe it. I mean, seriously, to hear David talk about it, you would think his dad was like some kind of god. So you're writing a piece about this?'

He pushed himself up from the sofa, moving purposefully back towards his desk, shoulders broadening.

He opened the drawer slowly, as if still unsure whether to show me or not. By the time he pulled out the folder, turning to face me with renewed purpose, he had me rapt.

'It gets worse.' His voice lowered as he sat. 'A lot worse, Anna . . . The problem with people like Clive Witherall, you see, is that they have friends everywhere.'

I nodded along, the dutiful student.

'And when you have the right friends in the right places and the means to take advantage of destabilised borders, there is no limit to what you can get away with . . . The problem is, right now, we've hit a wall. It doesn't matter what we know, because if we can't prove it—'

He cut himself off, his demeanour visibly shifting, as if suddenly aware of the line he had crossed.

'God, Anna, I'm sorry. You don't need to hear this.'

'No, I do.'

I unfolded my legs, on cue, turning my attention to what he was holding. After just enough deliberation, he took a step towards me, taking in my silence as he handed me the file – an A4 folder, neatly stuffed with papers and photographs.

Amidst the horror of what was being revealed, there was something so natural about sitting there with him, the intensity of the secrets passing between us. I felt his eyes on me as I flicked through pages of transcripts, studying my reaction to the images of dead bodies scattered across a dirt track; weapons, lined up like contestants in a beauty pageant – caring what I thought.

Yet, as I turned the page again, I felt my chest contract. The image had hit me in the chest with the force of a hammer.

At first my eyes were hesitant to settle on the lines of the child's face, but after that I could not wrench them away.

He would have been six or seven, the same age as Thomas, his eyes closed as if in sleep, peering out from under a white sheet. His mother's arms were locked around her son, her face twisted; it was the same expression I saw when I closed my eyes at night.

Here, in Harry's flat, in this image of someone else's child, stiff and lifeless under the sheet, I saw the tiny mound of limbs on the driveway of my parents' home, my own mother's heart being torn from her body.

I dropped the file as soon as I saw it, turning from Harry, my fingernails running down my arms.

'Anna?'

'Who is that?'

Harry's face gave nothing away, but clearly he knew he was safe to carry on.

'This is one of the children who died after a TradeSmart contractor was paid to dump seriously toxic waste at the edge of a playground.'

He let the words settle, waiting for me to soak them in.

'And that's just the tip of the iceberg. In that folder you're holding we have transcripts from women, children who . . .'

He must have seen the unease that spread across my face.

'I'm sorry, I shouldn't be telling you this.'

Taking a step back, he took a final pull of his cigarette before smearing the butt across the windowsill and letting it drop from his hand.

We were silent for a few minutes. I don't remember taking a single breath as I processed his words, leaning forward, the image of the boy's body soldering into me, intensified by my desperation for Harry's faith in me. Desperation not just to know, but to be the one he chose to confide in.

'Harry, please tell me.'

I could feel the burning in my cheeks as he sat back at the other end of the sofa, cupping his face with his hands. Closing his eyes, he circled his fingers over the dark lids, tracing the grooves of his skull.

Eventually, his hands dropped away from his face and he bent his knees, lowering himself beside me. I moved closer in response, holding out my hands.

'How can I help? Is there research, or could I . . .'

He shook his head.

'Oh, come on, Harry. I could do it, you know I could. You know how committed I am, I could help . . .'

He looked away, clearing his throat, preparing himself.

'Of course I know that, Anna. It's not that I . . . It's just . . .'

The more he resisted me, the more forcefully I pleaded with him.

'Come on. What's wrong with you? You have just told me this man is a child murderer, but you don't want as much help as you can get in exposing him? I live with his son, for God's sake, Harry. We're sleeping together. How could you not want to use me?'

How, in uttering those words, did I not understand what was happening?

'You would do that?' Holding my gaze, he sniffed. 'There are complications.'

I stayed quiet then, giving him the space he needed, the room to make the decision for himself.

'OK.' He had said it as if to himself. 'You really want to know, then I'll tell you. I don't really know how to . . . So I'm just going to come out and say it. I'm not writing an article about TradeSmart.'

I stared back at him blankly.

'What are you talking about?'

'I'm not writing a piece about Clive Witherall. I'm looking into him, yes, but it's not for an article. Not for a newspaper. The truth is, I'm working for . . . an organisation, an agency, let's say, to help bring down a man essentially responsible for genocide. And yes, we do need your help, desperately. I just don't know if I can . . .'

He looked at me for a final time before continuing.

'The problem is that Clive, he's an extremely powerful man . . . What we really need is someone on the inside, someone who can get close to him . . .'

The realisation slowly dawned. Drawing a cigarette from the packet he had dropped on the sofa, I let it roll between my fingers as I listened.

'Who is *we*?'

He held my gaze, unblinking.

My voice sounded more self-assured than I had expected, when I continued.

'Harry, if you expect me to trust you it has to go both ways. You can't ask me to be involved with something and not tell me who I'm getting involved with. You can't think I'm that naive.'

The truth, of course, was that he hardly needed to say, and I hardly needed to push. We both knew what we were talking about. MI5, MI6 . . . Did it matter which? I wasn't prepared to ask myself the right questions at the time, let alone to ask him. But the truth is, it can't have been that easy. There must have been a moment in which I stepped back long enough to question where all this would lead, a chill grazing the bare skin of my forearms. Yet, if there was any doubt, I have pushed it so far into the recesses of my memory that I cannot get it back.

'You wouldn't have to report to anyone but me. You would be paid a retainer.'

He said it as an afterthought, having returned from the kitchen with a bottle of whisky and two glasses.

'Obviously it would come from another source so it didn't look obvious.'

Had a smile formed on my lips? Or was it something else I was feeling, a sense that I was stepping with each second that passed towards devastating self-destruction?

It was hard to say right now exactly how much money I would receive, Harry added, but enough to make my life comfortable.

'Only this has to come from you. If you were going to get involved in this, Anna, it would have to be off your own bat. You hear me? For the right reasons – because you wanted to help.'

My expression must have sharpened, a pang of annoyance that he even needed to say this.

'No one will think any less of you if you decide you can't. Plenty of people know awful things are happening but choose – understandably – not to get involved. Even if they could help, they don't. And that doesn't mean that they're bad people, it just means—'

'I get it.'

He considered me for a while, as if noticing something in my face that he had not seen before. After a minute or so, he nodded.

'If you're serious . . . Either way, you need to go away and give it some thought. Let me know, when you're ready.

'More than anything,' he added, drawing a line under the conversation, 'you must know that I will always be there, if you decide to go ahead. If ever you need me.'

CHAPTER 11

Anna

David had already left by the time I woke up. Drawn outside by the light spilling in through every crevice of the house, the sound of the birds perched on the feeder outside the kitchen window, I took my cup onto the patio.

Following the curve of the garden, I walked towards the ornate iron bench which stood next to the door leading out onto the Heath, settling to feel the morning sun brushing against my face, the occasional call of a dog walker, the gurgle of a toddler, rising over the wall.

This is where I was still sitting, nursing a cup of cold coffee, when David appeared through the French doors half an hour later. It was a Saturday morning and the promise of spring danced between puffs of light cloud.

He wore a look of appreciation as he approached, the sun lighting him from behind. With the halo effect of the light around his head, I had a flash of memory: that first afternoon drinking together on the beach at Brighton. It was the same look, one that I could now recognise as adoration, which he wore then. Without the affectations of his university brand – the Camden Market-style jewellery traded in for a simple leather watch; the hooded jumper replaced with a casual light blue shirt – he looked younger, somehow, like a boy who had raided his father's wardrobe.

He was about to say something, I could tell, but he paused briefly, as if enjoying the spectacle of this moment together in the garden of the house he grew up in too much to interrupt. When he finally pulled up a chair, he pressed his lips on mine.

I smiled, pulling myself slightly away from him, meeting his eyes.

'I was thinking, we should get a gardener,' I said, once he had settled himself, leaning back against the bench, his legs splayed.

I had been working up to the suggestion over the past few days, still unsure whether it was within my remit to request such a thing. This was still very much his family home but, beautiful as it was, it had begun to feel frayed, the toll of David's once steady stream of parties having worn into the edges.

He shrugged. 'Sure.' The glint in his eyes remained intact.

I nodded, pleased at his easy reaction, looking away for a moment before feeling my attention drawn back to him.

'What?'

'Nothing.'

He was staring, the smile pinched at either side of his mouth.

'What, David?' I tried not to sound impatient, pushing playfully at his arm. 'What do you want?'

'I bought croissants,' he said, reaching down towards a shopping bag. 'And juice.'

I arranged myself in my chair, 'Excellent, thank you.'

'And . . .' he paused before reaching into his pocket, drawing out an envelope. There was a loaded silence and then he started to speak. 'These past months with you . . . I know, I know, but humour me, please . . . These past few months with you have been the best of my life. I know it sounds horribly cheesy but it's true. And . . .'

He made the sound of a drum-roll, then placed the envelope between my fingers.

Trying to read his face, I opened it and pulled out two tickets, feeling my heartbeat rise.

He watched me as I raised one hand to my mouth, the other hand clutching the plane tickets. 'Oh my God, David, I can't, this is too much . . .'

'It's not.'

He held my knee in his hand, squeezing harder with every second that passed.

'I know sometimes maybe you feel I'm pushing things too fast, but I really mean it when I say that you are the most extraordinary girl . . .' He corrected himself, 'You are the most extraordinary *woman* I've ever met. And I know how hard you've been working, and, well, it's a selfish act. I want you there, I want you to meet my family. My dad.'

He watched me, my teeth biting down onto my lip so that I could taste the blood inside my mouth.

'Sorry, that sounded intense. I just mean I want to spend time with you, away from here. I want you to be part of my life. Properly.'

I swallowed, looking up at him, pausing just long enough to see his desire grow a little more.

'I don't know what to say.'

'Say you'll come?' He moved closer.

Greece. I felt my stomach flip.

Placing my hand on the side of my chair to steady myself, I breathed in.

'I'll come.'

'He's invited me to Greece.'

I blurted it out as soon as I had stepped inside Harry's front door, the reality of what was happening jolting through me in fretful waves.

It was only the third time I had been at the flat since I moved in with David, feigning overnight stays with friends; claims I had been waiting for him to question, and which he never did – trusting me implicitly from the very start.

Harry was still standing with one hand on the front door, but after a moment a smile crept across his face and he pushed it closed.

'Really?'

He moved towards me and for once I moved away, unsure of what I needed, unable to stand still long enough to accept his touch.

He was gentle with me, careful not to push, always gauging his impact on me perfectly.

'And Clive, he'll be there too?'

'Of course.'

'You're brilliant.'

This time I stayed put as he placed his hands on my hips, pressing his palms against the gentle roll of the bone.

'What did you say when he asked you?'

'What do you think?'

He nodded, absorbing my words. I felt his eyes weighing me up, the balance of power between us shifting imperceptibly.

'And you are OK with this?' He spoke quietly, but his words were weighted.

'Yes.' My voice was less steady now, less convinced. I felt my body shake, my face turning to the table where his cigarettes lay.

Harry followed my gaze and leaned over to pick up the packet, pulling one out and pressing it into my hand.

'Are you sure? Because you don't seem sure.'

'Harry, for fuck's sake, I'm sure.'

I stooped to accept his lighter before looking up sharply. His lack of faith had provoked me. What did he think I had been doing these past months?

Sensing my unease, he clamped his right hand softly around the base of my neck, my flesh tingling at his touch. Closing my eyes, I felt the words fall from my mouth, 'I've missed you.'

CHAPTER 12

Anna

The airport that first time was an assault on my senses. Keeping close to David, I followed the endless lines, past armed police officers, parents with toddlers on leashes, women with fixed smiles seizing bottles of perfume; the cacophony of beeps and hums taunting me as I scanned the customs hall for cues as to how to behave.

It had not occurred to me to leave my second phone in my suitcase, and it was not the kind of question I had thought to ask when Harry was talking me though the plan, mistaking my continuous probing for direction in best practice, rather than a plea for basic information. Short of admitting I had never been abroad before, how could I explain to someone to whom international travel was second nature that other than knowing to take my passport, I had no idea what to expect?

While I had never directly lied to Harry about my past, there was plenty I hadn't mentioned. Our relationship, I was sure, relied on him believing me to possess a degree of sophistication that the full truth would instantly belie.

At security, I mirrored David's movements, laying my possessions out in a plastic tray, feeling the customs officer's eyes on me as she beckoned me through a metal arch that shot out a cry as I passed through.

Beckoning me forward, the woman pressed her hand against my body, her palms running up and down my thighs as perspiration stung the top of my lip.

'Could you empty your pockets for me, please?'

I nodded, not trusting myself to speak.

David, a metre or so away, was repacking the contents of his rucksack. My hands shaking, I reached hesitantly into the lining of my jacket.

The woman raised an eyebrow, as if to ask, *two phones*?

'One's for work.' I spoke quickly, my eyes moving to David, who was making his way towards me now.

'Everything OK?'

Working hard to hold his attention with my eyes, to distract him from my fingers, I arranged my face into a smile, the blood pounding in my chest.

When the customs officer spoke again, I missed her words.

'Sorry?'

'I said, you'll have to run them through the X-ray. Go back through.'

She was becoming exasperated, as were the family behind us, the toddler's screams growing louder with each second that passed.

Giving David a smile, I followed the woman's pointed finger back through the metal archway, moving as fast as was reasonable towards the stack of plastic trays, placing the phones side by side in the rectangular cradle. As I scanned my mind for possible explanations I could use to reassure David, all I could focus on was the sound of the child's voice rising in shrill peaks behind me; the wail of the metal detectors going off one after another across the hall, rising and falling like an air-raid siren.

I could of course repeat that it was a work phone, but he would be instantly suspicious as to why I hadn't mentioned it before. All of this, everything, relied on me giving him no reason to doubt anything I said. Ever. The moment he started to question me, even for something seemingly innocuous, would be the moment everything would start to unravel.

Besides, I wondered, could I lie to his face without giving myself away? It seems laughable now that I had credited myself with having so much integrity.

David's eyes stayed on mine as he continued walking towards me, trance-like, and I held them there, willing him with every inch of my body not to look away. If his gaze so much as slipped towards the glistening line of tiny crystals of sweat that had formed above my lips, the spell would be broken.

As I opened my mouth to speak – to tell the only lie my mind could fathom – there was a sound like a gunshot and every eye in the room swooped towards me. Instantly, the room fell quiet. A second later, there was a wail from the child behind us and it was then that I understood the source of the noise: a bottle of milk the boy's parents had been using in an attempt at placation being thrown and hitting the ground with the force of a missile.

Ever the helpful citizen, David leaned down to pick up the bottle. The moment he was down, I lurched towards the tray, shoving it through the curtain. My heartbeat still racing, I moved through the metal detector once more. In his enthusiasm to help pick up the bottle, David had moved back in the line, and now a customs officer put a hand on his shoulder.

'Sir, you're going to have to go back through the detector. If you can step back through the arch . . .'

The breath released from my body with a hiss.

David's exasperation was written across his face, but he wasn't one to make a scene. Instead, he compliantly followed the officer's instructions, holding out his arms as I moved back towards the conveyor belt, just in time to see the box containing my phones move out through the second curtain.

Hardly able to breathe, I ran at them, stuffing both devices in my pocket just in time to turn and find David standing in front of me.

'Shit!' I jumped and he half-smiled.

'OK? You look . . . sweaty.'

I laughed, my voice unnaturally cheery as I linked my arm through his. 'I know, sorry, gross. I need a drink. Shall we keep going?'

* * *

The flight to Athens seemed to take forever, every judder signalling impending doom, the roar of the engines marking the otherwise imperceptible shift into another life. When I looked back from the other side, I imagined the plane pushing through an imaginary seal, tearing a hole through the world I knew. On one side, the world I had left behind; on the other, the one that would be the end of me.

In all the times I had imagined what it must be like to sit in a plane, I had never anticipated the vibration, which shook through my body as the wheels scraped off the runway.

David rested his hand on my white-blue fingers, which were throttling the armrest. 'You didn't tell me you were scared of flying.'

'I'm not.'

I looked down at his open palm, my cheeks burning.

'It's Valium, it'll take the edge off.' He kissed me. 'I have a feeling you might need it for the next bit.'

Athens airport was swollen with noise and heat, shapes contorted in the stagnant hive of bodies. David reached for my hand, pulling me through the crowds.

By the time we caught the connecting flight, I felt the world slow down around me, colours bleeding into one another as we boarded the aircraft, which was barely big enough to carry the twelve passengers and our luggage.

I studied the seats, hedged into one another, the heads of the other passengers grey and distant, mine and David's the only English voices on the flight.

As the plane lifted off from the steaming tarmac, my eyes grew heavy. I took a long breath, studying the fine white hairs that lay flat against my thighs, like the wisps of bulrushes that snuck into the confines of our garden from the field at the edge of my parents' home. The thought triggered a memory: my brother's face disappearing towards the garden gate.

'Marianne! Come on!'

My own voice followed, too weak to be heard. 'I can't, Mummy said not to.'

Was it weakness or encouragement I was hearing? Had I failed to warn Thomas of the dangers he faced, or had I actively encouraged him to break the rules? Were the words I was remembering the uncertainty of a sister who was simply too young to have been put in charge of her twin – or was it rather the sound of a young girl sick of her brother always being the favourite, always being the one to get away with murder while she was the one upon whose shoulders too much responsibility rested?

'Anna?' David nudged my arm. 'Your seatbelt.'

Shuddering at the thoughts still clattering through my mind, I pushed my head back into the present. A woman's voice was talking through the crackle of the radio, first in Greek, then, less enthusiastically, 'Good afternoon, and welcome to this flight to Skiathos . . .'

'Oh, yes, thanks.' I reached for the buckle on either side of my legs and heard the click as I locked myself into the seat.

'So, once we land, we'll take a boat to the island. You don't get seasick, do you?'

I shook my head, already feeling the swinging bowels of the boat.

'My father will send a car to meet us at the port. We can go straight up to the house. He won't be there until the evening, so we can have a swim or whatever while we wait.'

I pictured myself on the other side, taking a long drag of a cigarette, imagining the tar rolling over my lungs, like hot concrete.

'You look a bit pale. Why don't you rest your eyes? I'll wake you when we're landing.'

Skiathos was another world again, winding roads tipping down towards the sea.

David and I left the airport, the wheels of our suitcases drumming against the pavement.

The hot leather of the seats soldered itself to my thighs as the taxi swung around corners, the radio hissing in and out of range. David reached over and took my hand in his, my attention fixed on the sheen of sweat on the driver's forehead in the rear-view mirror.

At the port, the gentle breeze cooled us as we awaited the boat, looking out on the expanse of water speckled with sails.

'This is beautiful,' I said, absorbing the shocking blue of the water, the warm embrace of the afternoon sun.

Taking a seat outside one of the cafés on the main stretch, we ordered coffee and orange juice, thick and bitter, cold and sweet. On either side, we were surrounded by gift shops selling marine-related magnets, postcards and cheap ouzo.

'Dad would have sent his, but he was using it this afternoon.' David adjusted his sunglasses, rolling his head back.

'I'm happy to get the ferry. When is it due?'

'Actually, I think that might be it coming in now. You see, that bright yellow one?'

I nodded, imagining the churning of the motor below the water, the vessel silently cutting its path towards us like a brightly coloured hearse.

Placing 15 euros under the ashtray, David stood, taking both our suitcases, leading the way towards the jetty.

'Shall we sit on the deck?'

He did not wait for an answer, leading me to a circle of seats at the boat's nose as the other passengers moved inside.

My stomach followed the undulations of the sea, the spray forming an arc where the steel cut a line through the water. Imagining the world that lay beneath them, I pictured hundreds of miles of darkness – secrets that would never be found.

'This is it!' David's face was like a child's as he led the way onto the sliver of port that lay inside the curve of land at the bottom of the mountain.

Facing the island, grateful to press my feet finally on solid ground, I let myself take a moment. The sun beating against the hillside, igniting against stone buildings, iron poles poking out from the top like executioner's spikes.

The port consisted of one small road. Below it, a strip of beach was spotted with seaweed and stones, a slick of engine oil shifting against the concrete jetty that formed a strip into the water.

To the left of the street, from where I stood, there were several bars and restaurants. Low, faded armchairs, blue upright chairs, chequered tablecloths, glass tanks crammed with lobsters clawing over one another for space.

'The best places to eat are in the old village,' David said as he rolled the suitcases in the other direction, towards the bus stop. 'But it's all pretty low-key. There are only three taxi drivers on the whole island, so make sure you never need to leave in a hurry. Where is Jorgos?'

He was talking to himself, scanning the road, which seemed to move in slow motion. Even the music wafting out of the taverna opposite seemed to be playing in half-time.

At that moment, a car emerged from around the corner, moving almost imperceptibly like a shark eyeing up its prey.

'Jorgo!'

David waved his arms above his head, revealing two circles of sweat. I followed his movements, shielding my eyes, dazzled by the silver glare of the Mercedes. The car stopped, engine still running as the driver, a large man with hands like cured hams and silver hair in a ponytail, stepped out and made his way towards David, open-armed.

As the men moved towards one another, David seemed small and child-like, his body folding into the older man's crisp white shirt. I could not make out his words as he spoke, looking over David's shoulder as he did so, pinning me with his eyes from behind his sunglasses.

'You must be Anna?'

Jorgos finally took a step towards me, a piece of gum rolling over his tongue as David pulled back and held his arms out, presenting me like a gift.

Before I could answer, Jorgos stepped forward and took my hand. His grip was hard and I could see my own reflection in his lenses, my yellow sundress clinging to me.

Turning, he picked up our cases in one hand, swinging his keys in the other.

'Anna, you go in the front.'

David opened the door, the rush of cool air from the sleek black vents sending a sweep of goosebumps over me as I lowered myself in.

The house jutted out from the land at the end of the dirt path, hidden behind a cluster of orange trees, the smell of the fruit clinging to the air around it.

David craned his neck from the back seat to see my face, enjoying the way my eyes opened wider to take it all in as the car moved slowly along the driveway. The whiteness of the building glowed against the blue sky, the flat roof sweeping effortlessly into glass, forming an exposed box at the end of the house where it met the garden. The pool stretched out to touch the horizon.

'David, it's stunning.'

His face swelled with pride as I spoke.

I flicked a glance to my left; Jorgos' eyes were fixed on the windscreen.

'Leave your bags, someone will bring them up later.'

David took my arm and stepped inside the door, which led straight into a huge room with floor-to-ceiling windows at the far end, offering views over a sweep of olive groves. The kitchen, to our right as we entered the house, was all sleek chrome fittings and marble countertop; a sofa and chairs overlooking the pool to the left.

Behind us, I saw the car quietly disappearing back up the lane. David followed my gaze.

'Jorgos is a legend. He's like my uncle, been working for my dad since before I was born.'

As he spoke, David started pulling open cupboards, lifting out bottles and discarding them again.

'What do you want to drink?'

The effects of the Valium were still pulling at my body, making my limbs heavy.

'I don't know, water maybe?'

'Sure, but we need a proper drink – we're celebrating.'

Drumming his fingers against the cold surface he peered through rows and rows of sealed bottles.

My head throbbed; all I wanted was to go upstairs and lie down.

'We could go and look in the wine cellar if you fancy champagne? Or . . .'

He pulled out a bottle of gin.

'G and T?'

'Perfect.' I pushed my lips into the right position.

David grinned back at me. 'I tell you what, I'll make these up, and then I'll grab some pool towels.'

'I'll do it,' I said. 'I need to use the loo anyway.'

He paused before agreeing, reluctant as always to let me go.

I was relieved to walk away, following David's instructions into the hallway where the breeze rushed through the atrium, trailing over marble sculptures, a glass table lined with artefacts made from shells, wood and pearl; up the cold tiled stairs, my fingers trailing the smooth bannister, and along the hall, lined with exquisitely framed paintings, before finally pushing at the door at the far end of the house.

Away from David's gaze, I allowed myself to take in the bedroom. The king-sized bed was made up to hotel standard with white cotton sheets and matching scatter cushions; a traditional woven rug by the bed, a selection of magazines on a low-lying table.

Somehow our bags had already been placed against the wall, next to a door leading out onto a small terrace. Through the French doors at the far end of the room, the side of the mountain rolled down to the sea like a blanket, dotted with olive trees.

The en suite bathroom stood behind me. Stretching out my arms, I slipped off my sandals and walked across the room, enjoying the coolness against the soles of my feet.

Running the tap, I let out a sigh as I splashed water against the heat of my cheeks. I reached for a towel and pushed my face into the plush cotton, inhaling deeply. When I opened my eyes I found David in the doorway, looking back at me in the mirror.

'There you are.'

'Shit, David!' I jumped, bashing my toe against the tiles. 'You scared me.'

'Babe, I'm sorry, I just wondered where you'd got to. Come down, the pool is begging for us to dive in.'

He was holding up a couple of white towels, which looked like they had just been pulled from the shelves of an expensive department store.

'I haven't got my swimming things out yet,' I told him as he hushed me, pulling at my hand, guiding me back towards the stairs.

'You don't need them. Dad's not going to be back for hours. You haven't lived until you've swum naked in that pool . . .'

Downstairs, David handed me one of the gin and tonics from the counter. 'I'm serious,' he said as I followed him out to the pool.

I screamed as I hit the water, bubbles rising up around me, my body writhing, twisting against its natural course.

Slapping my arms against the surface, I pulled my head up and took a gulp of air.

'Seven out of ten!' David called out, scraping his toes along the edge of the pool, swigging a bottle of Mythos.

'What?!'

I offered him an affected look, throwing up my hands.

'Bullshit, that was at least an eight.'

'Sorry, umpire's decision is final.'

He handed me a glass of rosé when I came out of the pool, and I sat sipping it on the steps at the edge of the water, my legs crossed.

'I tell you what, though . . .' David lowered himself into the shallow end and glided towards me. He looked up, his eyes following the bead of water that trickled down my stomach. Pulling me into the pool next to him, he pushed me back against the steps, kissing my neck, tasting the salt of my skin. 'I think you deserve a consolation prize.'

Before I could reply, I felt him pressing up against me, his slow movements amplified by the futile resistance of the water.

During our first weeks together, unable to push away the sense that I was betraying Harry, I had dreaded these moments, getting through them by allowing my mind to switch itself off, to shift gear, implementing the techniques the doctors had taught me to combat the panic attacks that crept in without warning in childhood. Slowly, though, the dread had softened, the guilt slowly, almost imperceptibly drifting away so that now, as David moved inside me, I felt myself quietly lean back into him.

Feeling my breath quicken, short, sharp stabs swelled and softened with his movements, I watched the cloudless sky, the thick, sweet smell of oranges mixed with sun cream.

'Shit!'

David lurched backwards, clambering suddenly in slow motion towards the edge of the pool.

I felt myself tipping backwards, my head scraping the stone, catching myself as David tore out of the water, leaning back down to grab me by the arm. As he hoisted me out, I felt my ribs scraping against the edge of the pool.

'David, that hurts!'

I resisted, watching the angry imprint of his fingers like burns against my pale skin, finally recognising the sound of wheels crunching against gravel.

With a sense of dread, I turned to see the Mercedes crawling down the driveway. Clive. I thought of the photographs Harry had shown me of David's father, spread out across the floor of his flat. The whole plan relied on Clive taking a liking to me, on him trusting me enough to bring me into the fold. While my access to David was the gateway, having David's trust alone was not enough. The crucial thing, Harry had emphasised, was that his father must want me in the family as well. First impressions were everything; those were the words Harry had used. If he saw me now, naked, frolicking in the pool with his son, I might as well admit defeat. There would be no second chances at first impressions – Harry had said that too.

Horrified at how easily I had let my mask slip, I lurched into action, pulling myself out of the pool, my eyes darting about for the towels, noting, with regret, that they lay on the sun lounger at the other end of the pool, just out of reach.

Before David could say anything, I turned and ran back towards the house, keeping my body low, out of sight; a slick of hair running down my back, leaving a trail of water behind me as I slipped back through the kitchen towards the hall, struggling to keep my feet from skidding on the tiles – unnoticed, I believed, by the men just the other side of the glass.

CHAPTER 13

Anna

'Have you been to Greece before, Anna?'

Clive was seated opposite me at the head of the table, Jorgos on one side, David on the other. The sky above the restaurant's terrace was black by now, a string of white lanterns hanging above our heads between bundles of bougainvillea, like paper bombs.

'I haven't, but I've always wanted to.'

I watched his face lift in satisfaction, as he barely raised his arm to the waiter, who obediently moved inside the restaurant and returned with another bottle of wine.

'Well, I hope you won't be disappointed. I'm sure David will make the trip very special for you both.'

He tilted his glass at his son, grinding his food deliberately between his teeth.

'I'm sure he will.'

I managed a smile, forcing down the mouthful of lamb, a string of fat catching in my throat.

'This was David's mother's favourite restaurant.'

Clive's voice didn't falter. David had been taking a sip of wine, which left a dark stain against his lips, and the stem of his glass hung in the air, a second too long, as he looked up at his father, his expression lost in shadow.

'Isn't that right, David?'

He had only mentioned his mother once, in passing, in the years that I had known him. She died when he was a boy, he answered quickly before attempting to change the subject when Meg asked. Meg, never one to take a hint, had failed to take the cue to stop and so I had intervened, aware of his grateful look as I stepped in.

'Mine too.' I had said it before I could stop the words from forming. Another lie, tumbling from my lips. But the words had had a soothing effect, I could tell.

'David tells me you lost your mother too.'

'Dad.' David placed his glass firmly on the table.

'I'm not sure this is the time.' Clive raised an eyebrow apologetically.

'No, it's fine,' I cut across David. 'I was very young, I don't remember much.'

'More wine?'

Jorgos leaned over to pick up the bottle, filling my glass before turning to the rest of the table. Lifting the glass, I smiled, meeting Clive's toast, as with the other hand he held a napkin up to his chest, the image of the stark white cotton striking me like a bus.

The noise that burst out of my lungs was a cry which seemed to come from somewhere outside myself. I heard the back legs of my chair scrape against the concrete as I stepped back, too fast. In front of me, as plain as the faces that watched us from the restaurant, Clive's features had become those of the child in the photo in Harry's flat, his lifeless body protruding from under the sheet, the mother's face beside him a contorted mask. The face in which I saw my own brother's reflection, the same hollowed-out look in his lifeless eyes.

Raising a hand to my chest, I stood, David's confused expression following me across the terrace and into the yellow glow of the restaurant. The heat from the kitchen rose out like a furnace as I passed, throwing open the door to the bathroom. Inside, I pushed at the latch, my fingers trembling. My reflection was little more than a colourless wash as I threw myself towards the toilet bowl, just in time, the sound of my own retching like a distant animal.

Running my forehead and cheeks under the tap, I gulped at the water before lifting my head, letting my vision settle on the mirror. My eyes were wild, my pupils like black stars.

Harry.

I whispered his name as I scrambled in my bag for my phone, the one he had given me the day before I left. I had put off leaving his flat, my arms clinging to his back as we said goodbye at the door. Closing my eyes, I pictured him in front of me, his arms around me, his fingers drawing protective lines down my back, the day my world split in two.

CHAPTER 14

Anna

David woke first the next day. From the other side of the bed, I felt him peeling back the sheets, the mattress lifting in his absence. Letting my head drop to the side, I made myself focus on the light breeze drifting in from the terrace, picturing the sun catching on ripples of water.

A few minutes later, I heard his feet slapping against the floor as he returned with a glass of freshly squeezed orange juice.

'How are you feeling?'

His face hovered above mine, scanning my skin for lingering signs of sickness.

From outside, I could hear the gentle scrape of a sun lounger beside the pool.

'Better, thanks. Is that for me?'

'Thank God. I feel so guilty, the food at Niko's is usually so . . .'

Leaning towards the side table, I took a grateful sip.

'Don't be – I think it must just have been from the flight or something. I'm sure the food had nothing to do with it.'

'Look.' He took my hand, his eyes falling to his lap. 'I'm really sorry about my dad, asking about your mum, that was—'

'God no, it wasn't.' I pushed my lips against his, silencing him. 'He was just curious about your girlfriend. I thought it was sweet.'

Smiling, he ran a finger through my hair. '*You're* sweet. And anyway, I'm going to make it up to you.'

* * *

'Don't worry about packing a bag, I've thought of everything.' David guided me through the kitchen by the hand, an hour later. An older woman was sweeping the stone decking on the terrace. She looked up at me briefly, her eyes taking me in before snapping her attention back to her work.

'Sun cream, hats, towels, swimming costume. And last but not least . . .'

He pushed me out through the double doors onto the driveway where a motorbike was propped up, two helmets hanging either side, watching the smile break across my mouth.

'Now, do you want something to snack on now or can you wait until we get there?'

'Get where?'

'I've told you, it's a surprise.'

I felt a pang of warmth towards him as I watched him carefully fill the storage unit under the seat, his body, warm with sweat, my anchor as I pulled myself over the bike, gripping his waist.

'Ready?'

He revved the handlebars, sending a plume of smoke and dust in our wake.

'Ready.' I laughed, my voice drowned out under the roar of the engine, the stench of petrol, hot black metal burning against my calves.

It was the first time we had left the confines of the house in daylight since we had arrived the previous afternoon, and with a growing sense of awe I watched the views unfold as we soared around the winding road that clung to the mountain. Swathes of sea, like precious gems, moved in and out of focus as the bike followed the tarmac. At points, the rock fell away, silent shrines marking the spots where the dead had fallen.

'Here it is.'

David's voice strained above the engine, which settled to a low purr as we pulled onto a strip of dirt track lined with tall shrubs. Silence replaced the purr of the engine as we pulled ourselves off the bike, and then the gentle lapping of the water.

Through a gap in the bushes, a stretch of powder-white sand revealed itself. There was a small taverna at one end, a cluster of rocks at the other. Fleetingly, I thought of the beaches I had visited as a child: sharp pebbles catching my toes, the slurring hum of the merry-go-round.

'Wow, this is so beautiful.'

David nodded as I took in the view, the headland jutting out to meet the cloudless sky.

'Isn't it? Now, choose somewhere to sit. Wherever you like, it looks like we're pretty much the only people here. I'm going to get our stuff.'

David disappeared back towards the bike and I slipped off my flip-flops, my feet submerging themselves in the sand, which was hot and prickly. Cursing under my breath at the unexpected heat, I stuffed my feet back into my flip-flops, moving further towards the water before settling on my sarong.

'Is iced tea OK or shall I go and get us a couple of coffees?' David had returned and was rifling in the cool-bag, pulling out two glistening cans. 'I even brought straws.'

'This is perfect,' I replied, pressing my elbows into the sand, my head rolling back in tandem with the crack of the ring-pull.

As we looked out across the beach, my eyes fell on two girls, who must have been around three or four, slapping at the sand with matching spades. For a moment, I thought of Thomas and my heart tightened. A second later, one of the children leaned forward and pushed the other, who instantly burst into tears. As their mother intervened to defuse the situation between sparring siblings, I felt David reposition himself on the towel next to me.

'Bloody hell, aren't you glad you were an only child?'

Taken off guard, my body flinched. 'What?'

He must have sensed something in my expression. As his eyes narrowed slightly, I pulled myself straighter on my sarong, following his lead.

'Yeah, I mean twins – can you imagine?'

'Nope,' David snorted, relaxing again. 'They run in families, you know that?'

'Do they?' I averted my gaze so that I was looking at a family settling themselves at one of the tables at the beach bar; the way they moved so naturally around one another was captivating, none of them ever bristling at each other's touch.

'Yeah, I mean fuck that.' His voice was emphatic.

I mirrored his tone. 'Massively fuck that.'

He made a shuddering sound and I laughed, picking up my drink, the bubbles fizzing against my throat as I swallowed.

The morning passed by in a wash of blues and golds, the sun lightly prickling my skin as I stretched out across the towel. After a while, the red glow inside my eyelids turned to black.

I could not be sure how long I had slept. When I came to a while later, the sound of the water breaking against the shore, I felt myself blinking against the sky's savage glare. Slowly lifting my weight up onto my elbows, I looked around for David, but he was nowhere to be seen.

Assuming he must have headed to the bar for a drink, I turned onto my front, undoing the clasp of my bikini top, watching the waves gently lap at the shore. For the first time all day, I let myself think of Harry.

He had already sent two messages since I had arrived in Greece. The sensible thing to do would be to reply then and there, while I had the chance, to let him know I was OK. Reaching into my bag, I let my hands glide over the hot surface of my phone for a moment before letting go; something about the idea of him thinking of me, wondering where I was, stopped me. Why not let him stew for a few hours longer? Taking a breath, I pulled out a cigarette instead.

With a passing flutter of guilt, I breathed in the smoke, exhaling the thought of him away.

* * *

'David, this is insane.'

I let him lift me into the speedboat like a child, squealing as he jokingly threatened to drop me back onto the deck.

'Are you actually safe to drive this thing?'

'Only one way to find out . . .'

As the boat set off, I was thrown back, the spray of the water slapping against my legs.

Steadying myself, I faced the beach, watching it shrink and then disappear as we cut around the headland, enjoying the longing in the faces that followed us from the shore.

David turned briefly to smile at me from the wheel. The wind tearing at my cheeks, I felt the urge to scream. What would my parents have said if they could have seen me now?

As unexpected as the rush of joy that had seized me a moment earlier, I felt a stab of pain as I thought of my mother, picturing her reaction if I had been able to tell her about David. There would have been the usual show of happiness for her only daughter, followed by an ill-disguised swell of pain. The surviving child, an unrelenting reminder of all she had lost. The loss of Thomas followed by the collapse of the business; my father's refusal to turn anywhere but inwards. The blame for all of it safely stowed at my door.

'Here we are!'

My cheeks were wet from the spray, stinging as the salt rubbed against my sunburnt skin. As I turned, another beach came into view, this one deserted, a cove at the far end like a gaping mouth.

Once he had laid the blanket on the sand, pulling the corners neatly in line, David pulled out a bottle of champagne and popped the cork.

Sucking the foam from the side of his glass, he pulled out a plate of fresh calamari, still warm, from the taverna, and a selection of dips and olives, with soft, greasy bread.

'David, this is perfect.'

It was, almost. Watching David scooping tzatziki into his mouth, I thought how proud Harry would be of me, of how far I had come.

Jealous, too? The thought pleased me as I let the straps of my bikini fall from my arms, tilting my head back to catch the sun.

'So are you. That's why I love you.'

The words made me freeze.

'Hardly.' I laughed lightly, turning my attention to the cooler bag. 'What else have you got in here?'

Pulling out a tub of fresh fruit, I willed him to look away.

'Anna, I mean it.'

Pushing against the sensation rising in my belly, I lifted my eyes to meet his. I opened my mouth and the words rolled out, round and easy on my tongue.

'I love you too.'

We returned from the beach in the late afternoon, the words that had passed between us earlier stirring behind David's eyes.

After showering, I slipped on a long dress and sandals, the pale pink of my shoulders fizzing under white spaghetti straps.

'I thought you were sleeping.' David looked up from the hammock where he was lying, his face coming to life.

'I couldn't sleep, I thought I'd have a shower instead. Hope that's—'

'There you are.' Clive's voice roared behind me.

He stepped into view, carrying his laptop and a newspaper, wearing a panama hat and linen suit, the off-duty Englishman.

'You're feeling better then? You gave us quite a fright at dinner last night.'

'Much better, thank you.'

He sat back in a wooden lounger, pushing another one forward for me to join them.

'Athena?'

A woman appeared from the kitchen, small but firm as a fist.

'We'll have three G and Ts if you don't mind? Extra ice, it's bloody scorching.'

'Anna, this is Athena, I don't think you've met.' David held out his arm towards the woman I had noticed earlier that morning, as she returned with a tray.

'Athena looks after the house and, more importantly, she looks after us.'

Clive held the last word a beat too long.

'Lovely to meet you.'

'You too. David and my daughter Maria grew up together. Every summer, the two of them were inseparable. They were like brother and sister . . .' Athena held my eye.

'Oh. David hasn't mention—'

But then David's voice cut across mine. 'We haven't seen each other in years.'

Did I imagine Athena bristling at his words?

Composing her face, she smiled though her voice was brisk. 'No, well, lives move in different directions. Anyway, I better get on. Nice to meet you, Anna.'

There was a moment's silence and then David nodded, switching his attention to the pool.

'You remember I'm planning a little soirée on Saturday?' Clive spat a stone into his hand.

'Of course. Who's coming?' David leaned back in the hammock.

'Oh, just the usual. The Campbells, the Earls and their kids, the Phillimores. Oh, and Jeff and May are thinking of heading over . . .'

There was a note in his voice, which David responded to with an unspoken question.

Clive waved his arm, silencing him, as I made a mental note. *Jeff and May*.

We spent the following day at another of the various beaches that lay in discreet inlets around the island, sunning ourselves until our skin burnt. Later on, we made our way back up the mountain, hot stones spitting against our bare, sun-drenched skin as David's bike swung around the sharp bends.

The house was quiet when we got back, the sun silently lowering itself towards the water that surrounded us.

'I'm going to use the outside shower. You can join me if you like?' David spoke as we entered the kitchen, the coolness of the air stinging against my skin.

'I might have that lie-down now, if that's OK?'

He nodded, watching me as I retreated upstairs.

Reaching the landing, I took a moment to drink in the house. The sweep of the staircase; the oversized ceramic pots like enormous urns at the corner of each room. Drawing a map in my mind, I processed everything only in small chunks, just as Harry had taught me.

The top floor echoed the footprint of the ground floor, before stretching out into the guest wing and then, separately, the staff quarters where the maid stayed while the house was in use.

The family wing, where I now stood, consisted of two doors along the main walls, and one more at each end. In the perfect stillness of the hallway, I moved slowly, studying the paintings that lined the walls on both sides. An orange grove in heavy slashes of paint. Sea views. A faceless woman crouched over the branches of an olive tree.

Recognising the brushstrokes from the picture which hung above the fireplace at home, and along the landing outside David's bedroom, I thought of David's mother, imagining her walking these halls in the months before she died.

Taking a step closer towards the bedroom, I caught the sound of a man's voice, Clive's distinct low vibrato humming from the second door on the left, which I now saw was partially open. There was a wall of books just visible through the crack. The study.

His voice rang with the affability of an English gent.

'Very good, Jeff. Well, I look forward to seeing you then. Will the kids be joining us?'

From the rise in volume it was clear that the call was coming to an end. Silently, I moved faster down the hall as I heard him ring off, the crack of his knees as he rose from his chair, followed by a low cough.

Holding my breath, I pulled open the door to David's room, pressing it closed as quietly as I could and leaning back against it. My heart pounded as I finally pulled out my phone from my bag. One message from 'Dad', sent three times since Saturday.

Anna?

I took a moment before typing, the thought of Harry calming my nerves.

Hi Dad, I'm here with David. So far so good. x

CHAPTER 15

Anna

'Don't worry, they'll love you.' David was in the en suite, a razor to his neck, chamber music wafting in from outside through the terrace doors.

I stood, moving in front of the mirror while he shaved, holding a yellow halterneck dress against my body.

Through the terrace doors, I could hear Athena talking to herself in Greek as the caterers laid out hors d'oeuvres on silver platters in the kitchen, the gentle murmur of her voice soothing my heartbeat.

'I wanted to give you this.' David walked around to the drawer by his side of the bed and pulled out a rectangular box.

'What is it?'

'Have a look.'

Turning, I saw the box in his hand, rectangular black leather, cracked open to reveal a cream-coloured silk.

He watched my face.

'It's amethyst. It belonged to my mother.'

'Oh David, it's beautiful.'

'Here, let me help.'

Walking slowly behind me, he took the necklace.

'It really suits you,' he said, pulling the chain lightly around my throat.

The final wave of guests started to pile in as if from nowhere at around 7 p.m., cars clogging up the drive. Women in garish reds and greens, lavish silks and pearls; men in linen suits strutted like peacocks, the smell of money oozing from their pores.

'Go out, I'll be down in a minute,' David whispered, heading back upstairs and leaving me in the kitchen where a team of caterers were distractedly piling crudités onto a silver platter.

'I thought it was just a few . . .'

I turned but David had already gone.

Pressing my hands nervously against my thighs, I spotted Jorgos for the first time since dinner the first night, just through the doors where the terrace gave way to the pool and the garden beyond. A gold chain glistened against his tanned wrist as he clamped his phone to his ear, his silver hair swept back in his signature ponytail. His eyes scanned the house behind his shades, taking it all in, not missing a beat.

For a moment our eyes met and then I felt a slight pressure on my shoulder.

'You must be David's girlfriend . . .'

Turning, I was met by a woman holding two champagne glasses, my mother's age but a different breed. Her skin, a thick mahogany, was pulled tight against her jaw, jewels clinging to her ears.

'I'm May. Clive has told us all about you.'

She handed me a glass, tilting it so that the rims almost touched.

A small smile formed on my lips and I nodded. 'I've heard so much about you too.'

The answer seemed to satisfy her and she leaned towards me. 'Do you smoke?'

I nodded, reaching for my bag.

'Shit.' Feeling the panic slowly seizing my body, I pictured it, ajar on the bed, both phones inside. Had I left it open? I could not think through all the noise, with May's eyes trained sharply on mine.

'Actually, I've left them upstairs, I'll just—'

'No need.'

She was already heading for the garden, gliding on impossible heels, willing me along with her.

'So, you're the one who's stolen David's heart.'

Her look was appraising. Taller than her even in flats, I was aware of my dress, the cheap material pulling across my body in all the wrong places.

Trying desperately to keep the fear from my voice, I started to excuse myself, my heart lurching at the memory of my bag on the bed, but she would not hear it.

'Well, I can't say I'm surprised, just look at you.'

She inhaled, keeping her eyes on me as I obediently took one of the cigarettes, thin and white, feeling the sheen of sweat rise across my chest as we stepped into the evening sun.

'May!'

It was David. A tingle of uncertainty rushed over me as he stepped between us, my bag, the clasp locked, in his hand. Had it been closed? Why could I not remember?

He leaned in to kiss the older woman. 'So, you've met, and you have drinks, excellent start. Here.' David discreetly handed me my bag, his eyes trained courteously on his father's guest.

Look at me, I urged him, desperate for a reassuring nod, a smile that would confirm that he had not seen anything out of the ordinary. But his eyes remained on May's.

'We have, but I've yet to probe her properly. Now, David, how are you? And university? Do they still call Sussex a university these days?'

David laughed, taking a drink for himself from a passing tray and another for May whose glass was already empty. I watched his inflection shift, the way he rolled his vowels, his whole demeanour straightening, so different from the one he assumed at home; visibly reverting to his heritage.

He was so good at this, so natural. A natural liar. The thought pricked at the top of my arms.

'I graduated a while ago now, and would you believe, I have a job?'

It was hardly deception, the ability to ingratiate oneself with one's parents' friends, I reprimanded myself as the conversation turned to David's work. Besides, if he had seen something in my bag there was no way he would be standing here now, having a conversation about the merits of the Russell Group.

Distracting myself, I let my attention drift across the party to the guests expertly moving between one another: the flow of kaftans, the chink of glasses, smoked salmon giving way beneath veneered teeth.

As if sensing my unease, David pressed his hand gently, reassuringly, against my lower back. Looking up, I caught his eye briefly and any residual fears instantly fell away.

Bolstered, I squeezed his hand before taking a step away so that I was standing a little away from the crowd, my back to the glass windows. Across the pool, my attention was caught by a young woman around my own age in the kitchen, thick dark hair falling in front of her eyes. Despite the heat, she was dressed in dark jeans and a black vest top revealing deeply tanned shoulders, black flip-flops drumming impatiently against the tiles.

Looking closer, I realised she was talking to Athena, whose figure was partially obscured by the fridge door.

My attention turning once again to the party, I reached into my purse, pulling out my phone and holding it in front of me, as if checking a text. Discreetly pressing the button for camera mode, I clutched it to my chest, an intentionally disarming smile pasted across my face as I turned casually from left to right, repeatedly pressing the red button.

Glancing down for a second, I saw Jorgos through the screen of my phone, less than a metre from me, his eyes concealed behind his glasses.

Flicking the camera off, I let the phone drop to my side and raised my hand in a gesture of hello, but could not be sure if he had seen.

'You OK?'

David was standing beside me once more and I turned, giving him my best smile.

'Fine.'

'Good. There's someone I want you to meet.'

CHAPTER 16

Maria

Like all of my mother's requests, my attendance at the party had not so much been a suggestion as a command. It was the day before our big blow-up but already tensions between us were bubbling just below the surface.

'Maria, I never ask anything of you. Please. How long has it been? Clive always asks after you and they know you are back from Athens. You don't have to stay long.'

Was it purely out of a sense of duty that I had conceded, or was there a part of me that wanted to see David again; part of me that refused to write him off?

The moment I arrived, regret had started to gnaw at my bones.

The house had changed almost beyond recognition. The dark stone kitchen where David and I used to seek refuge from the afternoon sun when we were children had long been bulldozed, replaced by Carrara marble. But the expensive alterations could not erase the memory of Artemis' face. It was everywhere, reflected in the brass taps, shimmering on the surface of the infinity pool.

As I watched my mother fussing with a tray of drinks, I remembered David's words screaming after me from the upstairs landing.

'Mama, I need to go.'

I kept my voice low as she fiddled in the fridge for no reason I could fathom other than to remind the caterers whose kitchen this really was.

The rage in her eyes was so immediate that it must have been bubbling under the surface, just awaiting a false move. Yet I persisted.

'It doesn't feel right. The house where Artemis . . .'

I restrained my voice to a whisper, aware of the staff moving in and out of the kitchen.

'Just being here makes me feel sick. Don't look at me like that; we owe that man nothing.'

'Nothing?' My mother's eyes shone with incredulity. 'You're living in a fairy world. Who pays for your university tuition? Hmm, Maria? Me. And who pays *me*?'

It was my mother's face that gave away his presence, her body pulling away from mine suddenly, righting itself, her tongue flicking over her lip where bubbles of spit had formed.

'David!'

I turned and there he was, inches from my face.

'Maria.'

The warmth in his expression was genuine, I was sure. In that moment, my fear that night, the visceral terror that had sent me running from the house, seemed irrational. It was a response to what had happened, I reminded myself now, just as I had tried to tell myself in the years following that summer, when the nightmares clawed me out of sleep.

Before I could speak he held me in his arms, his body so different from the one I remembered. The puny frame of a boy had been replaced with something more solid, more cultivated.

'Maria, I want you to meet Anna.'

He took a step back and beside him I saw the young woman from the restaurant. I felt a stab of jealousy as his arm touched hers.

She could not have been much older than me. Her eyes, with just a touch of mascara, were a pale green. As she smiled, there was something disconcerting about her, a wariness or a preoccupation that made her impossible to pin down.

When she spoke, she self-consciously pushed her hair behind her ear, the tone of her voice not matching her words. 'It's so nice to meet you.'

'And you.'

Did I imagine David flinching at the sound of my voice?

'Maria is my daughter.'

My mother accentuated her vowels, making it plain she was no longer the housemaid, but rather the family friend she had for so long been.

'She and David are very old friends, they were very close.'

I felt my cheeks blush. 'That was a long time ago.'

'Maria is studying in Athens now, David, did you know it? She was working as a teacher for a while and now she is at university. And . . .'.

My eyes flashed her a warning but she carried on nonetheless.

'Actually, she has been selected to do a year in London as part of her course . . .'

'Mum?' My eyes snapped to her face. 'It's not confirmed, there are things I have to work out first.' I shook my head, indicating my mother had got it wrong.

Anna's attention seemed to drift away as Athena rattled on. After a moment, she broke away, almost imperceptibly, and with a small, unconvincing smile disappeared into the crowd.

'I can't believe it's been so long.'

David accompanied me to the end of the drive, the huge iron gates slowly opening to reveal the pitch-black mountain beyond the gravel drive.

'Are you sure I can't call you a taxi?'

'I have my bike.'

I moved towards the scooter I had propped on the other side of the gates, as if preparing for a quick getaway.

'It's so good to see you again, Maria. You look . . . You look great.'

'Thank you. You look well, too.'

He leaned in to kiss me on the cheek and instinctively, I flinched. If he noticed, it did not show.

'Are you free for a coffee, or lunch? You could come over tomorrow. Anna and I—'

'I can't. I'm heading back to Athens in a few days. I'm working all the time, you know, I have so much to catch up on. My thesis is due after the holidays and . . .'

'It's wonderful, your course . . . You always wanted to go to university.'

Did he have any idea how patronising he sounded?

'The London thing, you know, if you needed somewhere to stay, or . . .'

There was a hint of hope in his eye, or had I imagined it? Maybe it was relief that whatever had stood between us all these years was falling away.

'It's fine, thank you. I have options, it's more that I need to work out stuff here.'

'Well, if you do . . . If you ever need anything, or . . . It would be lovely to see you. Thanks for coming tonight.'

There was something about the sadness in his eye, a hint of the boy he was, my friend, that made me reach for his hand.

'It's good to see you too. Your mum, she would have . . .'

I stopped, unsure of what I had intended to say, pulling my hand away as the gates started to close behind us.

'You better go, Anna will be looking for you.'

David nodded and turned.

I don't know why I said it. The words would strike me later as odd, but as I pulled my leg over the bike, I heard myself add, 'I'll see you again.'

CHAPTER 17

Maria

Of course I didn't mention that I had seen them, a few nights earlier.

I had been walking back through the square from the shops, the evening our lives fused together again after so long apart.

They were sitting in the far corner of the restaurant. Clive, Jorgos and David, the young woman I would later come to know as Anna seated between them. From where I stood, looking in across the taverna from the street, perfectly obscured by a trellis of vines, I could see her foot nervously tapping under the table as she moved her fork around a plate of food that remained largely untouched.

Would I have recognised David if it were not for my mother warning me earlier that day of the Witherall descent on the island? Was it coincidence that I walked by his father's favourite restaurant, just a few hours after I heard of his return? I told myself it was, but it is possible that I was seeking him out, in spite of myself.

I felt my body freeze. It had been almost ten years, after all. I had been just twelve the last time we saw each other, and he was fourteen. For a moment I pictured that night, heat clotting the air around us, his final words chasing me down the hill, muffled by the sound of my own snatched breath, the bones in my legs jarring as my feet slammed against the path away from his house.

There were changes, of course. The pale skin had grown warmer, more lived in; the stack of ratty cotton bracelets in red and greens and yellows he had worn up his arms that last summer had been replaced by a heavy silver watch.

From here, it was impossible to tell if it was Artemis' features that lingered in her only son, or Clive's.

A sudden breeze whipped through the trellis, so that if any of them had looked over, I would have been exposed. Ducking down, making to leave before anyone spotted me, I was distracted by a tremendous noise and I turned again to see the young woman at the table leap up, her chair making a cracking sound as it fell and hit the ground.

A second later, David stood too, ready to follow her into the restaurant when Clive, his demeanour unbroken, laid a hand on his son's arm. Straining to see what would happen next, I lifted my fingers to the foliage as the couple at the table directly in front of me stood, blocking my view.

At the same time, I heard my mother's voice calling from across the square.

'Maria?'

Crossing the road towards her quickly enough that she would not have a chance to catch sight of Clive, I glanced briefly back at the men and felt a chill inexplicably rolling through my bones.

CHAPTER 18

Maria

The tensions between my mother and me that summer were such that it was just a matter of time before one of us snapped.

I had woken first one morning. Struck by the lethargy that smothered me within hours of my return, I had fallen asleep on my bed the previous evening surrounded by the textbooks that provided a convenient escape from Athena's relentless tongue.

The house stood on the tip of the island, old and proud. It was already cloyingly hot in the room. Pushing open the wooden shutters, I was met with a square of perfect blue, the sea and sky blending in to one another, pressing everything else out.

It was still early. Following the quiet sloshing of the sea, which whispered to me through the kitchen window, I made my way down the familiar twists of the mountain path to the port.

The air was lighter down here. Yannis' bar was the furthest along the street running parallel to the sea, tapering out where a strip of bars and restaurants met the side of the mountain.

At this hour, it was the only place open. The plastic chair creaked as I sat.

'Just a coffee, please.' I smiled to the young waiter whom I recognised as the son of Carolina, one of the shopkeepers at the top of the village, his mother's solemn expression reflected in his pointed features.

I had been back on the island less than a week and already my body twitched with the sense that the land was closing in on me. A scattering of boats dozed on the horizon, illuminated by the morning sun, their distance a mockery, and for a moment my mind flicked to my father.

'Maria? I thought it was you! I heard you were back.'

I looked round at the familiar voice. Kasia's tone had been given an extra authority by the months she had spent training to become a teaching assistant. I had trained alongside her, at the only school on the island.

Phillip, standing beside her, had the same self-satisfied expression he had worn throughout school.

'But weren't you in Athens? I thought you were too good for us these days?'

'I'm visiting my mother for the summer.' I tried to match Phillip's jovial tone, aware of the light sting of humiliation on my cheeks.

Kasia placed a smug hand over the neat bulge of her belly.

'I'm having a baby shower in a couple of weeks, if you're around?'

For a moment I pictured the same faces from school, the same idle gossip; I worked hard to keep my expression neutral.

'Congratulations! That's such lovely news. And thanks, but I'm not going to be around long.'

I did not mention the flat on the mainland I had sub-let for the summer in a desperate attempt to recoup some of my rent.

'Really? I just thought you might have decided to stay and take over your mother's job—'

'Lovely to see you both.' I raised my cup at them, my jaw gritted, the tension still pulling at my mouth as I stood, leaving a handful of coins on the table.

If anything could be said for my encounter with Kasia and Phillip, it is that it was just the catalyst I needed. That same afternoon, I went back to the house and booked my return flight to Athens, for a couple of days later. Given that I had rented out my flat for the summer, I would have to sofa-surf while I worked out my next steps.

But it would be worth it. In fact, when I imagined the prospect of another month on the island, I knew I had no other choice.

I had been to see my course leader the day before I came back here. Her office had been dark, both curtains pulled against the glare of the sun.

She smiled when she saw me at the door, and I felt myself buoyed as I accepted a seat in front of her desk, though it was clear I would not be staying long. I was already stretching the boundaries of teacher – pupil relations to have turned up at her office uninvited, and I knew better than to push my luck.

The air in the room was thick and sweet with sweat, as she started to speak.

'I appreciate you coming to see me, Maria, and quite honestly I could not think of a single reason not to recommend that you apply. You are bright, you are tenacious and you are clearly driven, but I feel I must warn you, the placement is not cheap.'

However it might have sounded, this was not a plea for preferential treatment so much as an exercise in expectation management. If new tactics were needed, I would have to start work on them straight away.

'Maria, as I'm sure you are aware, mature students do not qualify for any sort of bursary and, well, I just don't want you to be in any doubt. London, it is not an easy place to make your money stretch.'

'It is not a problem,' I said, my features serene, despite the flutter of my heartbeat.

The professor's eyes smiled back at me as she nodded, holding out her hand.

'Well, in that case, I cannot think that there will be much standing in your way. With your grades, I can't think of a student more deserving of the year abroad. Of course there will be formalities, and nothing is a stone-cast guarantee, but I'll keep you posted.'

'Thank you.' I stood, dizzy with the prospect.

'And what are you doing this summer? You're staying around in Athens?'

I shook my head regretfully.

'I'm going to see my mother. She is . . . I haven't seen her for a while.'

'Lovely. The Sporades, yes?'

'Yes.'

My brevity had been well received.

'Beautiful. Now have a wonderful summer, and as soon as I know anything, I will be in touch.'

CHAPTER 19

Maria

The day I was due to return to Athens, I woke to my mother's voice, an instant reminder of where I was; the sound of her singing along to the radio seeped under my door like gas.

Already, I could picture the scene from where I lay, my body too big for the bed. She would be dressed for work, her apron pulled too tight around her waist, arranging flowers in a vase; tensing her jaw against the shooting pains that juddered up her spine as she moved.

It was the first time I had been home from university since the Christmas break, and given my premature return to the mainland – which I had put down to a summer job opening that was too lucrative to refuse – I knew exactly what would await me when I finally stepped out of this room. There would be freshly baked bread, piles of spanakopita laid out on the blue and yellow tablecloth she would have spread across the table on the terrace, two chairs squeezed into the gaps, although she would not sit. This was the setting of the scene for the memory she would use to rewrite the history of our time together.

My mother's voice had grown louder now. She would have sensed my waking up and would be finding some excuse to make noises outside my door.

'Maria,' she turned to me, her eyes shining, affecting a casual air as I stepped into the kitchen. I noted the apron, her greying hair pinned neatly into a bun.

'Are you hungry?'

I looked behind her, through the terrace doors at the laden table.

'Coffee?' My mother turned to the stove, too quickly. I heard a yelp as she placed one hand on the counter to steady herself.

'Hey.' I stepped towards her, but she pushed me away, her grip still strong.

'I'm fine!'

'For God's sake, Mum, you're not fine.'

'I am fine,' she hissed. I took the coffee pot from her hand and began to fill it under the tap.

As the steam started to rise from the stove, I took a seat at the small circular table in the corner of the kitchen, which was still exactly as it always had been, the low wooden counter stretching along the wall, beneath it everything hidden from view behind a blue and white curtain.

The basket of lemons by the door, which only my father ever took from, was still there, as if she needed the constant reminder of what she had been subjected to.

'Maybe you shouldn't go to work today.' I tried to keep my voice casual.

Athena ignored me, scuttling between the washing-up bowl and neatly stacked shelves above the counter.

'Clive relies on me. I can't just not turn up.' Her voice was clipped. Was she actually in pain or was this all part of her effort to show me how hard her life was?

'Mum!'

'Why do you keep on, Maria, as if we have a choice? We have no choice – your father made sure of that.' Her words hung in the air, pointed like arrows.

'Oh, come on, how much longer are you going to keep this up? It's too much for you now. You don't need the money that badly . . .'

My mother turned towards me, incensed. But I pre-empted her.

'Mum, I don't like you working for him.'

There was a pause, a momentary truce between us, and then she nodded slowly. 'I see.'

'That man . . . have you forgotten?' For a moment I thought my words might stick, but the scornful smile at the corners of her mouth told me otherwise.

'My dear, I think it is you who forgets. Who is it that has paid for this family ever since your father—'

'My father? *Your husband.*' I said it before I could stop myself, something inside me snapping with a ferocity that surprised even me. 'My father who was never quite good enough for you. Never quite rich enough; never quite enough like *Clive* . . .'

There was a sharpness to the silence while we observed the line that had just been crossed. Until now I had chosen never to acknowledge openly that my mother had lusted after her late friend's husband for years. But the rumours in the village were simply confirmation of something I had always felt, but been unable to name.

Reading my mind, her lip curled. 'That's it, isn't it, Maria? You blame me for your father leaving. It's always the woman, hmm? Men, they leave. They can just up and leave and it's never their fault. No one ever questions it.'

'Oh, please, Mum, don't make this about you as the victim again. This is about the fact that you were in love with Artemis' husband for years, and everyone knew it, and still, even though he has made it patently clear that he wants nothing to do with you, still you can't stop protecting him. Even though he's a *murderer.*'

The heat had intensified in the room so that the air suddenly seemed to vibrate with it, until my mother's cackle cut through it like a scythe.

'Murderer? Clive?' It was as if I had told her the sun only came out at night. 'Oh Maria. I know you loved your father, and Artemis. And I know that blaming Clive for Artemis . . . for your father leaving . . . I can see why that would be appealing. But speaking like that about the man who is the only person in this world who cares about us – who makes sure we have everything we need?'

'The man who *bought our silence* . . .' I spoke under my breath, but Athena caught every word.

'How dare you?' She was trembling with rage now. 'Since Artemis died, we are the only people Clive has, other than his own son, to remember his wife by.'

After that, what else could I say? Clearly, on one level at least, she believed her own lies.

'Anyway, I can see you won't be interested in his offer,' her voice was quieter now.

Imperceptibly, I lifted my head. 'What are you talking about?'

'He was asking after you, as he always does, and I told him about your plan to study in London for a year and—'

'Mum!'

'What? I happened to mention it while I was on my break and he said straight away that you can stay at his flat for as long as you like.'

I swallowed as Athena turned to take the coffee pot off the stove.

'It's just an idea, Mum. For God's sake, why are you telling people – why are you telling *him*?'

She carried on as if I had not spoken. 'He won't be there much. He's working abroad for months and when he is there, you would have your own room, of course. Oh Maria, it's so lovely. He showed me pictures. Right in the middle of Central London, on this grand square. The apartment is beautiful.'

'And what does he want in return?' I tried to keep my voice steady.

'Maria, he doesn't want anything. What more does he need? He is a rich man, and we are like family to him.'

I snorted, turning my head towards the door. My mother chose to ignore the sound, taking a step towards me, lowering herself so that she was kneeling in front of me. I moved to offer her my chair but she held me there.

'I'm telling you, Maria, I know you don't want to believe it, but

Clive Witherall is a good man. Artemis . . .' She breathed in sharply. 'Artemis wasn't well when she said those things. Do you understand me? Anyone who can do that to themselves . . . To her son . . . Well, she wasn't right, in the end. She was sick.'

My mother cupped her hand under my jaw. I felt her breath on my face. 'Maria, Artemis was my best friend and I loved her like a sister, but the woman was paranoid.'

CHAPTER 20

Maria

Did I imagine it, the picture I have of my father, his features strained through the gauze of sleep, the morning he left? It was Easter Sunday and I was seven, that much I know. In my mind, I see him lingering in the doorway of my bedroom, his fingers tracing the form of my face, from a distance; the creak of a floorboard decompressing as he lifted his foot, for the last time.

If he left a note, my mother never shared it. *That man*, she would call him from that moment on, the disbelief lodged in each syllable. *Your father*.

He is a giant, in my memory, a figure of almost mythological proportions. But when I saw his picture, smiling in the background of a wedding photo Yannis has framed above his bar in the port, I realised that he was no different from any other man; his features weaker than I remembered them. Whenever I went to the bar after that, I kept my eyes from straying to that frame.

The months after my father's departure haven't stuck in my memory; they are a free fall of feelings, snippets of conversation that don't involve me. Before my mother's mood finally settled into a low hum of embittered disdain, she had battened down the hatches against the outside world; the two of us barricaded inside that tiny house. My only escape was the daily walk to school, along the mountain path, the sea sweeping back and forth at the bottom of a vertiginous drop.

Artemis' arrival that summer saved us, or at least it saved me; her melodic voice lifted the air as she moved through the rooms of our house, pushing open the shutters that for months had been pulled tight. Her hand squeezed mine as she spoke to my mother using words I couldn't hear.

'You, Maria.' She lowered herself to look me in the eye. 'You're coming to stay with me and David, just for a little while, while Mama gets some rest. What do you say?'

Her eyes were bright and reassuring and I didn't say a word as she led me to the bedroom, pulling out a handful of clothes from the small wooden chest and placing them in the bag on her shoulder.

David was waiting for us as we walked out of the house, the shine of the sun too bright against a cloudless sky; the cicadas cheering me on as we made our way down the path.

'David, you remember Maria, don't you? You played together last summer.'

'Mum, I don't understand when you speak Greek.' David's voice was sulky, as if he felt threatened by a rival for his mother's attention.

Artemis gently rolled her eyes, but she continued in English, placing a hand lightly on both our shoulders.

'I said, Maria is going to stay with us for a few days. That's fun, isn't it? Now, who is hungry, or shall we go straight to the sea?'

Only years later would I recognise the note I heard in her voice that day, the sound of someone trying too hard to pretend that everything was going to be OK.

Any immediate resentment David had felt towards me that morning dissolved as we spent the following weeks on the beach, running in and out of the water, moving in unison, gradually becoming each other's shadows.

Artemis, her face partially obscured by a wide-brimmed hat, spent hours at a time on the shore, encased in her own private world, her eyes fixed on the sea.

My basic school-learnt English and David's refusal to engage with Artemis' mother tongue meant our conversations were limited, but we were young enough that we did not need language as a common bond.

I only remember one time that words passed between us that whole summer, as we lay in adjoining beds, the stars just visible through the crack in the curtain of his bedroom window.

It was me who initiated it. 'Where's your papa?'

There was a pause before David answered. 'He's in London, working. He is always working. But he is flying out next week to join us. Where's yours?'

It was the first time I had allowed myself to process the thought and my answer took me by surprise, 'I don't know.'

David's hand reached for mine, our tiny fingers entwined as sleep finally took hold.

In the days after Clive arrived on the island, something in Artemis changed. Her movements, once soft, tightened somehow, her eyes skittish as if constantly on the lookout for danger.

A week later, she drove me back to my mother's house.

'Things will be OK,' she said, her hand holding mine too tightly as she guided me back to the front door.

Even then, I could feel she was wrong.

CHAPTER 21

Maria

By the following summer, everything had changed, my mother having settled into the role of abandoned woman, playing on it when she spoke to neighbours in the street – 'Well, you know, now that it's just the two of us . . .' At this distance, it was a role that seemed to fortify her, give her new meaning.

When Artemis arrived from London, sometime in July, she was jumpy, distracted in a way that in hindsight I recognise as a woman who feared for her life.

'Why don't we see Artemis and David any more?' I asked my mother one morning as we walked back from church, the dust of the mountain path rising at our feet. It was August and since their arrival a month earlier, we had only seen them once.

My mother's voice was matter-of-fact. 'Artemis isn't well, she needs to rest. Clive is very worried about her.' She was not the kind of woman to soften her language for a child.

The next time my mother and I saw her was the night of the storm. We had no idea then that it would also be the last.

David had not left his father's side, the morning of Artemis' funeral, a year later. His eyes were set slightly above the open coffin, focusing on the window just above our heads.

I tried to catch his attention as my mother and I settled ourselves on one of the pews near the front of the church, but his mind was somewhere else. Throughout the service, which was short and perfunctory, a dustpan neatly brushing away the crumbs of a life, I watched him silently squinting against the glare of the sky, which had settled in streaks of dark grey and angry blues, following the storm.

His hand instinctively reached for his father's as the service came to an end, but it was unnoticed by Clive as he turned to embrace the handful of mourners who bowed their heads over his wife's corpse.

May her memory be eternal.

The words echoed through the empty church, lodging themselves in my mind.

I found David later that afternoon, a tiny figure crouched under a tree in the cemetery. He was ten years old, two years older than I was, but even to me, from where I stood, just out of the line of sight, he looked small and lost.

'What are you doing?' I didn't know what else to say as I pulled my skirt over my grazed knees, settling onto the ground beside him.

'They wanted to burn my mum's body.' He spoke thoughtfully, almost without emotion, as if mulling over a confusing spelling.

'Why?'

He didn't look at me.

'But Daddy wouldn't let them.'

He turned to me, apparently reassured by his own answer. With a flutter of unease, I felt his hand moving along the ground towards mine, this time his fingertips gripping my own.

Clive had taken David back to London the day after the funeral. He hadn't wanted to come at all, I heard him tell my mother at the wake; the funeral had only taken place on the island because this was where Artemis had requested it must be, in her will.

'You know what she's like,' Clive confided, quickly correcting himself. '*Was* like. She did what suited her, never mind the rest of us.'

Clive paused, closing his eyes. 'Forgive me. I shouldn't talk about her like that, to you, her best friend. It's . . . but I'm angry, you know? I don't know how she could have . . .'

My mother took Clive in her arms. 'You don't have to apologise to me. Oh, you poor man, and that boy . . . She never recognised what she had. What was she *thinking*? My dear friend . . . She was always selfish, but this?'

My mother and I had been in the shop at the top of the hill when we heard the news that the Witheralls were back on the island, the year following Artemis' death. The village was still quivering with the drama of it all, the lingering sense of shame.

Sensing my resistance to the idea of an unsolicited visit, Athena had attempted to lure my nine-year-old self there with the promise of using the pool.

'They might be busy. Should we not ring first?'

'Oh, come on, Clive is never too busy for us, Maria. I told you, we are the closest they have to family now. Artemis and I, we were . . .'

She stopped, an expression I could not read passing over her face, and then she paused to rearrange herself, pulling a tissue from her pocket and dabbing it across her brow.

'She was like a sister to me.'

It was the hottest day of the year so far, but a coldness rippled down my arms as we approached the house. By the time we arrived at the gates proffering a basket of freshly baked bread, David and his father had no choice but to let us in, though at just nine years old even I could sense a degree of hesitation that my mother was either blind to, or chose to ignore.

'Maria and I, we are . . . As you may know, Yannis left us penniless. Until now, we survived, but, well, I think I will have to sell the house . . . Unless I can find work . . .' My mother's voice carried across the garden. Quivering with embarrassment, I tried to blank out her words as David and I sipped on ice-cold juice, dipping our toes in the water, his skin pale against his red swimming trunks.

The pool in those days was a smaller, less opulent version of what it would be replaced with once Clive's business really took off. It would be years still until the diggers arrived, tearing up the home Clive and Artemis had built, brick by brick, replacing it with the lavish veneer that gradually took form as the summers rolled by: a slick, glossy polish to cover the cracks.

CHAPTER 22

Maria

The storm blew across the island like dragons' breath the night Artemis had come to the house.

The power was out across the village and from my child-size bed I watched the lightning fork through the window, ripples of light tossed across the Mediterranean Sea like shattering glass.

At first, I mistook the banging on the door for the sound of the wind, but when I poked my head out a few moments later I heard her voice, possessed, at the kitchen table. My mother held her friend by the shoulders as if, should she let her go, one of them might break.

'He's going to kill me – Athena, you have to believe me . . .'

The outside world seemed to be beating at our door, the elements whipping furiously at the path leading to the house.

Still, my mother was unstirred. When she replied, her voice was too quiet for me to hear the words, but her tone was calm, firm. Artemis threw back her head in response, her voice a hiss.

'*You have to believe me, Athena, I know too much!* I can see it in his eyes when he looks at me. The way he talks about me, as if I'm mad or . . . Please just promise me that if anything happens to me you will remember what I told you.'

At that moment a branch cracking outside the house caused the women to turn and see me, cowering in the doorway, my favourite stuffed rabbit hanging limply by my side.

My mother's face was fixed in a look I did not understand; her friend's eyes were black holes, wide with dread. As I stared back at her, something in Artemis' eyes reached into my own and held on with a certainty I knew even then that I would never shake.

'Artemis . . .' My mother stepped forward, limply reaching for her best friend's arm, but she pulled away, the regret shaking through her body.

'If you don't believe me, what hope do I have?' Her voice faded away as she turned, the wind chasing her from the house, biting at her bare feet, her white nightgown tangling around her legs.

My mother's voice chasing after her, begging her to return, was an infuriated howl, lost on the wind.

How many times I had reimagined the scene that night, in the years that followed: how Artemis must have felt, the skin on her soles slapping against the grit and pebbles as she made her way along the black mountain path, her fate already sealed; imagining it as if her pain was my own.

CHAPTER 23

Anna

'Anna, this is my husband.'

'I'm Jeff, good to see you.'

My hand moved inside his, and I managed a smile as May carried on talking.

'Jeff is TradeSmart's accountant—'

'That's why they call me the money man.' He wiggled his eyebrows and there was a cackle of appreciation from his wife.

'Oh really? That's so interesting.' I made to continue the conversation, but Jeff was momentarily distracted by a face behind my head. I turned and caught the profile of an ageing British actor I recognised from a recent interiors spread we had run, which featured his Hollywood Hills pad in return for a mention of its being for sale; he was leaning in to shake hands with the winner of last year's Man Booker Prize.

May noticed my eyes following the pair and smiled at me over her glass.

'He has a place on Skiathos, comes over every year. You have to have your little black book ready at Clive's soirées, as you'll find out.'

Smiling calmly to demonstrate how unfazed I was in the company of celebrities, I turned my attention back to her husband, but it was impossible to get a word in edgeways.

'Jeff knows a lot of people in the media, don't you, darling?'

But Jeff was distracted, shoving his leather briefcase into the arms of a passing waiter with a condescending wink, 'Be a sport and pop this in the cloakroom, would you?'

Returning her attention to me, May continued. 'What sort of journalism are you in? You really should speak to my husband . . . Although, you know what they say, never trust a journalist!'

She laughed sharply, her hand expertly lifting another glass from a passing tray, depositing the empty one on a table behind them, her heel faltering for a moment, steadying herself against a chair.

'Jeff is extremely important, knows everyone.'

Jeff rolled his eyes, mock self-deprecatingly. 'Hardly, dear.'

David, who had just moved in to join us, cleared his throat lightly, discreetly beckoning a waiter from across the pool who was carrying a tray of crab-stuffed mushrooms. Jorgos stood a little behind Jeff, his face tilted away from us. At the other side of the pool, I could just make out the tip of Clive's panama.

'Oh, come on, darling.' May leaned forward, Jeff stepping in to prop her up from one side. 'Don't be so bashful. It's not like you to resist the chance to spend time with such a lovely young woman.'

May returned her attention to me, a single bead of sweat following the line of her hair.

'My husband runs the foundation for Clive, set up the whole thing. I suppose you know all about the business . . .'

I swallowed, avoiding her gaze.

'Not much, really. I mean, what David's told me. It all sounds very interesting, I'd love to know more . . .'

David intervened, holding out a plate of food.

'May, why don't you have some of this? My father flew in the best caterers in Athens. I'm just going to borrow Anna for a minute, if you don't mind. So lovely seeing you both.'

David squeezed my hand as we strolled towards the back of the garden, stopping at the far end by the love-seat amidst the orange trees. Just in front of us, the ground tapered off as if we had reached the end of the world.

'I'm sorry about May,' he said, leading me to sit beside him on a bench.

'She's hilarious.'

'She's a bloody liability.'

I laughed. 'I liked her, actually.'

'I'm so happy you're here.'

I nodded, my chest bursting with everything that was happening, excitement and anticipation swirling uncertainly beneath a river of champagne in my gut.

He stopped suddenly, his face glowing with drink and sun and feelings he could not contain. 'Dad loves you too, I can tell.'

I felt my body tighten, the smile falling from my lips.

'Having you here, I think it's helped.'

'Helped what?'

He paused, thinking for a moment. 'Things have been strained in the past months. The business. Jeff, he's . . . he and my dad haven't been seeing eye to eye. Having you here has . . . it's been a distraction.'

'How so?'

I kept my voice light.

David paused. 'I don't know, you're just—'

'Not me, I mean, you said your dad and Jeff haven't been getting on.'

'Oh, God, work stuff . . . You don't need to hear about that. What you need is another drink, and . . .'

He leaned in to kiss me, pressing a bottle of champagne into my hand. As he pulled my leg towards him, I felt a sharp pain in my abdomen. Gently pushing him away, I moved my hand to my stomach.

'I'm sorry, I'm . . .'

David looked briefly dejected before composing himself.

'Poor you, you're still unwell?'

The pain was like a knife, slashing at me out of nowhere, and I gasped, trying to suppress the sound. 'I'm so sorry, I just need to lie down.'

* * *

I woke to a noise outside the room.

A dark blanket had fallen over the house by now, the roar of the party having faded to a low hum.

Sitting up, aware of the strap of my bra digging into my skin, I felt David's body slumped on the bed beside me. He must have come in after I passed out, the painkiller I had taken to soothe the pain in my stomach causing me to fall almost instantly to sleep.

Silently, I stood, letting my dress fall from my shoulders, taking off my jewellery, the clasp of the necklace pressing into the skin under my fingernail.

Dressing quickly in the nightie I had left folded on a chair, I pulled gently at the curtains in front of the terrace doors, slowly pushing the handle, desperate for a crack of air to alleviate the swell of pressure, the stale smell of alcohol and sweat secreting from David's pores as he slept.

The caterers, long packed up for the night, had been replaced by a white satin bar erected by the pool, lined with bottles of spirits; the moon a sliver of chalk rubbing against the distant sea; the remaining guests scattered carelessly across the grounds.

In the distance, where the pool gave way to well-tended gardens, I saw a flash of colour and two figures. Slowly they came into focus: Jeff, his shock of white hair shining under the moonlight, and Clive. From here, I could not hear their voices. For a moment I considered cracking the window open further to improve my chances of hearing what they were saying, and then I stopped.

Instead, flicking my eyes to David, I turned and headed, barefoot, towards the door.

The hallway was dark, the only light scattered through a spray of leaves silhouetted against the window. In the sultry glow of moonlight, David's mother's paintings loomed from the walls.

Feeling my way along the corridor, I let my hand rest for a moment on the door-handle of Clive's study. Pressing down, my clammy palm left a misty mark on the brass as the handle resisted until, with a final push, the door gave way. A barely audible click marked the shift from here to there, from safety into the unknown.

Nudging the door carefully open, I found Clive's office just as I had imagined it the day I had overheard him on the phone to Jeff, although it was now cloaked in shadow. Shelves of books covered two of the walls, the one to my left lined with framed photographs.

Glancing quickly over my shoulder, I took a step closer, into the room. The main picture showed Clive and Jeff, perhaps ten or so years previously. In the background was Jorgos, his ponytail thicker then. Between Jeff and Clive, smiling broadly, there stood another man, his eyes avoiding contact with the lens; his gap-toothed grin shining against black pockmarked skin. There was something about the picture that had my attention.

Pulling out my phone, I took a photo of the image, the glare of the glass catching in the corner.

I moved along the pictures until another caught my eye, at the far end, an image caught in shadow; a smaller print this time, faded. It was a man, a woman and a child standing against the backdrop of this house. It looked plainer, humbler, before it had been rebuilt, but I recognised the setting. The garden was less formed then, the orange tree nothing but a promise, the now perfectly tended lawn a heap of dirt, the sky behind them grey with dust.

I had to move in closer to see the faces. The light beating against their bodies, David's eyes peeped out under a bowl cut, his arm curled possessively around his mother's thigh, her face obscured by her hand as it guarded against the sun. To her side was Clive, towering above them both.

A cool breeze rippled over my skin as I focused on the woman's face. How old must David have been, eight or nine? The photo must have been taken not long before she had died. I found myself studying her silhouette for signs of decay, of the illness that would soon envelop her.

A flash of light swept across the room and I turned, my arms fixed in front of me, only to find it was just a headlight passing along the drive, another guest falling away.

Still, my nerves refused to settle as I scanned the room, unsure of myself now. Quickly, I moved towards Clive's desk.

It was dark wood with a leather top, drawers lining one side. Breathing in, I pulled open the first drawer, expecting some resistance; inside was an ivory letter opener and a wooden tray with compartments for staples, paperclips and several sizes of envelopes.

My disappointment tinged with relief, I pushed it closed and moved to the second drawer. This time, when I pulled the brass handle, the drawer refused to budge. I tried the third drawer, which slipped open, revealing a pile of unused printing paper.

Pausing for a moment, I tried the middle drawer again, bending so that my eye was level with the lock, feeling the metal jam against wood as I tried again.

I stood for a moment, casting my eyes around the top of the desk, anywhere that Clive might keep a key, already knowing it was a ridiculous prospect to expect anyone to keep a key in such obvious proximity. Then I remembered the paperclips, recalling how I had taught myself to fashion them as lock-pickers during one of the interminable summer holidays I had endured as a child.

Pulling open the top drawer, I went to take one out when my fingers grazed an envelope, slightly crumpled, standing on its side in the drawer.

Picking it up, I knew just by the weight of it what was inside. My fingers trembling, I pulled out the key, small and solid, bending down again and feeling the key slide into the hole; the lock shifted reluctantly as I turned my hand.

Inside, the drawer was bare but for an A4 cardboard folder. Pulling out the contents – a thin wad of paper divided into two files – I flicked through the papers, my hands clumsy with nerves. The first bundle, a list of TradeSmart shareholders, was the thicker of the two, the pages held together by a single staple.

Working my way through the neatly printed pages, careful not to leave a crease, I scanned the addresses – Venezuela, Japan, the US, Azerbaijan – searching for anything that might jump out, oblivious to what I was actually looking for.

The second file was a single sheet of paper, the words *Private and Confidential* written across the front, in marker pen. My chest thudded as I read the paper, a receipt, handwritten with the date in the corner, a fax number scrawled across the top, and a logo stamped at the top in faded ink 'THE MAJESTIC'.

Leaning back against the desk, I read the child-like scrawl:

Due to the high concentration of mercaptan sulphur and the highly noxious smell of your product, we 'The Majestic' agree to your suggestion, under the advice of a chemist, to dispose of the product in a properly prepared site away from the city.

We, The Majestic, agree to take all responsibility for the proper disposal and promise to do a good job.

The price for our service is a total of US$950.

We thank you for your bus . . .

Before I could finish the last sentence, a now familiar wave of nausea hit my stomach. Instinctively, my hand fell to my stomach. At the same time I heard a noise. Freezing, I waited a moment but it was nothing, a branch slapping against the window. Then it came again.

'Hello?'

The voice at first seemed to come from behind me, but when I turned there was no one there.

My body seized with alarm, I hurtled into action, my hands shaking as I pushed the papers back into their envelope. Dropping it silently into the drawer, I pushed the drawer closed only to find the key was no longer there.

My eyes blurring in panic, I scanned the floor for the key, which glinted at me from the carpet.

As I finally turned the lock, darting backwards, I saw a shadow pass the door.

'Anna?'

When he spoke again, I knew his voice at once.

CHAPTER 24

Anna

I recognised Jeff's presence even before I saw his shadow hovering in front of the crack of the office door.

How could I have been so stupid as to leave it open? In desperation I lunged back towards the open door, stepping out into the hall, my skin brushing against his, fire burning in my cheeks.

He turned, following me with his eyes, a smile curling on his lips.

'I thought it might be you, on the prowl . . .'

He was drunk; I felt his breath on me, thick and stale, as he took a step closer, forcing my back against the wall.

'I was just going to the loo.'

My voice sounded forced, too loud.

'David was asleep, I didn't want to disturb him . . .'

'Of course you didn't . . .'

His eyes rolled over my face, down my neck.

Drawing a sharp breath, the sickness heaving in my chest, I opened my mouth to speak, but it was Jorgos' voice I heard.

'Jeff?'

At first, I was not sure if Jeff heard him as he kept his eyes on mine, breathing into my face for a moment more before finally turning.

'Jorgo.' There was a tightness in his voice. 'Where have you been all night? I was just looking for you.'

Raking his eyes over my nightdress once more, Jeff turned and walked unsteadily away from me. I felt both men's eyes on my back as I turned towards the bedroom, my heart racing.

It was much later when I woke again, my mouth dry in the heat of the night, the house still dark as I made my way out of the bedroom towards the staircase in search of a drink.

Approaching the kitchen, drawn forward by the hum of the fridge, I almost didn't notice the briefcase wedged in the gap between the door and the frame of the cloakroom, so that it would not close.

I knew it immediately: the briefcase Jeff had thrust into the arms of the young waiter. Dark brown leather. The clips of the lock not quite fastened, it transpired, as I prised it open in the darkness of the hallway.

PART TWO

CHAPTER 25

Anna

An extra line. At first so faint as to almost be invisible; then so obvious it was as though it had never not been there.

'Hey, I'm just heading out, do you need anything?'

David's voice hummed through the door of the bathroom, the day after we arrived back in London. I could see the shadow of his feet from where I was sitting on the bathroom floor, the back of my head pressed up against the wall.

'No, I'm fine. I was just going to do some unpacking.'

My eyes didn't leave the plastic stick, which was still pressed between my fingers; I was terrified that if I so much as glanced away then what was happening might become real.

'OK, I'm just heading into the office, got some stuff to catch up on. I'll be home for dinner.'

'I'll make something,' I managed, the normality of the words at odds with the enormity of what was happening.

Harry was out of town. I had received a one-line response to my message the night after I broke into Clive's study.

Away for a few days, let's speak when I'm back.

I thought of Meg, pushing the tears away with my finger, the rest of my face still. Why did I not ring her then and there? Was it stubbornness or something else?

'Mum, it's me.'

The phone was warm against my cheek from having been held in my hand for so long. I knew I had made a mistake the moment I heard her voice, remote and businesslike.

'Marianne? It's a terrible line. Can you hear me?'

I nodded regretfully.

'That's better. Your father and I were wondering how you were,' she lied. 'It's been a while since you were last in touch.'

'Is Dad there?'

My lower back was gently throbbing.

'He's popped out.'

I pictured him in his study, closing the door against the sound of my mother's voice.

'Is everything OK? You sound . . .'

'I'm just out, it's a bad line.'

I pressed my hand against the wall, pushing myself to my feet.

'How was Greece?'

I could hear what she was doing, rounding the call to a close.

Silently, I begged her to ask another question, one that mattered this time. After a moment, I answered.

'Actually, I'm really sorry, can I call you back later?'

She paused a moment too long.

'I'm going to pop out to meet your father in a bit, but we'll speak soon. Don't leave it so long next time!'

It was past dinnertime when David got home. I had spent the afternoon unpacking and tidying the house, trying to distract myself from the gnawing sensation in my belly, between the repeated calls to Harry's phone in the hope that he might answer regardless, the automated voice on his answering machine a stinging reminder of his absence.

'There you are.'

I was on the sofa, my book, unread, on the armrest, my toes curled tightly under a cushion.

'Sorry, I got held up.'

He leaned down to kiss me. 'I'm going to head straight up, have a shower. Everything OK?'

The sun had streaked the front of his hair, which was at odds with the formal shirt and tie, knotted at a slight angle. There was something endearing about how unnaturally he wore his work uniform, how ill-fitting it seemed.

I had not intended to say anything, not yet, not until I was sure. But there was an urgency to my voice when I spoke his name. Instantly, dread spread across his face.

'What is it? Did you speak to the doctor?'

'Sit down.'

My hand lay on the sofa beside me, and he lifted it gently to his face as he sat.

There was no easier way to say it, and no way I could keep it to myself, the weight of it pressing down on top of all the secrets already buzzing inside me, like wasps trapped in a jar.

'I'm pregnant.'

His expression was suspended, and for a moment I thought I was off the hook. The decision had been made for me, I would have to go it alone.

But then his mouth finally opened and he gave a cry, faint but joyful.

'Oh my God.'

He squeezed my hand tightly against his face, pulling me towards him.

'Oh my God, Anna.'

'Is it good?' I asked, afraid of the answer.

He held me away so that I was at arm's length, his eyes shining. 'I think so.'

In that moment, despite everything, I actually believed him.

My sleep, when it eventually came, was deep and undisturbed. By the time I woke up, David had already left for work, the smell of his shower gel lingering in the hall. There was a note on the table, resting against a vase of flowers.

I didn't want to wake you . . . Rest! I love you. X

Knowing my colleagues would still be in conference, I texted

Clarissa and told her I was sick and would not be coming in for the next couple of days, pressing the reject button when she called back half an hour later.

By the time Harry finally rang me back, it was nearly lunchtime. I had spent most of the morning thinking of him, lingering over our moments together, which always seemed to end too soon. Longingly, I thought of the day we had created our joint email account, conspiring to save the world.

'Anna, this is serious,' he had reminded me, as if I needed reminding, making me commit to memory the login and password, forbidding me from ever writing it down.

'It's best to put together two random words. Let's see: hair, soup,' he said, looking at me first and then at the bowl of food, untouched on the table in front of us.

'That can be our username. Now you go, say the first two words that spring to mind.'

The words 'lips' and 'ache' popped into my head and, embarrassed, I lowered my eyes. 'Hand, spoon.'

He typed the words into the password box and then pressed 'confirm'.

'Done! Now, log in, create a new message and write your message into that, but never, under any circumstances, press send. Got it? Just save it in the drafts folder and leave it there, I'll find it. Once it says 'saved' you can log out. Be sure to always log out so you don't leave a trail.

Harry's voice had been that of a patient teacher speaking to an unreliable student. 'Once you've left me something, send me a text to let me know and I'll log in and leave my reply also in drafts. Whatever you do, don't download things to anywhere that could be hacked.'

By comparison, his voice, as I answered the phone this afternoon, was brisk.

'I'm pregnant.' I blurted it out as soon as I heard him at the end of the line. There was a silence before he spoke, his tone less self-assured now.

'Are you sure?'

I let the question hang there, useless, while he rallied himself.

'Wow, OK, how are you feeling?'

I was standing in the kitchen, facing the garden; the clouds through the glass appeared in layers, like holograms, above a bed of midsummer blooms.

'I'm OK. Tired.'

I knew it was not the question he was really asking, but I was not prepared to answer that one yet; something inside me refused to let him off the hook so easily. The truth was, although I was not necessarily averse to the concept of abortion, until that moment the possibility had not even crossed my mind.

'And you're . . .?'

'I'm keeping it.'

He could have held out a moment longer, could have feigned at least a moment's interest in my well-being before moving on.

'And David—'

'David's at work.'

'Have you told him?'

I paused. 'Yes.'

From Harry's silence I could sense he had expected something else of me – hysteria, perhaps – but I felt strangely calm.

'OK.'

What else had I expected him to say? Whatever it was, it was not this. I hated how easily he warmed to the idea, how readily he accepted the possibility of me carrying another man's child.

Without ever having had the faintest interest in interiors or design before, I had realised not long after joining the magazine that by simply watching and listening, carefully repackaging my boss's thoughts and tastes, lightly injected with a few key words which I read in the trend forecasts kept in bound journals, and selling them back to her, I could floor her with my great taste and meticulous eye for detail.

The more it became clear that Clarissa was not one to feel easily threatened – her vast wealth and superior social standing instilling in her not just a sense of her own entitlement, but an absolute belief in her own abilities – the more I had felt myself relax into my role. In my time as her assistant, I had become impervious to the pens gripped tighter around the table as I raised my voice in editorial meetings, tentatively at first, to add my thoughts on that month's theme, and in return any resentment from colleagues across the magazine for my obvious favour was suppressed under cool smiles.

Clarissa's message had arrived the day after I had taken the test:

'I've been trying to call . . . Hope you're feeling better. Ring me back, I want to ask you something . . .'

Something about her voice, as she picked up the phone, made me desperate to tell her. There was already so much deception, so many lies. If I had to add another, I might implode.

But before I could get the words out, she spoke excitedly.

'Now, this isn't public knowledge yet but Jessica is leaving us, and I want you to apply for her job.'

Features editor? It was a dream come true. If I told her now, though, about my pregnancy, I would be putting paid to any chance of being considered for the role. The only thing to do was wait until the offer was formal. She could hardly retract it then because I was pregnant, at least not openly. But, to my relief and shame, her reaction when I finally told her of my situation, weeks later, was one of genuine delight.

'Pregnant? Oh, Anna, that is . . . Well, it's wonderful.'

Her face was creased with compassion.

'Now, don't you look so forlorn.' Shutting the office door behind her, pulling the blinds against the watching eyes, she took my hand in hers.

'If you love David and you're both . . . Well, put it this way, there is rarely a perfect time.'

'I know,' I said, grateful for her wisdom. 'But I didn't want this . . .' I recoiled at my own words; already I had proven myself an unworthy mother.

'I mean . . .' I tried to rephrase it to sound less callous, but Clarissa raised her hand, 'I know what you mean, Anna, it's OK.'

'I'm sorry, obviously I'll understand if you don't want me to apply for the—'

'You bloody will.' Her voice was insistent. 'In the time that you've been here, you've been a more committed, and frankly more talented, employee than I've seen in a long time. So many of the girls who breeze through here think they deserve a career without so much as lifting a finger. Spoilt bloody brats. Besides, you'll have your pregnancy in which to get used to the role. I'll get some cover in for while you're on leave, and then you'll be back. And nobody makes for a more productive employee than a mother. Believe me.'

There was no regret in her voice, though I knew from earlier conversations with David that Clarissa and her wife had tried to conceive through IVF, with no success.

'Now you will apply, if I have to write the application for you.'

It was the first time I had cried about it. As I did so, Clarissa nodded and smiled.

'You're going to be a wonderful mum.'

I swallowed, pushing down the lump in my throat.

That evening, I returned from work ready for sleep, but as I stepped through the door, David greeted me.

'We're going out for supper.'

The excitement in his face was such that I had not the energy to argue. Besides, I was ravenous, and before I could speak he was pressing a bag into my hand.

'I know it's still early days and you're not showing or anything, but I nipped out at lunchtime, and . . .'

I pulled open the bag. Inside, was a black crepe shirt from a high-end maternity label, with a gift receipt. At the bottom of the bag, in perfect packaging, was a honey-coloured lipstick, and a thick body moisturiser which smelt of honeysuckle. The influx of gifts had gathered pace since we had returned from Greece, and as I opened them, it felt like fancy dress – each piece a new uniform to reflect the body I no longer recognised.

As we stepped out of the taxi in Primrose Hill, an hour later, the lights twinkled like tiny stars outside Lemonia.

'I thought we could pretend we were back in Greece.'

David pressed his hand gently against my lower back as we entered the restaurant.

'I can't believe it's only been a month since we were there,' I heard myself reply. Already it felt like another lifetime.

'They don't do those courgette and cheese fritters quite like Nico's but the calamari is to die for . . .'

David shook the manager's hand, and I spotted Clive looking up from the table. David leaned into me.

'I hope you don't mind, I invited my father. He was so excited about your promotion, he was desperate to come.'

He read my look, or part of it.

'It's OK, I know you don't want to tell anyone before the scan. You know you can trust me . . . Dad!'

When he turned, there was something in Clive's face that made me start, and then we moved closer and it was gone, and I wondered if it had ever been there at all.

'To Anna.' Clive lifted his glass as the waiter brought our starters, a selection of plates brimming with pastries and fried cheese, beans and yoghurt dishes, along with three glasses of Metaxa.

David shot me a look and rested his hand reassuringly on my knee as Clive lifted the glass to his lips, willing us to do the same.

Interjecting, David laughed. He was trying so hard to protect me from awkward questions that I felt a surge of love which struck me with such force that I felt tears pushing at the corners of my eyes.

'You won't believe it, but Anna and I have decided to lay off booze for a few days. After Greece . . .' He indicated his liver. 'Obviously getting old.'

He laughed and Clive raised an eyebrow, his face unreadable.

'Good for you. Well, I have not made such a decision, and I would like to raise a toast to Anna, for all her efforts.'

His hand rested where it was for a moment, poised in front of his lips, his eyes meeting mine. Cheeks flushing, I picked up my water glass, my fingers slipping against the condensation.

'Well, I haven't definitely got the job yet.'

Clive's mouth moved in a gesture I could not quite read, and I drank, thirstily, my fingers clutching the water glass, before looking up again just in time to see Clive look away.

The next morning I woke to find the sheets in the bed beside me had not been slept in. Clive had explained that he was due to leave town for a few weeks the following morning, and he and David had headed to his club, 5 Hertford Street, for a nightcap after the restaurant. David had winked at me before turning towards the cab, laughing to Clive at how short-lived his own efforts at teetotalism had been, the silhouette of his head disappearing as our taxis moved in opposite directions.

Reaching to the bedside table, the smooth lacquered wood soft against my fingers, I picked up my phone. As I expected, there was a text from David.

Crashed at my dad's in the end, too much to drink.

Stretching, I turned on my side, remembering, with a diminishing sense of panic, the cells multiplying in my stomach. It was extraordinary what hormones could do; within a month of discovering my pregnancy I had progressed from abject terror to tentative acceptance.

David's hair was ruffled and he was wearing the same suit as the night before when he finally arrived home, not long before supper.

'Sorry, I had stuff to do. I'm feeling rough, I'm going to jump in the shower.'

His voice was husky and unconvincing as he moved towards the stairs, turning at the last minute, barely meeting my eye.

CHAPTER 26

Maria

I had been living in London a few weeks when the call came from my mother, the first of many that would berate me over the following months, reminding me of what I already knew.

'You told me yourself, the flat is disgusting – and still you cannot afford to pay the rent.'

Her voice was insistent, hissing over the line, filling the room that was already over-capacity despite holding little more than a single bed.

'You are stubborn, like your father, but look what good it did him. The way I see it you have two choices – either you take up Clive's offer and move into his flat, or you come home.'

'Oh please.' This rhetoric – was there even any point trying to fight it? 'Mum, I am a student, not a prostitute.'

She shot me down, refusing to rise to my bait.

'You are a student who can no longer afford to study. I've told you, Maria, I cannot give you any more money. I have no money. You lied to me about how much the flat was going to cost you.'

'I didn't lie! The original place fell through and there is nothing else, nothing cheaper and . . .'

It was true, I was living on borrowed time. There was no way I could afford to stay on. Now that the reality of what it cost to live in London had hit home, the fact had become undeniable, even for one so firmly ensconced in denial.

Athena must have sensed my dejection for she softened then.

'Come now, darling. As for your insinuations, Clive has no shortage of female admirers, I'm sure. I can't imagine he would be unable to resist you. Even if he was living in the same flat, which I have told you a hundred times he would not be.'

'Mama, I can't talk right now. I'll find a way, but I have told you, please stop making me say it. I'm not living in that man's flat.'

But even then, as I said it, I was less convinced by my own words. Involuntarily, I thought of David and there was a tug in my chest.

Before I could say another word, I hung up.

CHAPTER 27

Anna

Summer was drawing on and the sky was thick with heat as David and I made our way to the hospital.

He had been working full pelt since news of the baby had broken. Something was bothering him, but the harder I pushed for information, the more he resisted. He was busy, he would explain over the phone from the office, where he was increasingly working late, after snapping that he just needed space.

I reached for his hand as we approached the front of the hospital building, which stood back from the road opposite Great Portland Street station.

As our skin met, I thought I felt him pull back, but then he squeezed my fingers before moving through the revolving glass doors.

Inside the lobby, the air was unnaturally cool. Huge glass bowls stuffed with orchids lined the foyer, where women with perfect skin were arranged behind a sleek white desk.

'You must be Anna?'

A well-built man in a pristine medical gown shook my hand first.

'Yes, hello. And this is David, my boyfriend.'

The medic held out a hand, which David took distractedly. We had not discussed the reason for our appointment at breakfast that morning. Still, the words remained unspoken between us as the taxi swung around Regent's Park towards Great Portland Street, talking around it, the tiredness, the ravenous hunger.

'Is it the baby? Are you having second thoughts?' I had asked a few nights earlier, feeling his hand flinch as I had laid it on my tiny bump.

'Of course not. I've told you, I'm just stressed . . . Please, stop asking.'

And so I had.

'Welcome both. I'm Manuel.'

The sonographer spread his hands in a show of openness, as he led us through to the examination room.

'I'll be carrying out your scan today. I take it this is your first?'

I nodded, following Manuel towards the reclining bed.

'This might feel a bit cold.'

He placed the ultrasound firmly against the unfamiliar mound of flesh that had begun to form around my belly. I watched it roll over my skin, left to right in deliberate sweeping strokes; there was a sharp pain as he pushed down hard against my abdomen.

'Sorry, I just want to make sure I've . . . Yes, it is . . .'

A smile stretched tentatively across his face.

'Do either of you have a history of twins in your family?'

'Twins?'

David spoke as if Manuel had been making a terrible joke. He turned to face me but my attention was fixated on the outline of the foetuses, mutating on the screen by the bed; two of them, entwined, dissolving into one. Instinctively, my hands moved to my belly, a wave of longing filling my body.

I could not speak. Instead I shook my head, hot tears pricking my eyes.

The humidity clung to my skin as I walked out of the house one Saturday afternoon a few weeks later, leaving David in the swelling silence of the house. Turning right, I followed the road towards the Heath, the usual parade of dog walkers, men talking too loudly into their phones, bristling past one another, settling my nerves.

Lowering myself onto one of the benches at the top of Kite

Hill, I gazed at London's skyline, reduced to a distant smudge of lines and curves under a haze of grey to the east; to the west, a single turret protruded through a thicket of trees at the bottom of a valley.

I thought of Thomas, placing a hand at the base of my stomach, imagining the lives growing inside.

'Would you mind?'

The voice was a pant. When I looked up, I saw that the woman was older than me, dressed in a neon-green vest top, a stretch around the clean curve of her belly, her flushed skin dewy with a light sheen of sweat. Catching her breath, she gave a pained smile as she leaned back onto the bench.

'No, please . . .'

My eyes grazed the woman's belly. She must have been a little further along than I was, five or six months perhaps, but she wore her pregnancy with such authority that it was as if it were her natural state.

I felt my spine straighten in response, pulling in my tummy as the woman stretched her arms out behind her head.

'Bloody muggy, isn't it?'

She took a long swig from a water bottle.

'Really muggy.'

I pushed my hair behind my ears.

'Especially in our condition.'

She paused for a moment as we both cringed.

'Sorry, awful expression.'

I laughed, 'Yes, it is.'

'How far along are you?'

'Three months.'

The woman's eyes widened.

'Twins.' I gave an apologetic shrug. 'I seem to have suddenly doubled in size . . .'

I smiled awkwardly, still unsure how to respond to the attention my new body was attracting. There were women who said their pregnancy made them feel sexy; mine made me feel like a toddler whose cheeks were constantly patted by strangers.

'You look amazing. Twins? Wow. I mean, I'm still getting my head around one. To be honest, I was slightly panicking that it might be twins – it was IVF, so it wouldn't have been uncommon, but . . . I'm Felicity by the way.'

She held out a perfectly straight arm.

I took her hand, enjoying the easy conversation, the way Felicity's eyes lifted at the corners when she smiled. There was something attractive about her. Magnetic.

'I haven't really got my head around it myself yet. My boyfriend, he's—'

I stopped myself.

'Panicking?'

She spoke softly, taking another swig before offering me the bottle.

'I'm fine, thanks . . . Sort of, yes.'

The woman nodded sympathetically.

'To be honest it's hard enough on my own. I can't imagine what it would be like if I was trying to negotiate someone else's feelings alongside my own.' She smiled conspiratorially. 'I've never been that great at compromise.'

'You don't have a partner?'

The woman shook her head happily.

I was about to reply when I felt my phone vibrate on my lap. Harry. How long had it been since we spoke?

I felt a surge of warmth running through my body as I held the phone in front of me, turning apologetically to Felicity.

She smiled, waving her hands dismissively, standing to stretch out her legs against the bench.

'Not at all, lovely talking to you.'

I turned, pressing 'answer', faintly aware of her eyes following me down the hill.

CHAPTER 28

Anna

'And how are things between you and David?'

'Fine.'

There was no reason not to tell him about the change in David's behaviour, except that to admit it would be to concede weakness.

Harry's eyes moved around the bar as I adjusted my legs to alleviate the discomfort in my lower back.

'Did you follow up on the information I sent, about the receipt?'

'We're working on that. That was, well, it was invaluable. And you're sure no one saw you?'

The muscles in my abdomen contracted, and I winced.

'I'm sure.'

There was a pause and then Harry nodded.

'OK. Good. Great. And the tension you mentioned between Clive and Jeff, is there any more on that?'

I shook my head, quietly exasperated. It was only a couple of months since Greece and with David working all the time, Clive was rarely around.

'Have you told him yet – Clive – about the baby?'

'No.'

'OK, good. Well, why don't you set something up? Get Clive and Jeff together – Jeff's David's godfather – it makes sense. Get them together to make the announcement and take it from there . . . Jeff's wife, you mentioned she likes a drink. Get her sloshed and see if you can get her to open up.'

I raised my eyebrows. 'Well, it won't take much encouragement, you can believe that. But actually, I think it's Jeff who is the weak link. He's a proper pervert, he practically threw himself at me in Greece. One smile and I imagine he'd tell me anything.'

'Perfect.' He nodded approvingly at me. 'Great. I appreciate it, Anna, more than you know.'

'We should have a dinner party.'

David was sitting at the kitchen table working on his laptop, which he closed as I walked into the room.

'What?'

'I've been thinking, and we should have a dinner party, to announce it.'

I placed my hand across my belly as a signal, working hard to keep my voice light.

'We could invite your dad, and maybe Jeff and May too – they are your godparents after all.'

David watched me move around the table towards him, his eyes narrowing. 'What's brought this on?'

'David.' My voice was hurt. 'We're having children together, don't you think that warrants a celebration – at the very least a formal acknowledgement?'

There was something about his face then that I did not like. He paused, and after a moment I began to move away in frustration, but he grabbed hold of my leg with his hand.

'I told you, I wanted to wait to tell my father in person. And yes, I think you're right.' His smile was tight. 'Of course we should. It's a great idea. I'm just . . . I'm having difficulty adjusting, if you want to know the truth.'

When I looked closer there was a sadness in his face and I gently placed my hand on his.

'I thought you loved me.'

It was a cheap trick but it worked.

'I've never loved anyone as much as you, you know that.' The words should have settled me, but instead they sounded like an accusation.

CHAPTER 29

Anna

'I was thinking of trying to get hold of Meg,' I suggested a few nights before the dinner, which had been arranged to coincide with Clive's fleeting return to town.

I was chopping vegetables in the kitchen, my back turned to the room, watching David's reflection in the window as he sat at the table.

'If you like. If you're sure. After what she did . . . Well, it's up to you.'

I did not reply, the sharp burn of chilli scratching the corners of my eyes. It was a relief, I suppose, the tone in his voice; the perfect excuse not to bother trying to track her down. In hindsight, perhaps I understood intuitively that being left in the dark was a far safer option than finding out the truth.

The chicken was bubbling in the pot as the doorbell rang, the night of the dinner.

I had been to the high street that morning, and taking inspiration from a proof I had been laying out at the magazine, the table was laid with bowls of Middle Eastern-inspired salads, between sprigs of freesia and nigella stacked in slender blue vases.

'David, are you getting it?'

After a few moments I called out again, but there was no answer.

Wiping my hands on the dishcloth and tossing it over the back of one of the chairs, I hurried to the door. The night air rushed into the house, whipping at my cheeks, for a moment throwing up my dress so that it billowed over the small bulge of my belly. Not that Clive noticed.

'Anna, my dear.'

His face was illuminated under the light of the porch so that I could see the blood vessels around his cheekbones.

'Welcome . . . to your house.' I laughed awkwardly, stepping aside, feeling the friction against my flushed skin as he kissed my cheek. It was more than two months since Greece and his tan had deepened, so the contrast when he moved was startling; the strap of his Rolex sliding down to expose a flash of white flesh.

'How was Bata?' I asked without thinking, as I took his coat.

He looked back at me enquiringly, and my mind flitted back to Harry's flat as we pored over the details of Clive's business dealings.

'Do you know Africa? You are a dark horse.'

My cheeks reddened and I turned, resting his coat over the curve of the bannister.

'Me? God, no. Sadly. David mentioned it,' I lied.

On cue, David emerged at the top of the stairs, his hair slicked impressively to one side. The white shirt, which was rolled casually at the sleeves, fitted him perfectly.

Something about him then, in the way he held himself, so perfectly poised, made me stop and watch him as he greeted his father, moving in, exerting a slight pressure on the older man's back. With a passing sense of sadness I realised how far removed he looked from the boy I had met that first day on campus, nearly four years earlier. His entire demeanour had shifted in a way that I couldn't put into words.

I was at the sink making last-minute preparations when Jeff's reflection appeared in the window that ran along the far wall of the kitchen, overlooking the garden. I shifted my attention from the broccoli I had been arranging in the steamer and turned to face him.

'I didn't hear you arrive. Can I get you a drink?'

'That would be lovely. White for me. I just wanted to apologise.'

His breath was sour. From the hall, I could hear May's voice, talking to Clive.

I gripped the wine glass in my hand.

'What for?'

'Greece, the party, I was . . . Well, I was pissed and I think I might have been . . . Anyway, I hope I wasn't offensive in any way.'

'No need.'

My face was tightly composed, trying to read his expression. Had he really bought my story about mistaking Clive's office for the bathroom? He had certainly been drunk enough, and something told me that Jeff was not one to register things that happened to other people. In his world only one person took centre-stage, and that was the one standing in front of me now, his ruddy cheeks glistening in the heat of the kitchen.

I was about to steer the subject towards Jeff's work when Clive's face appeared around the kitchen door.

'There you are! Come and join us, for God's sake, you two. Anna, you look like you could do with a drink.'

I struggled to catch David's eye over dinner, the conversation firmly divided between the men at one end of the table, and myself and May – who, for all her loose-lipped conversation in Greece, was apparently not in the mood for conversation tonight – at the other.

Whatever tension David had referred to between his father and Jeff, back in Greece, had clearly eased, or at least efforts were being made to overlook it now as Clive retrieved a bottle of whisky from the back of the cupboards in the dining room, where my fingers had encountered it, months previously, while David was working late one night. It had been the only thing I could ever find offering any trace of Clive's existence in the house; the furnishings and pictures had all obviously been down to Artemis.

'I'll get more wine,' I said to no one, pushing my chair back, the legs grating noisily against the floor.

Opening the fridge, I saw the bottles I had put to cool had already been removed. Placing another two in to refrigerate, I moved to the drawer to the left of the sink and pulled out a packet of cigarettes. I had not smoked since I had found out I was pregnant, but the urge was suddenly overpowering.

Wrapping my cardigan around my shoulders, I stepped out through the French doors, carefully avoiding the sensor so that the garden light would not flick on, giving me away to the guests seated in the dining room, which no longer felt like mine.

This was not the evening I had had in mind when I suggested the dinner. It was not so much nerves I struggled to allay as a sense of deflation. All along I had been telling myself tonight was about getting to Clive and Jeff, a chance to procure whatever information I could, but now I realised maybe this was more than that. The fact that David was clearly so loath to share our news irked me in a way it should not rightfully have done.

I stubbed out my cigarette with the heel of the black suede ankle boots I had bought especially for the occasion using David's card, the one he sent me out with to buy groceries, always encouraging me to buy whatever else took my fancy – in this case boots that, to my disappointment, he had not noticed.

The scent of cigarette smoke clung to me as I stepped back into the house. From the doorway to the living room it was clear the dinner guests were sufficiently distracted that I could slip up the stairs, unnoticed, to wash away the lingering smell.

Moving quickly towards the bathroom, I left the light off, grateful for the break from my own reflection, pressing toothpaste onto my toothbrush and working it around my mouth, the bristles sharp against my tongue.

Washing my hands and drying them on a towel on the rack, I rubbed a small amount of amber-scented hand cream into my fingers and my neck. As I turned to leave, I heard a noise on the landing, through the crack of the bathroom door.

I called out David's name, quietly at first, testing my nerve. But it was unlikely that I would have missed the characteristic sound of his feet thundering up the stairs.

Holding my breath in the relative silence of the bathroom, I strained to catch another sound. From the living room downstairs I heard a roar of laughter, muted from this distance. Exhaling, I realised it was just my imagination. The combination of the wine and my pregnancy, perhaps, setting my nerves on edge.

From the corner of my eye, I saw a shadow moving in the mirror, and then heard the creak of a floorboard. Instinctively, my hand moved to my pocket but my phone wasn't there.

'Hello?' I spoke loudly now, before I lost my nerve.

'Shit!'

The voice came from just in the hall, and as I pushed the door forwards, the eyes that stared back at me were wide with shock. It was only when she stepped back that I could place the face, recognition delayed by the absence of context.

'Maria?'

'Oh my God, Anna, I'm sorry, you scared me so much.' A mortified smile moved across her face, brightening her already perfect skin.

'What . . .'

There was an uneasy pause and then she blushed self-consciously.

'I am so sorry. I . . . This is so embarrassing. I needed the bathroom, but I saw these pictures and—'

'There's a cloakroom on the ground floor you could have used.' I cut her off, then wished belatedly that I had let her carry on. 'But what are you doing here?'

'I'm . . .' She paused. 'Wait, David didn't tell you I was coming?'

I pulled the bathroom door firmly closed behind me.

'I'm so sorry. He invited me a few days ago, I assumed you knew. And . . .'

She indicated the landing we were standing on, facing one another.

'The truth is, I went to find the toilet and when I reached the first floor I glimpsed one of Artemis' paintings up here and I thought I could just . . . I'm sorry, it must seem so rude. I just . . . I wanted to see them.'

We were interrupted by Jeff's voice calling up the stairs.

'Anna? Bloody hell, here you both are! We were about to send out a search party!' His eyes were glistening. 'Come down immediately, I have an announcement to make.'

I was still looking at Maria, but she was walking back towards the stairs, only turning briefly back to me, her face caught in shadow.

CHAPTER 30

Maria

They had been watching that night from across the street, I would discover later, their bodies slunk low in the front seat of a Mercedes, parked in the bay opposite, the tinted windows shielding them from view as David opened the door to the house.

Would they have seen his face from where they sat; would they have noticed it change as he saw me there on his doorstep, for the first time? Of course, it wasn't me they were interested in back then. It would be a while before I caught their eye. For now, they were simply watching it all play out. Biding their time.

It was just a meal, that is what I had told myself. Good food and an evening away from the flat. Besides, it was my first night off in as long as I could remember from the 24-hour burger bar on a dank stretch of pavement around the corner from my flat, and what did I have to lose?

From the look in David's eye when I walked into the house, it was as if he had not expected me to come, after all. Perhaps that was unsurprising. The phone call had been brief; he must have heard the reticence in my voice.

I had been drying my hair when the phone rang on the bed.

'Hello?'

There was a portentous silence and I felt my eyes strain, willing the voice on the other end of the line to speak.

'Maria?'

'Yes.'

I did not recognise him at first, though in hindsight it was hard to imagine who else it might have been. It was not as if I had had time for socialising since moving to London. My study workload alongside my schedule at the burger bar meant there was never any time even for talking to other students. Aside from snatches of conversation with my fellow workers, whose broken English allowed for little beyond communicating orders of refried chips and limp chicken nuggets to one another with only a degree of certainty, there was no one in the whole city I could really call an acquaintance, let alone a friend.

'It's . . . David.'

'David?'

Neither of us spoke again for a moment but it was he who broke the silence.

'My dad said you were in town – your mum, she rang him. I . . . I wanted to invite you for supper.'

There was a feeling in my chest – apprehension or relief? In retrospect, I could not say for sure, but in that moment I felt my heartbeat quicken.

Did I feel their eyes watching me as I moved into the house? Did they sense, even then, that I would become a person of interest?

CHAPTER 31

Anna

It was the first time all evening that David had so much as looked at me, his eyes lifting as I walked back into the room, two steps behind Maria, her slender waist, in a close-fitting polo-neck, serving to highlight my girth. David's gaze was glassy from the whisky, but that didn't stop his eyes moving over her body as she crossed the room.

'You found Maria, I see.'

He smiled, his gaze coming back to me.

'Yes, it was a lovely surprise,' I replied coolly, moving back towards my seat.

'Surprise?' He raised an eyebrow, his mouth twitching. 'But I told you Maria was coming.'

Aware of the rest of the table having fallen silent, I worked hard to keep my voice even.

'No, you didn't, but it's fine . . .' I turned to Maria. 'Honestly, the more the merrier.'

Jeff had positioned himself next to Clive at the head of the table. He was holding a knife in one hand, which he cracked against the side of a bottle, breaking an uneasy silence.

'Right, everyone, attention please!'

For a moment I thought that David had let slip our secret, and that I was about to be serenaded, but David's body language told me otherwise. Eyes positioned away from mine, he smiled tightly, keeping his body still, fingers interlocked, his elbows set on the table either side of his plate.

'Anna, darling, do sit. This concerns you.'

Jeff motioned towards my chair.

Once I had lowered myself warily to sitting, Jeff began to speak.

'It is my honour, as David's godfather, to announce that after twelve months with those useless sods at Spanner and Watts – not to mention, what was it, four years at university . . .?'

'I was doing a Masters!' David returned Jeff's humorous tone, but behind the smile there was something unsettling in his expression.

'Oh really? I heard student life was too much to give up; you were just having too much fun . . . Anyway, after far too long, this fine young man has finally agreed to come over from the dark side, to his father's firm . . .'

Before I could stop the sound from forming, I heard myself cry out.

'No!'

All eyes turned to face me. My skin was scorching now and I imagined the heartbeats I had seen on the screen in the scan drumming faster and faster, until my whole body was shaking.

'Anna?'

It was Clive, his face fixed on mine from the end of the table.

'Is there something you would like to share?'

'No . . . I mean yes, there is . . .'

I looked to David, but now he was facing the other way.

'I . . . the reason I wanted . . . the reason we invited you here tonight is that we have some news of our own, don't we, David?'

He turned to face his guests, his mouth held in a tight smile.

'Anna is pregnant.'

He made it sound like it was something that had been done to him. Nothing to warrant celebration. For a moment there was silence and then May let out a whoop.

'Bloody hell, didn't take you long, did it? Gosh, how marvellous.'

Her eyes shone as she watched me, my face turning pale.

I could not look up. Why was David not saying anything? The irony of the betrayal I felt was not lost on me.

'We're having twins.'

My voice was sharp as I skidded on.

'So you see, it just feels like a bad time to risk David's job . . .'

'Of course, I absolutely understand.'

Clive's voice was matter-of-fact. If he was surprised, it did not show.

'First and foremost, I'm sure I speak for us all when I say that this is truly wonderful news. I am utterly delighted.'

There was a warmth in his smile as I looked up, a hint of the grandfather he would become. He turned to David, whose face finally mirrored the gesture.

'Yes, it is. We are extremely happy.'

May lifted her glass, as if she needed the excuse.

Clive tilted his glass slightly, holding my eye.

'As for David risking a good job, there's really no need to worry. Whose hands would he be safer in than those of his own family?'

The taste of the cigarette I had smoked the previous night rolled around my mouth when I woke the next day. My breath rasping, I imagined the thousands of tiny hairs that lined my trachea trapped beneath a layer of tar as I walked into the kitchen, which was spotless, Maria having insisted on quietly clearing the table.

'It's the least I can do,' she had added when I told her not to bother. For a split second there was something about her face that made me want to cry on her shoulder, but instead I turned away and left her to finish as I made my way upstairs.

'David, aren't you going to speak to me?'

His face was obscured from view behind the newspaper when I entered the kitchen. He continued turning the pages of the Sunday papers slowly without peeling his eyes away from the financial supplement.

'David, what's going on?'

After a moment's pause, he slapped the paper onto the table.

'You're asking *me* what's going on?'

There was silence, and my hands gripped the countertop behind me.

'How about you tell me, Anna?'

'What do you mean?'

He shook his head.

'Well, we could start with last night, how you were a complete embarrassment? How about the fact that you arranged a dinner party, invited my family and friends and then behaved like a fucking tramp?'

His venom was so shocking that I struggled to know how to respond. His words were slow and deliberate, and my whole face stung.

'What are you talking about?'

'You don't know? Drinking like that, while carrying our babies . . .'

'I had one glass!'

'Smoking?'

A lump formed in my throat.

'To *forget* one of our guests, then belittle her in front of the whole table . . . And then to shout when my godfather announces that I've been given an incredible new job . . . Anna, is that what you think being in a family is? If this is the kind of mother, the kind of partner you want to be – is that the kind of woman you think I want?'

His voice dropped away, so that the last part of the sentence was almost a whisper, almost as if I could have imagined it.

'You know, sometimes I don't know who you are any more.'

His words hung in the void between us.

I breathed in sharply, turning to face the counter, closing my eyes.

'I just don't understand why you're taking that job.'

I said it as quickly and as devoid of emotion as I could manage, then flinched as his voice rose once more.

'I'm taking the job because we are about to have a family and moving into the firm makes sense. What about that don't you understand?'

'But you said you would never work for him!'

There was a silence before David spoke again, more quietly this time, 'What are you talking about?'

'You said . . . before, years ago . . . when you were talking about what your father does for a living, you told me you wanted nothing to do with it. You wanted to make your own life; you didn't want to live your life in his shadow.'

I still had my back to him but I could feel his body almost touching mine. I was not sure if he was going to push me or pull me towards him, but then he spoke, his mouth pressed up to my ear.

'Things change, Anna, don't they? People change. Sometimes life doesn't give you a choice.'

There was a pause, as if he had suddenly realised the full meaning of the words. 'Do you have any idea how much I love you? This whole . . . this whole situation is blowing my fucking mind.'

He scrunched his hair into his hands, then gave me one final look and walked out, the whole house trembling as the front door slammed shut.

CHAPTER 32

Anna

Five Months Later

I could tell David was not home as soon as I stepped inside, placing the bags of food shopping beside the dresser in the hall.

The hallway creaked with the unmistakable absence of life; nevertheless, I called out his name, the only reply a tap dripping intermittently in the kitchen.

At my most recent scan, the doctor had taken delight in pointing out the toes curled into my ribcage. I felt them now, their physicality both reassuring and painful as I leaned against the doorframe, taking a moment to imagine what it would look like once the builders had completed the designs drawn up by a fashionable young interior architect we'd featured in a recent spread on modern living; the new floor-to-ceiling glass doors which I had picked out, sanctioned by David with only the mildest hint of concern.

'I totally understand if you don't want to,' I had assured him as I broached the prospect of the redesign. 'This is the house you grew up in, and . . .'

I had not mentioned his mother, I had not needed to.

David shook his head. 'Whatever it takes, I told you . . .'

True to his word, he had managed to find builders who were prepared to work over Christmas. With Clive in the Maldives, where he was holed up on one of his 'working holidays', entertaining clients and flying out intermittently to meet colleagues in Sri Lanka and India, between luxury boat trips and spa treatments, the plan was to move into his central London flat while the work was completed, and we settled in with the girls.

The *girls*. To be honest, it was hard to imagine anything beyond the pregnancy itself, and the C-section which was planned for the following month. On cue, I felt the babies move, pushing against one another for space, the discomfort making me wince.

The prospect of Christmas was always dangerous, steering David towards questions I could not answer.

'What about your dad? Would he want to come and stay? There's plenty of room. It seems crazy we haven't met yet.'

I rubbed my hand against my lower back.

'I told you, he can't get leave this year, but he's planning a trip for next summer.'

The lie rang in my head as I fetched the bags from the hall, groaning as I bent over, a sharp pain tugging at my lower back.

Pulling out a stack of containers from the deli in Hampstead Village, I scooped a few spoonfuls from each pot onto a plate, eating my lunch at the kitchen table, musing on the merits of Elephant's Breath vs Dimity for the kitchen walls. There was the temptation to go bold, especially in a room of this size, which could certainly take it. But classic is classic, as Clarissa liked to remind us on at least a weekly basis as we met to brainstorm issues for the months ahead. Besides, I had spent my life trying to fit in, not stand out.

Holding the plate under the tap to swill off the fatty residue, I had to use the full force of my wrist to get any kind of grip before finally the tap exploded with unexpected force.

'Shit.'

Dabbing at the greasy water spattered across the dress David had picked out on a recent shopping trip, tiny blue flowers on white cotton, I cursed, reaching under the sink, pulling out a bottle of Vanish and turning towards the door.

Taking each stair to the first floor carefully, stopping to allow the stitch which pinched at my sides to subside, I moved into the bedroom, stepping out of the dress and pulling on a loose T-shirt. Turning to leave, my eyes flashed to David's bedside table. The laptop had not been there when I left the house earlier that morning – and was now perched on the ledge, its low humming light flashing like a silent alarm.

Taking a step forward, I looked again and caught a memory of Clive at the desk in his study, in Greece. Surely not; but then whose else was it? David's computer was at the office, being mended, and it certainly was not mine.

Moving reluctantly towards it, as if approaching an unknown animal, I ran my fingers over the smooth curve of the lid.

I paused for a moment, a limb clawing its way into my ribcage. The babies seemed to have jammed themselves into every available crevice of my body. I tried to think of them in the abstract, it was easier that way, avoiding the image of their fully formed bodies contorted inside my own.

Stretching my upper body away from my stomach, I pulled open the lid of Clive's laptop, expecting to find a blank page, a box demanding a password to which I would clearly not be privy. But it was worse than that. I felt the shock hit me as I was met by my own eyes staring back at me, David and Clive's faces beside me in the photo blotted out by a row of folders on the desktop; given the yellow dress I was wearing, the photo must have been taken at the party that night in Greece. Something about the image made the hairs on my arms stand on end. Allowing myself a moment to gather my breath, I sat more squarely on the bed, then there was a whirring sound as a series of emails flashed in the right-hand corner of the screen.

My hands, tingling with sweat, stroked the mousepad as Clive's inbox opened up on the screen before me. My heartbeat rattling against my chest, ears keenly attuned to the throbbing silence, my eyes darted through a list of emails . . . The first was from Clive's secretary, Moira, about the following month's AGM. Warily, as if at any moment an alarm might sound, I watched the screen as I clicked open the attachment to a list of shareholders' names and addresses.

Continuing to scroll down, my chest tightened as I spotted another message, dated three weeks previously.

Clive

I've been speaking to our boys, as well as friends in various territories following our rejection by the Dutch water police. There are a number of options at this stage, if we want to be creative.

The main storage companies in US/Singapore etc. no longer facilitate the use of caustic soda washes since local environmental agencies don't allow . . .

Getting the shit on-land is proving tricky, also looking into possibility of boats disappearing in case it is an option worth pursuing.

Let me know your thoughts.

Ben

- – - Original Message – - -

From: Clive Witherall
To: Jeff Mayhew
Subject: Update

I would like to be kept abreast of all developments in relation to the disposal as per our discussion this afternoon. C

I could feel the blood throbbing in my chest as I highlighted the rows of text, fingers shaking as I opened a new page in Google, logging into Gmail with the address Harry and I had set up together that day at his flat – the one we would use to share information. Entering my username and password, I opened a new message and pasted the highlighted text from Clive's email into it.

Following his instructions, I left the message containing Clive's email there for him to find when he logged in. Finally, my fingers still shaking, I scrolled up to History and deleted recent searches.

Breathing in, I looked back to the home page. Still, I could not shake my unease at how easily it had been done, scanning the screen for some sign that something was wrong. But all was as it should be. Exhaling heavily, I moved to adjust my position on the bed, and felt another pain in my gut, sharper this time, swiftly followed by another.

Crying out, I felt the corner of the bed I was perched on give way, followed by a spasm in my leg. Instinctively, I pushed myself backwards, sending the computer lurching from my lap.

'Shit.'

I watched the computer hit the carpet, unable to move fast enough to stop it, the pain moving from one side of my stomach to the other now. Gasping, leaning forward into the stabbing sensation, I grabbed the side of the bed with my hand, the other hand pressing down on the dull throbbing which moved steadily through my belly.

As I pushed myself to standing, I felt the gush of warm liquid down my leg.

Please, no . . .

Letting myself drop to my knees, I felt my breath quicken, the pain rolling from my belly to my back.

'Hello?'

The voice travelled up the stairs as I trained my breath in and out.

'David?'

Flooded with relief, I called his name again but my voice was weak and as I cried out I saw the white veneer of the computer flickering on its side, the screen still lit. My face, David's and Clive's, reflected in the glare.

'Anna?'

I could sense him in the downstairs hallway, slipping off his shoes, placing his keys on the side table, glancing into the kitchen, spotting the bags of shopping on the table.

Teeth clenched, I pushed myself forward onto my hands and knees, sliding myself towards the laptop as David's steps padded on the stairs leading to our bedroom.

The carpet chafing against my skin, I gritted my teeth.

'Anna, are you up here?'

Sweat breaking out on my forehead, I reached out, my fingers fumbling across the mousepad, my whole body trembling with pain as I slid closer to the computer. As his footsteps reached the landing, I simultaneously slammed my foot down on the lid of the computer and tugged the duvet down from the bed, the effort of it causing me to cry out as the cover landed on the computer, a split second before David ran into the room, his face pale with dread.

'Oh my God . . .'

He lunged at me, taking in the scene: my body curled like a foetus at the side of the bed; the pool of liquid. Reaching down to pick me up, he stopped, stepping back, scanning the room for a phone.

'I tripped, I . . .'

My voice was crushed under the weight of my own body.

'Sssshhh, don't try to talk.' He placed a hand on my head before running to pick up the receiver from the phone on the landing.

'It's OK . . .'

Holding the doorframe for stability, he punched the numbers into the phone. 999. For a second I could swear I saw him pause, his eyes flashing towards the computer, the corner of it poking out from under the duvet, and then back to me.

'What's the emergency?' The operator's voice filtered across the room.

David's voice was strained, 'It's . . . my girlfriend.'

'Anna, my name is Dr Singh. I'm one of the consultants here.'

His face hovered above mine; a throng of nurses moved briskly around me, the sickly white of the hospital room forcing me to squint.

'You're at UCLH, you're in very good hands . . .'

'What, why am I not at . . .?'

'When there are complications sometimes we need to bring you to somewhere better equipped than your private hospital to deal with the situation, but not to worry, Anna, you are in the best possible hands and we are going to take you into theatre now. I've spoken to your partner, and . . .'

David. Where was he? Struggling to sit up, I was struck by a wave of sickness. The doctor placed a firm hand on my shoulder.

'Anna, you had a panic attack and we gave you something to help you calm down. We've also given you an anaesthetic which means you are numb from the chest down.'

I felt the room move around me, struggling to focus as a doorway flashed above my head. Dr Singh was talking faster now.

'We are taking you into theatre, and you're going to meet your babies very soon . . .'

'But it's too soon.'

My voice faded away and the doctor smiled.

'Thirty-six weeks is absolutely fine – often with twins, women have a section around this time.'

That wasn't what I meant. *But you don't understand,* I wanted to shout out. *I'm not ready.*

'My colleague is going to ask you to sign some forms, just a formality.' The doctor's attention moved to the job in hand as the trolley swung through a set of double doors into theatre, my body instantly turning cold. Any detachment I had felt suddenly transformed into horrifying lucidity. Every flicker of light was illuminated; the metal sheen of the surgeon's trolley dazzled my eyes; a fuzzing sound like a radio hissing in and out of signal was coming from somewhere near my head.

Rolling my eyes upwards, I saw a woman in a hairnet talking to me, her face bright with optimism.

'I'm going to be sick.'

The woman stroked my head reassuringly.

'That's just the drugs, I'll give you some anti-sickness.'

'Where is David?'

I could not turn my head to look.

'David is next door, he will be here in a moment. Would you like some music?'

I tried to process the woman's words. Music? I needed my boyfriend. The realisation struck me like a weight across the back of my head – I needed David.

'I'm here. It's OK, I'm here . . .'

His face appeared above mine, perfectly formed against a fuzzy backdrop as he leaned over me, the skin around his eyes blotched and red.

I felt the tears come as I looked back at him, my hands feeling for his face but never quite making contact.

'Please try not to move.'

The woman at my head indicated the needle that had somehow been inserted between the bones on my hand; the tube running up my arm towards a plastic bag hooked onto a metal cage beside me.

'It's antibiotics, just a precaution against infection.'

I looked at my hand, wondering how it was possible to feel so disconnected from my own body.

'David, what's happening? I can't . . .'

'It's OK, there was something wrong with one of the babies.'

His voice was choked.

'They're going to get them out . . .'

Wrong? What did he mean, wrong?

'Right, Anna.'

It was one of the nurses, a face I had not seen before.

'I'm going to spray you with this cold spray, and I want you to tell me if you can feel it. OK?'

'I don't feel anything.'

'That's good – how about now?'

I shook my head, tears streaming down my cheeks, the only part of my body that still felt like my own.

'They're starting now, Anna.'

The woman with the spray-can was suddenly beside me.

'Just a minute, maybe less and . . . Oh, I can see your baby, Anna, she's . . . Here she is!'

The air seemed to crack with the sound of its cry. The child resisting, thrashing its limbs, held above my head for a fraction of a second before being whisked away towards a plastic table on the other side of the room.

I watched, through a mute haze of tears as three of the medical team rushed towards the furious child, moving between pieces of equipment, calling out words I did not understand.

'OK, and here is number two!'

Trancelike, I turned to see another baby, smeared in white and red mucus. This time, the body was curled in on itself. For a second, I waited for the familiar shrieking, the immediate protest against the world into which it had been pulled. Instead, I felt the atmosphere shift as the baby was suddenly lowered, a tacit agreement passing between the strangers around me who, without another word, flew mechanically towards the child as, finally, a cry erupted from her lungs.

'Good!'

The midwife called out, moving towards the plastic cot on the far side of the room. 'Good! That's right, you have a good old scream.'

'Oh God.'

David leaned forward, his body crumpling in relief.

'We'll just get them cleaned up and weighed and then you can have a quick cuddle before we take them to ICU for checks, OK? So far everything seems perfectly normal but we just need to have them checked out. All right, Anna?'

The surgeon remained where he was, studiously repairing the severed muscle as my eyes rolled back, deliberately pushing out the sounds around me.

People talk of that all-consuming love that rushes in the moment you have a child, blotting out everything else. I felt like I had been steamrollered and my body was slowly setting in the concrete.

* * *

The weeks following the birth passed by as if the world and all its colours and sounds had been dampened somehow. David spent the majority of his time hovering over the twins as if they might disappear if he so much as looked away.

Maria descended within hours of us returning home from the hospital. Arriving at night, she used her own key, as instructed, slipping into the role of surrogate mother with unnerving ease.

'An extra pair of hands, that's all,' David placated me as I lay on the side of the bed one morning, my face motionless, tilted towards the window, the girls writhing and cooing in the other room.

'She has taken a break from studying and she needs the money.'

Should I have felt the jarring of a nerve at the prospect of an old friend of my husband's coming to stay within hours of my giving birth – a woman who understood his family in a way that I never could, whose history and connection superseded my own? A woman whose body was untainted by the pushes and pulls of pregnancy, and birth? It seems obvious now, but in that moment, jostling for position was the furthest thing from my mind.

'I am glad she is here,' I replied, my voice barely audible, simply relieved that someone else would be there to satiate the swarm of needs that had suddenly taken hold of the house so that sometimes it felt the whole place was shaking with the weight of the things I could not do. Perhaps I should have noted the significance of an extra pair of eyes to watch over me, but I was too tightly woven inside my own darkness to notice, or care.

Like the answer to an unspoken prayer, Maria took the reins without ceremony, looking after the girls, bringing my lunch, removing the untouched tray hours later without remark.

'You want to try to feed her?' She knocked quietly before stepping into the bedroom holding Stella who was making up for her initial silence after her birth with feverish screams that rang through the house like an alarm.

I closed my eyes gently, whispering under my breath.

'She wants the bottle.' My voice was flat.

Maria looked like she was going to say something, but instead she nodded, hushing the baby to her chest, moving out of the room without another word.

It was weeks since I had heard from Harry. I had been so caught up in the last-minute organisation before the girls' arrival – design tweaks for the builders, wrapping things up at work – that I had hardly given him much thought. What was it that made me think of him then? Was it really him that I needed, or rather the knowledge that he was thinking of me?

The landing outside the bedroom felt unnaturally bright, the glow radiating from the ceiling lamps causing me to squint.

Letting my body rest against the wall for a moment, I felt the searing pain cut across my abdomen, a visceral reminder of the blades neatly laid out on the surgeon's stand, before making my way to the bathroom, the solid brass door handle trapping into position behind me.

With the door shut, the ceiling seemed to loom over me, concealing memories, secrets etched into the yellowing cornicing. The walls were dark emerald green to match the carpets, thick layers of curtain hanging from the window. In one corner there stood a circular cabinet in heavy, detailed wood.

Along the surface, a row of cut-crystal perfume bottles secreted waves of musty vanilla from the dark amber-coloured liquid that stained the glass, bottles I increasingly found myself inhaling – the scent of David's mother, this strange proximity to her haunting and reassuring in equal measure.

It took both hands to turn the tap on, an angry gush of steaming-hot water roaring from the wide brass spout.

Turning towards the sink, I avoided the reflection in the mirror. Bending down, I opened the cupboard, reaching expertly through the rows of bottles and clothes, my hand feeling its way towards the back of the shelf.

Twisting so that I could reach it, wincing at the sharp pain that jabbed at my ribs as I did so, I prised the phone from where it was wedged between the panel at the back of the cupboard and the shelf. My hand lightly trembling, I held down the button until the light flashed green.

From the hallway, David's voice reached in through the crack under the door. I had not realised he was home, and his return meant it must already be late afternoon. My skin bristling, I paused, listening to him singing to the girls in that giddying voice he had affected since their birth.

Bring back, bring back, oh bring back my Bonnie to me, to me . . .

It was another few seconds before I risked looking down at the screen. For a moment, I could picture a message from Harry, the connection between us having already alerted him to trouble. But then I blinked, and the screen was blank.

I've been in hospital . . . The girls are here, we nearly died . . . I started to type before deleting the message and starting over.

Did you get the thing I left for you? I need to see you.

Hearing David's voice getting louder, I pressed 'send' and pushed the phone back into the cupboard.

'Everything OK?' His shadow passed under the gap of the door; I heard his mouth pushed up against the wood.

Carefully easing the door of the cupboard closed, I answered. 'Everything's fine. I'm coming.'

CHAPTER 33

Maria

The sky was low as I stepped into the concrete basin that stood between Euston Road and the British Library, taking a moment to savour the building, red bricks containing the answer to the questions I would not have dreamt to ask.

Fleetingly, I thought of my childhood, my father's body bent over at the end of my little bed as he regaled me with the same stories his parents had told him, the sound of his voice vibrating reassuringly through the sheets as I watched the skin on his face stretch and crease. After he left, the stories went too.

Shaking away the thought, I pushed my body against the heavy metal doors that led into the library. Inside, a security guard scanned the contents of my rucksack while my mind drifted across the space, taking in the vertiginous ceiling and endless balconies. From where I stood, I imagined myself looking up at a giant human organ, sliced in two, every cell and valve exposed.

It was my day off from the twins and I was sitting on one of the single tables lining the wall in the coffee shop of the library, my notes spread in front of me, the first time she approached.

'Do you mind?' Her expression was so English, a look designed to convey how *loath* she was to impose.

'Oh God, don't worry, I won't be long,' she added, smiling, holding up her hand in an act of surrender as I scraped together the books that were sprawled out across the table.

'Gosh, that looks intense.'

She pointed to a book on the political economy of good government, brimming with Post-it notes. It had been bought with money from my first pay cheque from David, something to take the sting out of my abandonment of my course. Just because I had taken this time out of university, I told myself, there was no excuse to lag behind.

What had it taken for my mother to finally convince me? How many calls had it required to wear me down to her way of thinking? The truth was, there had been no choice. I had run out of money, and working twelve-hour shifts scraping fat off an industrial fryer was occupying more time and energy than my studies. However I looked at it, it was a false economy.

'So why not take this nannying job, darling,' she had pressed on. 'Surely it is wiser to defer than to be forced to pull out altogether. Just for a few months, and then when you have savings, you can go back to university. It's David you would be working for, not Clive. It's not David you're angry at, is it?'

Tears had run down my cheeks but I had not made a sound.

The woman opposite me was casting her eyes enthusiastically over my books.

'Intense is one word for it.'

I rolled my eyes, pleased to have someone to talk to. After the mood at the dinner to which David had invited me, I'd worried how Anna might react to my arrival. But the reality, when it came, was far more unsettling.

In the weeks since the birth, Anna had hardly left her room. Occasionally, I would hear her, feet dragging along the corridor. Peering through the gap in the door of the nursery I would watch her from behind, her ribcage protruding beneath her nightgown, above the swollen mound of her belly, as she moved towards the bathroom, the sense of unease following her like a ghost.

* * *

'What are you studying?'

'Political Science and International Relations – well, I was before, back home.'

'Sounds impressive.' The woman raised her eyebrows. 'Where are you from?'

'I live in Athens, or I did, but I'm from the Sporades originally. It's a series of islands on the east coast of Greece.'

'Oh my gosh, you lucky thing. I used to have a friend who had a little place on one of the smaller islands; it's so beautiful there. Which island do you come from?

I pushed the lid of my laptop closed and told her the name. She gasped when I said it.

'No way! Gosh, what a small world. I'm Felicity, by the way . . .'

It seems ridiculous now that I fell for it, but then what was I supposed to think?

CHAPTER 34

Anna

After a couple of weeks the health visitor arrived to sign me off, my stitches removed with a single tug by the accompanying midwife, who pulled and prodded at the girls while her colleague bombarded me with a stream of meaningless questions. How was I feeling? Was I struggling? Did I ever feel *at risk*?

For reasons I couldn't explain, my mind flashed to the pot of pills that sat by my bedside. I blinked, suddenly aware of my clenched fists, fingernails digging into my palms.

'David would never hurt me.'

I was perched uncomfortably on the sofa in the living room, a pile of leaflets by my side. Was there a hint of uncertainty in my voice?

'Good. Well, keep the phone numbers just in case. You'd be surprised what goes on in even the happiest seeming relationships, and children can create a strain.'

Smiling weakly, I closed the door, dropping the papers into the wastepaper basket as I made my way towards the stairs, stopping in the doorway of the kitchen where Maria was washing up our cups.

'Could you watch the girls? I need to sleep.'

Padding slowly along the hallway, I made for the bathroom to check once again for the message reassuring me that Harry was thinking of me when I needed him most; that perhaps, without me needing to tell him, he had sensed the girls had arrived. But the screen was blank.

I made my way back to the bedroom and pulled the sheet up higher around myself, never wanting to get up again.

'Don't you think you should get out of bed?'

David was standing at the doorway of our bedroom, his hair pulled to the side in the style he had gradually started to adopt since joining the firm. His wardrobes were filling with expensive suit jackets and crisply ironed shirts, which seemed to appear from nowhere; the smell of soap at some point had been replaced by a heavy aftershave.

'It's been more than two weeks, Anna. The doctors said it's important for you to move around, to help the healing . . . The girls, they need you.'

He said the last part of the sentence louder than necessary and when I turned I saw Maria in the hallway, delivering clean sheets to one of the bedrooms.

In the distance, the fractious waves of Stella's cry rang through the house, and Maria's footsteps disappeared. My eyes rested gratefully against their sockets.

'I'm so tired, my stomach is so sore I'm not sure I can walk. Could you bring the girls to me?'

Almost imperceptibly he turned towards the hallway. Noting it was empty, he carried on, though more quietly this time.

'Maria has them. I think it's probably best you leave them for now, you don't want to excite them.'

'But the health visitor said if I had any chance of breastfeeding, I . . .'

Stepping back inside, he lowered his voice. 'Breastfeeding? You really think that's a good idea, with the drugs you're taking?'

'There's no chance of infiltrating my supply, the midwife told me. The hospital prescribed those specific painkillers for that reason.'

'Anna, let's not kid ourselves. You're not . . .'

He paused, apparently pained by what he had to say.

'You're not safe, if I really have to spell it out. For the moment I think we need to lean on Maria.'

With those words, he walked away.

I cannot be sure how long I lay there before pushing myself up slowly, adjusting to the dusty light of the room.

My hip rubbed against the mattress as I slid to sitting position, confused yet again by the inflated barrel of flesh wedged across my stomach. Just along the line of pubic hair was the trace of the incision, a horizontal slit three inches across. Pressing lightly, my fingers followed the raised line of the wound, which was still numb. At any minute I expected it might rip open, my insides pouring out in hot red waves.

Pulling out a small white packet from the pocket of my dressing gown, I used my fingernail to pierce the silver film, pushing one of the pills into my mouth and then another. Taking a sip of water from the glass David had placed there the previous evening, I felt the medicine scrape against the back of my throat.

When I came round again, the light was more insistent in the room. David must have been in and pulled the curtains apart further while I slept, another weak attempt to lure me back into the world.

I glanced at the clock. 10.45. From the hall, I could hear him, his voice breaking into a fragmented lullaby, his shadow pacing back and forth in front of the door, head stooped over the bundle in his arms.

Somewhere in my subconscious I recalled a conversation through the gauze of sleep. Maria and David, discussing her next day off, away from the girls.

'I don't have to go, I can stay if you need me.'

'Don't be silly, we'll be fine. I know how much Mass means to you, and St Mary's is just around the corner, and I'll be here. Honestly, we'll be fine.'

I pictured Maria, her scarf pulled over her head, slipping quietly through the streets of Hampstead, lowering her eyes as she passed under the vast white pillars on Holly Walk.

It was Sunday, then. I felt a twinge of regret, imagining my mother waiting by the phone in the hall, worry tinged with relief when the call never came.

Over the years, I had taken to ringing every Sunday at the same time; since moving in with David I would leave the house on the pretext of picking up supplies from the high street before walking to the same bench by the call box on Well Walk. Giving myself a moment to switch modes, I would watch the well-heeled couples with their spaniels and perfectly turned-out children striding from lunch at The Wells to the lane that offered a short cut onto the Heath, while I gathered my breath. My mother always answered after the first ring, and my toes would press into the paving stones as I pictured her perched on the same seat in the same narrow hallway where she had scrubbed at Thomas's final footprints until the whole house stung with the smell of bleach.

During our last call, not long before the girls were born, I had been hit by a desperate surge of emotion, a suddenly overwhelming longing to be able to tell her the truth. To share my excitement, and fear, to ask the questions only a mother could answer.

'How is work?'

It was the same question every time.

'Busy.'

I fought back tears.

'I haven't received any of your articles in the post. I thought you were going to send some.'

'I'm sorry, there's just been so much going on, there never seems to be any time.'

'And the flat they put you up in, it's going well?'

I nodded, not trusting myself to speak.

'Your father and I would love to come and visit sometime. You know, it's just at the moment we're so . . . busy.'

My mother's voice trailed off, the silence ringing between us.

'Are you OK, dear? You sound—'

'I'm fine. Just tired, you know. Things are just so busy at work, but I'll be fine.'

There was a moment's silence. In that moment, I imagined telling her, practising the words; I need not tell her everything, need not mention David. I could just say I was pregnant and the father wanted nothing to do with the babies. Her grandchildren . . .

'Right, well, make sure you eat properly, won't you? We don't want you wearing yourself away.'

I exhaled, the moment gone. The possibility of a moment that I knew had never really existed at all.

David went back to work two weeks after my operation, kissing the girls on their foreheads before heading for the train station to a job I never allowed myself to fully imagine.

With weekdays spent at the office, he threw himself into the parenting role with a vengeance come the weekend, sending Maria off to enjoy her free time, his pointed comments about my retreat to the bedroom eventually fading to resigned silence.

'Which day are the builders starting?' I asked over supper one night, not long after his return to work, a takeaway I hardly had the energy to move around my plate with my fork.

He stopped eating, his eyes narrowing. 'I told you, I've cancelled them.'

'What do you mean?'

He inhaled, as if taking a moment to gather himself. 'You don't remember? I mean just that. I told you, I've put them off. Now is not a good time, when things are . . . Well, everything is a bit unsettled at the moment.'

'You didn't tell me that.'

He looked at me, unblinking, for a beat too long before nodding, turning his attention back to his plate. 'OK. It's OK, you're very tired. We're all tired. I probably didn't say it clearly enough, or . . .'

Something about his voice stopped me from answering. When he looked back at me, his eyes were shining with tears.

Late one Saturday afternoon, hearing his feet move on the stairwell, the steps creaking in time to the song he whispered in Stella's ear, I slowly eased myself out of bed, sliding my feet into the sheepskin slippers Clive's secretary had ordered as part of an elaborate care package, which had arrived along with an apology for his prolonged absence.

Can't wait to meet my girls. Not long now . . .

Pushing the thought away, I focused instead on the gentle crunch of the wool between my toes as I made my way towards the bathroom, where I found no reply from Harry since the last time I wrote to him. He could be dead, and there would be no way of knowing. Sometimes, when I thought of him in the middle of the night, the sound of the girls whimpering in the next room, David breathing steadily beside me, I found myself wondering if I had made it all up. And in those moments I could not be sure what scared me more, the possibility that Harry was not real or knowing that he was.

As I made my way along the hallway, I became aware of my husband's voice rising through the house. The bathroom on this floor was on one side of the hall; the carpet up here a deep emerald green, curling around the spindles of the staircase like the mouth of a snake sucking up its prey; the same carpet which had been here when David was a boy. I pictured him now, pressing his face between the wooden bars of the bannister, listening to his parents from the rooms below. What did he hear? Laughter, music, screams?

Poor David. Poor, sweet, trusting David. My eyes filled with tears for the boy I never knew, for the girl I had been. For the sea of lies that stretched between us, so that there was no way to cross without drowning.

I know how it must look, the hypocrisy of it; but the truth is back then I believed I was doing this in part for him too. He had a right to know who his father was, did he not? He had a right to know the truth. Or at least part of it.

My longing for a message from Harry led me towards the bathroom, but as I approached, I felt myself lured towards the door opposite.

The curtains in this room had been pulled tight so that it was pitch-black, but from somewhere inside I could hear shallow breathing. Taking my first hesitant step over the metal guard that marked the entrance, I felt a weight drop in my gut. Pressing my feet carefully onto the carpet, feeling like an intruder, I realised I had no sense of the geography of the room since David and Maria had moved it around, filling it with the pieces he had picked out in my absence.

My husband and the hired help playing happy families in my daughters' nursery, while I was recovering from an operation? What else had they done that I had no knowledge of?

The smell inside the room was overpowering, sweet and sour. As I tuned into the stillness, I could feel the movement from one of the cots, the one furthest away. Hesitant at first, repulsed by the sight of the beds, the slatted wood like tiny prisons, I was suddenly overwhelmed by a sense of urgency as I moved across the room, closing my eyes for a moment as I leaned over the cot.

Pausing briefly, I reached in, tucking my hands under the baby asleep at the bottom of the mattress; one palm cupping the bottom of her neck, the other holding her legs.

'Oh my darling, what have they done to you?'

Glancing around before bending my knees, I placed the child on the floor in front of me. As I did so I felt her body tighten, her tiny mouth torn open, her cheeks firing red.

'It's OK, it's OK,' I whispered, pulling frantically at the swaddle blanket, desperately trying to unleash her from its grip.

'What did they do to you?'

My hands shaking, I unravelled the final layer of the blanket and Rose's arms flew upwards, like an animal bolting from its cage. Tossing her head, fragile pink limbs flailed and then immediately calmed as

I once again scooped her up, pulling her into my chest this time, forgetting the shooting pain that tore through my stomach.

'It's OK, Mummy's got you. Mummy's got you, baby.'

'Anna?'

David's body cast an invisible shadow across the darkness of the room.

I turned to see him, Stella in his arms. The look on his face made me pull Rose tighter to my chest.

'She was caught up, she couldn't move.'

My voice was urgent.

'What are you talking about?'

David's eyebrows furrowed above a concerned smile.

'Rose. She was bound in a blanket, she couldn't move.'

For a moment he paused and then he laughed uneasily. He laughed at me.

'You mean the swaddle blanket?'

He took a step forward, regarding me with a pitying look. My eyes must have been wide, I felt them dry and unblinking, searching a face I no longer recognised.

'That's what you do with babies. They like it, it reminds them of being in the womb.'

'She didn't like it, she was crying.'

I looked down at my daughter, her mouth held in a tight O-shape.

'She's hungry,' David's voice hardened. 'She can smell your milk.'

'I don't have any milk.' I flinched, shifting into kneeling position so that one foot was pushed in front of me, preparing to stand. Realising I had no free arms, I looked around for something to lean against.

Noticing my pain, David took a step forward. Without saying a word, he reached out for Rose. For a moment, I clasped her to me; holding my gaze, David moved his arm slowly closer.

'Let me take Rose, then I can help you up.'

Reluctantly loosening my grip on my daughter, I watched David scoop the baby up and lay her in the cot next to Stella. Feeling him move behind me, I let him help me, pushing my weight against his as he pulled me up by the armpits, the pain shooting through my abdomen like a knife.

'Why don't you go to bed?'

'I'm not tired, I want to feed Rose.'

David regarded me for a moment. 'I'm not sure if that's the best idea right now.'

'What do you mean, it's not the best idea? You've been telling me how little time I spend with the girls – that I need to feed—'

'Anna, stop. You need to rest. And take your pills.' There was something in his voice that made me pause, and from downstairs, I heard the front door pull shut. Knowing she was home, I felt air seep from my body, the relief overwhelming. As the sound of Maria's assured footsteps rose up the stairs, David took a step back.

'I have taken them.'

David sighed. 'You haven't taken them, they're by your bed. I hid the packet so you wouldn't take more than you needed, so you can't have had any—'

'But I did . . .' Heat rose in my cheeks. Why was he questioning me? I distinctly remembered, this morning: two pills laid out on my bedside table, a glass of water. It was this morning, I remembered it clearly.

Opening my mouth to speak, I looked at him, both babies suddenly asleep in the cot beside each other, oblivious to whatever it was that filled the air around them.

There was no point arguing with him when all I had to do was walk back into the bedroom, to the side table and show him . . .

'I don't understand.' My eyes moved from the two pills laid out on the side table, and David standing in the doorway, his eyes filled with sadness. Without saying a word, he closed his eyes and turned back into the hallway, his feet padding towards the stairs.

Since the birth, the dream had started to return with increasing regularity, variations on the day it happened; the sense of inevitability growing with every night that I relived it.

The afternoon had been too bright that day, over-exposed. The trees that lined the bottom of the garden were smudged around the edges, like a warning.

My mother's voice was strained as she ran into the kitchen where my brother and I were gulping water from plastic cups at the table, escaping the heat.

'I've got to run into the office. Your father needs some papers typed up, I'm afraid it can't wait.'

She absent-mindedly brushed her hand over Thomas's head as she swept past towards her handbag, which was perched on the counter. Her only son's cheeks were wet with sweat, his fringe plastered to his forehead.

'Marianne . . .'

She picked her car keys from the hook by the door before moving to the sink. Two pumps of hand-soap, thumb between knuckles. Rinse.

'You're in charge, OK?'

'But—'

'No buts, Marianne. You know what boys are like. You're the sensible one and I'm relying on you to look after your brother, make sure he doesn't get in any trouble. You can at least do that for me, can't you?'

She gave me a knowing look, scrubbing her wrists with a clean tea-towel.

'Thomas, you do as Marianne tells you. You listening?'

She pulled her bag over her shoulder as she headed towards the hall.

'And no leaving the house.'

I watched her go, willing her to turn back around, my annoyance following her up the garden path.

'Let's play.' Thomas slammed his glass loudly on the counter and ran out to the garden before I could object.

I followed him into the garden, slowly settling myself under the tree.

'Come on, you're so boring.' He jumped from one foot to another as I pulled rhythmically at strands of grass, wondering when my parents would be home.

'OK, fine, let's play hide-and-seek.' I had said it to get rid of him, giving myself at least a minute's peace.

'Fine. I'm hiding first, start counting. Don't cheat!'

He fell for it every time. Believing I actually wanted to play, too. Oblivious to the contempt I felt for his very existence.

Before I had reached four, I sensed Thomas slip out of earshot. Satisfied by my clever ploy, I enjoyed letting the words fall away, letting my eyes fall open, returning my focus to the grass, sprinkled with tiny white flecks blown over from the bulrushes up the road.

In the dream, though, I looked up. In the dream I watched Thomas creep back through the house, along the silent corridor towards the front door. His shoes, the ones with the Velcro straps, leaving the traces of dried soil that our mother would later quietly scrub away with a mop.

I watched him glance back to check I was not peeking as he pulled at the latch. I watched myself wilfully ignore him as he shimmied himself up the window ledge at the side of the house, with glee, his grazed knees pushing him up onto the roof of the garage.

How could I have known, how could I have predicted what would happen next? And yet, in every incarnation of this dream, every flashback, it's there: the sense that I did. The sense that my parents were right to blame me.

In this version of events, I saw myself, bored now, distracted by the lurch of voices next door. Helplessly, I watched my own face freeze as I finally spotted him on the roof of the house, grinning back at me.

Did I move? Did I call out to stop him? No matter how hard I racked my brain for evidence that I had tried to stop him, none could be found.

I can still hear it, even when the dream is over: the screech of brakes sounding from the road on the other side of the house, my mother's car arriving home just in time to see the body of her youngest twin drop, like a discarded doll, onto the driveway.

I woke up once again, damp with cold sweat, sitting up too soon, forgetting the pain until it seized my abdomen.

The silhouette of the tree in front of the house streaked along the hall as I opened the bedroom door, David stirring under the covers behind me before settling himself.

A single light called out from the ground floor as I stepped into the hall, the one Maria liked to keep on at night in case the girls needed her. From the nursery, I could hear the gentle rhythm of the lullaby seeping out from one of the countless gadgets David had bought in those first weeks, to soothe and cajole, to offer love where mine was lacking.

Taking a tentative step into the room, I was struck by an urge to run to my daughters, to prise them from their beds and bolt into the night, to leave the door swinging behind me as I hurtled across the Heath.

Instead, I turned my head and stepped back into the hallway, my fingers running along the bannister as I headed for the bathroom.

Not daring to pull the light cord, I slipped into the darkness, my hands brushing over the corner of the bath, feeling my way towards the sink. Ducking down, I paused, a creaking sound causing me to draw breath. But it was me making the noise, I realised, mouth releasing air, my knees cracking as I pushed myself forward, stretching my fingers inside the cupboard.

Finally, my skin grazed the phone. Instantly I felt a connection to Harry, to my life before this.

'Anna?'

I heard the light click on as the room was suddenly bathed in light, the phone instantly dropping out of my hand, into the cupboard.

'Shit, David, you scared the life out of me.'

He was leaning against the doorway, watching me splayed out on the floor.

'What are you doing? Are you crying?'

I looked up at him, my voice stuck in my throat.

'I was looking for painkillers. My stomach, it's . . .'

He did not move.

'I'll be in bed in a minute.'

My hand still wedged inside the cupboard, I kept eye contact until finally, with a small sigh, he nodded and walked away.

For a moment I stayed there, frozen, until my body finally sprang back to life, the adrenaline shooting through me. With only a few seconds before David might well return, I fumbled in the cupboard, the palm of my hand scrambling between bottles of toilet bleach and expensive outdated bath salts before I finally felt it, hard and angular in my hand.

Glancing quickly towards the bedroom, where the light was now off, I hit a button and the screen came to life.

I hadn't expected him to get in touch, not really. I knew that in terms of the investigation, I had offered nothing since the birth to warrant him contacting me. But I needed to know, amidst all of this, that he was still thinking of me. And there it was, the sign that I craved. The reassurance which at this point in time I felt was the only thing I had left to hold onto.

New message.

My chest felt like it might explode as I read on, an address for a meeting point, on Millbank, and a date.

4.15 p.m. this Thursday.

CHAPTER 35

Maria

She had a habit of watching the girls when she thought no one was looking, as if surveying their faces for a possible explanation. Sometimes I would look up from the dusky haze of the nursery, lit only by a small lamp the shape of a cloud, and I would catch one of her eyes, unblinking, through the sliver of space between the door and its frame.

'Would you like to join us?' I had asked one morning a week or so after I arrived, when I looked up to find her watching us in the living room, her fingers pressed tight against the bannister. Rose was on her back on a play-mat, her attention caught by the sound of Satie's *Gnossienne* flowing in from the radio in the kitchen.

For a moment there was a flash of warmth in her face when I beckoned her into the room, and then she pulled back, a slight adjustment as she turned back towards the stairs, speaking over her shoulder. 'Actually, I'm tired, I think I'll go back to bed. I was just going to get some water.'

This morning, it was me watching her from the window of the girls' room, making her way back up the road, away from the house.

She told me she was going to buy clothes for the girls who at two months were almost out of the first wave of babygros. It might have been believable, despite her eyes looking away from mine as she spoke, but I knew better. I knew it from the way she moved; the way she looked back over her shoulder as she walked away, that she was going to meet *him*.

It was curious how instinctively aware she was that she was being watched, even if she had no clue from which direction the eyes came. And how could she? How could anyone expect to know who is on their side if they have no idea whose side they themselves are on?

CHAPTER 36

Anna

The wind rose off the water as I pulled the phone from my pocket. I pressed it to my cheek, my eyes closing as Harry's phone went to voicemail.

'Please, answer.'

I spoke under my breath, pulling the cardigan across my chest.

Not prepared to take any chances, I had given myself enough time to slip into Mothercare on the way, picking out two packets of babygros. Even so, it was nearly 5 p.m. David would be home soon. So where the hell was Harry?

I was about to stand when I saw him, his face a metre from mine under the glow of the streetlamp.

'Harry.' I felt the breath catch in my throat as he took another step towards me.

His hair was longer than the last time – how long had it been: six months, more?

'Anna.'

His eyes creased at the sides, the way they had that first night. He looked older somehow, worn out; but the memory of him, the warmth of it, had not faded.

'It's good to see you.'

He lowered himself to sit beside me, far enough away that our legs would not touch, but the sound of my name on his tongue reached out and enveloped me.

I felt tears prick at my eyes and I nodded, willing them away, not yet trusting myself to speak; unsure, even then, of what they represented. Tears of regret, perhaps, for the absence that had grown between us; relief for being able to be myself again, the version of myself I had created just for him, the version of myself he had created for me to step into. Tears, perhaps, of apprehension, a niggling reminder of what was still to come.

'Twin girls, eh? I was going to send a card, but obviously . . .'

The flutter of blood warming my chest turned cold without warning, the tears tumbling down my cheeks before I could stop them, hot and angry.

'Where have you been?'

He shook his head, lowering his eyes to the pavement.

'I've been away. I couldn't—'

'You got my messages?'

'Yes, I got them, but I—'

I felt a noise erupt from my chest, the pressure that had been building inside finally releasing with a hiss.

'Anna, I wanted to—'

My face turned from his then, the tears stinging my cheeks as I wiped them away. Leaning forward, Harry reached for my hand and I pulled it back.

'I can't do it any more.'

My voice was matter-of-fact. Using the base of my hand to dry my eyes, I stretched the skin outwards before brushing the palms of my hands against the bench.

'I've decided. I got you the emails, I assume you received them?'

'Those were very helpful.'

'Well, that's as much as I can do.'

What was I saying? The words were out of my mouth before I could stop them. All the anger, all the emotions I had repressed for so long pouring out of me at once; the numbness I had felt since the birth giving way to rage and self-pity.

'I'm leaving, Harry. I'm taking the girls and we're leaving.'

I can only imagine how ridiculous I must have sounded, but I needed him to listen. I needed him to know that my life was falling apart.

He smiled gently, nodding and then pulling himself straighter, keeping his eyes on mine.

'I can't live my life like this any more. I'm tired. The girls and I, we're . . .'

My voice trailed off. The truth was I had no idea who we were. Who I was. How, in my quest for meaning, my quest for love, I had become a woman trapped in a relationship with a man who no longer loved me, while the man I adored – the one for whom I had risked everything – thought of me as little more than an instrument. Something to be tugged at and pulled into position. A cog in a machine that I had never seen – one that, if I stopped to think about it, I could not even picture.

My fingers scratched at brittle wrists. Everything itched, and the more I tried to scratch it, the faster it spread.

'Anna, come on . . . I understand, it's been—'

'You understand?'

My eyes were like claws.

He took my hand in his, lowering his voice as an elderly couple stopped in front of the water a few metres away.

'Look, you know you can't do that.'

He paused for a minute, taking me in, and then continued, his eyes concerned.

'I mean, darling, how can you look after the girls when you can barely look after yourself?'

I stopped for a moment, seeing myself through his eyes: the nails chewed to the quick, the small but telling tuft at the front of my head where my hair had begun to fall out since the birth, clumps of it lining the shower, clinging to the towels along with streaks of red.

As if reading my mind, his voice softened with compassion.

'You are clearly under stress – and that is hardly surprising, in the circumstances.'

'I'll get help, we'll get a nanny.'

I made as if to pull my hand away, but could not bring myself to do so.

'Really? How are you going to do that?' He was not being unkind. 'Without this – without me, without David? If you leave, you have no income, no job, nowhere to live . . . What are you going to do, Anna? Go back to your parents?'

He held my gaze and finally I pulled my hand away, turning my face towards the bridge. What did he know about my parents? It was the first time I had let myself wonder how much of my life he knew beyond what I had told him. But the thought was pushed out by his earlier words.

Without me.

He had said it. Without David there was no Harry. That's what he was saying; a simple transaction – that's what this was to him. How could we ever come back from that?

I heard his lighter click. Silently, he handed me the lit cigarette.

For a moment I did not move, then I took it, pulling my hand back as quickly as I could.

Inhaling, I felt my head lighten, my body lifting from under me as I spoke on the out breath.

'Well then, I'll leave the girls. I'll come back for them later. Once I have things sorted.'

He pulled on his own cigarette, watching the angles of my face.

'Anna, listen to yourself. One minute you're running away to save your daughters, the next you're running away from them . . .'

When had I ever said this was about saving the girls?

He leaned forward, turning my face towards him. I pushed against the strength in his hand for a second before conceding defeat, rubbing my cheek against his thumb.

'Listen to me, OK? You've just become a mother of twins. You're exhausted . . . No, don't do that. Don't pull away from me. Listen to me, Anna. I know you and you're not thinking straight. I know you.'

Those final words rolled around my head, provoking unexpected sadness.

Under the bridge, the Thames flowed on, grey and thick and unrelenting. I felt the tears forming again on the edge of my lashes.

'We spoke about this, didn't we? You've made a commitment. You knew what you were doing . . . You've accepted money, a lot of money, and you can't just walk away.'

'I didn't know—'

'Didn't know what, Anna?'

His voice was colder now, his patience wearing thin. The couple turned from the wall, muttering something before continuing their stroll along the river. Nodding placatingly towards them, he waited a moment before speaking again.

'Anna. Listen to me, OK? You're not going anywhere. These people . . .'

He took a deep breath, stubbing out his cigarette before turning to face me.

'These people we're working for, they aren't the kind you mess around. You know? I told you that, didn't I? I warned you. This isn't a game. They're not paying you for you to decide you've had enough. You're privy to highly classified information. You think they're just going to let you walk away?'

'*They*.' I let the word hang in the air. 'Who are they, Harry?'

He laughed.

'You're seriously asking me that, now? How long has it been? You know who *they* are, Anna.'

I shook my head.

'You knew what you were doing. You knew. We had this conversation. I told you that if you got involved, if you signed yourself over to this, there would be no coming back. I told you that.'

I stared back at him, my eyes dull. Beneath the fear, I suppose, was a sense of relief. Relief that the decision had been made for me. There was no point resisting, I had no choice. Running away was not an option. There was nowhere to go. Without Harry, without David, I had nothing. And without one, there was no other.

'The fact is,' he said, taking both of my hands, 'We are close. The emails you sent us are a start, and there are other things. Every day we're gathering intelligence, but we need you to hang in there, OK? You need to sit tight.'

Looking over his shoulder, Harry shifted towards me.

'You want to know where I've been?'

He checked his other side before leaning in closer so that I could feel his breath on my face. 'I've been in Equatorial Guinea, meeting with people who might be willing to talk on record about TradeSmart offering bribes to officials there.

'I didn't want to tell you this right now. I didn't want to bother you, but the truth is we're getting so much closer to something tangible, something we can actually pin on these guys once and for all . . . But we need you more than ever. And you need to remember why we're doing this.'

The words filtered through my pores.

'According to the people I've been talking to in Africa, a few years ago TradeSmart were offered a heapload of a product called coker naphtha for sale, at rock-bottom price. It's a relatively unrefined gasoline – the main problem with which is that it has really high levels of sulphur, including high levels of mercaptan sulphur. In theory, this product could be worth a fortune if they were to sell it on to the right people. The problem being that in such a raw state, this product was potentially toxic as hell.

'In order for the gasoline to be sold in the developing world, where TradeSmart would be able to make money from it, it would need to have a very low level of sulphur, such as the type we buy at the petrol pump. However, in parts of the developing world, the key determinant for purchase is often the odour of the product, for example where sulphur levels can't be measured.'

I reached for another of his cigarettes, still refusing to look at him. But he knew me well; he knew this was what I needed, a meaningful reminder of what we were doing. An objective tangible yet abstract enough to draw me out of my own head. To appeal to the person I wanted to be.

'So, in order to shift the stuff, TradeSmart had to work out a way to make it sellable. When gasoline has high mercaptan levels, as this stuff did, it stinks. I mean it really stinks. But if you can reduce the odour and make the naphtha marketable . . .'

My mind jumped back to the receipt I had found in Clive's office. I kept my eyes on the river, still feigning disinterest, though the truth was the receipt was just the beginning of what I was capable of. He still didn't know what else I had found when I rifled through Jeff's briefcase the night of the party in Greece. Why hadn't I told him straight away, as I had about the receipt? I had been buying myself time. All I had to do was keep quiet and, in hindsight, this could have been the moment that brought it all to an end. This was the drawbridge pulling up and all I had to do was to stay where I was; to make no sudden movements. Following the path of least resistance, I could have edged myself out of this. But I chose another way.

'So TradeSmart decided to extract the mercaptan and then sell it on?' I asked.

'Exactly.' He gave me an approving look. 'Except, instead of paying to properly refine the product, which admittedly would not have been cheap, Clive and his team of fuckwits decided to experiment by mixing the naphtha with large quantities of caustic soda solution, allowing the mixture to settle before draining off the spent caustic. It's not dissimilar to a process called Merox washing, sometimes used on land – the key difference being that in the case of Merox washing there is a step involved which means the mercaptans are turned into a stable, harmless product – as opposed to what TradeSmart did, which was to create a volatile, potentially hazardous, caustic waste. So then they're left with the not-so-slight problem of where the hell to dispose of this stuff.'

Much as I hated to admit it, the sound of his voice was helping my body settle. There was something soothing about listening to him talk, evoking the memory of why I was in this, the memory of the person I was before – the one he had chosen to trust.

'According to stringent international laws governing this kind of thing, the only place where there was a specialist disposal company capable of treating the kind of waste that this process would throw out was in Rotterdam. Except, not only would it cost around $250 per kilogram to dispose of, but in the end the port decided it was too problematic, in light of its toxicity and local environmental laws.'

My fingers moved instinctively towards my bag, containing my phone, loaded with the photos that by now I knew I was going to share with him, even before I had summoned the courage to say the words.

Harry sensed the shift in my demeanour. 'What's the matter?'

Ignoring the voice in my mind screaming at me not to, I opened my mouth and it was over.

'So I suppose there would be an extraordinary value to having, say, shipping records showing the export and import value of each of Clive's products,' I heard myself saying.

Understanding the potency of this moment, if not yet fully understanding what was happening, Harry remained silent. Breathing in, I pulled the phone once more from my bag.

'What's this?' When I looked up he was looking at me, as if seeing me for the first time. There was a tension to his voice that I hadn't expected, given what I was providing him with.

'Photos.' I flicked through to the relevant album and then passed him the phone.

As he scrolled through the snatched images I had taken that night, silently praying no one would notice the flash in the hallway, Harry's face paled.

'They're shipping records from what I can gather.' I added, my voice quieter now.

'I know what they are, Anna. I'm asking how you got them.'

'When I was in Greece, the night that I found that receipt in Clive's study . . . I went downstairs to get a glass of water, and when I came back I noticed the door to the cloakroom was jammed open, and there was Jeff's briefcase with papers showing the codes. I—'

'What the fuck, Anna – in Greece? How long ago was that, nine months? More?'

'Jesus, Harry, I've had a few things to deal with myself, you know? It seems to have completely escaped your notice, but I've just given birth to the grandchildren of the man I'm supposed to be . . .'

His eyes scanning the pavement around us for signs of interest from passers-by, Harry leaned in. 'I am well aware of that, Anna, but what the fuck is this? You could send me the receipt but not these?'

'I didn't know what they were. I didn't realise they meant anything and, if you really want to know, I wanted to go through them first. I wanted to see if I could work out what they meant, first.' I inhaled, and then made eye contact. 'I wanted to impress you.'

There was silence while I let my words sink in: the pathetic truth.

Exhaling sharply, Harry buried his face in his hands. It must have been a minute until he spoke again.

'I'm sorry. I know it's been hard.'

'Oh, you know, do you, Harry? You know what that's like? You know what it's like to wake up every morning and remember that your whole fucking life is a lie? You know what it's like to spend every single moment of your life afraid that you're going to say the wrong thing; you know how exhausting it is to have to think about every single thing that comes out of your mouth so that you can't even have friends in case you let something slip? To be too scared to spend time with your babies, too scared to let your guard down in case you end up loving them too much to carry on? But all the time, you can't stop – you can't walk away. You're trapped because everywhere you look there's a wall, and you built it yourself and it's too late so you just have to live with the lies and the constant fucking tiredness, and you can't even tell anyone how shit it is, and the one person you *can* talk to – the person you loved so much that you gave up everything for him, can't even be bothered to answer their phone. And you have no control over anything in your life. Not one fucking thing. Don't you *dare* tell me for one second that you understand what that's like.'

Loved. That was the word I had used. Past tense. The thought slowed me down.

'Anna. I'm . . .' He breathed in such a way that it convinced me for the first time that he was actually acknowledging how much I had sacrificed.

There was a note of genuine contrition when he spoke again. 'I'm sorry. I'm so sorry I wasn't in touch.'

He laid his hand on mine and when I tried to pull my fingers back they would not move. For a moment I pictured our hands, side by side, on the train to Brighton. He had never been before and I revelled in the opportunity to be the one to teach him something; something personal enough, but still safe.

That weekend was the first time I felt that he belonged to me, in the same way that I belonged to him.

I had booked the hotel, overlooking the sea. I woke up to find him sitting in front of the window looking back at me.

'Hello,' I said, self-conscious beneath his gaze.

'Hello.'

As I pushed myself to sitting, he kept his eyes on me and I squirmed at the weight of his full attention.

'What?' My laugh was uneasy.

He shrugged. 'Nothing. I was just thinking how astonishing you are.'

'Oh please . . .'

'It's true. I just can't believe how long it took me to find you.'

I heard voices from inside the house as I made my way back up the steps, taking a moment to compose myself. My fingers were clammy as I held the Mothercare bag in one hand, the other struggling with the door.

As I pushed the key to the right, I felt the pressure give way from inside. It was Maria, pulling open the door, Stella in one arm, her pink face contented, lips puckered. I felt my body soften as my daughter stretched out her arms.

'I think she wants you.'

Maria made a gentle move towards me, smiling, as I dropped my bags to the floor. Stepping forward, I held out my arms nervously. 'Ssshh . . .'

I took Stella's swathed body in my arms, looking to Maria for reassurance.

'That's right.'

She nodded kindly.

Looking into my daughter's eyes, their black-blue rims, I felt a rush of love followed by a stab of pain. Leaning forward, nuzzling my face in her neck, I breathed deeply.

'There you are.'

David was standing in the doorway of the living room; his voice had a peculiar tone, and I felt my skin tingle in response.

'I'm sorry, I was in town.' I nodded towards the plastic bags at my feet. 'The Tube was—'

'It's OK, I was just worried.'

He took a step towards me, his hand rising to his temple.

'Anna, come in here for a moment, there's someone I want you to meet.'

He took a step back, turning into the living room. I thought of the way he had looked at me, that first day on campus. His face now was almost unrecognisable.

I looked to Maria but her gaze was fixed to the floor.

'Anna, I'm Dr Blackman.'

The stranger stood as I walked into the room, my eyes darting between David and the man poised in front of the sofa dressed in a faded white shirt and navy trousers, brown shoes scuffed at the toes.

'Please, do sit down.'

'It's perfectly normal to experience difficulties in adjusting,' Dr Blackman said, once we were all settled in the living room, his fingers locked together, elbows resting on his knees.

'Even in the least chaotic of circumstances, becoming a parent can be bewildering . . . I mean, children don't come with a manual, right?'

He looked at David as he said the last words, raising his eyebrows in a show of solidarity.

'But when the birth is surrounded by trauma, it can be even harder to adjust.'

The doctor allowed a few moments' breathing space. David leaned against the wall, nodding solemnly along, while I sat on the chair opposite, like a child.

My eyes roamed the room, desperate to avoid Dr Blackman's face, my gaze settling on David's mother's painting, looming from above the heavy stone fireplace.

'David tells me you've become withdrawn since the girls were born. Detached. He says you're not eating, and that you seem joyless. Would you say that's fair?'

He did not wait for an answer.

'I hear you're refusing to feed the girls. You've also become rather reliant on the painkillers you were given after the Caesarean? David says he found you a few nights ago, searching for them in the bathroom, that you were frenzied.'

His tone was firm but fair, like a teacher. There was no room for interruption, even when he paused for a moment, his voice softening.

'David tells me you lost your own mother, when you were young.'

I looked across at David, whose face was fixed at a point somewhere in the distance. He lifted a finger to his eye, turning further away from me. Before I could form any words, Dr Blackman spoke again, leaning inwards.

'He was worried.' The tone was confidential now. 'He *is* worried. About you, and the girls . . .'

I opened my mouth to reply. The girls were not in any danger. Did he honestly think I was a threat to our children?

I looked at David, but his face was still turned away from mine.

'I think, if truth be told, that you're probably experiencing some form of post-traumatic stress disorder, which is not uncommon after the sort of birth you've experienced. Combined with your own associations with losing your mother . . . It's certainly not something you need to be ashamed of, Anna. Frankly, I think it would be strange if you didn't have some sort of reaction in the circumstances. What is important is that you get help.'

David, who up to now had been silent, shifted his position against the wall, pushing himself upright.

'Dr Blackman and I were talking and we think it might be a good idea to get away for a while.' When he looked up, his face was stained with tears but the eyes that looked back at me were dull as rock.

'I've spoken to my father; he says we could stay with him in the Maldives. Get our own water-villa; I could work from there for a while. Maria could come with us, so we'd have plenty of help. I think it would do us good. A change of scene, sun, fresh air. Get away for a while . . .'

David's voice drifted off.

'We could have the work on the house done while we are away, too.'

My head felt light. I opened my mouth to speak but the room had moved on. The matter was settled. Obediently, I shook Dr Blackman's hand. He and David exchanged words I could not hear as they walked towards the front door.

'I appreciate it,' I caught David saying before closing the door, the lock clicking back into place.

CHAPTER 37

Anna

The seaplane circled high above a turquoise sea, golden atolls dotted below like dusty jewels.

David insisted I take the window seat as we boarded the privately chartered flight, which glistened red and white at Malé airport against the heat rising from the tarmac.

I had objected at first as we climbed onto the plane, my eyes moving anxiously to the cots, which were already fastened in along the back row.

'I'd rather not, David. I want to sit with the girls . . .'

'Don't be silly, they're fine, Maria's with them. And actually the back of the plane is the safest place to be, if there was an accident . . .'

I shot him a look, which he responded to by squeezing my hand a little too hard.

'I'm joking. Look, you can't miss this view, it's absolutely incredible.'

Pockets of land, so tiny they were barely visible at first, emerged from a blanket of blue. The pale sea stretched below, punctuated by flashes of green and gold where reefs and sunlight collided.

The landing strip was little more than a thread of land bolted onto the Indian Ocean. As the plane prepared to land, David leaned into me, his breath stale from a day of travelling.

'I told you, didn't I? It's not over yet.'

I turned to him, my hands gripping the sides of the seat, grateful for his renewed enthusiasm, and yet uneasy in a way I could not place.

'It's the wake-up call we all need,' David had stated once Dr Blackman had left the house, his voice flat but sure. I had felt Maria's eyes rise to look at me briefly as David left the room.

Perhaps he was right. In the weeks following Dr Blackman's visit, things had certainly seemed to be lifting. Perhaps it was the anti-depressants he had prescribed that were influencing my impression, but things felt more manageable at home; David, too, seemed brighter somehow, less weighed down by life.

Now, as the morning sun beat down on our heads, the sea unfolding across the horizon, I felt something akin to contentment, if not happiness exactly.

'I thought this might remind you of Greece.'

David turned to me as the speedboat arrived to take us on the final leg of the journey.

'You remember, don't you? That day. The first time we told each other . . .'

I felt a prick of unease as he stared at me, his eyes unrelenting.

'I still do, you know. Despite everything.'

I laughed uncomfortably, pushing my elbow self-consciously into his body, aware of Maria behind us with the girls.

'What, I can't tell the mother of my children that I love her?'

Smiling, I pulled my sunglasses over my eyes, the light too bright against the glare of the boat.

The speedboat cut across the ocean, towards a wooden jetty that snaked through the water on stilts. Across the shoreline, a series of shorter walkways led from the sand, each towards its own wooden hut on stilts, sprouting from the sea like an army of insects.

'Wilson!'

The hotel manager was perfectly groomed, his age impossible to place. David greeted him like an old friend as he walked out to meet us. David led me by the hand, the wheels of the suitcase thrumming against slatted wood.

'This one's ours . . .'

Through the gaps in the wood beneath my feet I could see flashes of water, darting precariously in the morning sun.

I looked up as David unlocked the door, standing back to let me push it open, giving himself a full vantage point from which to soak in my reaction.

From where we stood, the far end of the hut was a curve of glass looking out onto the deck with its own private pool; the sides of the deck were shielded from view by a wall of bamboo, the sea beyond stretching out to an unbroken horizon.

Taking a hesitant step inside the hut, which was divided into four spacious areas, I took in the bedroom, all plush silk sheets and duck-down pillows adorning a four-poster bed, adjoined by a living area with a low wooden table laden with fresh fruit in a wide glass bowl.

Moving silently into the bathroom, I leaned my arm against a wall of floor-to-ceiling mosaic tiles, like thick cubed shells.

'What's through there?' I asked, pointing towards a room adjoining the living area, separated by a shield of glass, with two raised wooden slabs looking out over the water.

'That,' David replied, pulling me towards him, 'is our own personal massage suite.'

My breath tightened as I cast my eye around the rooms for any sign of a cot or highchair.

'But where will the girls . . .'

'They will be next door, with Maria. I think it's important that you and I have time . . .' He led me onto the wooden deck, which dropped away to open sea. Taking a step back, I felt David's eyes on mine.

'This has to be where it ends.'

Watching the muscles in my cheek tense, his eyes softened though the pupils remained still. 'This resentment between us, whatever it is . . .' He swallowed, collecting himself. 'This is where we lay it to rest. A new start.'

I held my breath as he took a step towards me, my back to the sea. Raising my toes, imperceptibly, I found my body tense with adrenaline, the fight or flight response kicking in, as I wondered what was coming next. And then he took me in his arms and moved his mouth towards mine, holding my eyes with his all the while.

It was the first time we had had sex since the girls were born. I held my body defensively, afraid of aggravating layers of scar tissue, though the midwife had told me there was no need. David rolled off me once it was over and walked to the shower, the muscles in his calves stretching and softening again as he moved, like a cat's paw working at a mouse.

Listening to the water falling from the shower, I was finally struck by the impact of the journey. Stretching out my body, I slipped out of the rest of my clothes, my body sinking into the mattress so that as I slept I had the sensation I was falling down a dark hole.

I woke to find David at the side of the bed. There was a look in his eye I could not identify, but when I blinked and met his gaze again he was smiling, rubbing my forearm with the side of his thumb.

'Have you been taking the pills Dr Blackman prescribed?'

I shifted slightly away from him, nodding, trying to gather my thoughts, but before I could say anything else, David smiled and stood.

'Good. Good, I just . . . Anna, listen, I know things have been . . . They haven't been easy for either of us, but I just want things to get better.'

I watched his face and for a split second I imagined what could have been if I had never met Harry at all. The life David and I could be living now, a life that I knew, deep down, I would never have settled for.

'I love you,' I said, almost under my breath,

The truth was, I did love David. While I loved Harry for what he saw in me, for what he knew and didn't judge, I loved David for what he did not know. I loved him for what he could never see, nor even imagine; for the version of me he had been so willing to believe – that for so long had existed, largely untainted, in his eyes. But I'm not sure I would have ever allowed myself the simplicity of being with someone like David, if Harry had not been around to cast a shadow. He was the yin to Harry's yang. For any sort of equilibrium to exist, I had to have both.

'I've always loved you, despite everything,' David replied, his voice trailing off as he turned into the bathroom and locked the door.

I was caught off-guard by the tenderness with which Clive received his new grandchildren, later that morning. The way he stooped over their Moses basket, curling their tiny fingers over his own, his eyes glistening as he watched them, their faces fixed on the wooden fan which chopped silently at the air from the ceiling of the reception lounge.

'Anna . . .'

Clive looked up approvingly, as David and I walked in through the high wooden archway and into the reception area where a young man in head-to-toe white cotton discreetly proffered a tray of teacups gilded with ornate white petals.

My hair was still wet from the shower, pulled away from my face, the way David liked it, my skin glowing with one of the moisturisers lining the his-and-hers basins in the bathroom.

Dismissing the bellboy with his hand, Clive turned to us as we approached, both arms held out. Overcome by emotion, he took us in his arms in turn, me first, so that my head pressed against his armpit.

'I'm so sorry it's taken so long,' he said, pulling back after a moment, turning to David. 'I wanted to come sooner but things have been . . .' He held David's eye for a beat before looking back towards the young waiter, who was returning with a bottle of champagne and three glasses.

'We'll take it in the bar.'

Clive leaned down to pick up the Moses basket. David put an arm on his father's but Clive dismissed him. 'I might be old but I am not too old to carry my own grandchildren.'

He turned to face me, leaving David in the foyer. 'Now, how was the journey? What did you think of the old seaplane?'

* * *

David and Clive decided to take a boat-trip one morning a few days into our holiday.

'No, you two go, it will be nice. Father–son bonding time,' I said when David invited me along, my mind flashing to the spinner dolphins I had read about in the resort brochure, performing their tricks on the surface before sinking back under water to devour their prey.

Kissing David lightly on the cheek, I watched them leave, their steps merging into one as they disappeared towards the jetty.

I had spent the morning on the beach, wading in the shallows, miniature whitetip sharks playing at my feet. Turning occasionally towards the girls, I could see them sleeping under the shade of the palms, Maria watching over them, her body forming a natural barricade.

From this distance, I felt a swell of gratitude towards her, for the way she cared for my children so diligently. Gratitude increasingly tinged with the ache of regret that I could never be for them what she was; the easy confidence with which she tended to their every need always outstripping my own.

The truth was, I was desperate to be alone. Ever since we had arrived, David had barely stopped hovering over me as if checking for visible signs of improvement. Beyond that, he could not seem to settle. In the way I had noticed happen whenever he was around his father, he was like a child, desperate constantly for approval. The combination was exhausting.

The resort was arranged in such a way that even at full capacity, as it was at this time of year, it was easy to believe you were one of just a handful of people there. Clive's repeat custom meant that we were both left alone and fully waited on in the simultaneous fashion that only the most efficient hotels can manage.

As I walked back to my towel, Maria looked up, her mouth wide with warmth. Unlike me, she suited the sun: her body opening up like a petal under its touch; her skin had turned a nut-brown within hours of landing.

'I'm so sorry, I need to go back to the hut for a moment. Could you watch the girls?'

She stood, dusting the sand off her knees, her slight, boyish frame exposed in demure black shorts.

At the prospect of being left alone with the girls for the first time in as long as I could remember, I felt my chest constrict, my heart spiralling in a Catherine wheel of emotions. Pride trailed by joy, guilt, and then terror. The complex knot of feelings that clung together in my throat threatened to choke me. From nowhere, there was a flash and for a split second I saw the sea pull back, rising up and crashing down on us; a coconut swinging precariously at the top of the tree above my daughters' heads.

'Will you be long?'

The desperation was clear in my voice and Maria paused, placing her hand briefly on my shoulder, brushing away the intrusive thoughts.

'It is OK. You don't need me. I promise.'

And in that moment, I believed her.

CHAPTER 38

Maria

I left her there on the sand, the girls snoozing on their mats under the shade of a palm, anxiety coursing through her every movement as she shuffled to and fro, like a wolf guarding its kill.

Tapping my fingers against the pocket of my shorts, I felt the outline of the key-card I had lifted from her bag as she swam, without ever venturing more than a metre or so from the shore. It was tucked into the inside pocket of her bag, along with her second phone, the one she kept in the cupboard in the bathroom; the one she used to contact him.

The walkway was clear as I moved towards the beach hut. Just to be sure, I walked first towards the door of my own hut, turning briefly to survey the area. Only once I was certain the coast was clear did I move quickly across to the next-door suite, holding the key-card against the sensor and waiting for the consenting click.

Inside, the room was still in the same state as it had been left that morning, the maid yet to descend and perform her tricks. Briefly, I imagined her taking in the discarded underwear by the bed, the stain just visible on the sheet where the duvet had been pulled back.

A damp towel had been strewn over a leather armchair, half-drunk glasses of water abandoned on the bedside tables. Knowing I only had a few minutes, I set straight to work, moving quickly towards the suitcase, which lay unzipped in the corner of the room.

Feeling along the inside, with no luck, I moved to the cupboards, running my hands through the layers of David's soft cottons and silks, along rows of neatly hanging shirts and through to the back of the wardrobe.

As my hand made contact with the back of the cupboard, I sensed something that made my whole body freeze, the adrenaline rising so that I could almost feel it on the surface of my skin. It wasn't so much a sound as a transmission of facts, received by some receptor in my brain that worked with a sense I could not name. The same instinct that makes a person look around them when they feel they're being watched.

There was no way I could have heard the hand on the door, but in that instant I knew it was there. The inside of the cupboard was suddenly cloying with the smell of David's aftershave, Anna's elusive scent bleeding in at the edges.

If I were to bundle the clothes to one side, I could quite easily hide in here, holding my breath inside my body. But if I were caught like that, if it were David who had returned in search of swimming trunks? That would be the end of everything.

In a moment of lucidity, in what could realistically only have been a second later, I pulled myself back into the room just in time to hear the slight turn of the handle, and then a voice.

Before I could think it through properly, before I could be sure of what I thought I had heard, the words rushed out of me. 'No, please! Later!'

There was a moment's pause and then, just as I thought my heart would rise out through my throat, the tension on the door handle loosened, followed by a placatory mumble and the gentle clatter of the housekeeping trolley moving away.

I leaned back against the cupboard, just for a moment, before running to the door, lifting the paper sign hanging from the handle, turning it to 'DO NOT DISTURB' and stretching my hand out of the hut, my fingers fumbling for a grip; keeping my body hidden from view as I hung the notice on the front of the door.

Turning back into the room, aware that time was running out, I moved quickly towards David's side of the bed, and then Anna's, feeling with my fingers along the area between the mattress and the leather bed-frame. After a moment, I felt my skin strike against cold metal.

Closing my eyes for a moment, in gratitude, I pulled out the laptop and laid it on the bed in front of me. Working hard to keep my fingers steady, I pulled the stick from my other pocket and slid it into the USB port, waiting for a moment until the screen lit up.

CHAPTER 39

Anna

I enjoyed the feeling of the water beating against my back the following morning. It was a moment that was entirely mine, when I could luxuriate in feelings rather than thoughts; the scrape of the loofah against my arm, the steam rising from my pores, my fingers pressing against the hollows of my eyes. A moment in which I was neither Anna nor Marianne, a rare moment in which to simply be.

'I'm so sorry, I've had an email from one of our clients in Europe, they want to do a call . . .'

It was David in the doorway to the shower-room, his voice cutting through the gentle roar of the water. I jumped back, pulling my arms against my chest, scared, as I found myself sometimes when he caught me deep in thought, that he would see through me simply by looking.

The relentlessness of constantly pretending, of living various versions of my life that were never quite my own had started to take its toll. Despite the constant charade, there was one role-change whose power I had never anticipated. In becoming a mother, I found myself consumed with fundamental shifts, both physical and emotional, over which I had no authority. Sometimes it felt like that lack of control could be the thing to bring the whole world I had created tumbling down.

'Careful, who did you think it was?'

David raised his hand, by way of placation. Before I could reply, he had gone, the door slamming shut as he disappeared with his laptop.

I took my time dressing, flicking through the international news channels, cartoons and documentaries, until a film flashed on the screen – the same one Harry and I had watched that first evening together, my first night in Meg's flat.

The thought of him now filled me with a dull pain. The ease with which he had leaned in to kiss me, a few days later. The inevitability of it. How he had held my eye up until the last moment before our skin touched.

For a moment, I thought of Meg too.

By the time David returned to the room, the film was coming to an end. I was perched at the end of the bed, my wet hair still unbrushed, the bedclothes where I had been sitting by now cold and damp.

Aware of the tear-stains on my cheek, I leapt up, pulling at my towel, rolling my eyes.

'Are you OK? Has something happened?'

I laughed.

'God no, sorry. That film, it gets me every time. Are you hungry?'

Breakfast was still being served in the restaurant overlooking the beach. Inside the restaurant, each wall was lined with silver platters brimming with cold organic meats, obscure cheeses, sushi, hot plates of curries, exotic fruits and twenty different types of muesli, cereals and breads.

We ate on the terrace, the girls head-to-toe on a cashmere rug at our feet.

'What do you fancy? If you don't see it, they can make it for you.'

David was fiddling with Stella's sunhat, pulling the brim low over her sleeping eyes.

'I'm fine with toast.'

'I thought you said you were starving, but suit yourself.' David pushed back his chair, surveying the room as he made his way towards the cooked breakfast.

Standing, making my way to the edge of the terrace, drawn by the boats on the horizon, I spotted Clive a little way along the beach, his panama gleaming in the morning sun, his face the colour of cooked bacon as he made his way towards us.

About to raise my hand in hello, I realised he was turning towards the bar, which stood a way back from the beach. With David still at the buffet, his back to me, I pulled back slightly so that I could not be seen as I watched Clive take a chair, pulling out his phone and looking at the screen while a waiter brought him coffee.

He had just taken his first sip when I spotted someone walking towards him.

Noticing, too, Clive held his hand out to the man who was approaching the table. Dressed in a cream linen suit, which shone out against his black skin, there was something about the man that was familiar, and as he turned to address the waiter, revealing his face, I realised it was the man from the photo in Clive's office. At that moment Rose cried out in her sleep, her arms shooting above her head.

Moving quickly back towards the table, I reached down as David's footsteps sounded behind me.

'Are you going to pick her up?'

His voice was appraising.

'I am, I'm just supporting her head properly first.'

'I wasn't criticising.'

Rose's tiny body writhed in my arms with a surprising amount of force, and the power with which she resisted my embrace caught me off-guard.

'Your dad is over there.'

I stood in an attempt to soothe her as David followed my line of sight.

'So he is.'

'Who is that man he's talking to?'

I tried to keep my voice light as Rose wailed into my chest, the other diners turning their heads briefly to show their distaste.

David pulled a bottle of milk from the changing bag Maria had packed for us, watching my expression as he handed it to me. By this point Rose was screaming, her face strained and blood-red with fury.

'She won't take it.'

The tension in my body was rising to match hers as she swung her face from side to side, spitting the nib of the bottle from her mouth as though I were trying to gag her.

'Oh, for God's sake, Anna. Let me.'

It couldn't have been a figment of my imagination, the disgust in David's eyes as he pulled our daughter from my trembling arms and held her against himself, humming a low vibrato for long enough that her cry calmed to a low ripple. How could someone who seemed to love me so much one minute show such disdain the next? Worse still, the pain I felt in these moments when he suddenly blew cold reminded me that I needed him more than I cared to admit.

'Here you are, hush little one.'

Moving away from me, he shifted our daughter in his arms and placed the bottle against her mouth gently until she pressed her mouth into it, her eyes rolling in her head, her cheeks finally sucking gratefully.

I picked up my coffee cup, turning my face to the water as the other diners returned their attention to their meals.

'We have a reservation at the restaurant at eight thirty.'

David walked out of the bathroom, fully dressed, rubbing some sort of ointment into the tips of his hair. The smell of sandalwood drifted over the bed as he passed by where I lay back against a pile of cushions, browsing through the news channels, my hair swathed in a thick white towel, another wrapped around my body.

'You're going out again?'

'I told you, this is a working holiday. Given how much time I've taken off recently to support you, I can hardly swan off and expect—'

'I understand, I was just asking.'

'We can't both sit around all day, someone has to make the money.'

His tone was mock light-hearted.

'I'm joking, you know that. I just want you to rest. It's important you get better. That's why we're here. OK, so it's seven fifteen now. I'll meet you at the restaurant as soon as I can, but my father will be there at eight fifteen – why don't you meet him there and I'll be along when I'm done?'

David lingered in the doorway a moment.

'Wear something nice. Yes?'

There was something about the sight of Clive and that man on the beach that morning that I could not shake. Did I know what I was going to do as I pulled out my computer from my bag, minutes after David left the room? Did I know what I was looking for, let alone what I would find?

It took what felt like an age for the computer to warm up, the screen creaking to life as I pulled out the Wi-Fi code from the leather-bound brochure on the coffee table, remembering Harry's words as I tapped in the numbers – the words he had offered, that evening on the Embankment, once I had finally calmed down.

'As you say, these are shipping records. If you take the export and import data, you can see what each ship landing in Equatorial Guinea on any given day was carrying. Each substance has a code. Mercaptan isn't officially an import, as it's a waste product, but it too has a code. So we can see, on the week we're interested in, in the days leading up to the chemical spillage, two ships arrived in Bata carrying this mercaptan sulphur product.'

He sighed, running a finger over his chin as he continued.

'I can't believe you held out on giving me this,' he reprimanded me without making eye contact. 'But to be honest, I should have thought of it earlier. This kind of information, it can be bought, if you know the right websites to try. There are plenty of companies who collate trading data and sell it, normally to people interested in making investment decisions.'

I had nodded, my eyes running over endless columns as he continued.

'If you have the bill of lading, for example, you can see what goes onto a ship, and what comes off the other side. Once it is on the ship, the value of the cargo is frozen. In the oil trade that is important because you load up at a certain point and then you wait for the price to get to the right level again. That's pretty valuable information if you're wondering what to invest in, and when.'

'And what are these numbers?'

I had pointed to a series of codes.

'Those? I'm not sure . . .'

That was when his phone had rung, his eyes narrowing as he rejected the call. Was I imagining his skin burning as he turned back to me?

'You can take it if you want. She'll be worried – whoever she is.' I looked away.

He had shaken his head, but he wasn't denying that there was another woman, and I would have been a fool to imagine there would not be.

Before I could say anything he took my phone and selected the images, sending them to himself and then leaning forward to kiss me. I turned so that his stubble brushed sharply against my ear.

After what felt like an age, the computer came to life, a welcome sea breeze blowing in through the open terrace doors.

Glancing over my shoulder, out of habit, I opened Google, and realised I had no idea what to type. Scouring the photos on the phone in front of me for clues as to what I was looking for, I decided to start at the top and work my way down through the columns of numbers, typing out each into a customs data site in order to work out what they were.

My foot was dead under my leg, almost an hour later, as I finished working my way through deciphering the items on board the two ships that had landed in Equatorial Guinea in the days leading to the chemical spillage: cotton T-shirts, DVD players, construction materials . . . mercaptan sulphur. Still, that was nothing out of the ordinary – not officially at least, if one were assuming that the waste from the chemicals on board was to be disposed of responsibly.

Almost ready to give up, I shifted position on the bed, my eyes growing hot with tiredness, as I spotted another code, separate from the others, in the top left-hand corner of the first page. Studying it more closely, I noted the prefix: PEN, which I typed into the search engine, scrolling for three pages of Google links offering biros for sale, and websites for various organisations that could have no link to the shipping records in front of me. Then I saw it, the words Private Enterprise Number, and I felt a rush of adrenaline, a proximity to something that I could not explain. My finger hovering over the mousepad for a moment, I clicked the link and my body seized with excitement as the page loaded on the screen in front of me.

I could not have said how much later it was when I heard a knock on the door. Instinctively, I checked the clock at the corner of the screen. With a sense of horror I realised that almost an hour had passed since I had inputted the Private Enterprise Number from the shipping records I had copied from Jeff's briefcase into Companies House in order to draw up the shareholder history of the company that owned the boats. A British company, it transpired, named Strategic Services. My fingers, damp with sweat, had tapped out the words that led me to the full list of Strategic Services shareholders. Two of them familiar, Clive Witherall and Jeff Mayhew. The third was Francisco Nguema.

I had copied and pasted Francisco Nguema's name into a separate tab, waiting with a growing sense of unease as the picture of the man loaded on the screen in front of me. The man from the beach this morning. The same pockmarked skin I'd recognised from the photo which hung in Clive's office.

'Anna?'

My legs almost giving way, I stumbled off the bed, pressing 'sleep' on my laptop and pushing it and my phone under my pillow before moving towards the door.

'Hello?'

'Anna, it's Clive.'

Adjusting my towel around my chest, I took a moment to rearrange my face before opening the door a crack.

'Hi!'

'Oh, I'm sorry, I thought we could walk to dinner together. I saw David a while ago, he said you were nearly ready, but clearly . . .'

I rolled my eyes apologetically. 'I'm so sorry, I think it must be the jet lag. I fell asleep.'

Clive's eyes remained still.

'I'll be five minutes, I have everything laid out.'

'Don't worry, I'll just see you there.'

I nodded, pushing the door closed behind me and lunging to the bed, pulling the computer from under my pillow.

My heart pounding in my throat, I opened our email account, just as Harry had taught me. The thrill of knowing I had discovered something that he had failed to; the reassurance of knowing that I was good at this – better, even, than he was – was dizzying. Pasting the information I had gathered into a new message before leaving it in the drafts folder, as instructed, I waited a moment to make sure it had stored, before pressing delete on my history and closing down my computer, composing a text:

Dad, I've popped a letter in the post. Miss you.

Hesitantly, I added an 'x' to the end of the text before changing my mind and removing it. My finger hovered above the send button when a thought crossed my mind: whatever it was about knowing what I had discovered, without Harry's guidance, that thrilled me, it also made me pause. And without ever consciously making a decision, the decision had been made. Considering it for only a split second further, I deleted the text.

Drawing breath, laying the phone down on the bed beside me, I opened my computer once more. Before I could fully comprehend the choice I had just made, I found myself going back into the drafts folder and copying the information from the draft email I had just composed for Harry to find when he next checked into our joint email account.

Opening a new blank document, I then pasted the email onto the page and saved that on my desktop instead, under the header 'architect-transcripts-003-2013'.

Deleting the email draft and then purging the 'trash' folder, I erased my search history again and slammed my laptop closed.

It was a split-second decision, based more on a feeling than a rational thought. A feeling that if I gave this away now, it would serve a short-term goal of pleasing him; it would show him that I could do what he needed me to do. But, thinking ahead, what purpose did that serve for me? If I gave him what he needed too soon, there was a chance there would be no more need for me. I would have nothing left – no bargaining chip, should I ever require it. Nothing in my arsenal with which to defend myself against being discarded.

Did I mistrust Harry, then? Perhaps I did. Perhaps I was terrified of being tossed out of the warmth of this secret world in which, for now, we were jointly entombed.

CHAPTER 40

Maria

I was pushing the girls along a paved walkway lined with palms, which ran partially concealed behind the hotel bar, when I spotted David at a table where the terrace meets the sand. His laptop stood on the table in front of him, closed, and from my vantage point I could see his foot thrumming agitatedly against the ground.

Noticing the girls had drifted off to sleep, their heads bobbing towards one another in the double pushchair, I stopped. For a moment I stood there, watching him, savouring this opportunity to simply observe. There was something about his demeanour that prompted a flash of memory. That night at his house in Greece; the helpless rage that had consumed his teenage body as we watched one another, both of us terrified of what might happen next.

And then another feeling took over. The fear I had felt that night was replaced by a sense that I couldn't put into words, the sense of possibility, perhaps. At home, I couldn't deny the thrill of the conflicting emotions that took hold whenever he looked at me. The way his gaze followed me as I comforted his babies; the thoughts I could almost read running through his mind – the alternative reality in which it was me and him, just the two of us, and our own children . . .

But as I tightened my fingers around the handles of the pushchair, I heard David's voice, and it was only then that I noticed the phone pressed to his cheek.

'I've told Anna you'll meet her at the restaurant at eight fifteen.'

There was a brief silence before he spoke again. The tightness of his voice once more triggered memories of that awful night in Greece, the night that put an end to whatever it was that might have blossomed between us.

'I'm doing it tonight, at dinner . . . I know! For God's sake, Dad. Do you think I don't know that? I love her. I just don't get why you can't understand that? I loved her from the moment we met. I can't control how I feel.'

His voice by now was almost a hiss and his hand was shaking. When he spoke again his voice was quieter, almost grief-stricken.

'Of course I'm not. Do you think I don't understand what's at stake? It's just the lies. The constant lying that . . . I know. I know there's no choice, I'm just confused. Please, at least allow me that.'

'Madam?'

It was the hotel manager, his crisp white tunic almost blinding as I spun around to face him.

'Good evening.' I nodded, keeping my voice low, hoping he wouldn't see the heat I could feel rising in my cheeks.

'Is everything all right?'

Why did his words feel like an inquisition?

'Everything's perfect, thank you. I was just taking the girls for some air.'

Briefly, we held each other's eyes, and then he nodded, a tight smile crossing his face before he walked on, as I pushed the buggy back the way I had come, not risking another glance back in David's direction.

CHAPTER 41

Anna

The entrance to the restaurant was domed, like a mouth. I felt myself tipping forward as I followed the thick red carpet down towards the sound of the chamber orchestra, my heels digging purposefully into the floor.

'By the time we reach the dining room we will be five metres below sea-level,' my escort, a young Sri Lankan man dressed head to toe in black, explained in perfect English. As he said this, he pulled open large arched double-doors revealing a huge glass dome; above us and all around, fish of every colour and size darted through the water as if escaping an imaginary predator.

'Anna, my dear!'

I felt a hand on my back.

As I turned, Clive took a step back, moving his fingers to his chest. Any hint of his annoyance earlier had fallen away.

'My God, darling, you look extraordinary.'

Struggling to keep the smile from my lips, I let him kiss me on both cheeks, careful not to smudge the deep red lipstick I had selected earlier at the resort boutique, along with a black silk dress, the hem of which gently brushed against the marble floor as we walked together towards our table.

'Now, tell me, have you ever eaten under the sea before?' Clive pulled open the wine menu in front of his broad chest, widening his arms like a bear.

'We'll have the Sancerre. Or Anna, did you want something else? A cocktail, perhaps, to start?'

'Wine is perfect.'

I placed my hands in my lap agreeably, following his lead.

'David had to take a phone call but he said he won't be long.'

I filled the silence nervously, as Clive picked one of the rolls from a basket lined with a silk napkin.

It was the first time he and I had ever been alone together, and I felt a thrum of excitement but also reverence in his company. In the abstract, through my conversations with Harry and all my research, Clive had come to represent so much. Yet face to face, it was hard to reconcile the monolithic picture of him I had built in my head with the gentleman before me.

'Good, so I have you all to myself . . .'

He spread butter thickly on a bread roll before placing his knife on the edge of the plate.

'I've been thinking about you lately.'

The orchestra started up again, a waltz this time, as I shifted uncomfortably in my seat, the bread in my mouth dry against my tongue.

'The thing is . . .'

He lowered his voice.

'David tells me you've been struggling. With the girls.'

I felt a wash of relief, instantly turning to a sense of betrayal.

'Don't be angry. He needed to confide in someone. The truth is he's worried about you. But . . .'

He paused, picking up the bread again, tearing it with his teeth, careful not to let any crumbs attach to his beard. He chewed for a moment before continuing.

'It must be frustrating. I can only imagine what that's like, to suddenly find yourself . . . I mean, I sometimes wonder what that must have been like, to suddenly find yourself pregnant with a man – a boy, frankly – you've only been with for a few months – and twins! I mean . . . With your parents not around . . .'

The violins in the distance swooped in and out of earshot, the blood pounding against my ears.

Taking a swig from his glass, Clive fixed me again with his eyes.

'You know, David . . . he can be . . . Well, David is my son and I love him – you know that – I love him more than anything. I would do anything for him.'

The word 'anything' rang in my ear and I reached for my drink, a bead of condensation running down the side of the glass.

'I mean that, I really do.' Clive regarded me for a moment, long enough to top up our glasses and mop his forehead with the maroon silk handkerchief in the pocket of his suit jacket, and then he turned, a glistening in his eyes suggesting pain of some sort, a discomfort at what he was being forced to admit.

'But sometimes . . . He's highly strung. You know what I'm saying, don't you? He's emotional. It's his downfall, it always has been – his mother was the same way – and sometimes he lets those emotions get the better of him. The way he is with you, sometimes, the way he can be . . . it's because he loves you so very much. I need you to know that. There is nothing he wouldn't have . . .'

Following Clive's eye, with a pang of relief I spotted David talking to the waitress at the other side of the room, his taut frame perfectly held in a navy suit, the collar of his shirt buttoned to the top.

It was extraordinary to think that this was the same boy who had greeted me on campus all those years ago. From a certain angle he was a man who had grown into himself, the way some men did: shoulders pressed back, open-faced, the certainty of someone who was at peace with their lot. As he grew closer, I could make out the sinewy muscles in his neck, like snakes winding through the grass, just below the surface, waiting to shed their skin.

I felt my spine straighten as I saw other women notice him too, lifting their eyes to watch him cross the room.

David held his arms up in a placatory motion as he settled himself in a chair between his girlfriend and his father.

'What are we having?'

He kept his eyes on Clive. I took a gulp of my drink, surprised by the jealousy that was rising in my gut as I waited for him to notice me, the dress I had bought to surprise him.

'There you are . . . We haven't ordered.'

As Clive looked up, the waitress appeared at his side.

'Anna, what will you have?'

My voice, when it came, was sticky, as though it had been sitting too long in my throat.

'I'll have the reef lobster and the *légine*, please.'

I struggled again to catch David's eye, waiting for him to reach over and touch my hand.

'Fine choice! I'll have the lobster also, followed by the veal tenderloin.'

Clive looked to his son and David lifted his hand to show that he would have the same.

The evening passed as all evenings with Clive tended to, in a steaming haze; layers of food pressed down with wine and calvados.

I was pleased to see, when it came, that I had ordered fish. David had already finished three glasses of Sancerre by the time the first course arrived. With each glass, the composure he had demonstrated when he arrived unravelled a little more, a sheen of sweat glazing his forehead.

Catching his eye, I brushed my finger along his forearm.

'OK?'

He moved his arm, avoiding my eye. There was something unnerving about him tonight, laughing too loudly at his father's jokes, knocking back a tumbler of brandy before pushing back his chair.

'Excuse me a moment.'

Fumbling slightly, he headed towards the bathroom.

A moment later, I felt the room fall dark, followed by a collective intake of breath, the water in the tunnel above us glowing an eerie green. Following Clive's gaze to the door, I saw David walking towards me purposefully, with slow, steady strides. The rest of the room followed his progress as he approached, clasping his hands behind his back.

Feeling myself begin to shake, I rested my hands on the table in front of me, pressing my wrists into the edge of the table. The pressure steadied my breathing.

He did not speak at first and then, finally, my name formed on his lips. He halted in front of me, dropping to one knee. Leaning forward, he spoke so that only the two of us could hear, although I was aware of all eyes in the restaurant pinned on me.

His face was a translucent red under the tinted glare of the water, which seemed ready to rip through the glass as his mouth struggled to form the words.

The room started to sway. Above David's head, a shoal of fish seemed to be rushing at me. Clive, his face obscured by David's, looked on from the other side of the table.

For a moment, I thought he was going to be sick, but then he opened his mouth and drew a breath.

'Will you marry me?'

It was important to stay in the present; the past and the future both bulged dangerously with doubt. A side effect of the drugs Dr Blackman had prescribed a month earlier was that generally I had started to sleep better, but the night of David's proposal my body would not settle; damp bed-sheets clung to my legs as I tossed back and forth.

Meg, David, and then Harry. I saw them now as an island, a churning sliver of land in a sea of black, until gradually the land they stood on twisted and broke away, the gaping black hole opening up again. I was on the edge of a cliff. No matter which direction I took, the ground threatened to fall away.

Just before dawn, my body snapped awake, clammy and cold. Running a cool shower over my head, I wrapped myself in a white padded dressing gown, pouring a glass of water before sliding open the doors to the terrace.

Lowering myself onto the sun lounger overlooking the water, I watched the sun stretching to life over the Indian Ocean, letting memories of the night before slowly gather and take shape in my mind.

The prospect of a wedding was something that somehow, in all my preparations, all my deliberations, I had never really anticipated. I suppose I had never had time to wonder what the future, beyond next week or next month, might look like. I was pregnant before I had really had time to consider it – and once the girls were born, the web had already been so tightly woven, mine and David's futures so intricately laced together, that it never crossed my mind.

And yet, while we were already bound together by invisible threads, there was something meaningful about David's proposal. The pregnancy had been an accident; marriage was a choice. In asking the question, David had shown that he still wanted me, just when I had really begun to question it.

I could never have said no, it would have been far too inflammatory, and yet the prospect of such a significant gathering with all its potential pitfalls, its ability to expose the holes in our life together, meant that there was absolutely no way that a public wedding could be allowed to happen. It would raise too many questions. The prospect of drawing up the wedding list, name-checking old friends, negotiations over which relatives to ask . . . Then, of course, there was the issue of the father-of-the-bride.

Draining my cup, I rose, fixing my gown before heading back inside the hut.

'David?'

I pressed my mouth lightly to his ear but he did not budge. While alcohol made my sleep more fitful, it had the opposite effect on David, so that I had to lean the full weight of my body on his to elicit even a tiny stirring.

'David, I want to ask you something.'

I watched his face slowly come to life, his arms stretching above his head as he became aware of my legs entwined in his.

I kissed him, my lips running softly over his neck, the invisible bristles scratching against my skin.

'What time is it?'

He finally prised his eyes open.

Pulling the sheet so that it covered the scar across my abdomen, I kissed his mouth until I was sure I had his full attention, then I pulled back.

'Let's do it here.'

David lifted himself onto his elbows, his eyes narrowing suggestively.

'You know you never need to ask . . .'

'Ssshh, not that.'

I laughed back, seeing something in him I had not seen for months.

'I mean, let's get married now.'

'What?'

'I don't want to wait.'

I held his eyes, not smiling any more.

'I just think it makes sense. We're here, and I mean I literally couldn't think of a better place to marry. The girls are here, and your father . . .'

His face was unreadable. 'But what about our friends? Your dad?'

I pushed myself to one side of the bed, positioning myself against the pillow next to him.

'To be honest, I don't even know if I'd want him there . . . You know, he hasn't even bothered coming to see the girls, or to meet you. Honestly, he's never really been that interested in my life.'

Pausing, I held my breath, letting David adjust to the idea.

'And the truth is, I just want to marry you. It's not about anyone else. I love you, and being here, away from everything, it's given me time to think. About what I want from life. I just don't see the point in waiting.'

When I turned to look at David again, lines had formed at the edges of his eyes. He took a moment before replying, nodding his head.

'OK, let's do it.'

I moved closer towards him.

'Really, are you sure? You're not disappointed?'

He turned to face me, and I saw it then, a flash of love tinged with hope, and something else I couldn't read.

'Why would I be?'

CHAPTER 42

Anna

We had only been in the Maldives twelve weeks and yet in that time everything had changed. By the time we returned to London – a shiny new backdrop waiting for our return in our new status as husband and wife – not a trace of our old life together had been left intact. Downstairs, the kitchen shone with glass and marble, floor-to-ceiling doors revealing a garden transformed into the scene I had always craved: forget-me-nots sprinkled across a bed of freshly laid turf, borders brimming with crocuses and tête-à-têtes, twinkling under a blue sky.

It wasn't until you got closer that you would notice many of them had been killed off. It had been an early spring that year, the kind that fooled Mother Nature into believing it was safe, before a killer frost set in, wiping out swathes of frogspawn and blooms that had prematurely come to life in feeble patches across the city.

Even after having pored over the plans for months in advance of the building work, there was something disorientating about the absence of walls between the living room and the kitchen, once I saw it in person. Upstairs, David made me close my eyes as we approached the family bathroom. As I opened them, the words dissolved on my tongue as I spotted the new freestanding bath, which now stood centre-left, the cleaning cupboard that for so long had harboured my secrets having been wrenched from the walls, all traces of its existence filled in and finished in a pewter grey.

David's voice was close to my neck as I surveyed the scene, pushing away the sense of unease that crept like fingers inside my stomach.

His voice seemed to have read my mind. 'I've had them move all your things into our new en suite. No more having to fumble around the house in the middle of the night.'

In September that year, I finally returned to work. Despite the girls having turned nine months, and Maria's unwavering presence in their lives, David could not fathom my desire to leave them.

'I'm still not sure why you're going back. I mean, for God's sake, I'm earning enough and the girls . . . they need their mother.'

I appraised my outfit in the full-length mirror the builders had installed in the sparkling new dressing room David had added to the architectural plans, along with a few more additions to surprise me on our return home, a couple of months previously. Keeping my eyes locked on my reflection, I said nothing, though I knew my excitement at my imminent return to the office shone in my eyes.

'If I'm honest, I'm worried that you won't cope. The drugs you're on, Anna, they . . . Well, I worry they affect your judgement sometimes. You will have a team relying on you, and your memory. It's . . .'

'What are you talking about?'

'Oh, come on,' David's tone was placatory. 'I'm not telling you anything you don't already know – I'm not being cruel, Anna, I'm saying it because I love you and I care about you. I care about you pushing yourself too hard, so soon after . . . Well, you know as well as I do how hard things have been.'

His eyes took me in, noting how the former swell of my belly had settled into a gentle curve, imagining, perhaps, the spray of faint silver scars that ran across the surface of the skin, my breasts reduced to two tiny mounds under a soft silk shirt, my hair pulled loosely away from my cheekbones.

Tears pricked at the corners of my eyes. 'Well, maybe I'm thinking of stopping them, maybe I've realised I don't need them any more.' I stood taller but I felt light-headed.

'Anna,' his tone switched, and he took a step forward. 'For God's sake. Please tell me you're joking . . . Anna, look at me. That medication, it's not perfect – I know how hard this has been for you, how you've struggled since the girls – but if you stop the pills now, things will be a lot worse. Please, Anna, remember what the doctors said. OK? I will *not* let you ruin . . .'

His sentence was cut off by the sound of his phone, a faint drone calling out from one of the rooms downstairs.

As if too pained to look at me, he turned on his heels and walked out of the room.

He had made himself scarce by the time I made my way downstairs where the girls were lying on their stomachs on the new cream rug in the kitchen, in front of the doors out to the garden. Maria, who had been steaming vegetables for the girls' lunch as part of her carefully plotted weaning plan, looked up at the sound of my footsteps.

Her face broke into a smile when she saw me.

'Anna, you look beautiful.'

'Maria, are you sure you'll be OK?'

I hovered in the doorway, knowing full well I was as much use to the girls here as I would be at the office.

'Please, go, enjoy your first day! David is working from home, so if I need anything . . .'

I nodded, grateful for her reassurance, breathing deeply as I stepped out of the front door, the space rolling out in front of me as I made my way down the steps.

CHAPTER 43

Maria

Something changed in her, that holiday. Her movements, once languorous, had become lighter somehow, as if the wedding had buoyed her.

To the untrained eye, you might have believed it, if you had seen them there, the two of them, hands outstretched towards one another on the beach, David's white suit complementing the white silk sundress Anna had shipped in from Italy for the occasion, the pair of them barefoot. The girls, in matching bonnets, held by Clive and me, their only witnesses.

You might have believed, and I might have too, to see them now, back at home, the lightness passing between them. You would have been forgiven for believing everything was going to be OK, after all.

Except, of course, I knew better.

When I looked at Anna, I saw a woman driven by self-destruction; a woman who hated herself so much, she was compelled to ruin any chance she had at happiness.

CHAPTER 44

Anna

My return to the office had been marked by admiration and praise from Clarissa, whose levels of impeccable glamour seemed to have escalated, if that were possible, during my absence.

'My God, I can't tell you how delighted we are to have you back,' she had exclaimed that first morning after my return, as the lift doors opened onto our floor. 'And you look extraordinary, so bloody thin! The virtues of being so young, I suppose.'

Faces lifted, breaking into short-lived smiles as I followed her through neat rows of desks, past Features and the picture desk towards my new desk in front of her glass office.

David, it transpired without any attempt at disguise, did not share my boss's enthusiasm towards my journalistic progress. Rather, he interpreted my commitment to life outside the home as further proof of my inferiority as a mother. A slight to our family.

While his refusal to support me in my impressive rise through the ranks irked me, there was something reassuring, too, about him wanting more of me for himself. His possessive love for me, which had repelled me in those early days – the sense that he wanted me too much for me to give myself to him – comforted me now. It strengthened the stability, the sense of security, that life with him provided.

Even so, the mood between us gradually settled into semi-cordial indifference. There were the occasional moments of tenderness, still, which would creep up on us before we had the chance to question them; a shared look as Stella and Rose mouthed their first words, or his hand on my back as he passed behind my chair. But as soon as either of us became aware of them, there would be a mutual self-consciousness and our eyes would fall away to something less binding.

By the time the following summer came around, we had become little more than cohabitants of a shared space, two people joined together by a common history, rather than conspirators in a present life.

'Everything OK?'

I had walked into the kitchen to find him at the table, his eyes passing between his laptop and a leather-bound notebook that I didn't recognise.

'Yes, fine. Just trying to book these flights for Dad and the fucking system keeps crashing.'

'What flights?' I held my glass under the filter tap, before drinking and then refilling it once more.

'Just work stuff . . . He can run a company but he can't work out how to book bloody flights.'

It was the first time I had heard David talk about his work in relation to his father's company. It was another in a mounting line-up of questions I hadn't dared ask myself. What was it exactly that my husband did for a living now that he was part of the firm, and how complicit was he in his father's dealings? Words that were safer left unuttered.

Yet, while David being part of this was something I would rather put out of my mind, it would be foolish to suggest it didn't suit the plan. The greater access David had to his father's business, the greater I had too.

'Surely it's not your job to be booking his flights. What about his secretary, Moira, isn't that her name?'

'Hmm?' He looked up distractedly. He was wearing a pair of glasses I hadn't seen before.

'When did you get those?'

'What?'

'Those glasses?'

He half-smiled. 'Are you serious?'

I shrugged, by way of confirmation that I was, and he looked back at the computer screen, shaking his head. 'About two months ago.'

'Oh, come on.'

He flicked his eyes up only for a second but his look said everything.

Two months? Surely I would have noticed. Though it was true we had both been working so much that we rarely seemed to see each other these days, David often getting home after I went to bed, and me leaving before he woke.

I was grateful when David resumed our previous conversation. 'Yeah, well, it's not, but sometimes it's like I'm his bloody skivvy.' He paused for a moment and then continued. 'He's being a bit, I don't know, paranoid. Moira's off for a week and he says there's no one else in the company he fully trusts. So he's given me his diary and—'

I laughed. 'His diary? What year is it? Surely he doesn't keep a paper diary.'

'He's nearly seventy, Anna. How many people of his age do you know who trust a computer more than a piece of paper?'

'Fair enough.' I kept my voice casual as I walked towards him, carrying a glass of water, which I set beside him, giving myself the opportunity to cast my eyes over the book.

'That's for you. It's really hot today.'

'Thanks.'

'So he keeps all his dates in that diary and he expects you to go through and book his flights for him?'

'Nothing gets past you, does it?' His tone was mocking and I nudged him with my elbow.

'Oh, for fuck's sake.' From the hallway, David's phone was ringing in his briefcase. 'That will be Jeff. We're supposed to be having a meeting later ahead of the annual review. As if I haven't got enough on my—'

'I'll do this.' I held his eye as his brow furrowed slightly.

'No, it's fine, I can—'

'Honestly. David, look . . .' I sat on the chair beside him and caught his eye, softening my gaze so that for the first time in a long while we were on the same level, looking at each other, our bodies almost touching. This time neither of us made to move.

I resisted the urge to reach out and touch his hand, measuring my movements carefully. 'You're up to your eyeballs. I have the day off; let me help. Please.'

For a moment I sensed him swallow uneasily and once again I wondered how much he knew about the secrets his father's diary could reveal, in the wrong hands. But then he nodded, a strained smile forming on his lips. After all, whose hands would be safer than his own wife's?

'Well, if you're sure. That would be amazing. That means I can head straight into the office. The flight details are all selected on the screen, I just have to input the passport details, which are just there . . .'

He pointed to a piece of paper that had been inserted into the Smythson journal.

'And then you'll need to pay. You can use my business card.' He dropped a matt black credit card on the table in front of me.

For a moment he paused and I thought he was going to add something, but then he nodded to himself and walked towards the hallway.

'What time are you back?'

'Not until this evening. Maria's taken the girls out.'

He shut the door behind him before I had time to reply. As the lock clicked, I exhaled, my body loosening, my pulse suddenly rushing as if being released from a cell.

Waiting five minutes, in case David should have reason to return to the house, I took the stairs two at a time to the cupboard in my bedroom. Slipping my second phone into the pocket of the burnt-orange silk pantaloons I had paired with a cotton T-shirt, I headed back downstairs.

Instinctively looking behind me, towards the floor-to-ceiling glass windows that lined the back of the house, my fingers shook as I lifted the phone above the pages of Clive's diary, the camera silently capturing the private minutes of my father-in-law's life.

CHAPTER 45

Maria

The heat in London was oppressive in a way that reminded me of Athens. Even the sound of the car horns seemed to expand under the glare of summer in the city.

It was a Friday afternoon and I had spent the morning with the girls in the lido on the Heath. A few months from their second birthdays, they had taken to the water with varied enthusiasm, Stella plunging herself with the full weight of her body into the deepest area she could find while Rose held back, squealing with horrified pleasure as the water rose to her knees.

We ate our lunch on the verge of grass opposite the lido, watching a group of lethargic schoolchildren on the running track that stood to its left.

For once, neither girl offered resistance as I lifted them one by one into the double buggy and pulled the sun-shade down. Before we had even reached the gate back towards South End Green, both children were asleep.

It was a struggle to heave their weight up the flight of stairs that led to the house, but I had perfected the skill and made no sound as I turned the key in the lock. It was only once I had pushed the girls quietly over the threshold, so as not to wake them, that I spotted Anna, immersed in something at the kitchen table. Parking the buggy in the cool shady hallway, I removed the sun-shade and then made my way towards the kitchen.

When Anna looked up, it was as if she had seen an apparition hovering in front of her. With a yelp, she jumped back, her hand rising automatically to her chest.

'God, I'm so sorry, I didn't mean to scare you . . .' I raised a hand by way of placation and she shook her head.

'Maria, it's you. You nearly gave me a heart attack. I thought . . . David said you were . . .'

She was moving uneasily, edging away from the computer, and beside it a notebook of some sort, which was open on the table.

'It was so hot, and the girls are sleeping, so I thought this afternoon we would play here, if that's OK. Or . . .'

As I moved towards the sink to pour myself a glass of water from the ridiculously high-tech system, I noticed Anna's phone on the counter. Turning again, I noticed her hand dropping in a bid to stop me spotting the other phone she was clutching with a tight fist.

Working hard to pretend I hadn't seen, I lifted my glass to my lips.

'Sorry, you're obviously working in here. I'll go up to my—'

'No, no . . .' Her voice was a shield. 'It's fine, I was just helping David with something for his father . . .' She cast her hand towards the table and my eyes rested momentarily on what I realised was a diary.

'He needed some flights, but I'm done now. All yours.'

She smiled and if I didn't know better I might have believed it.

Only once her footsteps had faded and I heard her bedroom door close did I move towards the table and open the diary.

CHAPTER 46

Anna

'I'm taking you out for lunch,' Clarissa announced one autumn morning, leaning out through the door of her office.

I had taken to my new role with a trepidatious conviction, treading lightly along the delicate line between competency and deference, alert to any signs that I was overstepping the mark. Features Editor was a very different prospect to Assistant, and the lines were even more important to observe.

Since sending the contents of Clive's diary to Harry, replete with every appointment with every associate mapped out until Christmas, I had earned myself a brief period of respite from the constant prying. With Harry not just appeased but apparently delighted by the access my role in the family afforded him, my attentions turned sharply to the job of working my way up the ranks of the magazine.

I heard the brisk clacking of Clarissa's heels before I saw her that morning, Margaret Howell suit in pristine order, hair pulled into a tortoiseshell clip at the back of her head. Pulling myself straighter, I ran my hand over my own hair, my fingers catching at the ends.

I had hardly slept. The girls were teething with their molars and while I had tried to tune out Stella's low growling as Maria padded gently back and forth in the hall, her voice remaining even as she comforted the baby, it had felt as though my daughter's distraught moans were emanating from within my own head.

'It's just a maternal response to the sound of a child's pain, which can't be switched off. No matter how hard you try,' David had said under his breath as I sat at the dresser, pressing concealer under my eyes, earlier that morning.

'What's that supposed to mean?'

I kept my voice even, watching him tightening his tie in the mirror, turning myself in my seat to face him as he continued moving around the room.

He held up his hands but his voice sounded accusing.

'You're being overly sensitive again. You're clearly tired and . . . it's not surprising, given how much you've been working.'

It was the constant push and pull of David's remarks that wore me down, but I should have been more robust. That was the nature of family life. The tiredness, the resentment; these were textbook post-children domestic dynamics, and their mundanity should have been reassuring.

'Are you coming or not?'

Before I had time to reply, Clarissa disappeared back into her office, returning moments later with a trench coat folded over her arm.

I followed dutifully across the office floor, my back held straight as a sea of ponytails flicked right, and quickly back again, to watch us disappear into the lift.

'Do you know Frederick's? It's an institution.'

She swung out a wiry arm and a taxi ground to a halt in front of us.

'You'll love it . . . Camden Passage . . .' she called through to the driver. 'We timed that well.' Ducking in first, she shuffled along to make space for me as a roll of thunder clattered above us.

The rain started to fall as the taxi headed along the wide open streets that ran between Clerkenwell and Angel.

'Here we are.'

Clarissa stepped out first, leading the way into the restaurant with its high glass ceiling and leather chairs, the conservatory beyond, all exposed brick and made-to-measure wall art.

'Shall we sit in the bar? I can't be bothered with dining rooms at lunchtime.'

I was relieved. The idea of a formal meal in an upright chair made my body ache.

'What will you drink, red or white? I tell you what, I fancy the steak. You must too, it's exquisite. Let's go red, then. We'll have a bottle of the Montepulciano . . .'

By the time the main course arrived, Clarissa had swept aside the proofs she had laid out on the table, the conversation turning seamlessly from a spread on modern florals to idle gossip.

'You know Clive and I used to date, don't you? Oh, moons ago, before you were born, I imagine. Before I . . . well, I wasn't always so honest with myself.'

She took a sip of her wine, regarding me over the top of her glass.

'Sadly, they weren't nearly so rich then. That came later.'

'Really?'

'God no, it's only in recent years that Clive's company has really taken off. Since his wife . . .'

The waiter arrived with two coffees and Clarissa squared her elbows on the table.

'Frankly, I'm just thrilled for David. You and he, and the girls . . . I mean, if anyone deserves happiness it's that boy. After what he went through . . .'

I took my coffee, grateful for its strength.

'I mean, it's bloody criminal what he had to bear . . . That woman. I've never known anything so selfish in all my life, though to be fair I suppose there was no way she could have known that he would be the one to find her. Her own bloody child.'

I felt a knot gather in my belly, tightening and then releasing again. Swallowing, I pressed my napkin against my mouth, silently willing her to continue.

But as she met my eye, Clarissa faltered, her expression changing. The room was so hot all of a sudden, airless.

'Fuck. He hasn't told you, has he? Oh God.'

'No, I don't . . .'

I felt my hands drop to my lap, shame tingling over the tips of my fingers.

'Oh God, what have I done? I assumed, I just assumed he would have . . . Fuck. I'm so sorry.'

CHAPTER 47

Maria

Anna had already left by the time I woke with the girls. Settling them a safe distance away from the doll's house David had commissioned – a microcosm of their home built as an exact replica, from the plush velvet curtains to the mid-century furniture – I called out Anna's name as I padded down the hallway towards her bedroom.

As I moved through the hallway, I thought of Artemis, picturing her moving through this hallway, the day it had happened. Had she cried? I imagined her pain too far below the surface.

Satisfied that Anna had left the house, I moved quietly through the room towards the cupboard and slid my hand expertly into it, towards the clutch bag where she kept her second phone, as I did every few days. It was a mystery to me that she would so brazenly leave it here, where anyone could find it. Yet it never moved, and presumably David never found it. Why would he? Why would a man choose to rummage through his wife's clothes cupboards?

It only took a moment to enter her pin number, which was the same as the one on her regular phone: 1211. The numbers I had watched her key in so many times, occasionally wondering what their significance might be.

CHAPTER 48

Anna

He was lying on the sofa, a blanket spread over his legs, when I got home from work that evening, immersed in a book on the history of humankind, a beer balanced precariously on the arm of the sofa.

If you disregarded the geometric furnishings, the Scandi-inspired log pile and wood-burning stove where the traditional fireplace once stood, this could have been David when I first moved in with him and the memory of it warmed me briefly.

'The girls are already asleep.' He looked up from the book before taking a swig of his beer.

It was nearly 8 p.m. I had spent the afternoon walking around Islington, my mind whirring with what Clarissa had told me.

'Where's Maria?'

'She's out. It's her night off, remember?'

Did she know? The thought struck me for the first time. Their mothers were friends, weren't they? So there was no way she could not have known. It was the first time I had felt jealous of her in the whole time she had been with us. Despite her easy manner with the girls, her natural flair for parenting, which served to highlight my shortcomings, the confidence she was able to imbue in them as if by the process of osmosis, despite all that it was this new knowledge that really cut deep.

'What happened to your mother?'

The words came out before I was ready.

'Excuse me?'

David rested the book on his chest.

'Your mother – she killed herself, in this house, and you found her.'

There was a pause and then David moved to sitting position, his cheeks reddening.

'What the fuck are you talking about?'

'Why didn't you tell me?'

'What? Who told you that?'

'Clarissa, she assumed I knew. I am your wife, David. It would make sense for me to know something like that.'

He looked at me, and I felt a shiver across my chest, my nipples hardening.

'Why would you not tell me?' My voice was less certain this time.

'Are you serious?' There was a pause while he gathered himself. 'You are going to lecture me about openness, Anna?'

His eyes flared as he moved on the sofa.

'You? You tell me everything, do you? You tell me everything about your past, about your parents?'

'There's nothing to tell.'

David stood now.

'How fucking dare you? You tell me nothing, Anna. *Nothing*. And you know what? I accept it. Like a fucking mug, I accept all of it. And you know why? Because I love you.'

His eyes were shining with fury.

'I don't ask questions about your dad, who you refuse to introduce me to. I don't ask about your mum, who is also apparently dead, and actually no, I don't know how, either . . . You know why? Because I choose not to make you go through it. I choose to let you say as much or little as you like. Because I know that is the person you are and I know that I take that or I take *nothing*.'

David's words whipped through the air.

'But you? You expect me to go through it all, to relive all the sordid details, so that you can feel better about yourself? More self-assured in front of your boss?'

He wiped his wrist against his mouth and turned away from me momentarily. When he turned to face me again his eyes were wet.

'It's always about you, isn't it, Anna? Always about your needs. But what about me. What about *us*?'

There was a scuttling sound from above, followed by Stella's voice on the landing – she had managed to climb out of her cot.

'You know what? Fuck this.'

David's shoulder slammed my arm as he barged out of the room, the front door slamming behind him.

I knew as soon as I awoke that David had already left. He had arrived home some time before 2 a.m., when I spotted from the safety of the hallway his body splayed across the sofa in the living room.

I gathered the bag of snacks Maria had left out for me on the table, together with spare nappies for Rose and a stash of perfectly folded pants for Stella, who had, just shy of two years old, decided it was time to start potty-training, whether we were ready for it or not.

'Right, let's go then, shall we?'

I spoke to no one, giving my brightest impression of a young mother ready for a Saturday morning in the park with her girls. As I swung the bag over my arm, I turned to see Stella marching towards me, and for a split-second Clive's black eyes looked back at me. I stumbled before steadying myself.

'Mama!' she called out, and I moved forward to scoop her up, tossing the thought away.

'Gosh, aren't you a clever girl? Shall we go to the park, yes? Oh, you're a clever girl! Come on, let's get Rose.'

The weather, heavy and black for so long, had brightened into the kind of crisp late-autumn day that lifted even the dullest spirits. I had started to take pleasure in walking across the hills and vales of the Heath with the girls on Saturday mornings while David had taken to playing football on Market Road with a group of former colleagues, and Maria spent weekends studying at the British Library.

This morning we made our usual circuit of the playground by the running track, before heading up through the densely packed trees that led to Kenwood, skirting the house, following the dip of the valley.

Taking a seat at one of the benches overlooking the pond at Mill Lane, I let the girls out of the buggy to toss crumbs of bread for the ducks, hanging behind them as a band of coots and pigeons lurched towards us, a swan in the distance puffing her wings.

By the time we reached the bench at the top of Kite Hill, both girls had fallen asleep. I watched their faces, barely moving as they blew breath in and out of their lungs. It was a month since I had last called Harry. The distance between us by now was a matter of fact.

'Anna, isn't it?'

The voice came from behind, pulling me away from my thoughts. 'Gosh, so these are your girls . . .'

It was the voice I recognised first, followed by the face, sharp and self-assured.

'You don't remember me, do you? God, don't worry, you've been busy . . .'

The woman gave a warm glance towards the buggy.

'I'm so sorry . . .'

'Don't be. Felicity. We met, well, pretty much here . . .'

Spreading her hands towards the bench, she took a seat beside me.

'I was somewhat more rotund then.'

'Of course, you were pregnant too . . .'

Slowly the memory came into focus – the runner on the Heath, the woman who was doing it alone. She looked so different now, her hair folded over her shoulders, a Burberry trench pulled in at the waist.

Felicity noticed the memory click and nodded. 'Mine's a boy. Arthur. He's with the nanny, I needed to get out.' She gave me a knowing look.

I laughed. 'Sounds familiar.'

She smiled back at me. 'Hard, isn't it?'

The question caught me off-guard, or rather the way she asked it. Some days I saw being with the girls as a relief, a brief respite from the constant lies. Other days I would look at them and feel like I could not breathe.

'I'm back at work,' I said.

'What do you do?'

I felt a quiet stab of pride. 'I work at a magazine.'

Felicity raised an eyebrow.

'Fantastic. And how does your husband feel about that?'

Rose stirred under her blanket. Subconsciously clocking Felicity's interest in the stirring toddler, I leaned forward, moving the buggy slightly closer to my leg, adjusting the blanket around Rose's face, the soft angles of her lips rearranging themselves into a kiss shape.

I let the question hang awkwardly in the air for a moment, before she continued, as if to clarify her point.

'I just remember you saying before, he was . . . unsettled, by the pregnancy.'

There were so few times when I had the chance to be on my own, to stop thinking, to stop pre-empting, and I longed for silence now, for the chance to sit and look out over the distant buildings that disappeared into the haze of the skyline.

Felicity must have seen the look on my face, and for a moment I thought she was going to leave, and then she sat, close enough that I noticed the veins on the back of her hands as she pulled a cigarette from her pocket, holding out the box. I hesitated before shaking my head.

'No, I'm fine, thanks. I don't . . .'

'That's brilliant, though, about David, that he's come round. Sometimes men . . . Sometimes people aren't who they seem.'

David. I felt my throat constrict. When had I mentioned his name?

Suddenly, Stella cried out, and her arm shot out from under the blanket. Quickly standing, I lifted my daughter, her toddler frame going limp again as I held her to my chest, my other hand on Rose's arm, willing her to stay asleep.

Turning my head discreetly towards Felicity, I saw her profile, impassive, looking out across the skyline. Her mouth pursed around the white filter tip, leaving a thick print of red as she pulled the cigarette away.

The range of possibilities circled my mind like birds, swooping in and out of focus. Had Clive found out, sent this woman to draw me out of my hole?

'It must be hard.'

Her voice was deliberate, her eyes still focused ahead.

'I don't know what you're talking about.'

I felt my jaw tighten as I spoke, frozen to the spot, hoping my terror would not show. My eyes darted around us, over the brow of the hill: families wrapped in colourful scarves on weekend outings, men talking loudly into their phones.

'I'm a friend, Anna. I'm sorry to have to approach you like this but I need your help.'

The breath caught in my throat and for a moment I imagined that if I were only to stay still enough, if I could just maintain my silence, the woman might somehow disappear.

'Your father-in-law, Clive, I don't know how much you're aware of, but he is caught up in some serious business, and the organisation I work for, well, we need a friend on the inside.'

Felicity turned to face me, dropping her cigarette.

'I beg your pardon?' But as I said it, I was already gathering my scarf from the bench, while Felicity watched me, calm and unapologetic.

That was when she said the name of the organisation. Three tiny syllables, each of them a punch in my gut.

'Have a think about it,' she added as I kicked the brake of the buggy away. 'It's always good to know what you're getting yourself into.'

Struggling to pull together the words, I watched the embers of her cigarette slowly dying on the ground, glowing, then flickering faintly, until finally they were gone.

'Take this, have a think.'

She held out a card – but I turned, leaving it in her hand, the buggy pounding down the hill, my fingers holding onto the handles for dear life.

CHAPTER 49

Maria

The address on the piece of paper in my hand led me through Hatton Garden, a single road lined with jewellers on both sides.

Following the curve of the pavement, in line with the map I had memorised before I left, I turned right into a mews street and headed towards the inconspicuous entrance, as instructed, knocking twice before a man in a Metallica T-shirt stretched tight across his gut pulled open the door.

Inside, the beige decor in the narrow hallway was indicative of a shared student house. Following the man's bulbous silhouette, tentatively at first, up a steep flight of steps which wound round to the right, we emerged in a room with floor-to-ceiling shelves, each lined with a different form of camera.

'Not what you expected?'

'I didn't know what to expect.'

'So, according to the brief I'm looking at here, you're after a buttonhole camera.'

I nodded grimly, a lump rising in my throat.

'Used one before?'

I shook my head.

'Got the shirt?'

I pushed my hand into my handbag and pulled out a plain black button-down shirt, size small.

The man held it up for a moment before nodding.

'All right, you go off and have a coffee, and come back in an hour and we'll be ready for you.'

The following morning I headed to Liverpool Street station, first thing. It was my day off and Anna had already left for the office by the time I made my way down to the kitchen, leaving David, who sporadically worked from the house these days, in the kitchen tossing pancakes in return for whoops and giggles from the girls, sitting side by side in their highchairs.

I had arrived early, changing in the pub toilets before taking my place at one of the booths which stretched along one wall of the building so that I had a full vantage point of the concourse at Liverpool Street station on one side, and an uninterrupted view of the restaurant on the other.

The man arrived at 8 a.m. on the dot, as arranged. As he walked towards me, I noticed his brogues shining under the stark light of the bar. He ran a self-conscious hand across his hair, which was pulled slightly to one side with too much wax.

'Good to meet you.'

He held out his hand first, trying to take the lead. The man was twenty-six, according to the CV I had pulled off a poorly protected recruitment agency online, and had been working for the company for three years without enough movement towards the top to elicit any real loyalty to his employers.

'Stephen, isn't it?'

I kept my voice brisk, professional, remembering my brief training.

I ordered us some sparkling water, which arrived in a large glass bottle. Just before the waitress poured, I stood up, as I had been taught.

'Actually, I'm sorry, my chair is a little damp, do you mind if we move over there?'

I started walking towards a different table, slightly around the corner.

Stephen hurried after me, unnerved by the shift in tempo, followed by the waitress. Settling myself again with a clear view of each side, I smiled tightly as she poured out our drinks, casually surveying the room for anyone who might have moved tables after us; anyone who might be rearranging themselves closer to where we now sat.

After she left, I turned to Stephen.

'As I mentioned in my email, I am part of the team launching a new trading and commodities company, based here in London. We already have an office in Greece, which we launched in the wake of the crisis there, and we have grown so fast that we are opening a UK office and are currently scouting the best talent in Europe to be part of our team.

'We are offering our new recruits a very healthy salary as well as shares in the business. Given recent reports on insider trading, it is our belief that there is a great need for such an ethical company in the City.'

Stephen's smile widened. He was easier than I could ever have dreamed. 'Oh, definitely.'

'Well, I'm sure you have never encountered such things personally . . .'

He snorted, sitting straighter, relishing his chance to impress me. 'Don't bet on it. I've heard of tens if not hundreds of cases . . .'

'Surely not, even at a prestigious company like TradeSmart?'

I took a sip of my drink, feigning only a polite interest.

Stephen's eyes glistened.

'Oh, believe me, I could tell you some stories.'

I leaned towards him, ensuring the buttonhole camera in my shirt was level with his eye, the microphone picking up every word.

'Oh, I'd be fascinated. Please do.'

CHAPTER 50

Anna

It was nearly eleven on Monday morning by the time Harry finally answered my texts, his response brief, giving away nothing but an address. Informing Clarissa that I was going to a PR meeting, I gripped my phone tightly in my coat pocket as I headed out of the immaculate glass doors.

It was not so much an address as an alleyway, I realised as I approached. I paced the concrete, waiting for him to appear, the stench of bins flooding out from the back of the café on the high street. Finally, he arrived, turning into the side street and walking past me, instructing me to follow him like a dog.

'Now what did this woman say?'

He spoke once he was ready, carefully unpeeling the plastic from his packet of cigarettes.

Snatching the unlit cigarette from his hand, I waited for him to pull his lighter from his pocket, pausing before leaning into the flame.

'I've told you, she was asking about David . . . She said she had an interest in Clive's business and she . . . she said she works for MI bloody Six, Harry.'

His expression was cool as he digested the news, the two of us moving with the crowd along Charterhouse Street, wind pressing against our coats as we turned right towards Hatton Garden.

What must we have looked like to the outside world – friends, colleagues, lovers? Did they notice the sweat seeping from my pores?

'What the fuck is going on?'

My voice was low but persistent. He stopped and leaned against a wall, and I turned to face him.

'I don't know, but I'm going to find out, OK? Now you need to calm down—'

'Calm down?'

'Anna . . .'

He reached for my wrist and reluctantly I shook him off, desperate for him to tighten his grip.

'Anna. I don't know what is going on any more than you do, but—'

'You don't know? You don't seem to know much, Harry. For someone who claimed to know everything.'

My voice was low now, pleading.

'Just tell me, truthfully, does Clive know? Is this some kind of trap?'

'Anna, listen to me. You need to calm down . . . If Clive knew, you think he would send someone to play mind games with you on Hampstead Heath? Is that really what you think?'

I rubbed my hand against the side of my head, suddenly aware of a throbbing pain above my jaw. It had been a bad night's sleep again with the girls and I had forgotten to take my pills this morning, which I knew meant the headache would only escalate.

'I don't know what to think.'

He bent his head so that our lips were nearly touching, the sharpness of his breath on mine as he spoke.

'But what if he did find out, Anna?'

His eyes shone fiercely, seeming almost black in their intensity.

When I pulled my body away, his grip tightened.

'What's that supposed to mean?'

The smoke from his cigarette rolled into my eyes.

'It's not supposed to mean anything. I'm just asking what you think would happen if, by some means, Clive was to find out what you have been up to? A man like that . . . I can't imagine he would take too kindly to it.'

'Don't you bloody threaten me, Harry.'

Tearing myself free of him, I felt my voice trembling. A group of office workers huddled under the canopy of an estate agent's looked up from their cigarettes.

'Look, just calm down, will you?'

He held out his arms in a placatory manner.

'Jesus, look at you. I'm not threatening you. I'm just saying, if Clive did know, I don't think this is how he would approach the matter.'

I watched him, too confused to blink.

'Look, I'm the one under serious heat here, Anna. My bosses, they're getting tetchy. They've been pouring resources into us, into *you*, and well, frankly, we need more. So far, you've not given us much to run on here. I'm worried that if we don't get something to them soon, they're going to pull the investigation, move it on to someone else.'

Snatching a breath, I turned my back slightly so that the smokers enjoying the free domestic drama could not see my face. Recently, pictures of David and me had started to appear in the background of the society pages of the *Evening Standard* and I was conscious of the possibility of seeing someone who might recognise me.

'But what do you mean? You said it was OK – you said you were waiting for news and I needed to be on call, when you were ready.'

'Oh, come on, Anna. I didn't want to put pressure on you, not with everything else that was happening at the time. But what did you think, that they were going to keep paying you to swan off on fancy holidays, without providing anything in return?'

'What the fuck, fancy holidays? This is my *life*, Harry! I'm risking everything I have for this, my whole fucking life is a *sham* and everything I've done has been for them, for you!' There was a moment's silence as we both recovered from the admission I had made. But if Harry felt it, he didn't let it show.

Wiping away the tears forming at the edges of my eyes, I spoke again, more quietly. 'They can't just pull me off my *life*, like I'm some sort of fucking shift worker.'

'Really, Anna? You really think there is anything these people can't do? How long has this been going on now? Look, I didn't want to push you, and I still don't. I know it's been a difficult time, but . . . Well, if we want this not to be turned over to someone else, we've got to bring them something.'

For a moment, I paused. Would it really be so bad – being left to get on with my life, with the girls, with David, my job . . . away from Harry? Quietly, I let the possibility of it wash over me.

As if reading my mind, Harry continued, 'Of course, they would never let you stay.'

'What do you mean?'

A flash of disdain passed over his face,

'Oh, come on, Anna, you can't seriously think they're going to just leave and let you get on with life . . . You and David and the girls, as if none of this ever happened? You really think they'll trust you not to—'

'I can be trusted.'

Harry laughed.

'Anna, you're a spy – no one trusts you, no one will ever trust a word you say, not really.'

'What about you?'

He shook his head wistfully, pulling out another cigarette, his eyes pausing for a moment over the packet.

'I'm under no illusions.'

When he looked up again, there was something in his face I did not recognise, and then it was gone.

Moving forward, he gently curled his fingers into mine.

'Anna, we're on the same team, OK?'

He looked into my eyes, a slight pressure from his thumb against my face. Slowly, pushing a strand of hair from my cheek, he leaned in and kissed me carefully, his lips pressing lightly against mine.

A shock, like an electrical current, rippled across my mouth and from nowhere, I felt a tear rolling down my cheek. After a moment, Felicity's face appeared in my mind and I pulled back, sweeping the tear from my cheek and shaking my head before speaking again.

'None of this explains who the fuck that woman was, Harry.'

It was the first time I had ever rejected him and I saw the fact of it settle over him, his face adjusting accordingly. For a moment, he was silent, then he said, 'I'm going to make some calls, OK?'

Flashing a look towards the main road and then back to me, he continued, businesslike.

'What I think is that this woman must have been from a different department, and because of the nature of what we're doing – because Clive knows so many people and precisely because we're not going to let anyone find out about you, because our priority is to protect our assets . . .'

Asset. The word made me flinch.

'Because of all that, she might not know what we've already got in motion.'

How can I help? Those were the words with which I had pleaded with him, all those years ago, when initially he had refused to bring me in. Weren't they? I had pushed my way into this, and now that I had slipped through the door, the door had been bolted behind me, just as Harry had warned me it would be. Exactly as I had hoped.

His voice was softer now, tender almost.

'She probably doesn't have the clearance to find out, OK? Now you just have to calm down and stop worrying, and I'm going to sort it out. But, regardless, we need to step up our game.'

'Harry, there's something I didn't tell you, something I found while I was away.'

Was I aiming to ingratiate myself with him, to prove my worth; or was it that finally I was ready for this all to come to an end, in a way that I had not been before?

There was something unsettling about his demeanour as I continued talking, against my better judgement.

'I should have told you straight away, I just thought maybe I could find out more first.'

By now I knew this was a lie. In truth, I had been worried that once he found what he needed, once the pieces of the puzzle had come together, there would be nothing left to hold us together. That was why I had not told him about what I had found out in the Maldives. Maybe it was not so much happiness that had lifted my spirits over the past few months as the feeling of control.

'On its own, I don't know how much it means, but I did some digging on the shipping records I got from Jeff's bag, and the company who owns the boat, Strategic Services, has three shareholders: Clive and Jeff, and the third is a man called Francisco Nguema. He's some kind of African businessman; as far as I can tell he's involved in all sorts. I saw them together, in the Maldives, him and Clive, having a meeting one morning.'

I watched his face close in on itself, his fingers forming a fist at his side.

How long did that silence between us last, before he spoke, his voice taut with anger?

'Why the hell didn't you tell me about this the last time we met?'

I swallowed, unable to tell him I couldn't risk it being the end of the case.

'I only just worked it out. I'm sorry—'

'You lied to me.'

'I didn't lie. It's like I said, it took time . . . Anyway you had this information, why the hell didn't you figure it out? Why is this on me?'

I had hit a nerve. Harry shook his head, the vein in his neck pulsing.

'You have no fucking idea how much work I've had going on, Anna. You think this is the only thing I'm dealing with?'

'Harry, where are you going? Come on . . . Shit.'

I reached for him but he brushed my hand away and walked, his rage pulsing through the air around me as he disappeared into a thrum of bodies weaving towards the Tube.

CHAPTER 51

Maria

I woke early with the girls. For the past few days Anna had been tetchy, unreachable. I knew from the stream of one-sided texts and emails, the unanswered midnight pleas, that things between the two of them had been strained in recent months. She was slowing down, her output weakening. I wondered if she was already beginning to question everything.

It had been nearly two years by now that I had been working as the girls' nanny. Already, I had been a part of the family almost a year more than I had planned. But everything had changed. What would have been the point of returning to my degree now? I was already resigned to what I had to do, and I was good at it. I was learning fast. Unlike Anna, I knew what I had got myself into.

There had been moments during my time at the house that I had found myself a hair's breadth away from telling her. The truth was, for all her weaknesses, I liked her. I wanted to trust her. From an operational perspective, it made sense; together, we could have formed an alliance that would have made bringing them down infinitely more achievable. Yet, there was something that told me not to. Something that stirred uneasily inside me when I looked into her eyes; something that told me Anna could be the one to get us both killed.

After all, how could I really trust someone who had no idea of what part she played? It was just as my father had told me, one night as we sat with our backs against the wooden slats of my bed, quoting his favourite philosopher, Thales of Miletus. 'To know yourself is the most difficult thing.'

PART THREE

CHAPTER 52

Anna

After that, there was silence.

For a few months after our meeting on Charterhouse Street, the money kept trickling into my bank account just as it had for nearly three years, before, one morning, it stopped. Just like that. From then on Harry, and any trace of him, ceased to exist. The harder I searched for him, the further away from me he seemed to slide.

The girls' second birthday passed by in a blur, as though I was looking in from the sidelines through frosted glass, David and Maria tending to their every need.

The newspapers I tried, on the pretext that I was hoping to consult with Harry on a piece he had once written, were adamant they had not heard from him in years. The payments, when I finally dared to try and trace them with the help of a seemingly indifferent employee, were registered to a bank in the Cayman Islands which refused to disclose any information whatsoever. It was as if Harry had simply cut a hole around himself and stepped out of the world.

Over the months that followed his leaving, the memory of him, which presented itself frequently and often without warning, mellowed until it was a brief stab of pain that gave way to something else: more a sensation than a feeling, a ripple of cold air over my skin as I tossed in bed at night, David beside me; a prick against my finger as I absent-mindedly ran my fingers along the roses that lined our garden.

In time, I would allow myself to apply the same techniques with Harry that I had been taught to use when unwanted thoughts of Thomas arose. I would learn to allow myself to compartmentalise the swell of memories as they threatened to crush me. But at this moment, I was not ready to forget. The thought of him, the thought of our mission, was all I had to hold onto. The thing upon which I relied to push me through the guilt, the fear, the irrepressible feeling that something was very wrong.

Once my computer had come to life, I opened the search engine, taking a brief glance over my shoulder to make sure the office was empty before typing in his name. It was a ritual I practised again and again, the monotony of it, the certainty of his name right there before me, his face like a calming hand on my shoulder. An assurance that I was not losing my mind.

There was no expectation, no real belief that I would find anything new. Only this time as I clicked through the familiar pages of links and articles, before moving on to a stream of images relating to Harry and his various reports, my eye hovered for a moment longer than usual over one particular photo. It was a repetition of the byline shot I had first spotted that morning in the smoking room, in what felt like another lifetime. Now, rather than skimming over it as I had done previously, having mistakenly taken it for a piece I had already read, I clicked through to the article.

On closer inspection, the photo was attached to a syndication of the article I had seen years earlier in my parents' house the first night I looked him up. It was a report on Harry's dismissal from the paper the night that we first met, the one I re-read over and over that night at my parents' house so that I could almost recite every line – except in this version, a tweaked version published in the paper's Irish sister title, there was an additional detail.

According to our sources, the paper's editor, Eddy Monkton, saw off the writer, who was raised in Cork, in characteristically pithy style.

Cork? The room went very still. Was it possible that I had misremembered? Running the conversation back in my mind, I could picture his face as he spoke of his childhood, a distance in his eyes. Galway. He was born in Galway. He had been born there and had never left. He had talked about it, reluctantly at first and then with a weary nostalgia in his voice, the quaintness of it, the romance, and ultimately of his boredom.

Cork was miles from Galway – the paper must have got it wrong, I told myself. It had to be a simple mistake. And yet, for an Irish paper? It was quite a splendid error, if that is what it was.

She answered after two rings, when I called the following day from the playground on the Heath, leaving the house moments after David had left for his football match.

'Mrs Dwyer?'

There was a moment's hesitation. 'Yes?'

'Mother of Harry Dwyer?'

'This is she.'

In the background I could hear the hum of the washing machine. I imagined her in the kitchen he had described, the garden tumbling down towards a dry-stone wall, her hand pulling at the cord of the phone hanging on the wall. And yet how much of that was lies? Did she even live in the countryside at all?

I knew from the dialling code of the number I had acquired from one of Harry's former colleagues at the local paper where he had started out, that the house in which Mrs Dwyer stood was in a totally different part of the country, some 100 miles from the one he had described during one of our early heart-to-hearts.

'Hello?'

'Sorry . . .'

My mouth was dry; I held my hand over the mouthpiece of my phone, blocking out the sound of the girls playing beside me.

'My name's Anna, I'm . . . I'm a friend, of Harry's.'

'I see. I'm sorry I don't . . . Have we . . .?'

'We haven't met. Harry and I, we worked together. It's a funny thing, actually, I got a new phone recently and I can't seem to find his number. There was something I needed to follow up on with him and I'm so sorry to bother you, but I just wondered if you wouldn't mind passing on his number?'

The pause was longer this time, and then her voice came again, resolute.

'I'm sorry, I don't have that information. Harry calls here, I don't . . .'

There was something about her voice I could not read. Was she lying, or was she simply trying to convince herself it was normal not to have a phone number for her own son?

'That's OK.'

I reached out a hand to steady Rose at the top of the slide.

'I wonder, I'm sorry to ask, but might one of his siblings . . . As I say, I wouldn't usually ask, it's just that there's something we really need to follow up on.'

'Siblings? I'm afraid Harry doesn't have any . . . Sorry, what did you say your name was?'

'Mama!'

At that moment, Stella launched herself from the top of the slide and the phone slipped from my hands as I lurched forward to catch her. There was a second of horror as her face clipped the curve of the metal, but my hand reached her soon enough to pull her back.

'You're OK. Shhh, you're OK.'

I soothed her with one arm, scrambling with the other for the phone, which had fallen to the concrete in the commotion. But when I lifted the receiver to my ear again, she was gone.

'Hello?'

I had to ring the buzzer twice before the young woman answered, her voice short, as if I had pulled her from something more important.

The taxi driver insisted on keeping his engine running so that the fumes from the exhaust hovered at the side of the buggy as I pushed it back and forth in sharp motions, desperate for the girls to stay asleep.

'You can leave them in the back, I'm not going anywhere,' he had called over the microphone as I ignored him, steadily heaving the buggy from the back of the black cab, which I'd hailed as we exited the Heath at Parliament Hill.

It was the third time I had tried Harry's old flat in the months since he had disappeared, but this time I heard the click of the intercom, and then a woman's voice. My momentary relief was instantly replaced by unease.

'Hello? Is anyone there?'

It took a moment for me to gather my thoughts clearly enough to speak. 'Sorry, hi, look, I'm so sorry to bother you. This is Anna. I'm a friend of Harry, is he here?'

'Sorry, I don't know who you're talking about.'

I twisted my head quickly to check the taxi. The driver was on his phone, his eyes looking forward. I moved closer to the intercom. 'I'm looking for my friend, he used to live here. I thought he might still. Harry. He owned the flat – I wondered if you knew how I could find him.'

Whatever patience she might have had was fast disappearing. 'There's no Harry living here, but maybe it was before my time. I've only been here a few months. Listen, I was in the middle of working, I need to get back. I'm sorry I can't help, but the man who lived here, he wasn't called Harry. He was an old guy, Mohammed; he lived abroad and the flat was empty most of the time. Maybe your friend stayed here sometimes, when Mohammed was away.'

The taxi driver called out the window, causing me to jump.

'Love, are you going to be much longer?'

My eyes turned to his and he looked away, muttering something into the receiver.

'That can't be right. He owned it, he had lived here for years . . . He told me—'

'I'm sorry, I don't want to be rude but I have to go now. I hope you find your friend.'

CHAPTER 53

Anna

It was my fourth year with the company when Clarissa announced she was side-stepping to become Editor-in-Chief, leaving me to deal with the day-to-day running of the magazine.

My promotion to Editor did not go unnoticed within the industry, where my youth was commented on with a mixture of reverence and disdain. By way of contrast, at home my new role was greeted with indifference by David, whose disappointment in me and the life we had built together seemed to expand weekly, after the brief spell of peace that had followed the wedding. Two years of contempt, trapped in a purgatory of my own making.

Nine months had passed since I last heard from Harry. In the same length of time it would take to grow a life, part of me had died. Without him, I couldn't be sure who I was any more. Sometimes I wondered if I ever knew.

With the girls due to start at the nursery of a local private school that September, my regret for the extra hours my new role involved would creep up occasionally in the early hours of the morning, and then I would push it away again.

We spent a long weekend in Provence in October, escaping the interminable rain of London, with the usual tag-alongs in tow.

It was unseasonably warm, even for the South of France. On the Saturday morning Jeff and May were due to arrive from their pied-à-terre along the coast, and I woke to find the three men playing cards on the terrace, the smell of lavender swelling under the morning sun.

'Jeff, good to see you.' I leaned in to kiss him before pouring myself a cup of coffee from the pot.

'And you, my dear. Looking delightful as ever.'

'David, where are the girls? I thought I might take them into town for an ice cream.'

'Maria's taken them out for the day.'

Without warning, I felt myself overcome with a rage that was impossible to repress, even in front of the others.

'What the fuck, David? We're supposed to be spending time together as a family.'

'Well, you hadn't bothered getting up and they were bored, and Maria offered, so—'

'My alarm didn't go off.'

'Your alarm?' David snorted, releasing a short laugh. 'Right.'

'What the hell is that supposed to mean? I set my alarm, David.'

Why did my voice sound so unconvincing?

'It just seems unfortunate you had trouble passing out, given how much you put away at dinner.'

'Excuse me?'

David said nothing as Clive intervened.

'Give the girl a break, David, for God's sake. She is on holiday, she is allowed to have the occasional glass of wine . . .'

'"Occasional" . . .' David muttered under his breath, flicking through a handful of cards.

My cheeks burning with fury, I turned and stormed back upstairs towards the bedroom, plucking my phone from the bedside table and dialling Maria's number, but her phone was off. Pausing for a moment, I pressed the settings buttons, scrolling through to alarm.

It was off. But how could that be? Since the pills Dr Blackman prescribed had stopped having a soporific effect, my insomnia had returned. While the doctor still insisted that was no reason to stop taking the pills, emphasised with knowing looks and clichés about how depression is a disease like any other, I had started to rely heavily on additional tranquillisers, and had taken one around 2.30 a.m., having held off as long as possible before giving in.

Knowing the impact they had on my ability to wake naturally, I had made sure the alarm had been on before I finally passed out, sometime around 3 a.m.

My thoughts were disturbed by the sound of the wheels of Clive's Bentley crunching against gravel. When I looked out of the window I saw the car flanked by Jeff's soft-top, he and May visible in the front seats, exiting the drive.

Once the sound of the engines had faded into silence, I wandered back along the empty halls and down the wide curved staircase, the panelled walls sticky with beeswax. The silence in the kitchen was overwhelming. Pouring myself a glass of wine to allay my nerves, I moved outside and settled on a blanket on the lawn where I finally dozed off under the shade of a tree.

It was the sound of the girls returning later that afternoon that woke me.

'Mama!'

'Hello, darling . . . Have you had a lovely day?'

'Why didn't you come with us?'

Stella threw herself at me as I attempted to pull myself up, my eyes still adjusting to the light.

'Maria?'

My voice stopped her in her tracks and she smiled, turning and making her way down the slope of the gardens, which led down to an elaborate ornamental pond with lily-pads and a thin coating of moss.

'I'd rather you didn't take the girls out for the day without asking me.'

My voice was uncharacteristically reprimanding. It was not my way to speak to Maria like an underling, and the fact was I had always encouraged her to be autonomous when it came to looking after the children.

'I'm sorry. David asked me to, and I—'

'He what?'

She stopped, as if checking herself.

'I mean, he . . . Or maybe it was me. I'm sorry if it wasn't what you were hoping for today.'

'David asked you to take them out?'

'I'm sorry, I really can't remember whose idea it was, maybe it was mine. But I will ask next time. I won't do it again, I'm sorry. Would you like a cup of tea?'

I nodded, unsure for the first time whether I believed a word she was saying.

Clive poured me a second large whisky as we awaited the dinner David was preparing in the kitchen that evening, waving his hand against my protestations.

'Nonsense. This holiday is a celebration of you. You and David, how much you've achieved, despite everything. Don't think we don't see all you do.'

His eyes held mine as I knocked back the drink before standing on unsteady feet, resting my hand briefly on his shoulder, a flash of electricity shooting up through my shirt.

'Anna, where are you going?'

David appeared at the doorway as I reached the bottom of the stairs.

'Nowhere, I was just going to check on the girls.'

'Maria has them. They're fine, they're having a rest.'

'But it's suppertime, I wanted to—'

'For once, Anna, this isn't about what you want. The girls need rest. Besides, the food is ready. You look like you could do with something to eat.'

There was a moment of silence, the words I wanted to say ricocheting around my head, and then I nodded and followed him back into the kitchen.

* * *

'Well, that was a triumph,' Clive announced as Maria cleared the table once we had all finished our mains, refilling his own glass before passing the bottle to May.

'Anna, are you OK? You look unwell.'

He was seated at the opposite end of the room, David for once having offered me the head of the table.

'I can't imagine why.' David's words were pinched.

The taste of the beef swam around my mouth, bitter and heavy. Gradually the room seemed to contort and it was all I could do to hold onto the side of the table, in an effort to ground myself.

'Actually, I'm . . . I don't feel very good, I might . . .'

May reached out a hand to help steady me.

'I'll take you upstairs, maybe you should have a rest.'

The sheets were cool beneath my head; the last thing I heard before the room went black was May's voice.

'Anna, really, I know it's not my place to say anything, but you've really got to . . . David's very worried. We all are.'

CHAPTER 54

Maria

It was past the time when Anna usually left for work as I padded softly down the stairs one morning, the twins trailing behind me, Stella first, Rose dawdling, running her hand along the bannister.

They had been out the night before, she and David, and had arrived home around midnight, unaware of the sound of their raised voices echoing through the house.

This morning, from the final step, I could see her through the kitchen door, seated at the table, her skin pale, her hair unbrushed. She flinched as I stepped into the room flanked by her daughters.

'Rose.' Her face softened as the girls ran towards her legs, Stella pulling herself onto her mother's lap.

Rose followed, and they sat for a minute, their faces wide with satisfaction as their mother nuzzled their ringlets.

After a moment, she whispered something into their ears, and their faces fell as she made to stand.

'You two sit and have your breakfasts.'

The false brightness of her smile was not lost on her children.

'Help yourself to coffee, Maria,' she added, pointing to a pot that stood stone-cold on the table, before re-emerging twenty minutes later, fully dressed and businesslike, with that manner she could adopt, the one that warned you not to come closer.

I watched her from the window, the trail of her perfume following her down the steps and onto the pavement, her daughters' little legs hanging over the side of the sofa where they sat.

Without warning, an image of David shot into my mind, like a hairline fracture appearing across a glass; his hand on mine, held there a beat too long, as he passed me the girls' bag, that first morning in Provence.

'I was . . .' But my words failed me, sticking in my throat as David's eyes fixed on me.

'Daddy!' Stella stumbled across the room towards us, as David pulled his hand away, his thumb moving across my palm, so lightly that I wondered if I'd imagined it.

It was a few hours before Anna returned. Even from the living room, I knew it was she who had arrived home first; I could tell from the way she closed the door, too self-consciously, the way she does and thinks no one hears.

'Anna?'

I called her name quietly, afraid of waking Stella, who had finally gone down after hours of tossing her head.

Her voice broke as I reached the bottom of the stairs, the phone pressed between her shoulder and ear. Pulling back, I peered through the bannisters down to the hall where she sat, a bag of bones collapsed on the floor, face tight with pain, the phone clamped to her ear, tears silently streaming down her cheeks.

CHAPTER 55

Anna

The house stood in the middle of the cul-de-sac. As the car turned the corner, I held up my hand, signalling for the driver to stop at the end of the street.

Breathing deeply, I stood tall as I stepped out of the cab, taking a moment to absorb the lonely sycamore lining the curve in the pavement in front of my parents' home. The flat roof of the garage that they had never pulled down, a permanent shrine to the misery that still defined them.

As I walked towards the house, I pulled my jacket tight around me. Was that the curtain twitching in the top room, the one that had been Thomas's, or had I imagined my mother's silhouette quickly moving away, heading towards the stairs?

It was too easy to visualise the inside of that room. Though the door was kept locked, I could picture it exactly from the times I had returned home to find my mother, her eyes like glass, perched on the edge of the bed; the same small white bed in which he had slept the night before he died. The same teddy bear, his fur past its best, his limbs stiff, perched in the middle of the pillow.

'Marianne?'

My mother's face appeared at the door before I had a chance to press my finger against the plastic buzzer. I watched her face, the corners of her mouth lifting involuntarily in what might have been a smile. Reading the pause in my response, she dropped her eyes for a moment.

'Can I still call you that?'

'Mum.'

Tears pricked unexpectedly at my eyes as I took a step towards the doorway, feeling my mother's body collapsing into my arms – an injured bird, too weak to fly away.

We sat together in the kitchen, in companionable silence, before heading through to the living room, my mother making tea, busying herself as ever.

'I can't stay long.'

I looked out of the window towards the garden, then back at my mother.

'How is he?'

'Here is your tea.'

She set down the cup and pulled tentatively at a chair, slowly lowering herself to sit, as if entering a freezing cold bath.

'I'm sorry I had to tell you by phone.' She paused briefly. 'You're married?'

It was more a statement of fact than a question. Caught off-guard, I reached for my cup.

'I've seen his picture, in the paper. Lovely-looking man.'

It was a relief more than a shock and I smiled quietly.

'David.'

'Yes.' My mother paused, 'And you have children together?'

It was too late for guilt on either side.

'Twin girls,' I nodded, wondering if I had ever really believed I was truly keeping my family secret, and if indeed I ever really believed she would be falling over herself to get to my daughters even if she had known.

'They're nearly three,' I added, as if it made any difference.

Of course she had known. One of the women on the street would have seen my photograph in one of the magazines they loved to read, arming themselves with facts about other people's lives. They would have recognised me, of course. It was not that people around here had ever forgotten who I was, more that they had chosen to ignore it, to ignore us – 'It's just so hard to know what to say!' 'I know, so *awkward*,' I'd once overheard some of the school mothers sigh. How much easier it would have been for them years later when I became the source of an altogether more palatable sort of gossip.

I imagined the women on the street arriving at my parents' door armed with cake, after they heard the news. Perhaps they had finally invited Mum to join their book group.

My mother's fingers reached for her tea. I watched them tremble as she lifted the cup, the porcelain as thin as her lips.

I paused for a moment, ready to muster an excuse. The girls were still so young, you see, they hated to travel, it was so disruptive to their routine. Perhaps one day she could come to them, in London . . . But then what would be the point?

'Can I see Dad?'

My mother kept her face still, the pain held in the space between her eyes. Carefully, she stood, her hand pressed against the back of the chair, taking the pressure off her bones.

'He's through here.'

She walked round the perimeter of the table before moving towards the hallway. For a moment her fingers rested on the handle of the living room door, before pushing down, an exertion that seemed to take the full weight of her body.

The curtains in the living room had been drawn tight against the outside world, casting a red hue across the room. Along the opposite wall to the sofa, there was a bed. The outline of my father's diminished body was laid out beneath the sag of white sheets. For a moment I thought he had already gone.

'A nurse comes, every morning and afternoon,' my mother announced with a forced note of enthusiasm, sticking to the particulars, as always; facts were safer than feelings.

I took a step towards the bed, towards the face I could hardly bear to see, the smell of him heavy in the air. There were many ways to say goodbye, but this was not one.

I felt my fingers move towards the thin skin of his wrist, before withdrawing; wary of taking advantage, of the intrusion of my unwanted touch.

'I'm glad I got to see him,' I said, turning towards my mother, my voice cracking.

'He's still here.'

Her voice threatened to break.

I nodded compliantly.

'Will you call me when . . .'

She moved her head towards the window. 'Thank you for coming.'

'I'm sorry.' My voice was brittle as the blown-glass figurine on the windowsill, where my mother's gaze rested. Pulling the door closed behind me, I took a breath, my vision blurry through the tears. The overbearing silence of the house followed me back out onto the street.

'How was your day?' David was in the middle of the kitchen at the marble island, his brows furrowed, concentrating on the newspaper.

Looking up, his expression transformed when he saw me. Moving forward, he pressed his fingers against the skin around my eyes, puffy and red, my cheeks smeared with black.

'It's my father.'

My voice was detached; it was all I had to say before the tears ambushed me. I felt my body deflate as David scooped me in his arms, my head pressed against his chest. How long had it been since he had held me like this? And yet still his arms were not enough.

'Oh, Anna.'

He whispered into the top of my head, gathering me towards him as I struggled to breathe, focusing on the weight of my legs.

The funeral would take place on the same day as the girls' third birthday, I told David sometime later as we sat at the table, a glass of whisky in front of each of us. That much, at least, was true.

'We can celebrate another time . . .'

'I can't.'

'Oh, come on, they're turning three, they don't know what date it is. We'll just tell them their birthday is the following week . . . You can't miss your father's funeral.'

'It's a day's flight each way. I can't leave the girls.'

'Don't be silly, the girls will be fine. Maria's here. I could come with you—'

'David.'

My voice was enough to stop him dead.

'I'm sorry. I'm just . . . I just want to get on. You know, it would be a military thing and I'm not . . . I don't feel connected to that world. I want to remember him as he was.'

My voice settled again.

David remained silent across the table, his hand moving to his glass, his eyes pulling away from mine.

CHAPTER 56

Anna

'Don't you think you've had enough?'

Even above the clatter of glasses, the voices, raised and narcissistic, moving in Mexican waves across the room, David's voice had an edge to it that I had come to recognise, to savour even, as a reminder to stay on guard.

Holding his eye, I necked the rest of my glass before returning it to the waiter who hovered next to us, his champagne bottle suspended mid-air, his tuxedo stiff with embarrassment.

'I'd love some, thank you.'

Smiling pointedly at the waiter, I turned my attention to the enormous ballroom, which rippled with diamonds and silk. Across the floor, at round tables overflowing with discarded glasses, men lifted their hands, perfectly polished women whispering into their ears.

At the front of the room, an auctioneer was talking into the microphone while the crowd whooped with amusement.

'Aren't you going to bid, David? Come on, don't be shy. Don't I deserve a Caribbean cruise?'

He didn't even acknowledge me speaking, and my hand moved back to my glass.

It had been a long night and the lipstick had started to pull against my mouth. As I lifted the drink to my mouth, a man with a 'press' badge hanging from his neck raised his camera.

'Mr and Mrs Witherall, isn't it? May I take your picture?'

David stood to block his view, and then turned to look at me and paused. 'Well, we were just leaving, but I suppose a quick one . . .'

Using my hand to steady myself, I felt David lean into me, my eyes struggling to focus against the glare of the flash.

As soon as the photographer had moved away, David reached for my wrist.

'Come on.'

'I'm not ready. What about my drink?'

'Anna. We're going.'

The room was alive with voices, so no one but David heard me cry out as he closed his hand around my arm. Keeping his voice level, David pulled me to my feet, leading me towards the door.

At the cloakroom, distracted by one of his ex-colleagues, he finally released the grip on my flesh. Turning, grateful for the freedom to slip my arm into my coat, I found myself face to face with him.

'Anna?'

The strip-lighting of the atrium was startling compared to the darkness of the auction room, and I thought my legs might give way as the blood slid to my feet..

'What are you doing here?'

My mouth would not form any other words, my eyes refusing to leave his face, refusing to look away in case I should look back and see that I had imagined him, after all. Him, here, in front of me, after so long. I opened my mouth, as if to speak, but it was David's voice I heard.

'Are you ready? Oh . . .'

He stopped beside me. For a moment I couldn't breathe, but then I heard the words fall from my mouth.

'Harry . . .'

His name stung on my lips, my eyes pressing back tears so hard they ached. 'This is my husband, David. You know Harry . . .' I swallowed, my eyes closing for a moment. Remembering just in time, I added, my voice slow, 'My God, but it has been . . . years.'

There was a pause while David gathered himself and then he took

Harry's outstretched hand. I remembered that same hesitant movement, the time we had met at the Crown and Goose, what was it, four years ago?

'Harry, of course. Good to see you.'

All I could feel was Harry's eyes, not looking at mine, and then David spoke again, more warmly this time.

'Andrea?'

When I turned I saw that he was addressing the woman at Harry's side; I had not even noticed her arrive. Again, there was a barely perceptible pause and then Harry filled in the gaps.

'You two know each other?'

Talking to no one in particular, he added, 'Andrea works for the firm who put on the charity ball.'

'Of course, that's my old firm. Andrea and I, we did work experience together, back in the day.'

Andrea's face, shining with foundation, was pursed in an expression of curious amusement as she kissed David on both cheeks. She held out a sinewy arm to me, and I looked at it, unsure for a moment what I was expected to do with it.

'This is Anna, my wife.'

My face rearranged itself into what I hoped was a smile and then I felt David's hand on the small of my back, my muscles flinching.

'Well, lovely to see you, Andrea. Harry . . .'

He nodded.

'We'd better be off, our taxi . . .'

'Please . . .'

It was Harry speaking this time, and for a dizzying moment I thought he was going to move forward and claim me, but instead he laid his hand on Andrea's arm.

'Good to see you.'

With that, his voice was sucked away as David led me out of the high swinging doors and onto the Strand, the February night air scouring my cheeks.

* * *

In the time since Harry's absence my phone had become my most treasured possession, the one reassurance that he had been real after all. The only line of connection left between us, a map of our lies.

It felt strange to be holding it in public, so openly, so close to my office, as if it were nothing to hide. But it was early enough that the bar was practically empty, and besides, by this point I was almost past caring. I had lost my father, I had lost the man I loved. The vision of Harry the night before, arm in arm with that woman . . . well, it would understandably be enough to drive me beyond rational behaviour, and that was exactly what I needed Harry to see, too.

Taking another sip of my drink, I began to type.

Dear Harry,

I don't know if you're reading this, but after seeing you again I've realised the guilt is too much. I can't do it any more. For so long, I've been lying to so many people. I have let everyone down. I can't see any way to absolve my guilt other than to be honest with the people who have stood by me. My family. I'm sorry if that means I've let you down too, but I suppose that makes us even.

His reply came within twenty-four hours. I am not sure what pleased me more, his words or the fact that he had still been checking for my messages. In any case, I did not realise how long I had been holding my breath until I finally exhaled, my fingers trembling as I held the phone out in front of me, my eyes passing again and again over his words, allowing them to sink through my skin.

It was Rose who found me there, on the bedroom floor, tears streaming down my cheeks, the phone still in my hand.

'It's OK, they're happy tears,' I told her as she hovered in the hallway.

Moving reluctantly into my outstretched arms, she let me hold her there against my chest, like a trapped bird.

'How can you be happy if you're crying?' she said at last.

'You just can be,' I whispered into her hair.

And in that moment, I was.

I had already decided I would spend the morning in the office, needing the distraction of other people, other thoughts.

It was a good twenty-five-minute taxi ride from the office to the place Harry had suggested. On Goswell Road, I hailed a black cab, my heartbeat drumming as the hyper-branded bars and offices of Shoreditch gave way to the hubbub of Dalston and the leafy, wide open roads of Hackney Downs, before finally the smog of Upper Clapton Road.

The trees across Springfield Park were naked and exposed under a rare glimpse of morning sun. Letting the jacket fall from my shoulders, I settled on the bench at the top of the hill, allowing the warmth to soak through my skin.

Across the valley below, I watched the boats moored along the canal-side, plumes of smoke rising in discreet warnings, their smell tracing across the light wind to where I sat.

'Anna?'

The voice made me jolt. Allowing myself a moment before I turned, I prepared for the worst.

'Anna, I'm Mimi.'

I stood up. As we made eye contact, instinctively I took a step back. The woman wore a mauve cardigan, the sleeves of which hung around her wrists as she lifted her hands in a placatory fashion.

'Harry sent me.'

Her voice was reassuringly soft.

'Please sit . . . I'm sorry if this is not what you expected.'

In my mind, all the millions of words I had planned fell away and in their place was only silence as I followed her towards the bench.

'I don't have a huge amount of time, but I need you to listen to what I'm saying. Is that OK?'

'Where's Harry?'

'Harry asked me to come here and speak to you, but the fact is we do not have much time, and I know this is difficult but I need you to listen to me . . .'

I nodded, my fingers running over the flask of whisky in the inner pocket of my bag.

'My brother Charles, he was one of the drivers for the company in Equatorial Guinea who were paid by TradeSmart to dump the waste that Harry told you about . . . In the village where we lived, near Bata, there were a number of men like him, low-paid employees who were just doing as they were told and had no reason to question it. The man who owns the waste disposal company, Francisco Nguema, he's the one . . .'

Her voice trailed off; she was working hard to keep it level.

Handing her the flask, I saw her hesitate for a moment and then take the drink, her eyes squinting as she took a wary sip.

'Charles had been working as a driver for a man called Joseph for about three months. The company disposes waste in dump-trucks, at sites across the country. Mainly for foreign companies, but it takes smaller jobs too. Whatever is needed. The money was not good, but it was at least some money when there otherwise was none.'

'I'm sorry, I don't understand. Why are you telling me this?'

'You don't need to understand, you just need to listen . . . One day, Joseph comes to my brother and four other drivers, and tells them they are to meet a boat at the port in Bata. The boat is called *Miracle*, and it is their job to unload the waste from *Miracle* and drive to several spots outside Bata and up along the coast towards the nature reserve.

'Immediately, once he unloaded the canisters into his truck, my brother knew something was not right. He asked the men what was inside, but the men said it was not his job to ask questions. The smell, though, got worse as he drove.'

'The mercaptan sulphur?'

I remembered Harry's words. According to experts at Greenpeace, the smell of the stuff was so potent that if you were to deposit a small amount in Trafalgar Square, it could still be smelt outside the M25.

'That's right. Not long after he started driving, my brother's skin started to burn. He said it felt as if his arms were on fire. He panicked. He didn't know what it was but he knew he had to get rid of it.'

Now, Mimi's voice became smaller.

'He didn't know there was a village so close by.'

'It was him? That was why so many people got sick.' I finished the story for her, my body involuntarily shifting away from her.

'The people were so angry, but it wasn't his fault. He didn't know – my brother, once he found out what happened and what he had done, he wanted to die too.

'One day, a man came to visit my brother. Charles didn't know who he was. He was a white man, he spoke English. He told my brother he was not sick because of the mercaptan. He told him he had been sick for years. He leaned over his bedside and told him he needed to give evidence to say he was wrong, that he had been sick a long time.'

Mimi closed her eyes and held her sleeve against her mouth, before continuing.

'Across the area, villagers whose babies had died, whose respiratory and skin problems were so severe they could never walk again, who were left injecting themselves six times a day with medicine they could not afford, were intimidated into not giving evidence . . . Except Charles would not have had the chance to give a statement in court, anyway. He knew he was dying, so he recorded his story.'

'Everyone was scared to speak out, scared of what the company might do if they found out . . .'

It was Harry's voice I was remembering again now, the memory of it sliding down my skin like fingernails.

He had been so proud of himself as he explained how he had been talking to an employee of an NGO on the ground in Bata, which had been helping deliver medicine to victims of the disaster, and how he had been working to find victims to come forward.

And I was jealous because it was taking him away from time he could have been spending with me.

'The problem is, we've dealt with cases like this before and people like Clive are very good at handing down blame.' Those were his words at the time. 'Unless we can prove he knew about the deal – that he was explicitly aware of what was contained in the waste units, and the fact that they had been rejected by the water police in a number of other countries on grounds that they needed to be properly disposed of, as chemical slops, then he'll find a way to wriggle out of it. He'll say he was unaware, and pass the buck to some other sucker.'

'Your brother, did he . . .?'

The sentence petered out on my lips.

She nodded, looking down at her hands.

'Yes, he died. But it wasn't the sickness that killed him. The villagers, parents of the children who died, after what happened, they blamed him. One day they came to our house and . . .'

She stopped then, and I took my cue.

'What do you want from me?'

She paused, possibly questioning whether it was hostility or willingness that tinted my voice.

'The receipt you sent Harry a picture of, the one in Clive's study in Greece. We need the paper. We need you to go back to Greece and find it.'

'*What?*'

She didn't repeat herself, so after a moment I carried on. 'But that's absurd. I mean, we don't even know it's still there!'

'Why would he move it?'

'Well, I don't know. Why wouldn't he?' My voice reflected my growing impatience. 'I'm sorry, where is Harry?'

She paused, her expression settling into one of concern, and then I heard his voice behind me, a ripple of cold air bushing against my neck.

Mimi looked down, perhaps aware that she was intruding on a moment that should have been ours alone.

'Anna?'

I stood, allowing myself a moment before I turned, waiting for my body to tell me how to respond. For a moment, I didn't move, letting him take me in: my pressed white shirt tucked into light-grey woollen trousers skimming black leather boots.

In all the times I had imagined the moment of our reunion, as I had so often over the years, I never saw myself in his eyes, only him in mine. And every time I had imagined him, I realised now, I had pencilled in an extra detail.

'I needed to make sure you were alone.'

He answered the question I had not yet asked. His voice was rushed, less controlled than the one I remembered.

'It's too much to explain now. I still can't be sure you're not being . . .'

Without warning, he took my hands. The shock of his touch was sharp and I felt my body pull back.

'I'm sorry.'

He was struggling to sit still, his voice speeding up as he continued.

'I had to check you were alone. I needed to know you weren't being watched,' he added, noticing my hesitation and rephrasing so that he and I were once again in this together.

'Things have been happening . . . Things . . .'

What was he talking about? I looked to Mimi for reassurance, but she was ringing her hands, her face turned away from mine.

'I can't explain, other than to say things are more urgent than we expected. Your message, it came at the right time . . . The woman you saw me with – David's old colleague? She is working for us too.'

He saw my face fall.

'I'm sorry that I can't explain further right now. There isn't time. But you just have to listen to me, Anna, you have to believe me when I say that all I know is that we are in danger and the only way to get out of this is to get that receipt, get Clive locked up, and then leave.'

'What are you talking about, Harry? How can you turn up here out of the blue and expect me to— What? What is it that you are even asking?'

He took a moment. 'Out of the blue?'

'It's been a year and a half, Harry.'

He looked at me then as if I were a stranger.

'Anna, I'm sorry if all this hasn't been linear enough for you, swift enough. I didn't realise we were working to a timeline.' He paused, finding his flow. 'I mean, really, what did you think we were doing here?'

Mimi threw him a look that made me question the true nature of their relationship.

'What Harry is trying to say is that these things take time. I can only imagine how distressing it has been for you, waiting so long, not understanding what was happening; but Harry has intentionally tried to shield you, where he could. But now the time has come for action, and we're asking you – I'm asking you – for those children, for my brother . . .' She paused. 'Only you can help finish this.'

Amidst the turmoil, my mind scrabbled for something tangible to hold onto.

'The receipt, I don't understand. Why do you need that? You have the photograph I took of it, surely that's enough?'

'It's not.'

Harry shook his head, the flourish of anger having dissipated. Not wanting to meet his gaze, I focused on his fingers, the smooth curve of the nails I barely recognised. The hands that once held me so close against his chest that I could feel his heart beating as if it were inside me too were now those of a stranger.

There was an unnatural calmness as he spoke.

'With a photograph, when the case gets to court – which it will, by the way – his defence could easily argue it's a fake. We could have just photoshopped it. Whatever. If we have the signed paper, which clearly sets out the deal TradeSmart was striking with the owners of the *Miracle*, with Clive's fingerprints, that is a far tighter hole to squeeze out of.'

I felt Mimi's eyes on my cheeks. My perfectly preserved skin, which I layered each morning with moisturiser that probably cost more than a week's worth of the medication her brother had desperately needed. What must she think when she looked at me? What would she think if she knew what I had done, the choices I had made?

'Once we have the document . . .' Harry resumed his explanation. 'Once we have it in our hands, then we can get the ball rolling. Without saying too much, Nguema has a lot of power in his country, but we have ways of making things happen. Once we have the receipt, an arrest warrant can be issued for Clive Witherall's arrest.'

'But will the British courts really be able to try him for something that happened in another country?'

'With the scale of this case, and the involvement of various international charities who are prepared to condemn the environmental impact of the waste deposits, as well as the human cost, it could be that this is considered more than a local issue. Besides, this is essentially a British company and it's been breaking international trade laws left, right and centre.'

With the help of the emails I had found, Harry continued, he was able to hack the company's internal emails and weed out a chain of messages in which high-level employees debated how to dispose of the mercaptan without paying the proper $40,000 fee.

Did he notice how I flinched at how casually he raised our collective past?

'We've got at least thirty or so emails with employees talking about dodgy contacts in corrupt countries across the world who might be able to offer a way out. At one point, they discuss the possibility of buying a ship, loading it with the mercaptan and sinking it, in order to save a few thousand pounds.'

I could feel the movement of Mimi's body as she rocked her foot gently from side to side, her eyes still darting across the park, where a group of nursery children in high-visibility vests were being led to a picnic.

'The bottom line is, we don't want TradeSmart on trial in Africa.

We want it done here, and we have the means to bring about a serious class action case. We've got everyone on board, but the one thing we don't want is for Clive to give us the slip. And the only concrete evidence we have linking him to the waste dump is that receipt.'

I shifted again in my seat. It was cold, I realised. The sun had abandoned us and the flesh across my shoulders rippled with goose-bumps. I could feel Harry growing restless beside me. Seeing him now, this man I barely recognised against the vision that had kept me awake at night, I wondered if I had redrawn him in the image of a person who had never really existed at all.

Briefly, I felt a tug of pain, an almost overwhelming longing for what had abandoned us now. I turned to face him, the words I had practised waiting to be said. And yet, something stopped me, the inevitability of it all offering some relief. He was right. It had, of course, always been leading to this. How many times had I imagined this moment in my mind; how many hours had I spent with David snoring lightly beside me, deliberating the move that I always knew would eventually come? The final epoch. The action without which everything else would have been nothing but a charade. Or so I thought.

CHAPTER 57

Maria

Anna was working late one evening, the girls already tucked up in their beds, when I came down to find David alone in the kitchen, his face stained with tears. The girls' picture books were still scattered across the table, and he had a bottle of whisky hanging from one hand. In the other was a letter, which he refolded as he heard me enter the room, but not before I saw the girls' names printed on the lower half of the sheet.

His face changed when he saw me, a pitiful smile lifting at the corners of his mouth. Pulling out a chair beside him, I slid my hands towards him and held them there.

'Is everything OK?'

'No, it's not. I've just . . . Never mind . . .' He shook his head wearily, closing his eyes. 'Maria, I'm so sorry. I don't know what came over me. That night, in Greece, I . . .'

It was the first time he had mentioned it, in all these years.

Shaking my head, I squeezed his hand.

'Stop. It's OK. I know, you had lost your mother. You were a child. I shouldn't have reacted so . . .'

Something in his expression changed and he pulled away from me.

'Don't do that, Maria.'

I stood, moving towards the sink. 'Do what?'

'Don't be disingenuous. Don't lie to me. I've had enough of people *lying*.'

There was a glint in his eyes that made me question, for a moment, how much he really knew. He took another swig of his bottle.

'I wouldn't have done it.' His voice was quiet, his body sitting straighter against the back of the chair.

I knew, even before he touched me. My eyes held his as he crossed the room, in silence, my breath quickening as he approached.

He paused for a second, our faces a breath apart, before our mouths finally touched. I was the one who pulled away first.

'I . . .' My reply barely penetrated the silence, which was broken as the jingle of keys in the door interrupted us and I turned, moving out of the room seconds before Anna walked in.

CHAPTER 58

Anna

When I think of the life I am leaving behind, my first thought is always of Rose. Rose, who had been born fearful, as if something inside her had always known.

'You can't take them with you,' Harry said that afternoon once Mimi had left us, her part in my transformation complete; just the details left to iron out, like my children, which Harry referred to now as if they were a piece of hand luggage.

I looked away, my eyes filling with tears. But the fact was, no matter how you looked at it, I was not the parent the girls needed. It was debatable, perhaps, why my parenting was so inadequate. Possibly I did not have it in me to give them the love, the security they needed, because of my own emotional weakness, the lingering sense of failure that made me too afraid to try to protect them from a world I struggled to navigate for myself. A world in which I could not even protect my own twin.

Perhaps I simply did not have it in me to put their needs above my own; perhaps, somewhere along the line, I had fabricated my insufficiency in my own mind in order to justify my escape; the means to the life that I had wanted so badly that I had been prepared to give up all else.

Had I kept them at a distance in order to protect them, or to protect myself?

So many potential reasons why, but in the end it hardly mattered;

whichever prevailed, the result was the same – the girls would be better off without me.

I shivered as a breeze blew over the top of the hill.

'I just have to make the best decision I can for them in the circumstances. David is a good father. He's a good man . . .'

My voice trailed off. Sitting up straighter, for a moment it struck me that perhaps I could stay after all. How would Clive know I had been the one to steal the papers? If he was behind bars, surely then the threat would disappear? There was no reason for him to know anything . . .

Harry saw it in my face.

His voice was gentle but firm as he cast me out.

'Anna, you have to go. It's going to come out. These things always do.'

'Not necessarily.'

My tone was so rational that for a moment I almost believed it myself.

'Even if it did . . .' I was holding on to the idea with both arms. 'I mean, everyone will know why I did it. David, he will understand, once he knows what his father has done. It's Clive who is the criminal.'

As I said it, I felt my voice falter.

'The choices I've made were honest, surely they will see that? I'm not the one who's to blame here . . .'

'You really think David will see it like that, when he finds out the truth? And he will find out, Anna. You have to know that. Besides, the reality is, whether or not you get the receipt, you're not safe any more.'

'What about Rose and Stella? If I'm not safe, what makes you think—'

'Anna, whatever Clive might be, those girls are his grandchildren. David's children. You really think he would . . .'

I shook my head, unwilling to hear him test the words.

'Will they even remember me?'

He didn't answer, and I wondered if his thought in that moment was the same as mine: maybe it's best that they don't.

I turned away, so that he would not see me, pushing my sleeve across my cheek. I would not let him see me cry.

'You made this choice, Anna. I'm sorry if it sounds harsh, but there is no one else to blame here.'

'Blame?' I turned on him now, years of unspoken rage pouring out of me in a hot, sudden burst. 'No one else to blame? *Fuck* you, Harry.'

Silence swung between us. When I looked down at my hands they were shaking. A dark cloud had settled above our heads. On the horizon, where the Walthamstow Marshes faded into a too-bright sky, a train cut through the Lee Valley like a snake arrowing towards its victim.

'Where will I go?'

I kept my face turned away from his.

'Anywhere. I mean, I'd suggest somewhere people won't come looking.'

'Aren't you supposed to help, in these situations? Don't you usually provide somewhere . . . a new life? I mean, where am I supposed to go?'

I felt the panic seeping in, filling my throat.

'Trust me, you don't want us knowing where you are. There are too many people on the inside who . . . Clive has friends. You know that. The fewer people who know where you're going, the better.'

'People know who I am, Harry. My picture is in the paper. I can't just disappear.'

Though, of course, I could. It was what I had been doing all my life, disappearing into a crowd, slipping through the cracks. There was something chameleon-like about my demeanour that meant that even with my recent notoriety, people rarely recognised me. It was both a gift and a curse.

'You must have plenty of money saved by now. I mean, my God, you've been paid enough.'

He was right. I had barely touched the money Harry had facilitated over the years. I had never needed to; I could hardly spend all the cash David poured into our joint account every month. Aside from that, there had been my more-than-sufficient wage from the magazine that had been piling into a separate bank, without David ever questioning it. Yet, without a job – and I could hardly expect to tout myself in anything other than cash-in-hand, low-skilled work – how long would it actually last?

'We can get you a passport.'

Harry spoke quickly, speeding through the finalities, ticking off the boxes.

'We'll try to keep your name out of the press, of course. For the sake of the girls as much as anything. Anyway, they are young. By the time they're old enough to take it in, everyone else will have forgotten. And maybe by then they'll understand. What you're doing, it's heroic.'

I looked away, biting the tip of my tongue until it bled.

CHAPTER 59

Anna

'Have you seen this?'

Millie stands by the door to my office, holding a magazine spread in my direction above the swollen curve of her belly.

I take a moment to finish the sentence I am writing at my desk, pushing the open bottle of wine with my foot so that it will not be seen, placing my pen neatly to one side before looking up, folding the letter I know in my rational mind there is no reason for Millie to take notice of, a letter to the girls that I will never send.

'What is it?'

I know the answer even before she scuttles inside, brandishing the photo-spread taken from the society pages of one of the fashion magazines she devours. I see my own face and David's staring back at me, the colours weeping into one another.

'I can't believe you're throwing that away,' Millie had proclaimed one morning, not long after joining the editorial team as my assistant, when a photo of David and me at a book launch surfaced in the diary pages of the *Evening Standard* under the caption 'One of London's youngest power couples, TradeSmart heir David Witherall and his wife, editor and fashion icon, Anna.'

I had shaken my head dismissively, ignoring my assistant as she pulled the paper out of the waste-bin, flattening it out with the palm of her hand, which was left smeared in ink. The truth was it pained me that, despite having the more hard-won career of the pair, I was still referred to as David's wife.

From then on, Millie had appointed herself personal keeper of the growing paparazzi archives that relentlessly charted what was often cited as one of Britain's most profitable marriages.

'I'll be leaving in a minute, Millie.'

'OK, no problem.'

'Millie?'

I call her name too quickly. She stops and turns, a question flashing in her eyes.

I smile, shaking my head as if I have just remembered the answer. 'Don't worry. It's nothing.'

Rain drives against the side of the plane as the wheels skim the runway at Skiathos. My stomach tensed, I prepare for the inevitable lurch, the tightly controlled skid towards my final destination.

Looking down the length of the plane, I am one of fewer than twenty passengers gathering their bags, arms stretched above their heads, the overhead lockers springing open. The insistent beep of phones like hostages calling out to each other across the seats.

Feeling my own phone vibrate in my pocket, I take a breath, bracing myself for a message from David. A photo of the girls, reminding me of what I am missing. It would have been simpler if I could have dropped the phone in the drain at the end of our street, along with the house keys I had not quite been able to let slip through the bars. Eking it out like this, prolonging the process, makes everything harder, but I cannot risk raising the alarm too soon. I need to be able to text David and tell him I have arrived in Thessaloniki, as I have promised to do. Otherwise he will know something is wrong; he will worry, as will the girls. This is what I tell myself.

The image of my daughters huddled around their father's phone, listening to my voice on the answerphone message – *'Sorry I'm not available at the moment'* – telling them what they already know, makes my body lurch.

Stella will be the first to walk away, of course, distracted by something more interesting, more immediate. Rose, though, the natural worrier, the over-thinker; I picture her chewing the skin around her nails, her fine blonde hair falling across her face.

Taking a moment to steel myself, I pull the handset out of my pocket. One message, Unknown Number:

David tells me you are coming to town soon. If you send me your ferry details, I'll meet you at the port. Best wishes, Jorgos

Pushing back the lump rising in my throat, I draw a long breath. It is fine. No one is expecting me for a few days. As far as they are concerned I am heading straight to Thessaloniki and will be staying there until Wednesday.

I let the words ring around the inside of my head, rolling from one side to the other until I start to believe them.

Jorgos won't be around until the afternoon I am expected to arrive, in a few days' time, and Athena, I have gauged from conversations with Clive, only works alternate weekends this time of year, when the house is rarely used.

For a moment, I think of Maria and an unexplained sadness washes over me as I picture those dark, solemn eyes. What will she think of me when she knows what I have done? I blink the thought away.

I have until tomorrow to ditch my old phone. Once I have been to the house and have what I need, and have returned on the ferry to Skiathos.

Gripping the handset, I picture letting the phone slip from my fingers at the railings of the ferry, before catching my onward flight. The temptation to keep it, to hold onto the memories it contains – the photos, the videos of the girls – is overwhelming but I cannot risk anyone tracking me down. I feel a bubble of air expanding in my gut, imagining my daughters' faces plummeting into the depths of the sea.

The second phone, the one from Harry, is still safely stashed in the inside pocket of the small wheeled suitcase I have positioned on the seat beside me, my fingers curled around the extendable handle.

Indenting my nails against the leather strap, I wait for the cabin crew to announce it is time to deplane.

The mood on the aircraft has grown impatient as the passengers wait to be told they can leave. I hear limbs cracking around me as my fellow travellers stretch out their arms, limbering up for the journey ahead. In contrast, I hold my body very still, but for the fingers on my right hand, which strum silently against the handle of my bag.

What is taking so long? My eyes move quickly across the seats. At the front of the plane the flight attendants are leaning in towards one another; one holds a hand over his mouth and then there is a crackle from the intercom.

'OK, passengers, please leave the aircraft and remember to take all your belongings with you . . . Thank you so much for flying with us and we wish you a safe onward journey.'

Never before have the words held so much meaning. Holding my bag tightly to my chest, I keep my eyes down as we shuffle, single file, off the plane.

CHAPTER 60

Maria

I had not planned to come to the house at all that night, but a feeling lodged somewhere in my chest made me come looking.

The top of the mountain was black as I approached, the squeal of the brake on my push-bike the only sound as I slowed to a halt. The gate moved easily when I pressed it, giving way to the gravel drive I still remembered perfectly.

It was four years to the day since Artemis' death and I had spotted him that afternoon, at the foot of the tree, beside his mother's grave. At fourteen, David's face had filled out since the previous summer. A faint line of hair cast a shadow across the tightly held line of his mouth as he pressed a stick against the hard knoll of dirt, seeing how much pressure it would take before it snapped.

Not wanting to intrude, or perhaps not knowing what to say, I had left without saying hello, abandoning the bunch of wildflowers I had picked to lay on his mother's grave on the step of the church.

It was hours later that I built up the courage to go to the house.

'David?'

There was a light from somewhere inside as I approached. I knew his father was not home. I had seen Jorgos' car outside one of the restaurants in the port an hour or so earlier, and looked in to see Clive and a group of faces I did not recognise laughing at a large table.

'David, where are you?'

Even though the house was quiet, I could sense movement from somewhere deep inside.

Quickening my pace as I walked through the hallway to the stairs, I called his name again, and heard mine mirrored back at me from one of the rooms towards the far end of the house.

'What are you doing?'

When I peered around the door I realised it was a study.

'Maria?'

There was a wild look in David's face that I did not recognise. When I looked more closely, I saw he had been crying. From the over-extended movement of his limbs, the way his vowels curled on his tongue, it was clear he was drunk too, or high, or something else that my inexperienced twelve-year-old self could not quite compute.

Hesitating, I moved around the desk towards where he was sitting on a swivel chair. When I looked down, I saw he was holding a gun.

'What's that?'

They were the only words I could summon.

'This?'

He held it up, spinning it precariously between his fingers.

'What are you doing, David? For God's sake, put it down! Are you crazy?'

'Crazy!'

He laughed, as if I had hit on an idea.

'Maybe. Maybe not. They said my mum was crazy, do you know that?'

He laid the gun on his father's desk but kept his hand on it, beckoning to his lap with the other hand, my name playing on his lips.

I stayed where I was, my feet stapled to the floor.

'Maria . . . You know I've always loved you, don't you? My mother, she loved you too.'

'I loved your mother very much,' I said, keeping my eye on the pistol on the desk.

'What about my father?'

I looked up at him.

'Not so much?'

He nodded, as if considering something important.

'Me neither.'

'I'm so sorry about your mother, David.'

I did not know what else to say.

He nodded, closing his eyes suddenly, tensing his jaw, tears rolling down his face again.

'Do you think she . . .?' His grip on the gun relaxed and I took a step towards him as his eyes flicked open. 'Why would you hang yourself, though?'

I stopped before moving towards him again, desperate to offer some comfort but unsure how.

He held out his hand to stop me, as if he had something important to say.

'I don't mean why would you kill yourself, I mean why *hang* yourself, specifically?'

He stopped, his mouth gaping open as if paralysed by his own revelation.

'That's pretty fucked up, isn't it?'

Picking up the gun, he seemed to test the weight of it in his hand.

'Where did you get that?'

'It's my dad's.' He shrugged. 'Keeps it in the safe behind that false cupboard there . . .'

My eyes followed his towards a tall door by the window, fractionally open.

'David, please put it down.' My knees were trembling and I placed my hand on the table. 'Please, you're scaring me.'

But it was as if he could not hear.

'You know, I've been thinking. If it were me I'd use a gun.'

He held it up, the barrel dipping slightly in the uncertainty of his grip.

'Please, David.'

'I wonder, though, what would my dad say? If I did it. Because he's not too bothered about my mum. Do you know how many times I've seen him cry over his wife? Over how her body was swinging from the bannisters outside my bedroom. Why did she have to do it there? Do you think she wanted me to find her? Do you think she hated me?'

His whole chest started to shake then and it was only when I felt the tears rolling down my cheeks that I realised I was crying too.

'He's saying she was mad. I mean, to do that to yourself, you would have to be mad, wouldn't you? I think you would. That's what my dad thinks. What about you? Do you think she was mad, Maria?'

'David, please . . .'

I went to take the gun from the desk but he seized it and held it against his temple.

'It would only take a second, wouldn't it? If I did it like this. Much less painful, surely.'

I could see his hands were trembling from the movement of the metal against his cheek.

'Would he cry? Do you think? Would he cry for me?'

At that moment there was a sweep of headlights across the drive, and David's eyes, suddenly aware, followed the line of light towards the window.

'Shit.'

It was as if he had emerged from a hallucination and he looked at me, suddenly confused by what I was doing there.

With the sound of David's voice calling after me, I turned and ran down the stairs, tearing past the car, back through the gate, Clive's eyes following me from the driveway into the night.

CHAPTER 61

Anna

The rain is easing off as I step off the boat and onto the quay, where a group of drunk teenagers who have fashioned themselves macs from bin bags are drinking shots in one of the bars along the front, next to the bus stop.

Lifting my suitcase so as to spare it the puddles that have formed in the potholes, I keep my head down as I head towards the car rental office a couple of roads behind the main street.

'*Kalispera*.' I nod as I enter the hum of the too-bright room, a fan pushing stale air to and fro. A squat man looks up from the small screen on his desk by way of welcome.

The moped has a holdall on the back, just big enough to accommodate my luggage, the man points out, barely lifting his arm.

'And I can drop the keys through the postbox in the morning if no one is in the office?' I ask for the second time. The Skiathos to Belgrade flight leaves at 2 p.m. tomorrow, which means I must be on the first boat out of here in the morning.

The man nods in a way that says *no problem*, although ordinarily, I understand, this would be a big problem, knowing all too well one is expected to leave a driving licence, if not a passport, as collateral. But it is amazing what special service paying three times the ordinary amount, for less than half a day's use of a clapped-out moped in the quieter time of year, can buy you.

I feel in my purse for the driving licence that was delivered a month or so earlier, in my new name. The one with which I will drive from Serbia, where I will stay overnight before heading to Spain for the start of my new life.

The strangled roar of the bike's engine gasps and finally falls into silence as I reach the top of the hill, where a path veers left from the road, rolling discreetly towards the house. As I pull the key from the ignition, the beam of light from above the front wheel dissolves into a wash of black.

Lifting my leg over the seat, I dismount. Taking a moment to check my suitcase is still securely fastened onto the back, I push the bike along the path, the familiar gravel gently stabbing at the soles of my feet.

The house is in darkness, as David said it would be, its long white lines silhouetted under the hollow glow of the moon.

Jorgos is not expected back until the following afternoon, though David had offered to ask him to return to the island early when I told him of my plan to cover the fair in person.

'So, what, you only need to be in Thessaloniki on the Wednesday and the Saturday?' he had asked, the first time I had raised the itinerary for the trip, a month or so previously.

'Those are the only days when the two curators are available, annoyingly. I'm arriving on the Monday so I can have a look around then, get some background. I think they're expecting me to write a daily blog for the website, but to be honest I'm not that bothered about hanging around for the fair. I'm sure an intern or someone can pull together a daily schedule. I've got so much other work to be getting on with, and if I don't get that done I'll have no time to be with you and the girls the following week . . .'

Had my voice faltered?

'Why don't you take the ferry to my father's house, after your first interview on the Wednesday? That way you can work from there, in peace, for a couple of days before you head back to Thessaloniki on the Saturday, and then fly straight home from there.'

I had turned my back to him, facing the kettle, flipping the switch, reaching for the tea bags. Everything as it should be.

'OK, maybe. Thanks. I mean it would be more comfortable . . . if Clive wouldn't mind?'

Did my voice slip, then?

'Why would he mind? You're family, and he isn't using it, so . . .'

We hadn't talked of it again until the morning I left, but I knew by then he would have sorted it out. That was David. No sooner had he made a promise than it had been rendered unbreakable.

Pushing the moped along the gravel, the heat of the engine against my calf, I force back my tears. Despite the tension that has silently grown like bindweed between us, despite everything, he has never let me down.

In that sense, we are not so different, he and I. We have just made different promises; our commitments are not aligned. But that is good, in the end. If there is anything that can be said for David, it is that he loves those girls and he will protect them fiercely from the inevitable fallout. Collateral damage, that is what the Americans call it in war. At least they do when it is their own men who are the ones spraying bullets.

Propping up the moped in the empty driveway, I head towards the house, feeling in my handbag for the key David has entrusted to me. The sharp leather of my passport holder catches against my skin as the wheels of my suitcase drum steadily across the gravel.

I expect some resistance as I push the key in the lock, some small reminder that I should not be here. But the door gives way easily, too easily perhaps, to the familiar shapes of the kitchen.

Despite the obvious absence of life in the house, I move cautiously, my eyes trained on the shadows pinned to the wall. Slipping off my shoes, I feel the familiar coolness of the tiles against my feet, my fingers hovering over the light switch before pulling back.

There is something comforting about the darkness, a cave in which I can shelter from myself. Moving towards the island in the centre of the kitchen, I feel along the side of the unit for the handle, feeling the rattle of the bottles as I pull open the drawer, drawing out a bottle of Clive's favourite single malt.

As I lift the glass to my lips, I savour the gentle burn of the liquid against the back of my throat. It is impossible to drink without thinking of Clive; how impressed he had been by my taste for whisky, taking pleasure in showing me the nuances of the flavours in the selection of bottles he kept stocked in each of his houses, like a kindred spirit.

'Does your father drink whisky?'

'No,' I had answered. I did not add that he had his own methods for self-destruction.

Taking a final sip of the drink before refilling my glass, I move through to the sofa overlooking the pool.

I love this house, the way the moon trembles across the water like an open mouth, ready to swallow. The times I have sat here with David while the girls tottered around the terrace, their arm-bands biting into their skin, dance on the surface of my memory. Stella, bombing into the deep end.

'Mummy, watch!' I can see my daughter last summer, a toddler desperate to be a big girl, squeezing her legs together, hurtling herself off the stone edge, the slap of her arm-bands hitting the water.

Instinctively, my gaze had shifted towards Rose, standing back, as the water gushed over the edge of the pool.

'Eight points!' David had shouted from the sun lounger as Stella lifted herself up the steps, pulling the goggles away from her face, the corners of her mouth falling as she looked at me and noticed my face turned the other way.

David's sharp round of applause had pulled my attention back to Stella.

'Excellent, darling,' I joined in, the palms of my hands stinging as I clapped along. Wondering, even then, how long we had.

* * *

By the time I open my eyes, my head buried in one of the cushions that line the sofa, the moon has risen high above the house so that I can almost feel it pressing down on me.

My eyes settle on the bottle in front of me as I lift myself to sitting position. I had hoped to sleep longer, wishing the night would fade into oblivion and with it the thoughts that had inevitably followed me into sleep.

The original plan, as I had developed it, had been to wait until just before the sun rose before making my way upstairs to Clive's study. Shielded from the judgemental glare of morning, but close enough to my return to the airport that it would only be a matter of hours that the papers would actually be in my possession, their significance burning into my thigh through my bag.

Once I have handed them over to Harry at the café just inside the terminal building, I will buy my ticket and then I will be gone.

I breathe in. It will be 2 a.m. in London. This was the time I most often woke at home, hearing Rose calling out in her sleep, David's body, slack and warm, in the bed beside me.

Reluctantly, I picture the girls, their faces pressed against the pillows we had bought just a few days previously. It was an Inset day and David had insisted on bringing them into my office rather than waiting downstairs while I finished up before we had lunch together in town; proudly, he escorted them across the editorial floor, their little faces glowing with excitement.

'You're early,' I had mouthed at my husband as he led my daughters through the doorway to my office, urgently kicking off my moccasins under the desk. I had only walked in from my driving lesson five minutes earlier, and so I discreetly slipped my feet back into the heels I had been wearing when I left the house that morning.

'No, you said 1 p.m.' David let the girls in first as I moved out from behind my desk, smoothly nudging out of view the theory book on the floor by my bag.

'I'm sure I said one thirty.' I kissed my daughters on the head, pressing my hands against their cold cheeks. Clarissa had been in that day, and had let out a squeal of delight at the sight of the girls, their hair pulled into matching plaits.

I imagined the scene through the eyes of my colleagues: the dutiful working mother and her successful, doting husband, hands linked with their children as they weaved their way through the desks, off to a family lunch.

Stella had insisted on us going to a fancy new pizza restaurant with long benches instead of chairs, then refused to eat, ostentatiously picking at the congealed cheese while she and Rose squabbled about who had more ice in their drinks.

'Mummy's going to Greece in a couple of days. Is there anything you want her to bring you back from the airport?' David said, slicing at the crust with his knife.

I had felt my cheeks sting.

'I want to come.' Stella had placed her fork on the table, setting her face against mine.

'It's just for work. You would be bored.'

'I want Mummy.'

'Well, unfortunately you have to go to nursery.' I had taken a mouthful of rocket salad, chewing slowly, the leaves bitter and stringy, keeping my eyes on the plate as I reached for my wine.

When I looked up, Rose was watching me, her expression unreadable.

Swallowing, pushing against the feeling that I might throw up, my lips forced themselves into a smile, which Rose mirrored weakly before looking away.

I had been drunk by the time we finished our meal, the clouds glaring back at me as we stepped out onto the street, avoiding eye contact as David kissed me lightly on the cheek, steering the girls away with the promise of ice cream.

'I'm sorry, darlings, I need to go back to the office, but Daddy's going to take you to buy new bedding for your rooms.'

I turned back to see Stella's eyes following me, before I turned the corner and leaned my back against the wall, shaking, waiting for them all to leave.

Pushing my hands against the sofa to steady myself now, I stand. There is no point putting it off. The longer I stay in this house, the longer I am stretching out an attachment to the past, dwelling on memories rather than the facts.

The girls will be fine. They have David, and David is a more attentive parent than I can ever be. Does that make me a bad mother, or simply one who has created a necessary boundary in order to protect my children? What does it matter, now?

Walking through the kitchen, I focus on the soft light of the moon, which streams in from the window in the hallway, next to the door leading to what was once Athena's domain. From there, I shift my attention to the stairs. One at a time.

As I reach the landing, my eyes fall on the painting by David's mother, inky blues fading into dusty yellow skies. In a way we weren't so different, she and I, both of us forced, for reasons beyond our control, to leave our children.

What was worse: to walk out because you felt you didn't have a choice, because you couldn't cope with life – or because you had made the choice to leave, as the best possible course of action for everyone within the limited range of options available to you?

Clive's study is just a few paces away. I turn my head away from the painting, my eyes on the task ahead. Once again, I expect some resistance, but the door is unlocked; the two files, which I half expect to find gone, lie in exactly the spot where I left them all those years before, in the drawer of my father-in-law's desk.

There are no confidential warnings on the first page – no indication of the power they contain, the horror they promise to expose. Lifting the papers, I hold them against my chest, drawing out the moment until I check, the moment from which there will be no going back.

It only takes a few seconds to find it, even though I am cautious, careful not to bend or mark the pages, as if it will make any difference. The receipt from the shipping company confirming that TradeSmart had successfully attempted to shirk all responsibility for its refusal to dispose of its slops in an approved manner.

Leaning against the desk, I close my eyes, listening to the careful rise and fall of my own breath, controlling the flow of thoughts. Feeling my lungs contract and release in perfect symmetry, a fragile accordion pushing life in and out of my body.

It is cold inside the office, and I tremble under the gaze of the photos that line the walls, the faces that have framed my fate, beaming back at me. The rain beating down on the olive groves outside seems to have risen through the windows and doors, drawing itself into my bones.

Wrapping my arms around myself for warmth, the papers in my hand brushing against my chin, I open my eyes. I breathe in sharply, feeling the hairs on my arms rise as a band of light sweeps over my face. Pushing myself upright, I go to make a step towards the window, to prove it was just a trick of the light: a bird flying across the window, momentarily obscuring the glow of the moon; headlights from a car on the road at the end of the drive.

As my eyes rise to meet the view of the drive through the glass, I hear it, feel it, in fact, as clearly as if one of my own bones has snapped. The crack of gravel. And it is at that exact moment that I see him, staring up at me through a smear of glass.

CHAPTER 62

Anna

In the months after Thomas died, I had been made to see a doctor at a hospital almost an hour's drive from our home.

'This is going to make you feel better,' the GP had told me when he prescribed the treatment, which involved weekly trips in the car, the sound of Radio 4 accompanying the low thrum of the engine, my mother's blank face glued to the road ahead.

The doctor wore thick glasses, focusing on my face in a way that I hated. I willed his eyes to leave mine as he watched me for the full hour of each session, asking me questions about how I was feeling, in a way that was presumably supposed to resonate with a grief-stricken six-year-old.

What had he expected me to say? *I want my parents to love me . . . I want them not to blame me for my brother's death . . . I want to know it wasn't really my fault?*

One afternoon, not long after the panic attacks had started, the doctor had sat me down in his office.

'When you have these feelings, the ones that make you feel scared or angry, I want you to imagine a box. The box has a lid, and I want you to lift the lid up and picture all the thoughts that are making you feel bad, and I want you to picture lifting those thoughts up and placing them inside the box. Can you do that for me? Then I want you to picture placing the lid back on top of the box and closing it tight. So tight that those feelings can't hurt you any more.'

I pictured the box, small and dark. I imagined my brother's body inside it, rigid, covered in a white sheet, the soil we had buried him under pressing against the panels from each side.

I picture David in such a box, only a man-sized version, as I step into the car waiting for me outside the airport, my driver briefly attempting conversation before his voice falls away to silence as we move along the motorway, cars sliding across three lanes, just inches apart.

Pushing away the image along with the cascade of thoughts threatening to close in on me, I focus on the back of the man's head as we crawl along the Euston underpass, the taste of lead filtering through the windows as we move across Marylebone, finally pulling to a stop outside a large townhouse on Connaught Square.

For a second, I imagine throwing open the door to the car and running, but it is no longer an option. It is no longer a question of what I am running from, but who and what I am leaving behind.

As the car pulls up outside the house, I realise I have no money but, unfazed, the driver lifts his arm to indicate that the bill has already been settled.

There is a security guard in a black suit and an earpiece at the doorway to one of the houses a few doors along. I have not been to this flat before but I know the address by heart, from the Christmas cards, and the invitations over the years.

I press the buzzer and there is a crackle and then a woman's voice, a foreign accent I cannot place. According to her instruction, I follow the curve of the stairwell until I am standing outside a black door finished in glossy paint, which opens as I approach tentatively, finally allowing myself to wonder what lies inside.

The voice on the intercom is Aarti, the maid, who greets me at the entrance to the flat, her eyes falling as I step inside, like a death-row prisoner on her way to the gallows.

We move along the hallway in silence, the walls pressing in on me as I follow her to the living room, the Valium I slipped from my handbag in the back of the cab working its way through my bloodstream, wearing away the edges.

Clive is propped against the sofa on the opposite side of the room. When he looks up, he wipes a tear from his eye and it is as if something in him has died, too.

The funeral is held in the chapel on Rosslyn Hill. Close friends and family only, according to reports in the press, which note the tasteful, restrained ambience. David's daughters, in matching dusty pink shift-dresses, their mother in signature cream and black, the epitome of decorum as her husband's body is lowered into the ground.

'Anna.' I feel a light hand on my arm, turning to find a woman in front of me, a black fascinator pinned to the front of her head. It takes a moment for the face to register. The same defiant, feline turn of the eyes, same high cheekbones; the auburn Princess Leia buns now replaced with loose strawberry-blonde curls.

I shake my head slowly, disbelieving, as Meg nods, her eyes shining with tears.

Finally, the tears flow as I grip her arm so hard it is as though if I let go she might disappear, my fingernails forming grooves in her forearm.

By the time we reach the wake, my shock at seeing Meg again after so many years has settled into something hard and heavy: an accumulation of the sadness and rage that has simmered for so long below the surface.

'I just can't believe it. The report said the car was only going at twenty-five miles an hour when it hit him.' Her face instantly shows regret. 'Jesus, I'm sorry, I'm still no good at filtering my words.'

'I don't know, you seemed pretty good at holding back the last time I saw you.' I take a sip of my drink, turning away from her, my body longing for her to stay close.

Across the room, I see the girls sitting with Maria and May, who are attempting to reassure them with one of the bags of sweets I placed in the trolley as I hovered through the aisles at the supermarket, wondering which finger foods would be most appropriate to send off my dead husband.

I feel a cool rush over my skin and drain my glass. It was my idea to hold the wake at the house – for the sake of the girls, I had told myself. The truth was I could not bear dealing with the arrangements otherwise. Talking it through more than I had to, making decisions, watching my tongue.

My mother once told me the reason Thomas died was because I had no interest in other people. If only I had been paying attention that day; if only I had looked outwards, occasionally, rather than in. In self-appraising moments I have sometimes wondered if that is true. And as I thought through the plans for the wake, I realised she was right. How much I never knew. His favourite song, his most-loved photograph of us together, his favourite tie. How many questions I had never thought to ask.

Now, with all these people in our house, the weight of them, moving through our things, mine and David's, our life on display like this, I feel a sickness rising through my body.

Among the sea of strangers, old colleagues of David's, family friends to whom I have never been introduced, I cling to Meg like a strip of warm land in a cold black sea.

'Those poor girls. They're the spit of you. Nothing like . . .' She pauses. 'Oh God, I didn't mean . . .'

For a moment the sickness subsides and for the first time in days, I feel a smile push through the stillness that has taken hold of my body, like a cast.

'Told you,' Meg shakes her head, 'I'm nervous. I don't know what to say.'

'David's dead, Meg, there's nothing you can say.'

She disappears for a moment and returns with a bottle of wine, filling both our glasses.

'Anna, there is something I need to tell you.'

I look back at her, my face hardening again at the edges, reading the fear in her eyes.

'What is it?'

'Not here.'

Her eyes move around the room, and she leans in, her voice little more than a whisper.

'Will you meet me? Tomorrow?'

I hesitate. Although there is nothing I want more, there is something about the look on her face that makes me pause; an instinctive fear of what she might say.

It is midnight before the last of the guests leave, while Aarti and Maria clear the empty platters of finger foods and wine-stained glasses, pushing bits of broken glass into a dustpan and brush.

Clive remains, nursing a bottle of whisky on the sofa, Artemis' framed painting of a fallen tree clutched tightly between his fists.

After Maria has gone up to bed I move into the garden for a cigarette. The garden is still; the only sound comes from the foxes shrieking on the other side of the wall. I watch the smoke expand in the air in front of my face, lifting my head to the black sky. My eyes are met by the gentle glow of light from the girls' room and I realise I am shaking.

There is a sound from the living room as I re-enter the house, pulling the back door and dragging the lock closed. It is the static of a John McCormack record that has been left playing in the living room, and when I lift the needle from the LP, the room falls into silence.

On the sofa, Clive's body is slumped in a stupor. Moving towards him, I lift a blanket from the back of the sofa and drape it over his body, which is frailer than I remember it. Alongside my unease at his presence there is a lingering relief that I am not alone down here with David's absence wandering the halls like a ghost.

As I turn towards the stairs, I hear a hum from the side of the sofa where Clive is splayed out. Moving slowly back towards him, I spot his iPhone, vibrating, in the space between the sofa cushions. Leaning down carefully, I push my hands between the cushions.

Withheld number. Holding my breath, I freeze as my father-in-law stirs on the sofa. Pulling myself so that my body is taut, ready to fight back, I watch him; after a moment he snores deeply and I feel myself partially relax.

Working on adrenaline now, I move towards the door. Upstairs, hovering at the doorway to the bathroom, I imagine the message I will compose to Harry explaining that I have the phone. Just then, I hear a noise from the bedroom, Rose calling out, her voice small and helpless.

My hands rise to my face and for the first time in my life I know what I have to do.

Turning, I feel myself moving away from Harry, away from the prospect of a world in which my mission is complete, away from a man I thought I once loved, away from the brother who is long dead, and towards the ones I still have: my children, breathing in the room above my head. With a sigh of relief, I make my way back to the living room, slipping the phone back onto the sofa, before moving towards the staircase; towards a life of real redemption, towards motherhood, towards the right thing to do.

CHAPTER 63

Maria

The morning after the funeral, I wake in the same bed I have woken in every morning for the past three and a half years, but everything has changed.

There is a portentous quality to the light that spills in through the windows overlooking the garden as I pull open the curtains. Straining to hear the girls' voices from their room on the floor above mine, I am unsettled by the silence as I pull the bathrobe around my waist, a moment passing before I remember David has gone.

The sound of sizzling fat fills the hallway as I approach the kitchen. Inside, the girls are seated at the table, their heads glued to the iPad Clive bought them at Christmas. Sensing my presence, Anna turns, her pupils large and flat, her movements slow and deliberate; any anxiety flattened by the pills she keeps stashed in handbags and cupboards around the house.

Her face breaks into an unconvincing smile as I move into the room, surprised to find the remnants of last night's wake already swept away, the house a picture of domestic order.

'Maria, sit down.'

She joins me at one of the stools by the marble island, which always reminds me of the one at Clive's house in Greece. From the way she launches straight in, I know she has spent the night thinking this through, carefully selecting her words.

'You being here, it's . . . you've been like a mother to the girls.'

Her eyes move briefly to Stella and Rose, her voice lowering though they show no signs of interest in anything beyond the screen; the pair of them all cried out from the day before.

'I am so grateful to you for that. David, he . . . we both, we've loved having you here. But I think it's time you moved on.'

There is a moment when it occurs to me that perhaps she knows, perhaps he told her? And then I realise she is speaking to herself as much as to me, buoying herself for the next stage.

'I'll pay you, of course, for the next month – however long it takes. And I'll book you into a hotel. I don't want you to be left high and dry, but it's time.'

I nod, a lump forming in my throat.

'OK,' I say, knowing she is right, knowing this has run its natural course, though still I cannot stop the unexpected pricking sensation at the backs of my eyes.

'I'll miss you.' There were tears rolling down her cheeks, too. 'But I know it's for the best.'

Gathering my things, I step into the cab Anna has ordered me, and watch the street fade into a memory that I will never quite comprehend. As the car stops at the red light by Belsize Park Tube station, I feel my phone vibrate.

New WhatsApp message.

It is him.

Not long now. Can't wait until you're here. D.

CHAPTER 64

Anna

Work has offered me a fortnight's compassionate leave.

'More if you need it,' Clarissa added at the end of the funeral, her face stained with tears. 'Whatever you need.'

After wanting so much for so long, the thought strikes me as strangely unfathomable.

The one thing I know I don't need is time. A gaping black hole in which to ruminate on the choices I have made. What I need is to move forward, as far away as I can from a past that I hardly recognise as my own.

I plan to return to the office after a few days at the most. The girls went into nursery this morning on the advice of Sarah, one of the mothers I had met there, whose husband had also died when her children were younger.

'Best to keep their minds on other things,' Sarah advised, catching me off-guard as the girls and I made our way through the aisles of the Marks and Spencer in South End Green, in an attempt to induce a state of normality.

'You're right,' I had nodded, resisting the urge to pull away as she took my hand in hers, imagining the deferred maternal pain that I saw wetting the corner of her eyes bleeding into my own.

My fear when I first saw Jorgos outside the house, the quiet figure of him watching my betrayal through the window, was soon replaced with something far worse. My terror that Jorgos had caught me where

I should never have been – in the house where I had told David I would not be arriving for several days – was surpassed by the sharp realisation that he had hardly noticed this fact. Something far worse was occupying his attention

'Jorgos, what are you doing here?' Even as I asked the question I did not want the answer, my arms shaking as he held my gaze.

'I saw you at the port. I was in the bar and I assumed you had arrived early. I was about to get up, to come over to offer you a lift . . . I was, but there was a woman. I'm sorry. I was planning to come and see you in the morning but . . .' He stopped. 'But then I got the call from Clive . . .'

I took a step back then.

'Anna, I . . . it's David . . .'

I am dreading the prospect of being alone in the house, grateful that over the next few days there will be strings to tie up, papers to sign, the formalities of loss offering some respite from the aching unknown.

But for now I feel a fizz of excitement as I weave my way through the familiar copse of trees that stands a moment or two on the other side of the gate at the end of the garden, a hint of smoke on the air as I make my way across the Heath.

I am the first to arrive at the café in Kenwood House, taking a seat in the raised outdoor seating area.

The Heath is relatively peaceful at this time on a weekday. I pull my scarf closer around my neck, lifting my cup for warmth, distracting myself with the line of dogs tied along the railings a few metres away, heads cocked, waiting for their owners to return.

It is too cold to sit outside, but I need the horizon, the clatter of the canteen jangling against my nerves as I order an Americano, pausing to order something for Meg before realising I have no idea what she likes to drink.

The initial relief at seeing her again after so long has now settled to a quiet ache; my hurt at her sudden disappearance seeping through the edges of my smile as she makes her way up the paved steps.

Her skin without the heavy make-up I am used to seeing on her looks naked and over-exposed. She looks younger somehow, her hair lifted from her face, pulled into a clip at the back of her head.

Our embrace is more stilted this morning than it was at the funeral, a self-conscious smile passing between us as we pull away, me first.

'I hope you weren't waiting long.' She settles on the chair opposite me, smoothing her coat under her legs, her movements more considered, more self-conscious than the ones I remember.

'Not long. Do you want a coffee, or something to eat?'

'I'm good, I'll just have one of these.'

She pulls out a packet of cigarettes, admonishing herself with a raised eyebrow, before offering me the pack.

I shake my head, recognising one of the multiple rings on her fingers, the same oval turquoise stone she always wore.

Meg exhales, looking around. 'Do you mind if we walk?'

I am pleased to be moving as we make our way up the steps in silence, only speaking again once we reach the top of the hill that rolls down from Kenwood House towards the pond. My eyes move towards the climbing tree, to the right of the false bridge, where the girls loved to scramble from branch to branch, under David's supervision, whilst I peered out across the water, always too afraid to watch.

'How did you know?' I speak first.

'I saw it in the paper.'

The grey London sky hangs above our heads, heavy curtains drawn against the rest of the world, the seams frayed.

We walk side by side past the gardens, turning left down the hill before the dusty path gives way to bog.

'I knew you'd married, I saw that in the papers too. It was the weirdest thing – to see it there and not be able to get in touch.'

Unable? I feel Meg sense the words I am too weak to say.

'I was so happy for you. I wanted to send a card or . . . I didn't know where you lived.'

'Are you living in London?' It is unsettling, someone knowing so much about your life, but knowing nothing of theirs.

'No.'

'What are you doing here, Meg?' I stop walking, suddenly impatient to hear whatever it is she has to say. 'I mean, for God's sake, it's not like it makes much difference to your life, David being dead. We haven't seen, haven't heard from you. *You* could have been dead for all I knew.'

She pulls another cigarette from her pocket, and this time I reach for one.

'Well, you might have bloody checked!' There is a moment's pause and then she adds, 'I'm sorry . . .'

For a moment I think she is going to walk away and then she looks up at me, mouthing the words, 'Do you have a phone on you?'

'I don't know if it has any reception.' I look away as I pass Meg the phone, too tired to question it, an ache running across my chest.

She takes it from me, nodding. Pushing her hand into her pocket, she pulls out a keyring with a safety pin attached, which she carefully removes before pressing it into a tiny hole in the phone.

'What the hell are you doing?'

Meg looks up without answering, silencing me with her eyes as she prises the battery from it, moving towards a bench and laying the pieces out side by side before sitting.

'Please.' She pats the seat next to her and I pause for a moment before taking a step forward, reluctantly lowering myself to the other side of the bench, taking a drag of my cigarette.

'I need to tell you something, and I need you to listen. OK?' She nods encouragingly, pacing her words. 'The truth is, I didn't want to leave London. I had no choice.'

I remain still, exhaling a line of smoke, which is magnified in the ice-cold air.

'You remember Harry?'

For a moment, my whole body turns cold and then a little piece of my heart floats away like an iceberg breaking free of the glacier, into the abyss.

CHAPTER 65

Maria

'So let me get this straight, you're saying that the deliveries of mercaptan are a cover for arms dealing?'

It was nearly a year by then. A year after she'd first pulled me in, little by little, and then by the throat.

Felicity threw up her arms, businesslike.

'Exactly, they're a decoy. Arms, night-vision goggles . . . It doesn't really matter what it is they're selling. What matters is the influence these trades can buy you, in these sorts of places.

'Look at it this way. If you wanted to smuggle something into a country, what better way than to pad out your cargo with a trace of chemical waste and label it "toxic"? In fact, TradeSmart owns so many of the ports that it's unlikely the guards will check properly anyway. But even if they did, a low-paid customs guy? He's going to look at that skull and crossbones sticker and chances are after that he is going to take a cursory glance inside the box, if that. Thanks to the spillage, everyone in Equatorial Guinea knows the harm that chemicals can do, and for companies like TradeSmart, that makes for the perfect cover.'

I nodded thoughtfully.

'And David knew about this?'

Felicity looked at me and her eyes narrowed. 'Well, I'd imagine so, wouldn't you?'

The library café was closing soon, and a couple of women with trays were collecting used cups from one of the tables next to ours.

'OK, I see what you're saying, but . . .' I leaned in closer towards Felicity. 'What I don't understand is, if TradeSmart has its financial centre in Switzerland, as you say it does, to exploit the possibilities of secretive banking, and it has its head office in Holland, for the benefit of the tax loopholes there, why is any of this of interest to MI6?'

I felt her look me up and down appraisingly. Did she trust me? Of course, I knew she was in no doubt of my competence – I had after all been the one to suggest setting up a fake website for a non-existent new trading company as a way to lure Clive's colleagues to open up about any nefarious activity within the firm. But trust?

'Maria, if I'm honest, we're not really interested in Witherall's links to arms dealings in Equatorial Guinea. That, let us say, is his Achilles heel. What we're really interested in is the role his company is playing in destabilising our work in . . . somewhere else.'

Felicity paused, tapping her finger against the table, the eternal head-girl, simultaneously frustrated and reassured by the inability of us mere mortals to keep up.

'Look, the point is, Maria, you're doing a brilliant job. We're thrilled with you, we really are. But don't ask too many questions, hey? There's a good girl.'

CHAPTER 66

Anna

The ground is like ice beneath my feet as I scramble down the worn path that leads back towards Parliament Hill, Meg's voice still echoing around my head, calling after me. Pleading.

I take the steps to the house two at a time, my hand shaking as I press the key into the door, my boots smearing the carpet with crunched leaves, toes stubbing against the last tread as I reach the top of the stairs, my balance wavering, threatening to give way.

Harry and Meg. I push the image away, through the haze, shaking my head. Refusing to believe.

Running to the wardrobe in my bedroom, mine and David's, my fingers rummage for the soft-leather clutch bag. Collapsing back onto the carpet, I pull the phone from the inside pocket, my fingers pausing for a moment before tapping in my pin. The date we first met.

Despite my efforts, I think of him now, walking across the pub garden that first night in Canary Wharf, side by side with Meg. She is lying, she must be. Trembling through my whole body as I type Harry's number, I feel the quiet roll of the current wrapping itself around my ankles, preparing to pull me silently under.

The sound of his answerphone stings my ear. I close my eyes, letting the tears run down my cheeks, fear clutching at my stomach.

There is a beep in my ear and I hear myself speak. My lips tremble and I do not recognise my own voice, his name an unfamiliar shape on my lips.

'Harry, call me right now. I'm serious. Wherever you are. Now. *Please*.'

I throw the phone at the floor, as if it might bite me, before lurching into the en suite and placing my face under the tap, lapping at the water, which pours out of the sides of my mouth.

Startled by something, I lift my eyes and see David's toothbrush discarded on the side of the sink, abandoned.

'Anna?'

The voice is moving closer to the bathroom door. Standing, my body rigid now, I move back into the bedroom, the hairs on my arms alert, my eyes scanning the room for something to clutch, my palms beading with sweat. Before I can lunge at the lock, I see the handle of the door turn.

Once again, I freeze, and I cry out instead with fear as the door opens.

'Anna, my God, are you OK?'

It is Sarah, the nursery mother who has offered to bring the girls home. Behind her, I see my daughters looking back at me, their faces recoiling.

It is Stella who speaks next, but it's David's voice I hear.

'What are you doing?'

Twisting my head to face the girls, standing on either side of Sarah on the landing, I catch a glimpse of my own reflection in the long mirror on the far side of the bedroom and see wild eyes, my clothes scuffed with mud from where I fell.

'I . . . I went for a walk, I tripped. I'm sorry, I wasn't expecting you.'

'No, I'm sorry. We tried the bell but I thought perhaps you were still out, and then we realised the door wasn't properly closed. So I, the girls, we . . .'

Sarah pauses for a moment, her eyes catching briefly on the phone in the middle of the carpet, before continuing, her voice unsettled.

'I've left Mabel in the car, I should go back to her. Are you . . . I mean, I could take the girls back with me for the night, if you . . .'

'No. No, I really appreciate you bringing them home. Honestly, I was just going to get cleaned up, but I'm fine, thank you.'

I feel Sarah's eyes scanning my face.

'Actually, you know, that would be great. If you don't mind.'

Avoiding my daughters' eyes, I smile, the skin straining, and Sarah nods, placated, reaching out her hand as if to touch me, but I step back, unable to stop myself.

'No problem at all, Mabel will be thrilled. I was going to make cupcakes for dinner. What do you say, girls?'

There is an obedient mumble in response but I cannot make out their words.

Sarah places a reassuring hand on Stella's shoulder as she leads my daughters back down the stairs. Turning, she adds, 'I'm just down the road, if you need anything. You know what they say, a problem shared . . .'

I smile weakly, following them towards the stairs. Closing the door firmly behind them and pulling the chain, I notice the sky is already laced with black.

CHAPTER 67

Maria

They were doing to Anna exactly what they had done to Artemis, of course – the pills, the doctors who would attest to her madness, to her *instability* when it was all over; once they had silenced her for good.

The difference was that, unlike David's mother, Anna had no idea of the danger she was in. Unlike Artemis, she believed she had control, she thought she knew what she was doing. There is nothing more dangerous, more precarious, than a drunk who thinks she is sober.

CHAPTER 68

Anna

The sound of ringing from the bedside table lures me out of a heavy, medicated sleep, the grey sky already clawing its way through the curtains the following morning.

My head is thick, caught between day and night, teetering dangerously along the crack between two worlds, as I lift the phone. Looking at the screen I see it is not Harry but my new assistant, Lara, whose name flashes back at me.

Falling back against the pillow, I let the phone drop from my hand, rolling over into the blanket until I hear a beep, informing me of a new voicemail message.

'Anna, it's Lara. I'm so sorry to bother you, but a friend of yours came to the office and was very insistent that I call and tell you she is thinking of you and wanted to check you were OK. She asked me to pass on her number . . . Her name is Meg . . .'

As Lara started reciting the digits, I press delete.

Once again, my wallpaper blinks back at me: a photo of myself, Stella, Rose and David at the table outside the villa in Tuscany we had taken one summer, cypress trees lining the garden behind us, David's hands resting proprietorially on his daughters' shoulders.

I feel my finger move instinctively to his face, following the contours of his cheeks on the screen. The bed, once too small, is too big now, too still. The silence I had longed for as he had lain beside me is suddenly all-consuming.

It is the first time I have let myself think of him since he . . . I push back tears as the image of his body crushed and torn beneath twisted metal swells, unbidden, within me, rising through the pressure of the sleeping pills.

Hugging the pillow to my face, I hear the cries catch in my throat, the sound amplified through the duck-down pressed against my face. David would know what to do, he would know how to comfort the children in a way I could never fathom. Instinctively, he would place his hand on theirs, drawing them in, his breath pressing against their cheeks. He would make them safe.

But it is not just the girls who need him now, and there is only one person to blame. *This is your fault*. There is a hissing sound and it is a second before I realise it is my own voice, directed at Harry, blotting out the memory of Meg's words; the thought of him expanding in my head along with the endless lies.

Trying his number again on my second phone, the same automated female voice tells me to leave a message after the tone.

Fuck you, Harry. I picture his face and let the phone drop onto the covers.

The sound of ringing, a few minutes later, forces me to sit bolt upright in bed, picking up the receiver. But as I do so I see the screen is blank. It is another two rings before I remember my main phone, discarded on the floor beside my bed.

Lifting it resentfully, I read the words 'Unknown Number', my finger instinctively hovering over the 'cancel' button.

It will be Meg, no doubt.

Except, it could also be the girls' teacher. She had failed to hide her horror at the prospect of the twins returning so soon after their father's funeral, being more concerned at the prospect of having to confront the girls' grief, no doubt, than for the welfare of Rose and Stella. The truth is, while I believe the girls are better off busy than wallowing in their loss, it is equally true that I am too afraid of their sorrow, even more so.

I bring the screen towards my face. When I see his name, my body freezes, the way it always has; the spectre of him so much more overwhelming than the actual person.

For a moment I am grateful. Clive will know what to do. Clive, the only connection to David I have left.

Pushing myself to sitting position, I press the green button, clearing my throat before I speak, but he gets in there first.

'Anna? It's me.'

My voice floats somewhere outside my body as I listen to him read out the address of the solicitor's office where we arrange to meet the following day, a faceless building a stone's throw from Queen Square.

'David's will. We need to wrap things up.'

His words sound hollow; there is something in his voice I cannot read. I hear him topping up his glass at the end of the line.

'Where are you now?'

I need to picture him as he talks, picture his loss, as a separate matter from my own. I try to summon some sense of justice from the ultimate evening of scores. His son snatched from him, just as the children killed as a result of the chemical dump had been snatched from their parents. But in the end, I feel nothing.

'Can you be there by nine?'

I nod before speaking. 'Yes.'

'And the girls?'

'They'll be at nursery.'

Clive is quiet for a moment. 'Good.' He pauses and then adds, 'He loved you, you know?'

His voice has shifted. I inhale sharply, feeling my breath slice against my sides like a knife.

CHAPTER 69

Maria

David and I spent the morning in our usual spot, seated at the back of one of the chain coffee shops on Caledonian Road. It was a stone's throw from the football pitches where he played on Saturday mornings, and a short walk from the library where I had spent the past two hours staring at a blank page, no longer interested in the pile of books in my backpack, passing the time before his game was over and we would take our place opposite one another, the strip-lighting illuminating the Formica countertop.

It was the sort of place David could count on not being discovered by anyone he knew, and his hand rested on mine, his thumb moving back and forth against my knuckle.

He had been distant all morning. Driving from the house he remained silent, without so much as attempting to stroke my knee. By the time he finally joined me at the coffee shop, I was terrified of what might be on his mind. But then, with only the slightest prompting, the floodgates opened. If ever I needed proof that I was his confidante, this was it. As soon as he had started to speak, he could not stop.

'I didn't believe my father at first, when he told me. We had gone for dinner, the three of us, to celebrate Anna's promotion. It was the loveliest night, and then she went home early and my dad and I went on for a drink at his club. We had just found out Anna was pregnant and I knew she didn't want me to say anything, but I couldn't stop myself. I was so bloody excited.

'As soon as we were in the cab on the way there, I felt him change. I assumed, at first, he was distracted by work or something else. We got to the club, we ordered drinks and as soon as they arrived, I told him. I blurted it out. Anna was pregnant. We were having a baby. I didn't know then that there were two of them. But it turns out that was the least of the things I didn't know.'

David let out a laugh and shifted slightly in his seat, silent for a moment before continuing. 'When I told him, he didn't say anything at first. It was as if he hadn't heard me; he just answered that he had something important to tell me. I remember his words exactly. He said, "David, I'm not sure how else to say this, but your friend, Anna, she's not who you think she is."'

The movements of David's thumb stopped and he looked up at me, his eyes almost glazed.

'It was the night of my father's party, in Greece, that they had found out. The one where I finally saw you again. The funny thing was, he already knew there was a mole, he'd got wind of it from one of his contacts, but he thought it was Jeff. Jeff was always a loose cannon, and my father assumed he was the one selling him out. So he had Jorgos follow him, and Jorgos caught her coming out of the study. After that, my father checked the camera, and it was all there. My girlfriend, *the love of my life*, snooping around in his office.'

David shook his head, laughing to himself, before biting his lip.

'And you know, I still didn't believe him. Despite everything. I convinced myself it was an honest mistake, that she had just been looking for a pen or . . .' He shook his head. 'I know, fucking ridiculous. But what . . . I was supposed to believe that she was a *spy*? I was supposed to believe the woman I was in love with, the woman carrying my baby, was using me to . . .'

His voice trailed off, and then started again.

'For a while I blamed Jeff. I thought he and Jorgos must have been in on it together . . . setting Anna up in order to cover their own tracks.'

My throat was constricting. For want of something to distract my hands, I reached for my cup and took a sip, the coffee unexpectedly hot, scalding my lip.

'But my dad, he wouldn't give up; he wouldn't stop going on and on about how she was a fraud. He had seen her passport. She wasn't born in Wiltshire at the airbase at Boscombe Down, like she told us; she was born in Surrey, and that is exactly where she grew up. An unremarkable life in an unremarkable family, as she stayed until she met me . . . Her mother wasn't even dead.'

His fingers were pressed against the side of the table, his knuckles white. But his voice wavered with disbelief rather than anger.

'But even then, I kept thinking there's got to be an explanation. For months, I believed there had to be an explanation. But my dad wouldn't drop it, so eventually I set a trap. A few weeks before she was due to give birth, I went out and left my father's laptop on the table next to my bed. And I actually felt bad. Even doing that, doubting her just for a second. Then I came home, and it was the day she went into labour – in our room. I came back and her waters had broken, and next to her was the computer, under the duvet on the floor, and it was on. And when I looked at her, her face . . . That was it. I knew.'

Unaffected by my silence, David had hardly paused for breath, something inside him having opened that could not easily be closed again before purging years' worth of stale, festering emotions. And then he stopped.

For several minutes, we sat in silence, his eyes set somewhere in the distance while the memories churned around his head, until once more the words spilled out.

The coffee in front of me was cold and grey by the time he spoke again.

'You know, I might have felt like a fool, if it hadn't also been made clear that she had no idea who she was actually working for. All of this, and she hadn't even bothered to check. Can you imagine that?'

I felt a prickle of hairs along my arms.

'That man, that reject journalist scum she was fucking – did I tell you that bit? No? Oh yeah, she was bending over for him at the same time as taking every penny my family ever gave her, lapping up every opportunity we offered. And the girls, they—'

He looked up, and then something stopped him continuing with his sentence. He picked up the stirrer and moved it absent-mindedly around in his cup.

'You know, sometimes I try to picture her face the moment the penny drops at how she's been played. Oh, to be a fly on the wall the moment she discovers that all along she was actually working for one of the biggest crooks in Central Africa.'

He was talking to himself now. Whether or not I was present was neither here nor there. I was the one into whose arms he fell, believing he had already been more betrayed than he could ever be.

CHAPTER 70

Maria

It was nearly two weeks after that Saturday with David that I finally heard from Felicity again. I had been making my way back from church, when she stepped out from the shadows in Holly Walk. It was the first time she had ever approached me so close to home and the audacity of it unnerved me.

'Let's walk,' she said, leading the way along the backstreets towards West Heath. She stopped at a small café and ordered tea for both of us.

I had imagined she would jump out of her skin when I told her what David had said: that the corporate investigation into TradeSmart's business had actually been commissioned by Francisco Nguema, who hired the company to investigate the mercaptan spill in Equatorial Guinea with the sole intention of finding out how traceable his own role in the affair could be.

'From what I've been looking into, it seems Nguema used a company registered in the UK, Strategic Services – ostensibly owned by Witherall and Mayhew. Presumably this made it easier for him to move goods in and out of the country, undetected. British cargo: such a reputable nation – who would question it? In return, he offered TradeSmart the kind of contacts and access that a corrupt warlord can afford in Central Africa . . .'

But she hardly blinked.

'Oh, we know all about that.'

'You knew? But I don't understand.'

The idea to me was unfathomable at the time, but Felicity shrugged as if it was the most obvious thing in the world.

'Think about it. You're the client – you're paying this private investigations firm God knows how much money – so they are never going to hand you over to the authorities, regardless of what they find. It's the perfect testing ground, isn't it? Who better to pay to test your own fallibility – your own traceability – than an esteemed UK investigations company? The same company that has some of the country's biggest corporations, from banks and law firms to newspapers, as clients – using ex-MI6, ex-MI5, ex-coppers, journalists, some of the world's greatest analysts, to do its dirty work, without ever asking awkward questions – and without ever sharing the results with anyone but you?'

I nodded, letting her pick up the paper cup of tea before I spoke quickly, desperate to catch her attention.

'David's leaving. He's found out the girls aren't his, and he's moving to the Maldives. He's asked me to go with him.'

I expected her to pounce on my words, but slowly she took a sip of her tea before placing the cup carefully back on the table in front of her. 'And I suppose Anna knows about none of this?'

She didn't wait for my reply. We had never discussed Anna's role in all of this, though of course if I had figured out what she was involved in with Harry, there was little doubt that MI6 had too.

'Poor Anna.' Felicity rolled her eyes. 'We actually tried to recruit her for ourselves a couple of times, thinking if she would work for them, there would be little reason why she wouldn't work for us, as well. So we dug around a bit more and it turned out she had no idea what she was involved in. Frankly, I think she's a liability. I'm rather pleased we didn't get her on board. One has to be so careful.'

She sighed perfunctorily, before dismissing the thought and drawing breath.

'Look, Maria. The reason I wanted to meet you today is to tell you that the case has been pulled.'

'*What?*'

'The situation I mentioned, it's been resolved.' She smiled, as if this was good news.

'So they are being charged?'

She pursed her lips. 'Actually, no. But turns out it isn't our problem any more. The situation we needed to resolve in our territory has been otherwise dealt with, and, well, this is no longer our concern, or yours for that matter. So, you're off the hook.'

The breath caught in my throat as I processed the meaning of what she was saying.

'But, the arms dealing, the people trafficking . . . What do you mean?'

I felt my voice rising. A man on a nearby table lifted his head from his laptop and flashed a look in my direction.

Felicity shrugged.

'Like you said when we first met, TradeSmart isn't registered in the UK. The spill, it's a matter for the African authorities.'

'But you said they would just get away with it if it stayed in Africa – you said there would be enough back-handers to—'

'Oh Maria, look, I'm sorry but you're not getting this. This is no longer my case. Frankly, it's no longer anything to do with you. If I were you, I would go back to Greece, take the money you've earned and get on with your life. Or continue your studies here. Live. Don't take it so personally, hey? You've been brilliant. We have so appreciated having you onside.'

CHAPTER 71

Anna

'Is Clive not joining us?'

I follow the solicitor's brisk pace into his office, a large square space, empty except for a desk in the middle, one chair either side. A window runs the length of the room, exposing a blank sky.

'Couldn't make it, I'm afraid. He had an urgent appointment. Please do sit down.'

He is younger than I had expected, dressed in a suit with no tie, his hair pulled behind his ears. I half-expect him to perch at the corner of the table rather than to sit, but eventually he moves into the chair opposite mine, leaning back, his legs spread wide apart.

The room is airless and stale. Self-consciously, I press down my skirt, undoing one of the buttons on my suit jacket, feeling over-dressed, suffocated by the smell of my own perfume.

'As I believe Clive mentioned to you on the phone, I'm James McCann and I'm overseeing the estate of David Witherall. Please accept my sincere condolences for your loss. I didn't know David long, but he was, by all accounts, an exceptional man.'

I nod, wishing I had accepted the secretary's offer of a drink when I arrived. My mouth is dry, my tongue sticking to the side of my teeth.

'I won't keep you long. There are just some papers to sign, but first, although Clive couldn't be here, there was something he wanted me to give you.'

I hold the solicitor's eye as he hands me the envelope – A4, brown paper – his expression blank.

Not daring to look away, I let my fingers slip inside, slowly pulling out a larger piece of paper, folded in half to fit.

It takes me a moment to realise that I have to unfold the sheet. When I do, I see it is a printout of a newspaper article, with tomorrow's date in the top corner.

'Please do go ahead . . .' He hurries me with his hands, smiling as he flicks through papers on his desk. 'As I say, Clive really was gutted he couldn't be here with you for this.'

My throat closing in on itself, I focus my eyes on the words in my hands, alongside a photo of myself and David, taken the night of the charity auction; there is a slight smile on David's face, his eyes turned towards me as I stare absently at the camera.

The late socialite David Witherall has claimed responsibility for the dumping of tons of toxic waste in Equatorial Guinea, causing the death of innocent civilians including children and babies.

In a letter exclusively obtained by this newspaper, Witherall, heir to the leading trading company TradeSmart, admitted he and his wife, magazine editor Anna Witherall, had masterminded the chemical dump in a bid to avoid necessary treatment costs to dispose of the toxic waste product.

The CEO and heir to the TradeSmart business, which was worth $76 billion at the time of the dump, hired a small local firm to illegally dispose of raw toxic waste, near a children's playground in a residential area of Equatorial Guinea, along with his then-girlfriend.

Organised by the pair when they were in their early twenties, while living together in the Witherall family home in Hampstead where they hosted frequent parties, more than 300 tons of the deadly chemical compound mercaptan, referred to in emails between the company's staff as 'slops' and 'crap', was offloaded in a residential area in Bata. As a result, 22 died and hundreds more suffered symptoms including burns and respiratory problems. The case has also been linked to a spate of miscarriages in the surrounding area.

Clive Witherall, who is in the late stages of an aggressive form of cancer, has denied all knowledge of the dump, and has passed on copies of correspondence between his son and daughter-in-law. A receipt for the cargo, which was erroneously abandoned near a playground by local delivery drivers after they panicked over the smell of the toxic waste, has been handed to police along with a letter hand-written by David Witherall not long before he died, after being hit by a car.

The former magazine editor and mother of two, Anna Witherall, has battled mental health problems since childhood when she underwent professional treatment following the loss of her brother, and suffered extreme postnatal depression after the birth of her twin daughters in 2016.

In an interview with this paper, Clive Witherall, who only has months to live, also claimed an investigation would be launched into David's death, which he believes could have been arranged by those wishing to silence him once it became clear he planned to hand himself in to police.

In a statement yesterday, Mrs Witherall's former boss Clarissa Marceaux told this newspaper she was shocked by the revelations, and confirmed that Anna Witherall would no longer be employed by the company.

Clive Witherall added: 'It is with great regret that I accept a degree of responsibility for the actions of my company, TradeSmart. Although I had no knowledge of it at the time, it is only right that I recognise that I failed to prevent this terrible misdemeanour, leading to the tragic loss of innocent lives.

'I have always said that corporate responsibility stands at the heart of, and has been the driver for, all that we do at TradeSmart. In my years as a businessman I have always strived to hold the highest standards of corporate responsibility, not just through our

own behaviours but through our foundation and our sponsorship programme.

'It is with great personal remorse that I must tell you that in the weeks following the death of my son, David, I received a letter from him, confessing to what had become to him a very heavy burden. In the letter, David revealed that under a degree of pressure from his wife, who I have since learnt had been duping my son from the moment they first met, the pair hired a local firm in Equatorial Guinea to dispose of waste materials, to avoid costs.

'My son accepted he acted with terrible misjudgement after falling for the charms of his wife, who entered our lives under a veil of deceit – and he was subsequently plagued by the ramifications of his actions in the years leading to his untimely death.'

The lawyer keeps his eyes on the papers he is shuffling on his desk.

'As for the will, apparently David had a paternity test done in the months before his death and, well, it turns out he isn't actually the father, so there isn't any reason to leave anything to the girls, or, of course, to you . . . But I'm sure you already know that.'

His eyes suddenly flick upwards to meet mine, and I see he is no longer smiling.

'You have until this evening to clear out of the house, or this piece runs as the splash in tomorrow's paper.'

CHAPTER 72

Maria

The taxi David has ordered is due to pick me up at the hotel at 1 p.m., exactly as planned. I will be dressed in the demure button-down tunic dress he bought for me at one of the boutiques on the high street, together with a pair of pretty leather sandals, one of a number of parcels I found stashed in my cupboards or under my pillow over the past months. My final transformation into the image of the woman with whom he intends to live out the rest of his life is almost complete.

I have stayed the night in the room Anna booked me into by way of atoning for my untimely dismissal. The strength it must have required to ask me to leave gave me some hope for her future, what ever that may hold. The decision brings me some comfort as I brush out my hair at the dressing table in front of the window overlooking the church on Portland Place: an omen of sorts, I do not doubt, though whether good or bad, I cannot yet be sure.

There is no need to bring anything, David has explained. There will be a suitcase full of clothes waiting for me when we meet at the airport. For a moment I wonder whether if, in the days to come, Anna will wander along the high street and notice the shoes she gave me for my birthday in the window of the charity shop, where I had deposited my belongings on my way from the house.

I stop myself. What a foolish thought; there will be no time for window shopping. Not for her, not after today. Not once she has had her meeting with the lawyer. But it is imperative that I think of Anna as someone with a future. At this point, I cannot allow myself to engage with the alternative.

I leave my hotel room at 8 a.m., giving myself enough time to do what I have to and still get back in time for the driver David has arranged to collect me from reception.

But for now, I duck into my first taxi, the one about which David knows nothing. The one that forms the first stepping stone on the final journey to salvation.

As the car turns in a wide U before sweeping along Portland Place, towards Regent's Park, I think of those first days in London, having been brought in as much to watch over Anna as to care for her daughters.

'You'll be our eyes and ears, Maria. Anna, she's . . . volatile.' Clive had taken me aside one afternoon in the Maldives, talking to me like an old friend. 'We have our concerns. I know you can be trusted. You're like family to David and me.'

I had gripped the side of my shorts with my fists to stop my fingers from trembling.

At this time of morning it takes just twenty minutes to reach Hampstead Heath station. As I step out of the taxi, approaching the house on foot, the key I have secretly had duplicated pressed in my pocket, I think of the first time David touched me, in that room just there, the girls asleep upstairs.

Given this is the last time I will ever be here, I allow myself a moment to take it all in: the wisteria creeping up perfectly formed London bricks, the curve of the iron railing that lines the steps. To the random passer-by, this is London at its most picturesque. Few could imagine what secrets lay beyond these perfect windows.

'Arms dealing, people trafficking, a child brothel, frequented by older men at a very high price.' This was how Felicity had first described the horrors she was inviting me to help rally against.

The operation by MI6 into TradeSmart's extensive roll-call of nefarious activities, she explained, had been ongoing for years, but they were finally at a crucial stage. Thanks to an inside man, one of Clive's closest colleagues, they were near to bringing the whole thing down, but what they needed was someone else on the inside, someone who could get closer to the family without being seen, to keep an eye on things.

'Inside man? Who, Jeff?' Another thought struck me. 'Jorgos?'

Felicity's eyes remained impassive, holding mine a beat too long. 'I'm afraid I can't tell you any more than that.'

It is 8.45 a.m. as I make my way up the front steps of the house. By now Anna will already be on her way to see Clive's lawyer, as David has proudly made me aware. Yet still my eyes scan for signs of life within as I climb one tread at a time, stopping for a moment before knocking tentatively at the front door, pushing my fingers through the postbox and checking for any hints that I am not alone.

Only once I am sure it is safe to enter do I slide the key from my pocket and turn it in the lock.

Knowing I have to be as quick as possible, I only allow myself a moment to linger in front of the photo of Stella and Rose, the girls who I raised from birth, the girls whose lives will be destroyed along with their mother's. Unless . . .

Breathing deeply, I walk towards the kitchen and pull two notes from my pocket. The first is in my own handwriting. I have deliberated for hours over my wording, but in the end I tell her as much as I know. However you say it, it sounds incredible. How I wish that it was.

Anna.

I know this will be hard for you to accept but David is alive. He and Clive are planning to have you killed, just as Clive did with his own wife, when she started to question the business. They will make it look like suicide and they will tell everyone that you were mad. You must leave the house immediately. You are not safe here. Please, as soon as you have read this letter you must burn it – if you don't I will be uncovered and I will not be able to finish what we started. So please, burn the letter, take the girls, and run. I have made contact with Harry and together we will make sure of everything else. You can trust us.

Love, Maria

CHAPTER 73

Anna

My body moves on its own, back through McCann's office; the lawyer is still speaking, his secretary's pursed face following me towards the door.

I hail a taxi on Queen Square, my arm flying out of its own accord, my voice detached from my body as I say our address for the last time.

As the engine starts, I feel the seat slide under me. My body is unnaturally still, as if cast from stone. In the rear-view mirror I feel the taxi driver's eyes fixed on me, and when I look up he doesn't turn away.

There is a click and instinctively my eyes move to the light on the door, which glows red, telling me the doors are already locked.

Suddenly there is a crackle and then the driver's voice calls over the microphone in the back of the cab.

'You're ringing?'

I start at the sound of his voice. Confused, I put my hand tentatively into my pocket and draw my phone out, as if it were a blade. There is a missed call from Sarah, followed by a text.

I'll take the girls to ballet after nursery then give them supper at mine. See you 6-ish. Sx.

The driver's voice clicks back over the speakers, 'You all right, love?'

* * *

The moment I push open the front door, I know someone else has been here, though I cannot pinpoint what has changed: a smell; a feeling; a picture frame on the hall table, slightly off set. The letters stand on the kitchen table, two innocuous white envelopes, my name on the front of the first, drawn in looped ink.

The sight of Harry's writing makes my legs bow, and once again Meg's words roll through my head.

'He wouldn't leave me alone. A month or so after that night we met him in Canary Wharf – you, me and David – I bumped into him. After that, it was like everywhere I went he would suddenly be there. We started talking more. You know, he was really charming and made this joke out of the fact that I must be following him because we always ended up in the same places.'

I can taste the acid rising through my body. Clutching the envelope, I sink to my knees, placing my hands over my ears to blot out the sound of her voice stinging my ears.

'At first it was just sex. He was fun, you know. I wasn't in love with him or anything, but he was always up for a laugh and he had this amazing flat and . . . And then, one day, we'd done a few lines and he tells me he's a spy.

'I know, it sounds insane but that's what he told me. He said he was working as a spy trying to gain access to David in order to find information on his dad.'

This time she slowed her words, making space for me to interrupt. Desperate, it seemed, for an interception that never came.

'And you know what? It turned out all along he thought he could recruit me to get to David.'

She let out a shrill laugh at the idea, dragging deeply on her cigarette, coughing harshly into fingerless gloves. 'I mean, who the fuck did he think I was? David was my friend. The idea that he thought he could shag me and then get me to do his dirty work . . .'

Her eyes furrowed together as she took a deep pull on her cigarette, squeezing the filter so hard that it was almost flat.

She laughed then, the sound making me turn; above us, a pair of green parakeets shot out of a tree, followed by a piercing cry.

But it was Harry's voice I heard as I looked down on the Heath, pressing against my ear; the sombre cadence of the priest at the funeral service; the deafening sorrow of Stella's cries as David's casket was lowered into the ground, drowned out only by Rose's silence.

Through the swell, I became aware of Meg's voice, starting again, her hand reaching desperately for mine.

'I said no. Obviously I said no. I need you to know that. Straight away. I mean, I freaked out. What the fuck? He told me I didn't have a choice, that he knew I sold David drugs, and if I didn't do it, he would expose me. He said he had photographs, of me and David, that he would go to the police and the press, tell them I was pushing drugs to the son of this major socialite. The bastard.

'I was scared, really like freaked out, as you can imagine. I said I'd think about it. I didn't know what else to say. After that, I went back to Newcastle for a couple of weeks. Trying to sort my head out. It was when we had just moved in together, you remember?'

She didn't wait for an answer.

'When I came back, I told him I wouldn't do it. I mean, I thought he was probably talking shit about the photographs. So I called his bluff.'

Meg slowed suddenly as a man with an ageing Staffordshire Bull Terrier walked past, the dog stepping in time with his owner. The man looked up, aware of the growing silence between us, sitting at either end of the bench, our legs tightly crossed.

Once he'd gone past, Meg turned back to me, her eyes wild with need.

'Do you mind me telling you this? I know it's the wrong time, in a way. I know you don't need anything more, but also I needed you to know, now more than ever. With David gone, I've wanted to tell you why . . . You must have hated me.'

'I didn't hate you.' The words came out without me forming them.

Meg stopped, her shoulders relaxing, eyes closing for a second. 'Thank you.'

But I hated her now, as she pulled her sleeve across her cheek, drying the tears.

'I wanted to tell David. I wanted to warn him, but Harry . . . When I told him I wouldn't do it, he went mental. He started black-mailing me. One day he turned up at the flat with a picture.'

She stopped again, rolling her fingers under her eyes.

'The picture was me and David talking – we were just talking, I swear to God, Anna – but it looked like . . . I don't know, it looked like we were together, holding hands or something. But he never wanted that.'

There was a note of regret in Meg's voice and when I looked at her, she looked away, wiping a tear from her face.

'You and David?'

She shook her head. 'He never wanted me. It was always you. Once I knew that, I backed off. I never . . . But yeah, if you want to know the truth, I loved David. I really did. I'm sorry if it hurts to hear that, but he didn't want me; I could see how much he wanted you, and I would never, ever have hurt him . . . And then Harry sent me another picture of me handing David a wrap – it might even have been David handing drugs to me – I wasn't a dealer, for fuck's sake.'

She shook her head, lifting her thumb to her mouth, chewing the skin, her eyes wet at the corners.

'But Harry had looked up my parents' home address. He was going to send them the pictures, tell the police I was dealing to half of bloody London, if I didn't leave; he was going to tell my work. He had a couple of baggies I'd left at his flat, with my fingerprints on them, obviously, and he said he was going to give them to the police too. The other option was, he'd give me a few quid to leave. I didn't have a choice.'

She took a final drag of her cigarette before flicking it into the grass, tugging at the stumps of her gloves, one by one.

'Please say something.'

I was trying not to be sick, pushing away the image writhing in front of my eyes. Harry and Meg? For a moment I told myself she was lying. It was a set-up, another test, like Felicity. And yet.

Finally, my mouth opened and the words slipped out.

'Why didn't you tell me you were sleeping with him?'

'I wasn't. Anna, I told you, Harry was making it up. I would never. I mean, David and I were only ever—'

'I'm not talking about David. Harry, Meg. Why didn't you tell me you were sleeping with Harry? We lived together . . .'

My voice faded out as I pictured our flat. The nights Harry would be out and I would call him and he was never there. Working away, that's what he said.

She paused for a moment, bemused. 'I didn't want him to get in trouble. I mean, he said it would have made things difficult. I had been an intern at the paper the day he was fired; he was still in the middle of the court-case . . . He said it could have been misconstrued.'

I snorted a laugh, my body bending forward on the bench, but Meg did not stop. 'Anyway, it wasn't a big deal. I didn't think it was worth even talking about . . . I mean, Jesus, Anna, I've just told you some guy was trying to recruit people to spy on your husband and that's the question you're asking?'

'I'm just trying to get my head around it. What you're saying is very confusing . . . So you said no?'

I kept my voice controlled, focusing on the smell of smoke rising from the chimney of the park ranger's house in the distance. Counting the rise and fall of Meg's breath. Anything to distract from the image forming in my mind.

'Of course I said no, for God's sake. That's what I'm telling you. I said no and I left. I went to Bristol, like I told you, and got a bedsit with the money he gave me, which was enough to tide me over while I did work experience at the local paper and . . . I sorted my life out. You know? Met my boyfriend, who was working as a local MP, and in the end I got a job working in the PR department for the council. Can you believe that? Talk about selling out, but, you know, it was what it was.'

She took a moment to process the sorry minutes of her life, laid bare, strand by pathetic strand. A moment later she turned back to where I sat, my eyes transfixed by the movements of a large black dog, bounding away from its owner at the bottom of the hill.

Meg turned her body as if to move closer, but stopped herself at the last moment.

'And the next thing I heard, you and David were an item. I'm just so sorry, Anna, I should have told you sooner. I should have warned you, but . . . The whole thing was such a head-fuck. You probably think I just ran off and never thought of you guys again, but I never forgot. I never forgot what Harry had done to me, or David, but I got distracted. Tom and I, we had a little girl. Maisie. She was ill, she is ill. She has learning difficulties which make it hard to . . . Well, it was all quite hard, and for a while I had other things on my mind. But I never forgot.

'A few months ago, when Maisie started pre-school and I had a bit more time to myself, I started thinking about it again. About the things Harry had told me, and I just couldn't stop thinking that something just wasn't right. Things didn't add up. I mean, I was too scared to question it at the time, but then a few months ago I started looking into him, into his background, I even found out where he was living . . . It's amazing what you can find out when you put your mind to it.

'I wanted to confront him, but the truth is I was scared – as much as anything about what I might do. I was so angry. I think Tom sensed it. In the end, he offered to go to London, to look for Harry's flat and watch him for a couple of days. It was ridiculous. I suppose he might have been humouring me. If I'm honest, I'm not sure he believed me. I think he was trying to prove I had imagined it, that I'd built up this narrative in my mind to exonerate myself for leaving a perfectly good job, or something. Either that, or he just knew how badly I had to know.

'Anyway, one morning he went to Harry's flat and he nicked the recycling bag from outside his flat. Can you imagine? The whole thing was farcical. But actually it was pretty brilliant, because from his bank statements I found a series of payments from a company called Central Intelligence Solutions. It sounded like some sort of IT firm, but when I looked into it, it's actually this so-called investigation and defence agency. A sort of corporate spy agency, basically.'

The ground at my feet was cold and split. Hundreds of tiny fracture lines, invisible at first, rising steadily through the soil.

'I don't understand.' My voice was distant, as if coming through the end of a bad phone line.

Meg paused for a moment, slowing her breath to match mine. 'I'm sorry, I'm ranting. I've just been waiting so long to speak to you about all this, and I know it's too much to take in at once but . . .

She looked up. 'I'm sorry, this is too much. Right now, while you're grieving . . . It was selfish, but when I heard David had died, I just knew I had to tell you.'

The whole heath had slowed to match her pace. My lips moved.

'Did you ever think you could do it? If it was for the right reason.'

Meg flinched in her seat, pushing a strand of hair behind her ear, watching me pull my cardigan closer across my chest, my whole body folding in on itself.

Her forehead crumpled, her hand reaching out to mine at last. 'Come on, Anna. What do you think?'

She watched her words, not seeing how they rolled over my skin, singeing the hairs, forcing me to flinch in silent pain.

Meg stopped, pulling a cigarette from the packet on the bench. As I watched her, I felt my body constrict, the walls of my ribs pressing in so tightly that I felt I might crack. Making to stand, I placed one hand on the cold wooden slats, my body leaning into it, the smell of smoke from the park ranger's cottage seeping its way into my lungs. The hill in front of me seemed to sway, tilting sideways; my eyes fixed for a moment on a single crow lunging overhead as my head hit the ground.

CHAPTER 74

Maria

The day before I was due to meet David at the airport, I had taken a short walk from my hotel to Regent's Park. I already knew from my Google searches what to expect as I approached, the stretch of Nash buildings behind me, along the path that curved towards the bench where I had insisted we meet. I recognised his face from the photographs online, the unnaturally blue eyes the computer screen had failed to do justice.

'Harry?'

He looked up, his eyes narrowing sharply as they met mine before looking around, instinctively, for signs of company.

I could not be sure that he would come, after my call from the phone box the day after Felicity 'let me go'. I had stolen his number from Anna's phone with such ease that I wondered how she ever thought she was fooling anyone.

Taking a seat, I held out my hand.

'My name is Maria. Like I said on the phone, I'm a friend of Anna's. I also believe we have another person in common.'

'Another person in common, you say?' His accent was soft and I could instantly see from the way he held his face, the intensity of the eyes, what had drawn Anna in; though I would not be making that mistake.

Harry raised the cigarette to his lips and inhaled, the paper burning at the edges.

'Yes. I think until now, you and I have been working from different angles, towards the same common goal. And I think we could help each other, if we joined forces.'

Something clicked, a look of intent forming at the corners of his mouth.

'Is that right?'

Unnerved by the depth of his stare, I looked down for a moment and then lifted my head.

'If you're anything like me, you're not going to want to see him get away with it. After everything we've given to bringing them to justice?'

'We?'

'Yes, we . . .'

'What are we talking about here?'

Harry kept his expression cool, taking another drag of his cigarette as he looked out across sculpted hedges circling an ornamental fountain.

'I assume you've heard about David.'

Harry raised an eyebrow, his voice measured. 'I read something about it. The funeral was a few days ago, wasn't it?'

'David's not dead.'

I watched his face turn towards me, and I smiled.

'Now you're listening? David is alive and is fleeing to the Maldives – tomorrow evening – where, as I'm sure you know, there is no extradition treaty, so once he is there, he's free. MI6, they're no longer interested. The African authorities, from what I gather, because of Nguema's involvement and how much influence he has there, they aren't in a hurry to prosecute. If anyone does try to fit him up for it, there is a plan to lay the blame on Anna. So the way I see it, there are only two people left on this earth who care about bringing Clive to justice. And one of us has been asked to accompany David to the Maldives, as his mistress.'

Harry cocked his head, exhaling a long line of smoke, his face breaking into a smile.

'Well, I certainly didn't get the memo. OK, now I'm listening.'

'Anna is due to meet with Clive's solicitors about the will. David and I are meeting at the airport tomorrow afternoon. He wanted to be sure everything went smoothly in terms of Anna's reaction to the meeting she is due to have with his father's solicitors, tomorrow morning, so he has been lying low at his father's flat, "getting his ducks in order", that's what you say. Right?'

'I definitely don't say that.'

I paused then, unable to stop myself. 'Why did you do it?'

'Do what?' His expression was one of genuine bemusement.

'All of it. I mean, there must have been easier ways to make money . . .'

Harry raised a hand at this, as if the idea of being in it for the money offended him.

'Seriously, I'm intrigued. I know why I did it, but I can't work out . . .'

Harry smiled then, as if considering something for the first time. 'But life's not like that, is it? It's not that straightforward. You must know that as well as I do. You make decisions as and when situations arise; you take steps and you never really know where they will take you. You just do what you think is right in that moment; sometimes you're right, and sometimes—' His voice stopped abruptly. 'Well, maybe I was right, maybe I was wrong. Maybe we all were. It just depends what angle you're looking at it from.'

CHAPTER 75

Anna

A half-light falls across the kitchen through the doors from the garden. I hold the letter in front of my face, the words blurring through the tears which refuse to fall.

Dear Anna,

I could not let you leave without sending this note.

By now you'll no doubt have heard that I have not been entirely honest. My reasons were complex, but what you need to know is that I didn't know who the client was. I never knowingly deceived you, Anna. I promise you that – and I swear to you, in that sense, at least, my intentions were always good.

One of my great regrets is not being able to tell you about Meg. I have an inkling of how much it hurt you, her leaving so suddenly like that, and I want you to know it was my fault. She didn't choose to abandon you. I made a mistake, thinking she was the one who could lead me to David. And when she pushed back, when it became clear that it was you who I needed, I had to scare her off. If she'd stayed she might have let it slip to you and I couldn't risk her jeopardising what we were doing. If I'm honest, I was cross with myself for not seeing straight away that you were the obvious target, because in hindsight I should have seen that you were more vulnerable, more susceptible to my approach. But then maybe I was sensing something about you that told me, despite everything, you are stronger than you think. And I need you to know that, because if you let yourself, you will be everything those girls need, and more.

Another regret is that I even let you carry on. Twice, when you held out on me, I had the opportunity to let you go. Perhaps, subconsciously, you were giving me permission to cut you loose, or perhaps that's looking too deeply into what happened. But still, I could have taken the chance to free you from this. I could have made up a reason to the agency for letting you go; better still, I could have warned you, and you and the girls could have fled. Before all this unravelled. Before we came to where we are now, the point of no return.

But at the time, I thought what we were doing was for the greater good. I believed that we were sacrificing ourselves in the name of justice. I was, for want of a better word, an eejit. In my defence, I only found out who we were dealing with long after I drew you into this; the man who told me was the same friend who had recruited me to the agency in the first place, at that stage not knowing himself what sort of rotten ship he was hauling me on board; the same man who warned me once he discovered who the client was, and tipped me off that Witherall knew too.

There was an informant inside the agency, you see, pushing word back, all along. And then he was discovered. You might have thought an ex-spook would know better than to contact the man he was tipping off from a company computer belonging to the investigations agency he was betraying, but sometimes you can't make this shit up.

Anna, as soon as I found out, I tried to get you out, but you wouldn't leave. After you told me what you had found out about Nguema, that day we met by Charterhouse Street, I was so furious at you for having held out on me, but I was ultimately furious with myself. You were right, it wasn't your fault, but there were things going on, things I couldn't tell you about. I was getting threats warning me to drop the case, which I now know were from

Clive's people. That on top of trying to deal with the work-load, and my guilt over what was happening to you . . . I was falling apart. It gets to you, this life. Not that I need to tell you that.

After we met on Charterhouse Street, I took the information back to my bosses, expecting them to cheer me on, expecting them to be thrilled. But after that, the case was suddenly pulled. That was as much as the client needed to know, they said. The case was now closed. It didn't make sense and the closer I looked into it, the more I realised there was to uncover. All along it was Nguema who was paying our salary, trying to find out how easily he could be implicated; how easily evidence against him could be found.

That was when the threats started to escalate. But I never stopped looking for the truth. When I saw you that night at the charity ball for David's old firm, I was with another of my informants, an old colleague of David's – I hadn't expected you to be there, which was foolish of me. And then when you sent me that message saying you were going to expose yourself, and me, well, I had to get rid of you.

I had to save your life – and mine. Sometimes I wonder what you thought you were getting yourself into. And I blame myself, for not being a better judge, for bringing you into something you did not deserve to be made part of.

In any case, that is when I came up with the plan of sending you back to Greece. I imagine you will know by now that that mission was an invention. Of course, the receipt was of no use to anyone, and frankly I didn't have much faith that it would still be there at all. All I was certain of was that if Witherall was involved with Nguema, the only way to ensure your safety was by sending you on that final mission. By getting you to leave for good.

But then, David.

The truth is I no longer feel safe, and you are not either. The men we were working for, they are, for want of a better word, bad people, Anna. I am so sorry for bringing you into this. I hope one day you will find a way to forgive me, for everything.

You have to do as Maria asks, and leave. You are not safe. Please, take your girls and go. Anywhere. One day maybe our paths will cross again, and in the meantime Maria and I have a plan to see this through, but you cannot be part of it, and I am so sorry that you ever were.

Now, you must go, and so must I. It is getting late, but then it always was.

Yours,
Harry

In that moment, I feel my life stop. The world, as I know it, grinding to a halt, so that when I look up, a moment later, I am surprised to find my eyes capable of movement, amidst the freeze-frame. Through the window of this room, in the garden, I see my daughters, careering down the hill on the balance bikes David had spent days researching, insisting it was the way to get them to understand how to ride unassisted by stabilisers.

I blink and they are gone, and I know now that I will never see them again.

As I hold the letter in front of my face, I notice, for the first time, that it is raining, and I blink again, trying to clear the images that have begun to rotate in my mind; the thoughts tumbling over each other now; the faces skidding in front of me: Harry, David, Felicity, Clive, Nguema, Maria, Meg, the girls.

Crying out, I feel my chest constrict, then a knock on the front door as the letter box opens and even from here, through the hallway, I see two eyes fix me from the outside world.

Before I can turn to run, I hear the voice.

'Anna, it's me. Open the door.'

*Acknowledgments*

Being unashamedly nosy, and interested in the mechanics of writing, I've always ogled the Acknowledgments pages of a novel with a mixture of curiosity and baffled wonder. How could a single book require quite so many 'thank yous'? Having finally come to the end of the writing process, myself – after 35 years of dreaming of this moment – I now understand how many hearts and minds (both stretched to the point of breaking, at times) are involved. It is no exaggeration when I say that without my agent, Julia Silk, I may never have finished this book. From the outset, she has rallied, mentored and urged me along when I might otherwise have closed my laptop and succumbed to the voice telling me to give up. Julia's determination, composure and unwavering belief in me, and this story, has been a guiding light, and I couldn't be more grateful or eternally indebted to her for all the support – and the fun – along the way.

My editor, Ann Bissell, is a master and a true joy to work with. Unflappable and whip-smart, she instantly understood what I wanted to achieve with this book, and how to draw the best from the world within its pages. Together with Felicity Denham – my personal champion and publicist extraordinaire – she and the gang at Borough Press have been the real-deal dream team.

Huge thanks to my first reader Laura Gerrard, whose passion for this book, and wisdom, spurred me on when I needed reassurance.

To Jason Bean (AKA #ShitSpy) for all your insights, I salute you. Thanks, too, to my Greek goddess, Vilma Nikolaidou. And massive love to my friends and fellow writers who have fed me wine and words of encouragement along the way, not least: Rebecca Schiller, Rebecca Ley Ellson, Alicia Kirby, Clare Dwyer Hogg, Wendy Ide, Ruth Whippman, Jess Clark, Bridie Woodward, Hannah Foster, Tamsin Clay, Emily Freud, Aoife Ledwidge, Charlotte Haworth, Alex Joyce, Louise McMahon, my book-club babes, and my brother from another mother, Henry Kirk. And to those who send love and encouragement from afar – not least my dear cousin, the original Anna.

Ultimately, though, nothing would be possible without the endless support and tireless love and energies of my long-suffering husband Barney, and my mum, who between them have been the foundations of everything. Thank you, a million times, thank you. Special thank you, too, to Sandra Fordham, for all that you've done and do.

To my dad, who would have enjoyed raising a toast (or 12) to this moment: bottoms up, old boy! To Mandy, Jo, Tommy, Harry, Greg, Glen, Mark and Lorna, with love, and to Grandma Joan and Grandpa Basil, whom I can almost hear cheering me along. Not forgetting Grampa Kimsky, whose curious endeavours became the genesis of this novel. Last, but by no means least, to my dear children: thank you for being the most astonishingly joyful, unconditionally loving, and wonderfully bonkers souls – and for understanding when I snap, or forget, or simply fall short in one of many ways. I love you to the moon and back.

Read on for an excerpt from Charlotte Philby's
new novel

A DOUBLE LIFE

9TH JULY 2020

Prologue

The woman's lips were blue, the same shade as the evening sky that shone in through the window, calm and unbroken.

The knot around her neck had been pulled tight. The note, propped against the hallway table, was short.

'I'm sorry, I couldn't do it. I love you both, please forgive me.'

Chapter 1

Gabriela

It is hardly warm enough to warrant an evening in the garden, but something about the house is pushing her out. After all these years, and all the memories she made here in her teens and early twenties before Tom had so much as set foot inside its four walls, their home is already taking his side. So when he goes out for a smoke, savouring the single roll-up he still allows himself each day now that he is staring down the barrel of forty, she follows him into the starless night.

Pulling on a jacket, she brings with her the slightly too warm bottle of Sauvignon she picked up at the off-licence near Dartmouth Park Hill on her way home, partly to calm her nerves, partly for the excuse to partition off this section of her life, to annex it safely away from the day she has just left behind. The beginning of the end.

'Ten ninety-nine?' Tom takes a swig of his beer, incredulity written in the lines above the bridge of his nose. She follows his gaze to the bottle she is clutching by the neck and for a moment she feels herself on the cusp of laughter that will mutate into sobs if she is not careful. Screams that will reverberate through the house where their children sleep.

How the hell are they talking about the price of a bottle of wine? But he has no reason to suspect this is anything but an ordinary evening, the end of a day just like any other.

'How was work?' he asks as she takes a seat beside him on one of the worn garden chairs. It shifts precariously on cracked paving, the same shoddy stones that have been there since her father first bought the place, more than two decades ago. The memory of those days, however complicated they might have seemed at the time, soothes her briefly.

'Work?' she repeats, buying herself time, wondering if Tom notices her bristle as she pictures her desk; the job she fought tooth and nail to get and then to keep.

Before she can answer, he continues, uncharacteristically forthright. 'I'm worried about you, Gabs. This case. Ever since you came back from Moscow . . .'

'Jesus, Tom, it's not supposed to be easy,' she snaps, immediately holding out her hands by way of apology. 'I'm sorry, I'm just tired.'

It is true, she thinks: *I am so tired.* It is not the whole truth but what more can she tell him? She is bound to secrecy, her lips have been sewn shut. As he watches her from across the lopsided plastic table, she registers the sound of a car moving too fast on the street outside. She imagines the needle pushing through the skin at the edges of her mouth. Instantly, she is transported to the bedroom upstairs, just a few weeks after she and her father had moved in. She and her best friend Saoirse in matching crop-tops, kneeling on the floor, her head level with the mattress, her earlobe flat against the CD case, which Saoirse has placed on the bed.

'You've burnt the needle properly, right?'

'Obviously,' Saoirse says as she clamps Gabriela's shoulder with one hand and with the other removes the ice cube she has been holding against her skin. Cold water trickles down Gabriela's neck. As her friend breathes in sharply, Gabriela feels the remaining ice slide to the floor, Saoirse holding her shoulder a little too tight as she pushes the pin through the soft nub of flesh.

More than twenty years later, she touches her earlobe. The memory of her own cries of pain, tinged with defiant euphoria, ricochets around her head as she looks up to the window of that same room, where now stands the goose-shaped lamp that keeps guard on Callum's windowsill. The lamp which, now that he is five years old, her son claims to have outgrown, though he never pushes the point. Secretly, she knows he is no more keen to grow up than she is to lose him to the girls and then the women or the men who will inevitably step in to claim him. The hands that would have taken him from her even if she hadn't already made it possible for them to be torn apart.

Sadie is in the kitchen, already dressed in school uniform, fastening the clips on the violin she chose for her most recent birthday, when Gabriela heads downstairs the following morning. Seven years old: how the hell did that happen? Briefly, she wonders what the fall-out will be for Sadie, after all this. Will it send her over the edge? But there is no point trying to second-guess her daughter, whose emotions are always more nuanced, less discernible than her own at the same age. There is an air of pointedness about Sadie's refusal to cause trouble for them in the way that Gabriela is prepared for that she finds unsettling. No, she reprimands herself, her fists tightening – it is not Sadie whose behaviour she needs fear.

'Mum, have you seen my sheet music?'

As her daughter speaks, Gabriela's eye catches the wine glasses from the night before, which stand marooned on the table where she is packing her school bag.

'This what you're looking for?' Tom squeezes past cradling a cup and drops the pristinely kept wad of paper onto her school bag, winking at her as he settles on one of the chairs squeezed up against the kitchen table.

'Made you a tea,' he says and Gabriela fixes her jaw into a smile, moving forward to clear away the cereal bowls that will otherwise languish until she comes home, and then she stops. *I will not be coming home.* She hears the words as a whisper between her temples. There is a brief moment when she is struck by the enormity of it, but then she sees her son walking into the room and instantly everything is as it was. Once again she is Sadie and Callum's mother and she is preparing for a normal day at the office, for a job that Tom watches her forfeit so much of their life together, without ever making her explain why. The job in which he has watched her rise through the ranks while he takes bit parts as a freelance architect, picking up the pieces without so much as a suppressed sigh.

'Want me to walk you in?' he asks Sadie, leaning back in his chair, rustling open yesterday's copy of the *Guardian*. Sadie throws him the same look she has been giving him since she was a toddler – something between despair and total adoration. For the past few weeks, Tom has let her make the short journey alone and Gabriela can't tell him why it makes her so uncomfortable, their child being so far out of their reach.

Enjoying the familiarity of the rapport between himself and Sadie, the reversal of the traditional parent/child roles, he shrugs, widening his eyes as if to say, *What? We don't have to leave for five minutes*.

'Leave the girl alone,' Gabriela plays along, batting his feet off the table as she passes, sweeping up the trail of cups and bowls and opening the dishwasher.

'I'll do that,' he calls over from his seat, without moving.

Ignoring him, she stacks the crockery in a neat row.

'Are you out tonight or in?'

'Jesus, Tom . . .'

'I know, I know, I'm messing with you! I hadn't forgotten. It's on the calendar, right there, where it always is. So you'll be back on Thursday?'

'That's right.' She swallows, keeping her eyes trained on the dirty cutlery she is placing in the stand.

'You're going away again?' It is Callum's voice this time, and her heart strains so that it feels like it might tear.

'Oi, what's so bad about hanging out with your old dad? Come on, love, Mum's got to work, you know that.'

It's always Tom's instinct to dive in to protect her from the decisions she has made, and his refusal to let her defend herself grates on her.

'I'll make it up to you,' she says, the lie lingering in her throat. 'I promise.'

* * *

As she opens the front door, she watches Sadie disappear around the corner of their street. Part of her wants to run after her daughter, to throw her to the ground and to hold them both there – to stop time, her face buried in Sadie's neck, and somehow to go back and unravel the knot. Not back, she scolds herself as she loses sight of her daughter, for the last time on this street. How could she think that?

The walk to Tufnell Park tube station helps clear her head, gently easing her mindset from the domestic world to her other life. The trees lining Dartmouth Park Hill radiate new energy, their shoots a reminder that whatever happens, the world will go on.

Preparing to cross at the traffic lights, she starts to think through everything she has to do, and only now does it strike her that she has failed to buy credit ahead of time for the second SIM card she keeps tucked in the lining of her handbag. She swears under her breath as the green man fades to red, cursing herself for allowing such a pivotal element to fall through the net. But it's pointless berating herself for it now – it is not an option, at this stage, to let things fall apart.

Heading into the newsagent's diagonally opposite the station, she skims the headlines of the newspapers to distract herself from the fear that pummels at her stomach as she makes her way through the aisles, making sure there is no one here she recognises, no one to pull her up on why she is using a burner, probing her with their hilarious quips about her being not a civil servant after all but a spy, or maybe a drug dealer.

It was the kind of joke Tom had made when she was seconded to Russia, her first posting after joining the FCO. And her last.

'What are you, some sort of double agent? Working for the FSB now, Gabs?'

But the jokes had stopped by the time she returned. In the days leading up to her most recent stint in Moscow, Tom had long since ceased laughing. By the time she got back he looked at her as though he didn't know her at all – and he was completely right.

'Seven months?' His look had been disbelieving at first, as if he had been waiting for her to remind him it was April Fool's Day.

'I know, it seems like a long time.' She felt sick but she couldn't let him understand how wrong this was. The situation had to be presented as non-negotiable – a necessary but surmountable task.

'What about the kids?' His face changed then. 'We could come with you. It could be an adventure. You always said you wanted one of those.'

Her cheeks burn as she remembers how quickly she had snapped her reply.

No.

It must have been impossible for him not to notice the change in her since she came back, but he has worked so hard not to push her on it. He does not comment on the physical shifts, which she can't avoid when she looks at her reflection. Nothing about her body is unscarred, though it is her mind that will truly never be the same.

Leaving the newsagent with her phone topped up, she crosses towards the tube station. The carriage is unusually empty as she settles onto a seat, taking out the Burberry trench coat she bought to match the boots she denied to Tom when he asked if they were new.

Holding her bag tightly on her lap as if holding on for her life, she feels the outline of the car keys press reassuringly against her fingers, through the leather. Distracting herself, she looks up at the map of the Northern Line. For a moment, she pictures herself walking through the arch at King Charles Street, greeting the security guards who know her name and those of her children by now. She imagines familiar faces as she makes her way towards the main entrance, collecting her bag as it emerges from the scanner, nodding to the receptionists before heading through the turnstiles, the sound of metal grating closed behind her.

Except today this is not her route. Now, as the train stops at Embankment, she stands back to let an older lady off the train first, before stepping out onto the platform, walking past the exit sign, following the arrows indicating the District Line. There is a chance she will see someone she knows from the FCO but they will not question it; the sight of her heading away from the office in the direction of the Westbound District Line will not cause them any concern.

Taking a seat a few metres along the platform, she listens to the wind whistling through the tunnel. It is both warm and cold, and as the train approaches she stands, registering the air brushing against her face. Breathing deeply, taking a moment to gather herself, she steps forward towards the yellow line, looking to her right, watching the carriages tearing towards the crowd. For a moment, she meets the driver's eye and sees a hint of dread, and then he is gone and the train has stopped and her legs shake as the doors open and she steps inside.

It is fifteen stops until it's her turn to get off. There is too much time to think and so she closes her eyes, concentrating instead on the gentle rhythm until she hears the announcement: *Kew Gardens*. Opening them again, she is met by daylight as the train pulls into the outdoor station.

On the platform, she follows the familiar path towards the exit. The sun presses against her cheeks as she steps out onto the pavement, holding her head down, her hair falling in front of her face, reaching into her bag and pulling out a pair of sunglasses.

Putting the glasses on, she turns slightly and catches a glimpse of herself in the reflection of the boulangerie, and she is struck for a moment by the image of a woman she no longer recognises. Standing straighter, hardening herself against any doubts, she follows the familiar route, down Lichfield Road, past the perfectly manicured privet hedges, the pristine gravel and obligatory plantation blinds, turning right into an unsigned side street. A moment later she reaches into her bag, pulling out the keys and pressing the button to unlock the door. With a flash of the headlights, the Range Rover clicks open and she steps into it, breathing in the smell of fresh leather.

As she turns the key in the ignition, the radio blares a song she knows and the shock of the unexpected noise makes her cry out. It takes a moment to compose herself, palms pressed against the steering wheel, before she looks over her shoulder and reverses, taking her usual route along the wide open streets of South-West London, towards Richmond. It's a different world here and she feels not so much safe as anonymous. These are not her people, and in this car with its tinted windows and hyper-clean paintwork she is almost certainly unrecognisable.

On Richmond Road, she turns into the Waitrose car park and pulls into a space. There is silence as the engine cuts out, apart from the sound of her breath rising and falling in shallow bursts in her chest. Stepping out onto the pavement, she helps herself to a trolley, working her way through the aisles, selecting the sort of basics you might buy for a picnic. As she turns into the baby and toddler aisle, she gives a cursory glance over her shoulder. Once she is sure she is alone, she continues walking, picking out a selection of organic purees she would never have dreamt of buying for Sadie and Callum.

It takes several minutes to gather all that she needs, making her way to the till as she pulls out the phone and dials. When Polina answers, she speaks more quietly than usual, unable to keep the relief of this contact out of her voice.

'How are you?' Gabriela asks, affecting her brightest intonation, giving a polite wave of recognition to the cashier and an apologetic smile at the rudeness of talking into the phone while the woman begins to scan the items on the belt.

'How are you?' Polina's voice asks on the end of the line and she replies, 'I'm good. I've had a change of plan with work so I'm on my way back now – I'm just at the supermarket picking up some supplies. Is there anything we need?'

Before Polina can answer, Gabriela adds quickly, 'How's Layla?'

'I'll put the phone to her ear,' Polina says.

Reaching into her bag for her purse, Gabriela stops as she hears the child's breath. The lump that has been rising in her throat softens into something thick and expansive, so that she can only stand stock-still, drinking in the broken inflections of her daughter's voice.

Gabriela's voice breaks. 'Oh baby . . . My baby, I've missed you. Mummy will be home in a minute, OK?'